Double dead: *adj.*
Meat that comes from an animal that has died of disease.
Does not pass the necessary sanitary standards.

An Abaddon Books™ Publication
www.abaddonbooks.com
abaddon@rebellion.co.uk

Omnibus edition published in 2016 by Abaddon Books™, Rebellion
Intellectual Property Limited, Riverside House, Osney Mead, Oxford,
OX2 0ES, UK.

10 9 8 7 6 5 4 3 2 1

Editor-in-Chief: Jonathan Oliver
Commissioning Editor: David Moore
Cover: Joey Hi-Fi
Design: Sam Gretton & Oz Osborne
Marketing and PR: Rob Power
Head of Comics and Book Publishing: Ben Smith
Creative Director and CEO: Jason Kingsley
Chief Technical Officer: Chris Kingsley

UK ISBN: 978-1-78108-420-5
US ISBN: 978-1-78108-421-2

Printed in Denmark

THE COMPLETE
DOUBLE DEAD

CHUCK WENDIG

ABADDON
BOOKS

Double Dead

PART ONE
PREDATOR

CHAPTER ONE

The Vampire Awakens

THE BLOOD CRAWLED through tight channels and shunted cracks like a rat in a maze. It descended through shattered concrete. It crept down a length of rusty pipe.

Eventually it found an opening and dangled free in darkness before becoming unmoored and falling through shadow.

The first drop landed on the man's nose. Which did nothing.

The second dotted the flaky, cracked flesh of his forehead.

That also did nothing.

But the third drop. The third drop was the magic drop, tumbling out of darkness and falling upon his desiccated lips, from there easing down into his frozen, arthritic maw, moving past rotten teeth and touching the dark dry nub that once was a tongue.

When the blood touched that blackened stub, it came alive with a sharp sound: the sound of a spoon back cracking the surface of crème **brûlée**.

The tongue twitched. Swatches of crispy tongue-flesh fell away like flakes of char. Then the tongue did more than twitch: it flapped, flailed, seeking, needing.

The mouth widened.

The drops of blood from above became a steadier flow. The tongue shot out from the mouth, extended far, too far, *impossibly* far—and like a child catching snowflakes, it caught the blood.

It wasn't long before the blackened tongue was blackened no more. Now it was pink, bright, stained with red.

The mouth opened wider as the blood now fell in an unsteady rain.

THE SOUND OF an animal's cries and the coppery, greasy taste on Coburn's tongue cut down through his dreams like a machete: he reached for them, the animal's cries mingling with a child's cries, the memory of wallpaper and linoleum soon replaced with a wall of darkness and the feel of stone beneath the island of Manhattan.

He lurched forward. His spine cracking, his bones brittle as sticks.

Blood fell from above. He cupped his hands—around his mouth so hard to move, the fingers like the stiff legs of dead bugs—and made sure not to miss a single drop of the sweet stuff. He was a junkie, a blood junkie, a Noo-Yawk *vampire* who thrived on this stuff and he hadn't had it in—well, he didn't know how long, but judging by the condition of his body, it had been a long fucking time.

What fell in his mouth wasn't enough. Not nearly. He needed more. Would kill to have it—and had in the past, many times, too many times to count.

He tried to speak, but found his voice lost in the dead puckered flesh of his throat, his vocal cords naught but withered strings.

Coburn needed the blood.

And so he decided to climb.

COBURN MOVED LIKE a spider. Fingers mooring in the cracks of broken cement and crumbling brick, hauling himself up while still craning his neck so as not to miss any drop from the tiny waterfall of blood. When he found its source—the end of a rusted sewer pipe—he nursed on it like a baby.

It still wasn't enough.

Coburn pried his mouth from the blood—a task that borrowed from his last vestiges of will, a task that set off alarms and screams from the monster inside his head: *Go back, you're going to miss it, you need it, you fucking ape you can't exist without it, you're a moron, you deserve to die—to die for real this time, to die for* good. And yet he persevered despite the cat-calls of his own worst survival instincts, letting the human mind—the one with reason and sense and the ability to see beyond a few drops of blood—take over from the reptilian fiend that wrenched at the puppet strings.

He swung out, using what little strength his dead body still possessed, and swung along pipe after pipe, a nightmarish subterranean jungle gym.

Then: he smelled it.

A faint breeze from above.

On it, the scent of blood. And a curious smell of rot.

Echoing down through the hole again came the animal's cries, a kind of panicked bleating. Coburn hoisted himself through the hole, his mouth wet with blood, his jaw tight with hunger.

To HIS HUMAN mind, nothing here made sense. It was like that old game: *One of these things is not like the other, one of these things does not belong.* But it wasn't just one thing. It was a metric shitload of things. It was *all* things.

Coburn hoisted himself up into an old movie theater that tickled the back of his memory somewhere behind the wall of hunger that dominated him. The theater lay in ruins—the ceiling was half-caved in, the scent of dust and mold sat heavy in the air. Scorch marks crept up the walls, blasted across the floor in a sooty asterisk. The screen itself hung in tatters. Rows of seats had fallen to disrepair.

But the thing that really twisted the noodle was the deer.

And the two men eating it.

The beast was a whitetail buck. Not standing, so much as leaning against the broken row of seats, its head thrashing, the creature crying out some sound between a child's whimper and a beastly grunt. One man slumped against the creature's haunches, biting into it the way another man might bite lustily into an apple. The other stood at the front, pawing at the whitetail's face, fruitlessly snapping at the thing's neck—but the animal, alive but weakened, kept jerking its head away from the attacker's mouth.

Coburn didn't understand one lick of what was going on.

And frankly, he didn't give a shit.

Because *sweet goddamn* was he hungry.

He moved to feed. The deer no longer interested him. The blood of beasts was functional, but barely.

The blood of men, however, was king.

Coburn, his skin still tight, his bones and muscles still uncertain, stepped up atop a row of seats and almost fell—but he quickly regained his balance and walked across the seat-tops toward his prey.

He came first to the man chowing down on the deer's ass, wrapped his hands around the fool's skull and snapped the head back with a sharp, wet crack.

The smell hit him in the face like a thrown brick.

Rot. Decay. The sour stink of a wound gone bad.

We don't drink from the sick, said that horrible little voice inside Coburn's head, but really, hell with that voice, and so he bit down anyway.

Black blood as thick as motor oil filled his mouth. It tasted of pus and of pain, but worst of all it tasted *worthless*.

See, humans possess a spark of something. Coburn didn't care to ruminate on what that spark was: the divine, the soul, a glimmer of sentience, a social security number, whatever. Fact was, *life* was bright and alive inside every man, woman and child, and that glory dwelled—nay, *thrived*—in the blood. It was why the blood of a human was infinitely better than that of a beast: animals had an ember, a spark, but only a fraction of the total fire.

The blood of man offered the whole package. Life in claret sweetness.

This blood had none of that. It was dead. Inert. Diseased.

Black as tar and worthless as baby shit.

Coburn's head snapped back, recoiling with the disappointment of a starving man who'd just bit into a plastic fruit. His victim struggled, hissing, the hole in his throat gurgling and bubbling.

The man turned and lunged for Coburn with long, yellowed nails. His face was half-caved in, calling to mind a rotten pumpkin. A gobbet of super-fresh venison sat flat on the dead man's tongue, the meat thick with tufts of deer hair.

The man was dead.

Dead-dead. Not 'dead' like Coburn was dead.

But real dead. Double dead.

Shit.

The vampire had little time to parse. The gurgling corpse lunged at Coburn, letting go of the deer. He wrapped his hands around Coburn's throat and turned the tables: Coburn thought he'd be doing the feeding, but this dead sonofabitch was hungry, too. And strong.

That was when things went sideways.

The deer, sensing opportunity, kicked out with its back legs. A hoof caught Coburn's rotting assailant in the temple, going through the fucker's head like a broomstick through a block of softened butter. Whatever bullshit facsimile of life managed to animate him before was now gone, and the hands around Coburn's throat went slack.

The whitetail was none too happy about this and continued to thrash. It bucked its head and drove one of its antler points through the chin of the other feeder trying to get a taste up front.

Coburn backpedaled, almost tripped over a seat as the deer panicked. He watched, equal parts starving and stymied, as the deer struggled—it had stuck its attackers at both ends. Antler under one's chin, foot through the other's head.

And it couldn't get free.

It was then that Coburn's veins tightened. His dead heart stirred: not with life, but with a hollow paroxysm of *need* and *want*.

He stood.

He reached out.

He pressed his fingertips together, forming them to a single point.

Then Coburn corkscrewed his hand fast—faster than any human could manage—into the deer's side, up under the ribcage, and grabbed hold of the creature's heart and crushed it like it was a pomegranate.

The vampire removed his fingers, licked them clean, then pressed his face tight against the hole and drank. It tasted of grass and musk and animal stink but he didn't care, because at least it wasn't black blood, dead blood, *useless* blood.

The blood filled his throat, and for a moment, all was right in the world.

CHAPTER TWO

The Vampire Reflects

SITTING SLUMPED UP against a deer corpse, framed by two rotting pumpkin-heads, his mouth rimmed with gluey red, Coburn had time to reflect.

His first reach for memory was a stunted attempt: in the shadow of his own mind he found only broken pieces, like a photograph sliced into ribbons by a razor blade. He saw a flash of blonde hair: pigtails twisting, evading his grasp. The sound of a television announcer: *gonna be a rilly big shoe.* A shadow crawling in through the window. Then, time shifted, leapt forward suddenly, showcasing another flurry of images: a camping hatchet, an upturned middle finger, a bearded man, a gout of flame.

Didn't make any sense, and whenever he tried to look deeper, those images turned to roaches and scattered from the light.

But beyond those…

Blood. Excess. A woman laughing. A woman screaming. Limousines that stank of money and leather, and dark alleys that smelled like rotten garlic and stinking curry. The stars and moon above, always dark, never the sun, the provenance and kingdom of Coburn the vampire.

These were the images he knew. These came back to him comfortably. Like a warm blanket felt for in the dark.

It was a life—or an unlife, or whatever it was you cared to call it—bloated to the gills with the most wonderful of sins: gluttony and lust and revenge and all those glorious transgressions. An existence of endless pleasure.

And now, this.

Waking up in a ruined movie theater. Feasting on a dead deer. Attacked by—what? Homeless degenerates? Meth-addled plague victim freakshows who were too stupid or too jacked to know that they were a hair's breadth from death?

"Ain't exactly the—" His throat crackled. He coughed, and *ptoo*-ed a bloody wad of whitetail fur out of his dead throat. "Ain't exactly the Four Seasons."

Coburn stood. Walked over to a faux-gilded movie poster frame. The poster within was no longer recognizable, covered as it was with rampant mold, but the glass was still surprisingly intact. The vampire examined his reflection.

He didn't look so hot. Cheekbones, sunken. Eyes, too. His skin had started to soften—but some of it still lay cracked, like the skin around his eyes or the flesh betwixt each finger. His hair, once slicked back and lacquered to his skull, was now a hot, frizzled mess. Hell, all his roguish good looks had been run through the gauntlet. Coburn's lips curled into a sneer below his crooked nose.

His time below had ruined a perfectly good thing.

He swatted a fly away from his head, and in doing so, called to attention a curious fact.

"I'm missing a fucking finger," Coburn said, not sure who he was talking to. Did he always talk to himself? Or had his time underground tweaked his psyche? He didn't know and didn't care, and was instead more interested in his hand.

He held up his right hand, waggled all of his fingers except the middle one. That finger dead-ended in a shriveled stump.

It would regrow. Eventually. Once he had some *real* blood sitting in his gut and churning through his dead heart. The deer blood wouldn't do it. Not strong enough stuff—like light beer or wine coolers, it was a thinned-down version of the real thing. Worse, it wouldn't last long. Give it a couple of nights and he'd be back to starving, and when starvation was on the line, reason and higher thinking were out the window. Go without for too long and it was back to the crispy body, the muscles-gone-rigid.

Which meant it was time to hit the town. Would be easy pickings in this city: it always was. Head down to Times Square or Penn Station, wait for some tourist drunk off the newest Broadway fiasco, sweep them up, do a little of that *voodoo-that-you-do-so-well*, and drink them dry in an alley or a restroom. Then Coburn could clean up a little, because damn if he wasn't nasty-looking.

At least he still had his leather coat—a ratty, weathered thing worn by David Johansen of the New York Dolls, Christmas Eve, 1971. Band's first performance. And his boots: pair of derby swirl Fluevogs with soles that read: 'Resists alkali, water, acid, fatigue, and Satan.'

He looked back over the theater. Tried to remember how he got there. Something moved in the back of his thoughts, like a moth fluttering against a darkened window. But it refused to be pinned.

Coburn would remember. It would just take time.

And blood. It always took blood.

He marched toward the theater's front double doors and threw them open, ready to step into the bright lights, big city, and feast like a fucking king.

THE AVERAGE VAMPIRE had the nose of a pregnant woman: the olfactory sense was dialed up to 11, then the knob was broken off. Truth be told, *all* of a vampire's senses were ratcheted up, but right now the one that mattered most was smell.

The city stank of death.

A crowd gathered outside, as it always did here in the Big Apple. But this crowd wasn't like any other crowd.

This crowd was not alive.

A woman with a missing nose and hair like the tail of a dead horse dragged a broken foot, the bones jutting awkwardly from ruined flesh, a clutch purse still in hand.

A man in construction gear stumbled around in circles, his fat belly bloated with foul gases, his skin marred with the purple striations of death. With a rotten hand—literally rotten, so rotten it was just a mush of meat with bleached finger bones sticking out—he scratched divots in his cheek.

A little boy, his lower half just a squid's beard of guts and meaty fringe, dragged himself across an open manhole, then fell down into the dark.

And it wasn't just them. Dozens right here. Hundreds down the street in every direction. The city, thick with them.

The air, fat with flies.

The city lay dark and still but for the shuffling and mumbling of the damned. No power anywhere. No car horns. No music playing. Coburn couldn't smell food cooking, couldn't feel the subterranean rumble of the subway, couldn't even hear the scurrying of the rats or the fluttering of pigeon wings.

Only the swarm of flies and the slow dance of the dead.

The construction worker pivoted his head toward Coburn. His lower jaw unhinged—not like a snake's jaw but rather like a jaw whose tendons had long turned to mush—and he hissed.

Coburn pirouetted back inside, gently shut the door behind him.

As he closed the door, one final realization crossed his mind.

The city no longer offered a bounty of expected smells: burger grease, exhaust, cologne. But that wasn't the troubling omission.

Coburn couldn't smell blood, either.

No life, no blood.

No blood, no food.

That was not good news.

CHAPTER THREE
Dead City

PANIC CHEWED AT his guts like a nest of hungry rats. No blood. *No blood.* All dead? Not a whiff of life here in the city? Best case scenario put him, what, sucking the juice out of pigeons in Central Park? Worst case scenario put him starving on the streets and collapsing on the sidewalk before morning. Then he'd either be eaten by those freaks out there or he'd be scorched by the coming sun.

What was going on? None of it made sense. This was some kind of fever dream. He never woke up. Clearly—*plainly!*—he remained down in the dark, trapped in the throes of some undead nightmare.

Still, this all felt pretty goddamned real.

Coburn tried to find focus as the panic inside him was boiling what little useful blood he had in the cauldron of his vampire's body.

He gritted his teeth so hard together he thought his fangs would snap. What time was it? How soon was dawn? No telling. What to do? Wait here? Wait the rest of the night as his body rendered the blood inside inert? Or go? Go and risk the dawn, the dark, the dead city?

"Fuck it," he said. Coburn wasn't a timid creature. He wasn't a church mouse—hell, he ate church mice like they were Jalapeno peppers. Standing around like this, he might as well go and shove one of those antlers up his ass. The time for thinking was over. The time for doing had begun.

No windows in this room—no use having windows in a theater. But up above, he did see a vent.

That was where he had to go. *Up.*

The theater curtains—red, ratty, moth-eaten—felt uncertain in his grip, like they might fall apart at any moment, but when he tugged on them, they held. And so Coburn began to climb. For him the task offered little struggle: he wasn't some gawky teen hauling his bony butt up the rope in gym class. He was a vampire. That afforded him abilities and powers others could only dream of.

When he reached the top of the curtain, he kicked out with his legs, swung over and caught the ridged vent cover with his (remaining) fingers. He pried it off with a twist of his wrist, and then crawled up into the ventilation system.

Up top, the air didn't smell so thick with the stench of death. Coburn elbowed open the vent and wriggled free like a worm escaping from a foul apple, and he took a deep breath up here. The breath did little for him; fuck oxygen, because his vampire's body could thrive only on blood, but even still it was good to exercise those dead bladder lungs of his, if only to draw scent from the air.

And here it smelled clean.

Or clean*er*, at least.

No time to dwell.

The rooftop gravel crunched under foot as he hurried to the building's ledge. The darkness of the city below struck him. New York had always been a vibrant, living thing: a bleary neon beast with arteries of light and blood, a monster that never slumbered, a city that was as much a vampire as he was, awakening at night to drink the life of the weak.

And now, it had been rendered a dark ruin.

The moon rose fat above, highlighting distant windows—some broken, some not—but the rest of the city lay covered in shadow. Just black shapes. Silhouettes.

He couldn't be the only one.

It couldn't all be dead.

If it was...

Well. No time to contemplate that. No time to think about how without blood he'd turn into a dried strip of vampire jerky. That was not a future he decided to entertain.

Had to be blood out there.

He lifted his chin, urged his lungs to suck in a powerful breath through his nose—scents on the wind, the commingled odors of death. But somewhere beyond it all, he could smell a flower pushing up through broken concrete, he could detect a rat taking a piss on a ledge, he could smell a faint lingering whiff of gasoline...

There. It lit up his dead synapses like a circuit-board. Suddenly his gut clenched, ripples of *want* and *need* and *I'll tear down this dead city to get it* wrenching his esophagus closed. He felt like a dog watching his master eat: if he could have drooled, he would have.

On the wind, the faintest aroma of blood.

Human blood.

Vibrant and bright and alive. But far off, too. Distant, like the Dog Star.

Just then: a *hiss* down and to his right.

One of them—*let's just say it,* he thought, *it's an undead motherfucking smells-like-a-roadkilled-possum-stuffed-with-gorgonzola-   cheese asshole zombie prick*—lay against the ledge. Except, this one *didn't* smell bad—or, at least, not like the others. This one was practically mummified. Skin like that of fried chicken. Eyes white and bright. Teeth, too, like white pebbles in the dry cavern of its mouth. Lips pulled back. Gums just hard, parched nubs. Couldn't tell if it was a man or a woman. It just lay there, moving only its head, snapping its teeth in his direction. Equal parts 'comical' and 'pathetic.'

Maybe the sun did this. Thing got trapped up here. It wandered. The sun cooked it down, dried it out.

Coburn kicked it in the head.

The head came off easy as anything. Like flicking a seed pod off a dry stalk. It broke apart, the crispy head shards spinning off into darkness.

Down in the theater, one rot-fuck got a hoof through the temple. The other caught an antler up under the chin. This one stopped moving when he booted its head off the roof.

"Just like in the movies," he said. "Aim for the head, they go dead."

The rhyme pleased him, if only a little.

He turned, once again looked at the moon. It had already begun its descent toward the horizon. He didn't have long until morning.

Two hours, maybe? Three, at best.

He stood at the edge, caught that scent of blood once more. It waited for him *out there*. Out beyond Riverside Drive. Out beyond the river itself. Wouldn't be far. He could make it. If only it really *were* like the movies, he could think real hard, squeeze his butt-cheeks *real tight*, and—poof!—turn into a bat and flutter away without a second thought. But vampires, they couldn't fly.

Though they sure could jump.

CHAPTER FOUR
The Deader of Two Evils

COBURN LEAPT ROOF-TO-ROOF, a shape blacker than the night itself. He did so silently, the only sound being the thump-and-crunch of boots striking rooftops. Not every roof was parallel—sometimes he crashed hard into a fire escape, then bolted his way up to the rooftop. Not fifteen minutes later he stood atop a ten-story walk-up, the roof home to a pigeon coop whose only inhabitants were a morose display of long-dead birds, matted feathers hanging from rust-colored bones. The vampire didn't stop to admire the attraction.

From here it would be easy: this was the Upper West Side. From this roof to the river, he could plan his journey above the city with ease—in the moonlight he could see a path cut between the too-tall buildings, a path that would let him take a slow descent. At least, until he got to Riverside Drive: there, the buildings shot up again to ensure that the hoitiest, toitiest New York citizens got a view of the river. Of course, all those citizens were now food for the living dead. Or were perhaps themselves the living dead—Coburn didn't have to time to worry about the mechanics of it, as to whether this was somehow viral or bacteriological or mystical or whether it maybe fell from the sky as part of some kind of alien meteor. Didn't matter and so he didn't care. Wasn't his fault, so—*fuck it.*

Once he hit Riverside, he'd drop to the ground, cross Riverside Park, and throw his own ass into the river. The air here was cold, but not wintry—he suspected it was spring, or just on the cusp of it—but it wouldn't matter anyway. Temperature changes had little effect on his body. As long as it had blood in it, his body would self-regulate. He went to the doctors once on a lark, just to see what his temperature was: 89.8F. A lot lower than the average living human, and to most his skin felt icy—the 'chill of the grave,' he'd say, with a bullshit Bela Lugosi accent to go with it. But to him, he always felt hot. Feverish. Hungry.

He took another running leap, aiming for an eight-story brownstone—he sailed through the air, legs kicking like he was riding some kind of invisible bike, the wind caught under his coat, that lingering tickle of blood-scent deep in his sinuses—and he landed, looked up, and found himself surrounded by the living dead.

These, like the last one, were mummified: less *rotting corpse* and more *dried-out husk*, but unlike the last, these fuckers were all up and walking around. A dozen of them, milling about in a clumsy, drunken moonlit waltz. One in a ratty sweater. Another in a ruined suit—the fabric once dark and clean, now sun-bleached and tattered at the edges. Over there, a woman wandered around in a dress half-torn off, her shriveled tits like a pair of hog scrotums popping out, each a lifeless, milkless sack. Others shuffled in the dark of the roof.

Coburn landed, tucked, rolled, and stood up in their midst.

They hissed, raspy and wordless, and turned toward him.

He didn't have the time for a game of zombie grab-ass. Ratty Sweater reached for him and he caught its arm, snapped upwards, the bone splitting—the arm remained connected only by a tenuous, leathery cord of tendon.

"You my dance partner?" Coburn asked. Ratty Sweater's bulging white eyes stared, offering not a single lick of recognition or cognizance. The vampire jerked Ratty Sweater left, crashing him into Missus Hog Balls—they both went down.

Then they came at him, en masse.

They were slow, and he was fast. Faster than any human. By the time they reached him, he wasn't even there anymore: he was behind two of them, and he wrapped his arms around their necks, putting them in a headlock.

Coburn squeezed his arms. Their heads popped off with the sound of someone breaking a hard loaf of bread.

Then, because he didn't want to waste any more time with these assholes, he took off running for the next rooftop.

He leapt. Right leg forward, left leg extended behind him.

Something grabbed his foot.

He pivoted, mid-air, just in time to see Ratty Sweater already back up—the ugly mummy had reached out and caught Coburn by the boot.

Thus ruining any forward momentum he had.

He—along with Ratty Sweater, whose zombie grip on the vampire's Fluevog boot was unyielding—tumbled down through the darkness.

VAMPIRES? HARD TO kill. Or, since they were already dead, hard to *destroy*. But that didn't mean they were impervious to harm. Far from it. Their organs didn't work, no, so it wasn't like they could suffer liver failure or kidney damage or heart attacks or anything. But their bones were the same bones that humans had. They shattered just as easily. And if you put a bullet in their brain, that vampire would be done for. Game over, good night. All that would be left was to sweep up the greasy ash pile left behind.

No brain bullet here. But even still, Coburn fell eight stories.

With a zombie holding his ankle.

Ratty Sweater hit the ground first. He didn't explode so much as *fold up upon himself*, collapsing from head to foot into a cloud of skin-dust. The sweater held together. The rest of him, not so much.

Coburn hit, legs down, landing on his feet like a cat.

This was not ideal. All those movie images of a vampire dropping down from ten stories up and landing in some kick-ass dark hero crouch? Not happening. His boots hit asphalt, and the impact shattered his leg bones; osseous shards thrust through his skin at various angles. Coburn howled some unutterable profanity, some inhuman invective from the most primitive part of his reptilian brain, and then he collapsed to the ground like a house of cards, laying there in the remnants of Ratty Sweater.

He took a moment. Not because he wanted to, but because he had to. For a human to suffer this kind of trauma, well—the human would soon perish or, at the very least, be in traction for the rest of his pathetic life. And thus came the vampire's edge: yes, Coburn's bones shattered into a grenade of bleached internal shrapnel, but they damn sure weren't going to stay that way. Long as he had blood in his body, he could channel the red stuff to his injures and set the life stolen from others to work mending bones and stitching flesh.

But it didn't happen lickity-split. Quick, yes, but not so quick he'd be up doing a merry jig in a trio of seconds. It would take a few minutes.

He craned his head up and peered through the darkness. This was Broadway. He'd recognize it anywhere: the center lined with trees, now overgrown and spilling out into the street (nature had come to reclaim the city, replacing the asphalt jungle with, well, the *jungle* jungle). Further down, the shadowy marquees. The defunct buses and taxis, their windows busted out. Here, a Blockbuster video in ruins. There, a shawarma joint now just a darkened cave. The city left for dead. Or rather, for The Dead, because here they came.

They did not move quickly, but they did come without hesitation. Dragging limbs. Drooling fluids. A steady stumble, a certain shuffle.

At first they were just shadows—a ring of them encircling him at all sides. A hundred feet away. Then ninety. Then eighty. And by then his eyes adjusted as they stepped into the moonlight. At first? Dozens. But it didn't stop there. They came like dark water seeking to fill a low valley, gravity drawing them ineluctably toward him—a slow-moving piranha frenzy, a sluggish army of hungry hyenas.

As individuals, he realized, they were dumb. Almost harmless. Even two or three of them, well, fuck 'em. They were like cows: just stupid animals.

But get a bunch of those stupid animals together, and they might stampede.

They became dangerous in numbers.

They're going to tear me apart.

The irony was not lost on him. He was long an undead predator, plundering life from the living by feasting on their blood. And now he would perish in much the same way: these were not predators, these shambling rotters, but rather, scavengers. Just the same, they'd pick him apart and eat him: the dead feasting. Even when a lion fell, the vultures came to eat the hunter's flesh.

No.

Fuck that. To Hell with them. They were slow and stupid. He was fast and smart. He wouldn't go out like this.

He gritted his teeth, willed the blood to work faster.

Coburn rose on half-shattered kneecaps, steadying himself with the flat of his hand against the street.

Here they came. Moving around the back end of a ruined bus from one direction. Filtering around two collided taxis from another. Some just climbed over. Many that did slipped and fell, face-planting on the asphalt.

Coburn tried to stand, but his legs didn't support him—he fell to his knees as the circle closed in around him.

They were at fifty feet, now.

Forty.

Thirty.

Fuck.

He churned and burned blood. The whitetail's life—only recently measured in his dead arteries—was fading fast, soon gone from Coburn, its carrier. His mind felt stripped bare. The pain was clarifying. Every part of him: one raw nerve.

Coburn sprang up on half-shattered legs and broke into a run—straight at the collapsing ring of moaning, groping zombies.

He ran straight toward some stumpy undead *hausfrau* in a nappy pink bathrobe. Half her scalp was peeled back, revealing an equally-pink ridge of scalp.

To Coburn, this looked like an excellent stepping stone.

Plan was: leap up, plant foot firmly on skull patch, vault over the zombie housewife and then bolt toward freedom.

As he approached, she belched a frothy stream of spit and blood.

Coburn leapt.

Or, tried to, at least.

His legs were like mushy brownies: they weren't done cooking and the bones were still soft in the middle. As he raised up on his heel the leg folded underneath him and suddenly it was all *jumpus-interruptus*. He hit the ground with his shoulder. The sting was almost worse than the one his pride took for having fucked up two easy jumps in the last fifteen minutes. This wasn't like him. He was better than this.

The zombies fell upon him. They were all rotten hands and snapping teeth. One pressed the heel of its palm on his face, pushing his cheek into the macadam. Others tugged at his legs. Someone stepped on his hand. All the while, they bit down—gumming his jacket, mostly. Leather was tough, and they couldn't bite through it. A flare of possibility lit up inside his *cornered animal* mind: he wasn't weak, he was strong, all he needed was a little leverage and—

The bathrobed housewife ripped into his neck with her teeth. She nuzzled her face like a dog digging into someone's crotch and ripped a hunk of his neck flesh out. Then she lapped at the hole with her ruined tongue.

So this is what it feels like, Coburn thought.

The blood fled him. While the other living dead chewed fruitlessly at his clothing, the housewife pushed aside his flap of neck-flesh and supped at the slow-drooling blood creeping from his neck wound. His eyes were suddenly covered by dirty pink bathrobe.

Numbness tingled at his fingertips.

A red haze crept in at the edges of his vision.

His skin tightened. Soon it would begin to crack and split like dry lips. Not long after that, he would—what? Well, he didn't really know. Never happened before and he didn't know many of his own kind. His flesh would split apart like a red pepper over a grill's flame, maybe. Or it would flake apart and fall to the wind like dandelion seed.

Then, a curious thing occurred.

The *hausfrau* paused in the consumption of her bloody meal.

A sound first came from her throat, a kind of halting, choking sound, as if something very unpleasant were lodged in there. She lifted her head up, her tongue jutting from her mouth. It began to swell.

Her eyes, too, turned from pink to red as fresh blood overloaded the capillaries and they began to burst.

She began to weep runny red tears.

Whatever it was that was blocking her throat was suddenly gone: she lifted her head to the sky and let fly with a barbaric, guttural cry. The other hungry dead paused as if gazing at something shiny, their heads tilting like curious cats.

The hausfrau went apeshit. She began swinging wildly, biting at her undead cohorts, clawing at them with broken, yellowed nails. She struck one with her taloned fingers and tore half his face off in a powerful swipe.

Coburn felt dizzy, weak, confused.

But he knew this was his only chance. And so the vampire began to crawl. He no longer had the strength he possessed before, and his bodily repairs were only half-formed, the bone shards fitting awkwardly together in the meat sacks that were his legs. He didn't know how long it took him to escape that scene—he belly-crawled through an alley, the sounds of carnage and undead wails behind him, the living dead occupied by their rampaging compatriot. He dragged himself through greenery, over a shattered bike path, pulling his body by whatever park bench or shrub root he could grab.

The sun began to bleed across the horizon like the yolk of a runny egg.

He smelled flowers: tulips, he thought. He put his palm down on a carpet of pink: cherry blossoms. It really was spring.

His jacket began to smolder as dawn's fingers caressed the length of his body. In a minute or two, that caress would become a fist, and that fist would enclose him in a fiery grip and cook him like a hunk of meat. A small part of him felt okay with that: this, after all, was the first time he'd seen the dawn in a very long time. He'd long learned that even the opening fanfare of sunrise was enough to give him a bad case of sunburn, and so come 4:30AM every night he'd retire to his Soho apartment (his belly fat with the blood of some club whore), shutter the windows, lock the dozen locks, and climb into his bed in a perfectly darkened room.

That was a damn nice bed, too. Memory foam. Way he sank down into it gave him the embrace of the grave with far greater comfort.

And his sheets! Egyptian cotton. A thousand-thread count. Cost him a pretty penny. Well. It cost *someone* a pretty penny. All luxury like blood, always pilfered, never his own.

But all that was gone now. He couldn't imagine going back to that apartment any time soon. The place was probably overrun with a bunch of hipster artist asshole undead, milling around in thick black eyeglasses and drinking shitty working class beer and spilling it on his glorious sheets and divine mattress.

He felt his skin grow warm.

He continued crawling, but he wasn't even sure why.

He shut his eyes.

And then: mud.

His fingers sunk into mud and before he knew what was happening he was sliding down on his belly like some dipshit penguin—the brown turbid waters of the Hudson rushed up to meet him and he took in a mouthful of the foul river.

Coburn drifted down, the lazy current dragging him along.

All went dark as morning rose.

CHAPTER FIVE

Blood and Dreams in Dark Water

ONCE MORE, COBURN dreamed.

Daysleep was often without dreams, the landscape as lifeless and black in his own mind as it would be in the crypt. For all intents and purposes, during the day he fell into the same slumbering coma enjoyed by all the world's corpses (except now, where the world's corpses were a restless army of the hungry undead). It was different when he was hungry, though, and even worse when starving. If he went to bed in the morning without feeding, the dreams crept in at the edges: the darkness brightened at the margins with gray images as spectral as cigarette smoke.

The dreams were shaky, uncertain, hard to find.

But they were there.

He could feel carpet under his hands.

A dark shape—an *evil* shape, far more evil than he—stood behind him; he could not see this shape but could only sense it. Eyes at his back. A shadow lurking.

Somewhere he heard a girl's cry: a young girl.

A lock of hair in his hand—the girl's hair, he thought. Blonde. Curled at the end; a pigtail. Smooth and sweet and smelling of honeysuckle.

Then: blood and pain and screams and a curtain of misery drawing tight across the dream until—

Until as before, he was awakened by blood. This time, not running down from above but rather caught on the river's murky current.

His eyes opened. The dream fled to the darkest corners of his head. He found himself underneath a sunken, overturned rowboat. Catfish, slimy and slick, fled him as he jostled to some semblance of life.

The blood was like a trail of breadcrumbs. He planted his feet on the boat—which had stuck partly in the mud and rocks at the bottom of the Hudson—and pushed off, swimming up-river, a shark in search of a meal.

CARL TOOK HIS rusty pocket knife, slit the tabby cat from neck to nuts, worked his dirty fingers up under the feline's pelt. He'd already bled the cat out and burned all the fur off, which elicited a smell that once upon a time would've made his throat close up, but these days, it only served to make him hungry. The cat still had a little blood in him, though, and it dribbled into the cloudy waters as the sun set at the far edge of the dead city across the way.

From behind him: a low and little growl.

He turned to the skinny black-and-white rat terrier in the rusty cage behind him. It was really just a guinea-pig enclosure, but still served as a make-shift trap.

"Shut the hell up," Carl said. "Your buddy here is dinner, and tomorrow morning, you're breakfast."

The dog keened in the back of his throat. Carl didn't care. He didn't like dogs, he didn't like cats. Didn't like people, either, actually. This whole zombie apocalypse was working out just fine for him. Gave him lots of time to himself. What few survivors he'd met, they didn't know how he so easily stayed alive. Or stranger still, how exactly he'd kept his paunchy belly.

"It's easy," he told them. "I stick by the river. The rotters won't cross water. I just wade in and go far enough out and they mostly gather at the shoreline till they get bored. A few might stumble out into the Hudson, but those dumb fucks don't know how to navigate. They get stuck in the mud or pulled along by the current, and I just watch and wave. If I got to, I get in a dinghy and hang out in the middle of the river for a few hours."

But, they always asked, *that doesn't explain how you're so well-fed.*

Carl laughed, then, and taught them his trick.

A few hours later, they'd be cooked up over a fire. Parts of them dried for jerky. Bones saved for broth. Thigh meat in his belly.

Guy's gotta do what a guy's gotta do to survive.

But it had been a while since he'd seen any survivors. He'd camped at this spot for a good six months now, because it was a great place to lure the living. He clung to the river's rocky shore, yes, but right there—no, really, right over there by about fifty yards—was a helipad, and next to that, a parking lot.

And beyond the parking lot was a hospital. Palisades Medical.

People loved hospitals. Thought they were safe. Thought they could find *medicine*. What assholes. Hospital was the *worst* place to go during the apocalypse. Medical services were barely enough to handle the day-to-day of normal living. Carl once sliced open his thumb when he was preparing a pheasant for taxidermy (that was what he did in his former life, and what made him so good with the knife), and he waited in the emergency room for six hours. Bleeding on the floor. Nurse would come along periodically, drop a towel under his hand and collect the one she'd deposited an hour before—a towel soaked with red.

If they couldn't cope with a bleeding thumb, did people really think a hospital could handle the end of the world?

Hospitals were the first place the military hit—flamethrowers in the hallway to cook the sick and make sure they didn't come down with a bad case of the corpse-walk flu. Hospitals were the first place that looters hit, too. It was a goddamn charnel house in there. Burned bodies under sheets. A handful of rotters trapped in the hallways, fumbling around like idiots.

And yet, survivors always showed up. Few got away from him. He offered them a meal: some fish, some cat jerky. Then he drugged them with the tranquilizers he found inside the Medical Center. Or, if he didn't have the opportunity, he beat them over the head with a bat or stabbed them repeatedly. Death was death however it was achieved, and he found that drugging them made the meat a little goofy. Which was fun to eat, but it slowed him down.

Still. By now Carl wondered exactly how many survivors were left out there. Last batch he saw come through here didn't stop in the hospital: a big ol' rickety RV came bouncing down River Road. They were here, then they were gone.

Headed West, he suspected. Lots of survivors talked about heading West. They'd all heard the stories, and he guessed in a way it made sense. Midwest was the breadbasket of America, but was suspiciously devoid of people. Most of the country's population lived at the country's edges: East Coast, West Coast. Middle was a mushy nowhere wilderness. Iowa? Indiana? Arizona? Not a whole helluva lot out there. But people spread apart meant the sickness didn't spread so fast. Gave people time. Let them get smart and prepared.

Rumors went that the country's breadbasket was a safe haven. That the country still 'lived,' now out there in the middle. Red States, triumphant.

Whatever. Carl didn't buy it. World was fucking ruined.

Besides, this was his home. He'd rather die here with his belly full than live a full life as a resident of, what? Nebraska? Piss on that.

The terrier behind him started to growl again as he let the cat's internal organs plop down and splash into a pot he held beneath the dead kitty.

"Pipe down, pooch," Carl said, growling right back. Except in the evening light he could see the dog was no longer looking at him.

The dog was staring out at the dark waters.

Strange. Or not, since dogs were basically morons.

Carl went back to gutting the tabby.

Then: a bloom of mud up through the dark waters. About twenty feet off the scum-slick waters. *Might be that the catfish are restless*, Carl thought. They were morons, too—didn't take much to nab a catfish. Few pieces of bread in the water and they came up with their big dumb mouths open. Easy to hook. Could just reach in and grab 'em if one were so inclined.

Carl set the cat down on the rocks, gingerly took a few steps out into the water. It was cold, but he didn't mind. Later he'd light a fire and dry off (if it brought the rotters, he'd just burn the lot of them—the pile of charred zombie bodies around his campsite showed just how willing he was to make a stand).

He let his hands float into the water. He pulled a few dry bread hunks—he called them 'croutons' even though they were just rock-stale moldy chunks of French bread—and let them float out into the water.

The mud stirred.

Gotcha, he thought as he saw a shadow rising from ten feet away.

Oooh. This catfish was a big sucker. Good eats.

He bent his knees. He leaned forward.

Then the catfish shot up out of the river and Carl screamed.

COBURN KICKED UP out of the water and wrapped his hands around Carl's throat—he didn't know the man's name, of course, and didn't much care. This sodden fool with his pooched-out belly and his greasy, matted beard was going to serve as the first *true* meal that Coburn had consumed in a good long while.

As Carl screamed, Coburn ripped into his prey's neck with his pair of mean fangs. His incisors were curved in and back—like a snake's. When he closed his mouth, they fell neatly betwixt his lower teeth, his tongue slumbering atop them. But even better, the toothy curves let him bite down and dig in real good; anybody wanted to rip away from his bite they'd have to lose a big fat chunk of neck to do it.

Normally, he wouldn't be this crass. Generally, he *wooed* his victims a little bit: a little talky-talk, a little hypno-gaze, a little *here, listen to my suddenly eerily lyrical voice*, and then settle in low and slow for a bit of bloodletting.

But hell with it, Coburn was hungry. This was the equivalent of ripping into a candy bar with the wrapper still on.

Carl cried out. He beat uselessly at Coburn's side.

Blood, hot and sticky, filled his mouth. He was like a kid guzzling chocolate milk: he couldn't stop and he didn't want to. He needed this.

Wasn't long before Carl went limp. Coburn kept drinking.

He kept drinking until his tongue played in the neck wound, licking up whatever last vestiges he could of his victim's juices.

The body fell into the water. Well, all of him except the head: the head smacked against the rocks, thudding dully like an unripe cantaloupe.

The rest of Carl just bobbed there in the muddy river.

Coburn laughed. Wiped his mouth. Then, with his legs—wholly repaired now, not a bone chip or taut tendon out of place—he marched his ass out of the water.

Further, he felt an itchy tingle in a space above his hand, a phantom twitch. He watched as his middle finger grew back, sinew threading around a stretching bone, blood and flesh knitting together.

The vampire stretched.

He noticed then the dead cat. The vampire couldn't help but wonder if it was curiosity that killed this beast.

Then: a growling. He spotted the little terrier in some kind of makeshift bird cage. The stubby little dog snarled at him. He met the animal's gaze and did a little of the old *eye hoodoo*, then shushed the dog.

"Shhh," he said. "Chill the fuck out, pup. Last thing I need is for you to call a gaggle of undead assholes my way. Is it a gaggle? What is it? It's a school of fish. A murder of crows. A parliament of owls. What's a bunch of fucking zombies? A cluster? A cadre? You know what? I'm going to go with a *fuckbucket* of zombies. Sound good to you, pup?"

The dog kept growling.

That was unexpected. This little snarling cur was resisting his blood-sucker mojo. Had that ever happened before?

Instead, he tried a different approach: he snapped his fingers.

The dog sat down in the cage, and quieted its growls.

"Yeah," he said, feeling pretty good about himself. "See how I did that, pooch? I did that *old school*."

He bent down and unlatched the cage. Coburn reached in and grabbed the dog under his front legs. If the dog tried to bite him, he'd just snap its neck.

But the dog didn't bite. Instead, it panted.

Coburn grinned, licked a little blood off a fang.

"I hereby name you *Creampuff*," he said, chuckling. "Because you are going to be a delightful little snack tomorrow night."

Then, dog under his arm, he took off walking.

CHAPTER SIX

Chuck Wagon

IT STRUCK HIM, then, as he walked down the two-lane road—a road littered with cars shoved into one another at odd angles, a surefire sign of the Apocalypse if ever there was one—that the clock wasn't going to turn back. Things had changed (*duh*), and they weren't going back. Sometimes you break something and make it better, but this wasn't that: this was a broken world that wasn't merely content to stay broken, but would continue to break down even further.

Just as rot had claimed the zombies, it had also claimed New York. It had probably claimed the entire planet, for all he knew.

Coburn approached this thought charitably, with a spreading sense of warmth and satisfaction—a good meal had a way of casting one in a pleasing glow, even if the rest of the world had gone to Hell in a hazmat suit. The blood in his belly was now working its way through his blackened heart, through the withered channels. It felt good to be fed. It always did.

And before last night, getting fed had been easy.

The vampire led an easy, spoiled existence. The last fifty years had been an endless all-you-can-eat buffet. Manhattan had a population of almost two million, and that didn't even count the millions who came in and out of the city each day as workers and tourists. Coburn sat in the midst of this like a glorious tumor, funneling fresh blood supply into his mouth night-in and night-out. He wasn't really all that good-looking: his nose was a bit crooked, his teeth were a little fucked up. He was lean and lanky and had dark gray eyes that nobody in their right mind would've called 'friendly.'

But being a vampire came with an unholy host of perks. With but a thought he could turn his voice into an angel's song or a devil's cry, he could blink and make his eyes as calming as a hot spring or as bleak and endless as a black hole. Didn't hurt that he could snap even the toughest sonofabitch alive clean in half. Anybody got wise to his hypno-bullshit, he could break their necks easy as snapping a rib of celery.

Hell, most of the time none of his tricks were even necessary. The city that didn't sleep was also a city that supped on sin. Drunk chicks. Meth-heads. Party-till-dawn-with-sex-drugs-and-techno-music. Blood thick with narcotic bliss.

God, he hated that fucking music. Didn't anyone know how to play a goddamn *electric guitar* anymore? And the things they drank, the drugs they did. Nobody seemed to enjoy a good shot of cheap whiskey. Or a spoon full of black tar heroin. It was all *artisanal cocktails* and *designer drugs*. Made him sick. Made him want to puke up a bucket of blood.

This generation was the worst. Generation of weak-kneed hipster emo shitbags. A poor facsimile of their parents—and, frankly, those people were awful versions of their own parents, too. Generation after generation of bad duplicates. Like a letter run through the copier too many times. After a while, you couldn't even tell what it was trying to say anymore.

That was why he didn't feel bad about killing all those people. He went out of his way to select victims from the ranks of the douchebags, the asswipes, the hypocrites and bullies. Not because he had a conscience but rather because…

Well, it satisfied him.

Sure. Once upon a time he'd held onto some faint memory of a conscience. A glimmering, fragile little thing. Like a snowglobe or a porcelain pony.

That fragile thing had long been crushed under a black boot. The reality of what he did—of what he *was*—didn't leave much room for guilt or shame.

Besides, it wasn't like he killed *every* victim. Most of them he let go on their merry way. If only because disposing of bodies was an arduous task. Dumpster? River? Acid bath? Who had the time? Far better to drink a little, then send them on their way drunk and confused and without the memory of what they had done (or what had been done *to* them). Of course, sometimes they tasted so good...

At which point, well. Dumpster. River. Acid bath.

Now, though, everything was different. An obvious statement—what with the plants pushing up out of broken highway, the pile-up of rusted cars, the roaming hordes of slavering undead, only a mule-kicked blind dude could suspect that the world hadn't pretty much shit the bed. But what struck Coburn was how it had changed for *him*. He had always been solipsistic, of course, occasionally convinced in the wee hours of the morning that all of the world was but a figment of his diseased imagination... but now it really hit home. The buffet had closed. The endless line of willing and drunken and drugged-up victims (*queue forms in the rear*) was done funneling their life source into his open and eager mouth.

No more gravy train.

No more chuck wagon.

Maybe it was just the warm glow of Carl's blood talking, but that gave Coburn a sick little thrill. It was time once again to be the hunter. Before, he was like the spider grown fat in the center of the web. He let the flies come to him.

But now, if he wanted to eat, he needed to roam. He needed to *hunt*.

It was time to become the predator once more.

And it was with this thought that he saw something on the ground, something that caught a band of bright moonlight.

On the side of the road waited a wet puddle. Small—no bigger than a tea cup saucer. The dog whined in the back of his throat and Coburn shushed him as he knelt down and dipped two fingers into it.

His fingers came away black and sticky.

Motor oil.

Fresh, too. The wheel rut next to it was new. Someone had just been through here. Drove on the side of the road to avoid the gauntlet of wrecked-up cars.

Vehicle meant humans.

Humans meant food.

Maybe the gravy train wasn't dried up just yet.

"Let the hunt begin," Coburn said, and Creampuff yipped in agreement.

THE *HAUSFRAU'S* BELLY distended against the pink bathrobe, poking out past the frayed fabric belt. It was so bloated that the belly button stuck out, fat and shriveled as a dead man's thumb.

Around her lay the bodies of her undead cohorts, all of them ripped asunder, bitten into with great gobbets of spoiled meat taken from their thighs, their guts, their brains. Some of them were still... well, not *alive*, not really, but animated, at least. They moaned and twitched and pawed at the earth, their bodies too ruined to get up and amble around in search of fresh meat. Each as dumb as a bag of sand.

Hausfrau wandered among them, the taste of their foul flesh still lingering on her empurpled lips. It did nothing for her. It did not sustain her.

But the blood. The blood had changed her.

She moved her disintegrating fingers, the bony tips poking through puckered skin like a second fingernail—like an animal's claw—and she used those fingers to feel along the inside of her mouth.

Her teeth came out in her hand.

That in and of itself was not unusual. They were, of course, rotten.

But they had been replaced. Beneath them: a row of razor sharp canines, one after the other. She could not count, but if she could, she would count dozens. Both in the top of her mouth and the bottom. Her bony fingertip clicked along—*tik-tik-tik-tik*—like a child's stick dragging along the pickets of a fence.

She wanted more of that blood.

It wasn't just need. It was want. Desire. *Agency.*

That was new. It was like parts of her brain—an organ which before now was just a lump of dead tissue sheltered by her misshapen skull—

suddenly flared to life. Not the parts having to do with higher thought. Or rationality. Or intelligence.

But rather, the parts having to do with instinct and desire.

Right now, desire overwhelmed her: the desire to run, hunt, fuck, and kill. Her body ached for it. She ran her tongue along her razored teeth, and they cut clean through the muscle and severed the tip. But the *hausfrau* didn't care.

She was hungry. She smelled the air. She wanted blood.

COBURN TRACKED THE vehicle by the dots of lost oil and by the fading stink of exhaust caught on the wind. Whoever was driving the car—no, not a car, but a truck or something bigger—headed north on the highway away from town. Along the way, Coburn didn't see much of the walking dead. Once in a while he caught sight—or scent—of them wandering around in a stumbling cluster, but the living dead were not capable hunters. They were merely reapers of opportunity, attacking when prey stumbled nearby.

At least, that seemed a pretty good theory. Coburn in turn stayed far away from them: any time he heard their distant groans or soggy gurgles, he kept to the shadows, creeping quietly. The dog, too, seemed to understand this, knowing that it didn't want to become a late night snack for the horde of undead. (Though the dog did not seem to have that same sense about Coburn and had calmed down some since the river, perhaps because he was choosing the lesser of two evils.)

Coburn wandered the highway. Stars above. Moon often hidden behind bands of rheumy clouds, as if it refused to show its face or cast light onto such a broken, shameful world. He wasn't alone out here: the dead milled around on the highway, sometimes staggering about in the bands of pine trees to either side of the road. They were slow. If they got in his way, he obliterated them. A new way each time: he put one through a car window, then jerked the dude's head *just right* so the glass decapitated him. He stuck a branch through another fucker's head. He beat a one-eyed little girl to death—or, rather, beyond death—with a hubcap, her skull in the end looking like a treacly blood pudding.

By day, Coburn slept in the trunks of abandoned cars, his jacket pressed up against the cracks in the trunk to ensure that no light would creep in and burn sun-touched scars across his body. Creampuff lay curled in the crook of his arm.

At night, he wandered. The first night, he forgot that the dog needed food. And bathroom breaks. The animal squirmed and whined and such an expression of weakness grated on the vampire. He thought about dashing the dog against a car bumper and cracking the pooch open like a can of bloody soda, but rationing food was wiser. And these hard days demanded a wisdom Coburn wasn't used to. So he let the dog walk along with him and do his business off in the weeds. He wasn't sure how to feed the animal, not exactly, but he suspected after surviving in a world gone mad the dog had his ways.

Sure enough, Creampuff returned with a fat bullfrog in his mouth. He trotted back, offered it to Coburn first.

"Fuck off," Coburn said, shooing the animal. "What do I look like, a French chef? I'm not Escoffier over here. Go eat that somewhere else."

The dog did as told. He sat down, ripping into the frog and eating the guts first. Coburn didn't wait. The dog caught up five minutes later, muzzle slick with red, and the appearance of even that small amount of blood lit a fire in Coburn's belly—he did think about licking the blood from the terrier's snout, but decided against it. Coburn was not given over to great fits of shame, but making out with a skinny, dirty rat terrier would destroy what meager dignity he still possessed.

The end of the third night came, and Coburn was getting hungry.

"No food out here," he told the terrier, who looked up at him with small, dark eyes. "I don't smell anything good. Just the rot on the wind. And that trail of exhaust pushing farther away."

Made sense, really. His prey had a vehicle. They could outpace him—not easily, as they had to navigate ruined roads and abandoned vehicles. Sometimes they had to double-back and take a different exit just to avoid a gummed-up highway blockade. Coburn, however, had no such limitation. He could walk over the tops of cars if need be. To a man on foot, the apocalyptic wreckage offered few transportational challenges.

Even still. They were steadily escaping.

And he was increasingly hungry. The terrier was starting to look like a stopgap measure: he carried the dog under his arm and with every hour was more keenly aware of the animal's little fluttery heartbeat. A heartbeat that pumped blood—food, drink, *ecstasy*—through the beast's wan body.

Fuck it, time to eat.

He opened his mouth, tilted the dog's head back, and bit down.

But then, he paused—fangs not yet puncturing the dog's hide. Creampuff panted, seemingly happy at the attention, as if this was tantamount to affection rather than an attempt to suck the pooch dry. He tasted the dog's musky canine odor, tasted the dog's desperation and hunger and loyalty, and then stopped. It wasn't guilt that stopped him, or at least, that was what he told himself.

Rather, it was the fact that eating the terrier would provide so little food that it was almost not worth the energy: it would be like handing a starving man half of an old cookie. No satisfaction to be had.

When the terrier gave him a curious look—a damning, accusing glare—Coburn shot back: "Calm down, frog-muncher. I'm not going to eat you. Not tonight, at least. Tomorrow is a different matter." The dog continued to stare, as if to lay blame. Then the animal looked at the cars around them and offered a sharp bark. "I can't drive a car, you little shit. I've been dead for 50 years and I lived in Manhattan. Why the fuck would I learn to drive?"

He might've known once. He wondered about that, sometimes. His old life—meaning, the life he actually *lived* as opposed to this dead mockery—was lost to him, swallowed whole the night he awakened in an empty grave north of the city. Even still, that was so long ago, what did it matter? Cars were different now anyhow. All the buttons and fiddly bits. Kids watching cartoons about sponges on screens fixed to the backs of seats, turning their pliable little minds into the intellectual equivalents of sea cucumbers. This was the future, and the future was dumb.

So, no, Coburn didn't drive. He took taxis and limos. Or, his preference, he walked. He liked the feel of the city under his feet, the people around him moving like cells in a bloodstream.

The terrier whined. Coburn said, "I hate you."

They kept walking.

That night, after crossing from New Jersey into Pennsylvania along I-78, Coburn slept in the back of an overturned trailer. Before settling in for the night he cleared the area of the living dead—they reached for him, rotten teeth snapping at the air. He beat them all to death with a 4-way lug wrench he'd found in the last trunk—part of a tire-changing kit. They went down fast, and the last one—a bloated old man with his guts already hanging out, all twisted up in his shirt like a bundle of apples—dropped when Coburn flung the lug wrench at his head like a goddamn Chinese star. It lodged in the old man's head, cracking through the forehead like it was brittle as an egg. Coburn reclaimed the weapon, then joined the dog in the back of the trailer.

The next evening, good news awaited.

The stink of exhaust had grown stronger, not weaker, during the day.

"They've doubled back," he told Creampuff. A smile spread across his face like butter in a hot pan. He licked a fang. "Let's go eat."

CHAPTER SEVEN

Fat is Flavor

BLOOD PUMPED INTO his mouth and down his throat, his tongue playing in the wound like a boy splashing in a kiddie pool, and as he drank, Coburn was reminded of something an old chef friend of his used to say: "*Fat is flavor.*"

Even in blood.

Salty. Sweet. Thick.

Equal parts *milkshake* and *liver pate*.

Fucking delicious.

The fat man wobbled and swayed but did not fall, his hand still idly fingering the button on his jeans as if he still might decide to stop and take a piss here along this overgrown fencerow, the tall needled pines on the other side playing home to an army of complaining nightbirds. Coburn cupped a steadying palm under the man's chest—his tit, really—and dug in deeper, savoring the warm and buttery blood.

Only an hour before, Coburn and Creampuff came following the dots of oil and the trail of exhaust down a back country road until it wound down a gravel drive. A sign, choked by ivy and mold, read: LAKE TOWHEE.

And there, parked on a knoll overlooking a scum-topped lake, sat a big, clunky RV. A low fire, now mostly glowing embers, lay smoldering, the smoke and ash drifting in whorls toward the pregnant midnight moon above.

Coburn could smell them. Not one, but several—used to be he could identify humans by the smell of perfume, the scent of leather, the odor of mouthwash or toothpaste. Now it was mostly just a gross mélange of body odors: sweat and bad breath and piss and scum. And maybe, just maybe, an undercurrent of soap.

Oh, and blood. Coburn could *always* smell the blood.

Must've been four or five people up there. The buffet, it seemed, was open once more. Good thing, too, because Coburn was on the edge of a keenly-honed hunger, and hunger made a vampire do very strange things.

He and Creampuff hid amongst a nest of dry reeds, watching. A fat man came out of the camper, a windbreaker as big as a four-person tent draped across his body. Coburn marveled at the man's size. Here it was, the end of the world, the gates of Hell ripped open so that all of its rotting souls could come tumbling out, and this shit-heel somehow managed to remain morbidly obese.

But hey, the vampire thought, who cares? Big boy means big blood. Buckets of the stuff. Gallons. His toes curled just thinking about it.

The big dude had a rifle. He leaned it up against the RV, next to the door, then tottered off toward the forest's edge.

He was going to take a piss.

Coburn looked to Creampuff, then pressed his finger to his lips. He thought again about trying to coerce the dog to do as commanded, but before he had to, the terrier hunkered down on his belly.

"Wait here," Coburn said, and then he stalked the fat man.

And now, here he was. Dumb fuck came up. Coburn threw a stone to distract him—and as soon as big boy turned around to look (pivoting his prodigious mountain body), Coburn bit down from behind.

"Guh," the fat man said. Way his lips worked made him look like a fish, gasping. The blood was wonderful. Oily and sweet. This was what the Japanese called *umami*, Coburn thought. The salty satisfaction of fish sauce.

Then—

The sky split with the sound of thunder.

Coburn felt struck, as if by a fist.

The sweet smell of the blood in his nose gave way to another odor: the acrid, rankling stink of gunpowder.

It took all his will, but he wrenched his fangs free of the fat neck and let the poor bastard bleed like a stuck pig.

Behind him, a fireplug of an old man. No—not old, not exactly. Late 40s, early 50s, maybe. Weathered face. Small dark eyes. Hair going silver even now and an ill-sculpted gray beard clinging to his chin.

In his hand: a lever-action rifle. A .30-30, by the look of it. Probably the same one that fat boy here left by the RV door.

Coburn grinned, licked a goopy drop of blood from his lip before it slid down his chin and he missed the chance. He released the fat man, let the corpulent bastard drop into the brush, moaning like one of those rotting fuckers.

Then he turned to face his attacker.

The silver-hair jacked another shell into the breach.

A woman hurried over—younger, with perfect hair and makeup, even in these mad times, even in this dead world (it was on her that Coburn had smelled the soap)—and stood by him, holding his hip protectively.

"Again," she seethed, a fire in her eyes. Coburn knew that kind of rage. Didn't expect it in a girl who looked like that, like a painted doll.

Rifle raised, the silver-hair stared down the sight. The barrel wavered.

"He doesn't look like a rotter," the older man said. "Pale. But not... coming apart at the seams." Behind him, one of the windows of the RV—protected by a clumsily-cut chain link mesh bolted into place—showed movement. A white curtain parted. Another woman stared out: a black woman with fear in her eyes, drawn by the sounds outside.

More blood! Coburn thought. This buffet was bigger than he'd imagined.

"Shoot, Gil!" the girl hissed.

Gil winced, pulled the trigger.

Bang.

Coburn felt a hard tap on his shoulder, not far from where the other bullet had gone in. He looked down, saw the hole in his leather jacket.

Stuck a thumb through the fabric and into the wound, wiggled it around. Bummer.

"You're a piss-poor shot, pal," Coburn said, chuckling. "You couldn't hit the broad side of a barn with the broad side of a barn."

He popped out his thumb, thick with the black blood that populated his withered veins, then stuck it in his mouth like a lollipop.

"It's a cannibal," the girl said. "You saw what he was doing to Ebbie."

The fat man—Ebbie, apparently—groaned in response to his name.

"That what you are?" Gil asked, the rifle quivering in his grip. He jerked the lever, put another bullet into play. "Goddamn man-eater? Like it isn't bad enough we got the walking dead out there looking for a taste, we gotta worry about your type, too? You get the hell away from Ebbie. Go on. Move."

Coburn didn't move. Not yet.

Instead, he just shrugged. "Survival of the fittest, am I right?"

"You go to Hell."

"Your big boy's bleeding over here in the weeds."

"Step away, I said."

Coburn took one step toward Gil, grinning still. His words took on a sing-song quality: "I'm just *say*ing. He's *go*ing to waste."

"Kill him!" the girl screeched. "*Gil.*"

Time collapsed in on itself. Coburn saw the man's finger tighten around the trigger, saw it pull taut, saw the girl's eyes go wide and the corner of her lip curl into a mean vulpine smile, saw the woman at the window close *her* eyes because she didn't want to watch, saw a pair of moths dancing a herky-jerky tango in the headlights of the RV, saw the doorknob to the vehicle twist *oh-so-slightly*—

Coburn moved fast. Faster than any human could.

In the time it took to almost pull the trigger tight, Coburn was behind the silver-hair, jacking the rifle lengthwise up against the man's throat. The plan was simple enough: gun was lateral, the mean end pointed toward the dolled-up darling, and she'd catch a bullet as Coburn helped the man pull the trigger. Then before the man could cry out at the loss of his cradle-robbed prize with the ruby-red lipstick, Coburn would yank back on the rifle and collapse the man's trachea, turning it to a gurgling paste.

Then he would feed.

Fill his coffers with many pennies.

Fill his jug with the finest claret.

Fill his belly with—

Well. He'd guzzle blood, that was what he'd do.

Then, everything changed.

The door to the RV swung open as Little Miss Lipstick caught up to what was going on, realized that Coburn wasn't where he had been and was now behind her silver-haired sugar daddy. She screamed.

Another girl came hurrying out of the RV—not the black woman from the window, no, this one was even younger than the dolled-up darling, maybe in her mid-teens. Frail, bird-like, even. Big wide eyes glistening, capturing the light of the moon.

Coburn smelled peaches and cigarettes.

She walked out, held out her hands, palms forward, as she tried to catch her breath. With those doe eyes she looked him up and down, her white-blonde hair bobbing atop her bony shoulders. Her eyes were ringed with dark shadows—like faint bruises. The girl smiled: nervous, excited, terrified.

"I like the jacket," she said. Not *wait*, not *stop*, not *oh my god*.

I like the jacket. Well, shit. Flattery. Coburn liked flattery.

Gil gasped, struggled in Coburn's grip, rifle tight against the man's throat.

"It's old," Coburn said, smirking.

"It's slick."

"It's seen some times."

"I bet it has." The girl circled around, still facing him. "You've been around."

"Pshh. I'm young. Look at me. Tall, lean like a coffee stirrer, barely any salt in my pepper. This guy here"—Coburn demonstrated by lifting the gun and, with it, Gil—"*he's* old. Older than his years."

"And you? Younger than your years?"

"Maybe so."

Gil was starting to turn blue. Eyes bulging.

The girl looked to the man. "It'll be okay, Daddy."

"Daddy?" Coburn asked, then offered a barking laugh. Still, he loosened his grip just enough so as not to kill the man, not yet. "Huh.

Didn't see that coming. The painted lady there, she's damn sure not your Mommy, though. Not unless she had you when she was barely done playing with her E-Z-Bake oven. Pregnant at the ripe old age of eight? Nasty to think."

"You sonofab—" The doll started.

"*Cecelia*," the teen spat. "Shut the fuck up."

"Oh!" Coburn said, surprised. "I like that. Lippy little girl."

"What are you?" she asked.

"Doesn't matter."

"Are you dead?"

"Do I look dead?"

She took another step closer. "Dead isn't the same as it used to be."

"Fair enough. Even still. I don't smell like spoiled meat. Maggots aren't using me like a condo complex. And all my organs? Still inside my body."

"I know what you are," she said.

"I doubt that."

"You're dead."

"Am I?"

"But not like them. Not like the others."

He chuckled. "I don't smell like a dead goat that's been bloated in the sun, for one. Don't attract flies, either. And all my parts are still inside my body, so that's a plus."

"Still," she said. "You're different."

Coburn showed her his set of bloody teeth. "Could be, rabbit. Could be."

"What's your name?"

"Coburn," he said. What could it hurt?

"I'm Kayla."

"Great. Whatever. I don't normally name my food before I eat it, but whatever works for you."

She was scared. But she crept closer just the same.

"I want to make you a deal."

"A deal. For me. Cute. Ballsy. Not interested."

The girl's eyes twinkled. Something about them: she didn't have much to lose. That intrigued him. Would've been the easiest thing in the world to continue with the plan: shoot the brat, choke the man, then take his time with the teen.

But something stopped him.

"Look around you," Kayla said. "World's gone sour. People—like, *all* people, society, civilization—didn't make it. Not many of us left."

"Getting bored over here. And peckish."

"That's the point. Bored now? Wait 'til all you got left are those rotters to keep you company. Think you're hungry? What happens when there's none of us left?"

If his heart still worked, it would've skipped a beat. Even still, the blood in his gut curdled, the dead muscles tightened. Fear and panic scrambled against his mind's walls like a cat with its tail on fire. He remembered last night. He remembered the hunger.

He narrowed his gaze, then cleared a clot-bubble of blood out of his throat. "Go on."

"The deal is this," she said. "You help us, we help you. We show you food. We know where others are. Living people. *Bad* people. People who'd kill us just as soon as say hello."

"And in return?"

"You keep us safe." She looked to her old man. "But first you have to stop choking my Daddy. I think you're killing him."

CHAPTER EIGHT
Tête-à-Tête

THE RINKY-DINK PARK playground was rusted, its equipment just a tangle of shadows—the torchlight played along its edges as the vampire Coburn followed Kayla and her torch. The girl—herself just a tangle of shadows, like a handful of coat hangers that got caught together— plopped down on the edge of a slide and lit a cigarette. A Virginia Slim. Comically too long, too effete, for this girl.

Off in the distance, Coburn could see the RV. But, more importantly, he could see the moon glinting off a rifle scope. He was in the old man's crosshairs. The man—Gil, the girl's Daddy—was not particularly keen on letting his daughter wander off into the darkness with Coburn. And yet, the girl persisted: she muttered about dreams, about the future, said something like 'he's what I was talking about.' Then Gil waved her off, angry but acquiescing.

"You gonna sit?" she asked, blowing a dragon's plume of smoke from each nostril. "You can. It's okay. I won't bite. Get it? Bite?"

"Funny," he said. But he could tell that she was scared, just the same. "I'll stand, thanks. Just in case your Daddy over there falls asleep on the rifle and *accidentally* pulls the trigger."

"You sit, he'll have a harder shot."

He crinkled his brow. "You think?"

"I do."

Shit, she was right. Coburn shrugged, and sat down on the edge of a squeaky playground carousel. He planted his boots on the ruggedized rubber ground so he didn't drift and spin like an idiot. He had some veneer of cool to keep, after all.

From here, the shot would have to go through a jungle gym. A dozen chances for the bullet to go astray.

"How's your shoulder?"

He wormed a finger into the hole the bullet tore into the leather. He pressed the finger deeper so it pushed into his own dead flesh. Didn't hurt. Finger didn't go that deep, either. Coburn watched Kayla with an unblinking stare. Watched the smoke wind around her like a pair of ghosts. "Right as rain, little girl."

"You wanna eat me?" the girl asked. It was not, despite the way it sounded, a come-on. When she asked it, her hands were shaking.

Coburn smelled the air. "Funny thing is, no, no I do not. Something's wrong with you. You sick?"

"Just a cold." She flicked ash from the Virginia Slim.

"No. Uh-uh. It's more than that. You're too thin."

"Hard to get food out here."

"Dark shadows under your eyes."

She shrugged. "Hard to get sleep out here, too."

"You're sick," he said again.

"And you're a vampire."

The word gave him pause.

"Not many people are willing to say that word out loud," he said. "I've killed a helluva lot of people, my teeth in their neck, their blood in my mouth, and not one of them dared to call me what I so obviously was."

"They didn't want to believe."

"Yeah. Maybe."

She laughed—but it was a sound without mirth. "Times have changed, though. Like Leelee says, these are the end of days. Gotta start believing in something. Might as well be vampires."

Coburn didn't know who the fuck Leelee was and he really didn't care, either. Probably one of those blood-bags in the camper. He still planned on eating them all. Wasn't sure how he'd do it, yet. Kill one? Kill them all? Blood from an already dead body swift became a non-nutritious snack—'nutritious' being a relative term and all. He wasn't even sure why he was here, now, with this sick girl. Could be that the human part of him was bored, and this was one way to fill the hours. Plus, it let him ask some big questions.

"When did it happen?" he asked. He swept his hands out as if to indicate the world beyond this quiet, peaceful night-time park. "This. The end of the world. When did these shambling assholes start running the show?"

"You really don't know?"

"I was sleeping."

"Sleeping?"

"Let's just say I was *forcibly detained*."

She flicked the cigarette over her shoulder, lit another off her oil-rag-on-a-chair-leg torch. "Daddy's been keeping track of the days. Said it happened about two years ago, I guess? But it feels like a lot longer."

Two years ago. Christ. So he'd been out of commission for at least two years, and who knows how many before? He tried to conjure up the last year he remembered, but the information escaped him.

"How'd it all go down?" he asked. "What the hell is it?"

"They say it's some kind of bacteria. Someone dredged up some long-dormant bug-a-boo from an oil well, I guess. Drill, baby, drill. They figure that Patient Zero was one of the rig workers. With the zombie disease, you get bit, you turn. Usually within twenty-four hours, sometimes forty-eight, maybe it depends on your immune system. But it gets you one way or another. Doesn't matter if it's just a little teeny-tiny bite or if they ate all your guts out. Even if they kill you, you'll get back up, half-eaten and dumb as a bag of cat turds. You wanna know the funny part?"

He shrugged, the message being, *Eh, not really.*

"You know how in the movies the zombies are always like, *Braaaains, braaaaains*? And they crack open skulls like Cadbury eggs and suck out the head-meats?" As if to demonstrate, Kayla made a slurpy noise.

"Nuh-uh, not true at all. They got that part all wrong. That's the one part the zombies *don't* eat—brains. And that's the one place you gotta hit 'em to kill 'em."

"That is funny," he said without laughing or actually thinking it was funny. No part of this was funny. Just plain fucked up, was what it was. And when a vampire thought shit was fucked up, well, it probably was.

"You're being sarcastic."

"Me? *Never*."

"I see what you did there."

"Uh-huh. So—" Coburn tilted his wrist toward his face. No watch hung there (he didn't need one; he knew when dawn was on its way), but even still, he tapped two fingers against his wrist bone. "You've got five more minutes to tell me just what the hell this deal is all about. After those five minutes, if I remain unconvinced—and let's be honest, I'm totally not going to be convinced by this bullshit— then I'm going to break your neck, stalk back over to your friends in that rat-trap Winnebago, and I'm going to turn each one of them into a blood sprinkler. Then, just to be a *real* bad dude, I'm going to roll around in the blood the way a dog might roll around in a smeary pile of gopher shit."

Kayla visibly tightened. But she laughed in a piss-poor effort to cover up her fear. "You're a man who doesn't mince his words. That's real good. Here it is, then. I want you to protect us."

"Uh." He laughed, too, this time, for real, because *hot damn* if that wasn't the funniest shit ever. "How's about, *no*? Malnutrition has made you dangerously delusional. Let me guess: you're a girl who likes ponies and unicorns, yeah?"

"Think about it. Your food supply is dwindling. You kill all of us, eat us right up, how long that gonna last you?"

He clacked his teeth together, leaned forward. "Maybe I can turn you all into jerky. Or blood sausage. Maybe your bodies will last me into summer."

"Maybe. Maybe you're just playing with me. Either way—what then? You think you can find more of us out there? You won't find many beating hearts still in the world. We're few and far between. Look at the biology.

You drink blood and we humans always make more of it. Provided, of course, that we're alive. We make blood same way cows make milk."

"You want me to milk you?" This was absurdity, but he kept listening.

She almost looked stung, as if he was mocking her really good idea. "Well. Yes. In a manner of speaking. You keep us alive. You protect us. And we'll keep you fed. Not just from us. Like I said, we know of others out there. Bad people. World went to Hell and so did the human spirit."

Coburn clucked his tongue. "That's not how I figure it. I figure the end of the world just ripped off humanity's mask, and now the true face of mankind is out there grinning like a mad skull in the moonlight. But you think what you want. Keep talking."

"I'm just saying, you travel with us, you protect us, you stay fed. You just need to get us out West. There's people out West. Lots of 'em, if the stories are true. That's where they're rebuilding. That's where the people are. And where you got people, you got blood. A near endless supply."

"So let me get this right." He sucked a little air between his teeth, licked some of the fat fuck's blood off his teeth. "You want me to play farmer."

"Shepherd, really. Don't think of us like crops. Think of us like livestock. Think of it like you're driving a cattle train. You're just moving the herd. We're your food supply."

"Food supply." He let those words hang out there. This wasn't how he did things. Save people? *Protect* them? The thought made the fat man's blood curdle inside him. Still. He had to give it to this girl. For a teenager, she was a lot smarter than he'd figured. His gut reaction to her plan was the vampire's reaction, the *monster's* reaction: *kill her, lap at the sick girl's blood like you're at a water fountain.* But his human side saw the reason in it. New York City alone had gone from millions of people to millions of *dead* people. Dead people whose blood was as good as road tar. Rest of the country couldn't be much better. If he went ahead and gobbled up these fools tonight, in a few nights he'd be back where he started. Hungry. Wandering. Hunting night to night, looking for shelter for the day, watching out for those rotten fuckers at every turn. The thought didn't thrill him.

Even still. The old man shot him. The fat man was delicious. He wanted more. He wanted it now. Every time he blinked his eyes, there it waited in the darkness behind his lids: a red haze, a bloody curtain, a crimson hunger.

Fuck it. Coburn made his decision.

He moved fast against the girl. Backhanded the torch out of her hand—it went spinning off into the shadows, rebounding against a set of monkey bars.

Then he grabbed her by the throat and lifted her up.

And he started to squeeze.

"I am not a good man," he hissed. The girl's eyes started to pop. "Point of fact, I am worse than a bad man because I am *no longer* a man at all. I am a monster."

Bang.

Gil, her father, started shooting. But with the torch gone, he and the girl were mostly just shadows. The rifle barked an echoing report—a bullet whined off one of the bars of the jungle gym.

"I don't like people except as *tasty treats.*"

Another shot ricocheted. If Gil got lucky and scored a hit—and *if* it hit Coburn smack in the head—well, that would be bad news.

But he kept on squeezing.

"I don't especially like taking orders from some smart-ass teenager. I could break your neck just by twitching."

Bang. This one hit the monkey bars on the other side: Gil overshot.

"But you know what? You got yourself a deal."

He dropped the girl. She landed on her feet, but her legs were wobbly and didn't hold her—her butt bone clanged against the metal slide.

Kayla gasped, wheezed, clutched her throat.

Just then, he saw her eyes flit to the space behind him. Creampuff the terrier stood there, watching all this unfold.

Coburn went over and scooped up the dog under his arm.

In the distance, Gil and the others were racing across the open ground between the RV and the play area, calling out Kayla's name.

"Nice dog," Kayla said, coughing.

"I'll see you tomorrow night. Don't leave without me. You do, I won't be so inclined to be reasonable the next time we meet."

And with that, he moved fast, exerting his vampiric will. Coburn and his dog vanished into the shadows.

CHAPTER NINE

A Day in the Life of a Dead Girl

KAYLA HATED HAVING to pee in the coffee mug. It was bad enough having to pee outside, though by now she'd pretty much gotten used to that. But Leelee told her she needed to see the urine, which meant having to contain the urine by pissing into a coffee mug, which *further* meant frequently whizzing on her own hand.

This morning was no exception.

"Shoot," she said, wiping her hand on the grass. She hiked up her panties, then lifted the **World's Best Grandpa** mug and swirled it around. The urine was dark, turbid—the color of beef broth. Leelee wasn't going to like that.

Kayla extracted herself from underneath the blue spruce and wandered down toward the lake's edge, where Leelee was washing clothes and where her father, Gil, was sitting on a park bench oiling the rifle.

She thrust the coffee mug under her father's chin.

"Coffee?" she asked, bright and chipper. "Still warm!"

Gil wrinkled his nose and waved her away. "Christ, Kayla. Quit fooling around. I got a gun here."

"Ain't loaded."

"You don't know that. Besides, that's still no reason to go waving a cup of piss under somebody's chin."

"Pssh, Daddy, you are the same old stick-in-the-mud that you always were, and I love you for it." She set the mug down and kissed her father on the bridge of his crooked nose. He was a tough old guy—not big, and actually kind of short, but even still. Serious gray eyes, salt-and-pepper at his temple and in his beard, and a stripe of silver up top. Skin like saddle leather.

He just grunted at her affection, then pulled her close and tilted her chin with his thumb. It was a gentle adjustment; he had never been rough with her.

"Looks like someone strung you up in a tree, left you there overnight." From the back of his throat, a low growl. Then he turned his eyes away from her—a flash of shame crossing his face. "I should've been able to take that sonofabitch out before he hurt you. Damnit, Kayla, you should've stayed back at the Winnebago."

Before she should respond, Leelee was behind her. The woman dried her hands on an old shammy. "Here," she said, turning Kayla toward her, "let me see, girl. Come on, now, let's have a look."

Kayla rolled her eyes and did as asked. Didn't stop her from adding, "I am *fine*. Doesn't even hurt." A lie, given that with every beat of her heart her neck throbbed with waves of echoing pain, almost as if he were still choking her. "I am, as you have noted in the past, one tough little bee-yotch."

"I think I said *tough little cookie*," Leelee mumbled. "The bruising's bad. But it's just that. Bruising."

"I bruise easily. You know that."

"Mm." Her nurse wasn't convinced. "Let's see the cup." She peered into the coffee mug, and Kayla saw the woman's face fall. She knew it wasn't good; Leelee's forehead scrunched up into a little consterning 'V' whenever she was genuinely concerned. "That's a lot of blood."

Kayla felt Gil's eyes following all of this. He wouldn't say anything. Not now, anyway. With him, it always simmered low and slow: the man's heart was like a tough cut of brisket. Took a while to break it down.

"Pshh. I'm fine. I feel good."

"It's getting worse."

"I am as healthy as a bear. A big bear. A big happy *healthy* bear. Come on, Lee, you know me. I should've been dead six months before the world went and turned to spoiled meat. But I keep on keeping on and it's because somebody—God or Buddha or John Travolta—wants me to keep going." The other two stared at her, each worried in their own way. Her father's dark pinprick eyes were the tell, with him. With Leelee, the 'V' in her forehead just grew deeper and deeper until it looked like you could shove a dime in there and lose it forever. "It's just a thing, a temporary *my pee looks like cranberry juice* thing," Kayla said, fetching her last cigarette from her pocket.

She popped the Virginia Slim between her lips like a lollipop. Her father quickly grabbed at it—she was too slow to lean back, and he snagged it. Then he flicked it into the lake where fish promptly began to nibble at it; it twitched and hopped like a bobber.

"*Dad*," she said. "That was my last smoke."

"Last smoke is right. You're done with that shit. You're not healthy, and sick little girls should not smoke cigarettes." Before she could protest, he continued—more firmly this time, thrusting his finger up into her face. "You're also done with this delusion about what's going to happen tonight. We're not waiting around for that mean crazy sonofabitch to come back."

Kayla sneered. "I'm not a little girl. I'm fifteen years old. And *he* is a vampire. Mean and crazy, maybe. But he's a vampire. You can say that word."

"What I can say is that he was some nut-ball cannibal cranked to the gills on methamphetamines or horse tranquilizers or some-such. We can only hope that he didn't have some kind of other disease before he decided to bite into Ebbie like he was a tube of summer sausage. Last thing we need is Ebbie getting Hep-A or something. We don't have the means to deal with that." Just six months ago or so, Ebbie got an infection from a cut on his calf—the skin turned red and dark tendrils spread out underneath the skin looking like earthworms under dirt. Leelee said it was blood poisoning, and that they were lucky to find some antibiotics in the medicine cabinet of an abandoned house or Ebbie would've been a goner. Didn't help that Leelee discovered the big guy had diabetes (though Ebbie strongly disagreed with that diagnosis and made no effort to confirm it). "Ebbie's already laid low today, thanks to that monster."

"Ebbie's going to be fine," she said. "Besides, he could stand to lose some water weight."

Again with the finger in her face. She felt a stab of guilt in her heart because she knew what was coming: "Abner could've been killed last night. And there you were cozying up to the one that almost put him in the grave. If we had it your way, he'd be stuck on a spit somewhere. We might all be. Hell, your buddy from last night damn near collapsed my throat." He craned his neck, showed her his own bruises—mottled shadows from where the rifle pressed. "You should be ashamed of yourself, little girl."

Leelee offered a steadying hand and gently eased Gil's finger and hand back toward the rifle. "It'll all be okay."

Kayla tightened her lips. She wanted to say she was sorry, wanted to tell her father and Leelee that it *would* all be okay, that she dreamt about how it would be all okay in the end—but she felt angry inside, a storm of broken feelings like a tower of teacups pushed over so they shatter.

"You shouldn't talk to me that way," was what she said instead, her words betraying her feelings—or was it the other way around? "Tonight, he's coming back here no matter what you say. That's just the way it's going to be. We're going to give him what he wants so he helps us get out to California. You don't like it? Too damn bad, Daddy. Because if you really believe I'm so special like you keep staying, then you don't want me doing something rash, do you? Running off by my lonesome? Maybe taking a big old fistful of Tylenol and Advil and swallowing it down with a gulp of Cecelia's vodka? You think I'm so special, then it's time to start doing things my way."

The anger came out of her like fluid from a lanced blister. Her father, rarely a man to wear his emotions on his sleeve, looked taken aback. He tried to say something, but she just shook her head and marched off.

Leelee called after her, but she dared not look back.

*   *   *

INSIDE THE RV, Ebbie—short for Abner—slept on his side on the pull-out couch. The couch had long developed a cruel lean, and it looked like it would soon spill him out onto the floor.

Kayla crept in and placed the flowers she had picked—just a handful of early spring tulips coming up out there amongst the trees—on an overturned bucket next to Ebbie's head.

"The hell are you doing?"

Kayla spun around, her heart jackknifing inside her chest as Cecelia appeared—skinny, eyes ringed with shadows (both real and painted on), long dark hair draped over a ratty old robe. She looked like she had just awakened, even though it was already coming up on the middle of the day. Dad didn't let anybody sleep past seven (or six if he was in a mood)—anybody except Cecelia, who did whatever she wanted, whenever she wanted it.

"Shh," Kayla said, pressing a finger to her lips.

Cecelia waved her off. "Whatever. That blubbery dipshit wouldn't wake up if you stuck a firecracker in his ear and let it explode."

As it to confirm this, Ebbie grunted, groaned, then pulled the sheet up around his chin. When he moved, Kayla could more easily see the square patch of gauze covering the wound on his neck. Her father's voice echoed in her head: *You should be ashamed of yourself, little girl.*

Kayla tried not to think about it.

"You should be nicer to him," she said, instead. "He likes you."

"He also likes Snickers bars. In fact, I think he likes those a lot more than he likes me," Cecelia said, poking around the vehicle's interior—kitchenette countertop, seat cushions, console dashboard. "Gimme one of your cigarettes."

"I'm out." She paused, decided to tell her the truth: "Dad threw my last one in the lake. Food for the catfish."

Cecelia eyed her up, obviously suspicious. That wasn't unusual: Cecelia was suspicious of everything and everyone. Years back, her father told her that people like that—people who can't trust, who always think the worst of everybody—act that way because they themselves can't be trusted. Most people, he said, figured they were as good as or better than all the other folks around them. So, bad people couldn't ever see the good in folks because they were the only example. Funny, then, how her father couldn't see the same in Cecelia. Funny too how he'd become like that—suspicious all the time—ever since the world went to Hell.

The woman came up on her, stood in front of her, looking down. Her breath smelled like mouthwash—did her father sneak her some? Or did she have a stash of it somewhere in the Winnebago? Kayla felt privy to too many secrets already. She knew that Ebbie had a cache of candy and junk food in the back of one of the RV's luggage compartments. She knew that sometimes Leelee went off by herself to just cry—not just *cry a little* but great big heaping gulps, the kind of sobs that wrack your body and hollow you out. Given how the woman was normally a rock, normally so level-headed, that was not comforting news.

Cecelia, ironically, bent down and tried to smell Kayla's breath. It wasn't subtle. Nothing about Cecelia was.

"Guess you're telling the truth," she said to Kayla, apparently satisfied that she wasn't catching any whiff of recent *cancer intake*. "Your Daddy's too much of a goody-goody." The corners of her mouth turned to a salacious smile. "Though not when he's with me."

Outside, as if on cue: two gunshots—reports from the rifle. Kayla felt her heart kick, and she turned to pull back the curtains on the little porthole window, but Cecelia grabbed her hand.

"He's just out hunting," she said. "Calm down, little girl."

Little girl.

"You don't call me that," Kayla said. "Hell, you're not but five years older than me. You don't get to talk down to me."

Cecelia ignored her. "Your Daddy's a good shot with that rifle."

"Yeah. I *know*."

"He always hits his target." The smile on her face broadened: she was no longer just talking about the rifle, and she wanted Kayla to know it.

"Gross."

"Your friend from last night rolls up in here, he's going to kill him. Figures he probably won't show because by now the PCP or whatever he was jacked up on will have worn off—he won't survive those other bullet wounds. But if he does show?" She made her finger into a gun and held it against Kayla's temple: the nail, cut and painted, dug into the teen's skin. "Pop, pop, pop. Three to the head."

"You're disgusting."

Cecelia licked her lips and winked.

"Coburn's going to come back. I dreamed about it."

"You're too old for that kind of fantasy. Bet you also believe a unicorn's going to come out of those woods and whisk you away on its back." Her laugh was as much a growl as anything; it was almost enough to put Kayla off smoking. Then, Cecelia changed gears suddenly. "He and I are gonna get married, your Daddy and I. Soon as we find the perfect spot away from the rotters. Out West somewhere. During the sunrise. We've talked about it. Maybe one day you'll call me Mom."

Kayla couldn't take it. She shoved past Cecelia and exited the RV. Just to be sure that Cecelia got the message, she slammed the door.

Hard.

Hard enough, in fact, to break it.

The door didn't stay closed when she slammed it; that was the first sign of a problem. The latch didn't catch. The door just bounced off it and drifted open.

Kayla felt panicked. That wasn't good. The door needed to close. The zombies, they were creatures of opportunity, not intelligence— ironically, even though shooting them in the brains put them down for good, they didn't have a whole lot going *on* in those brains, either. Something as simple as a door presented a problem for them: best they could do was swarm up against it until they broke it down by sheer weight and volume.

She hurried back over, gently closed the door. Heard a *click*. Let out a sigh of relief, then stepped back down to the ground.

And the door drifted open again.

"Oh, no," Kayla said. "Shoot shoot *shoot*."

Cecelia appeared in the open doorway.

"You gotta be shitting me, Kayla!" she said—Kayla couldn't tell if the anger and outrage was real, or just Cecelia trying to pour gas on a fire. "You broke the damn door? For real? I swear, you are nothing but a problem. First you invite some kind of cannibal back to our camp, and now you break the 'Bago door? You are something. Now somebody's going to have to fix it before the damn rotters show up. Nice one. It's like you *want* us to get killed."

Kayla didn't even hear this last part—because, by then, she was weeping and running for the woods.

IT WASN'T FAIR.

You're special, they told her. Again and again. *You're different. You're not like everybody else. You should be dead. We have to take you somewhere.*

We have to take you Out West.

Then, of course, times like these came along and she didn't feel special at all. Matter of fact, she felt the opposite: she felt lower than a snake's belly in a wheel rut. Her father treated her like a child. Leelee treated her like a fragile little thing, a snowflake that might melt with even the gentlest touch. Cecelia treated her like a bag of garbage. And Ebbie...

Well, Ebbie was the only one who was nice to her at all.

For a monster, something about him felt utterly *honest*.

Refreshing, in a kind of horrible way.

Kayla leaned up against a tree, wiping her eyes. She'd been walking now for... how long was it? She didn't even know. From time to time she'd hear her father calling, or Leelee (but never Cecelia), and when she heard their voices she either hunkered down and hid or traveled in what she could best surmise was the opposite direction. A part of her knew this was wrong—a bonafide *bad idea*—but even still, she wanted to punish them a little bit.

And another part of her just felt ashamed. Like her father said she should be. For getting him hurt. And Ebbie. For arguing with Cecelia— why couldn't she just shut up and try to keep the peace?—and for breaking the door.

Didn't help that she was just making it worse by being away. If her father was out here looking for her, who was back there fixing the door? Ebbie? Ebbie was an IT manager before the zombie guts hit the fan: the world no longer had much use for computers, and so Ebbie's place in the food chain had been supplanted. Survivors knew how to identify edible plants and siphon gas from cars, not quarantine computer viruses and search for porn on the Internet. (Hell, the Internet wasn't even *a thing* anymore. It had long gone away, as insubstantial as a distant wind.)

Shame dogged her. So did anger. And righteousness. And a whole other squirming bag of emotions—Kayla had crossed the puberty threshold and her body was a cauldron of warring hormones. It was like someone had overturned a bag of snakes inside her heart and mind and let them tangle all up together in one big crazy breeding ball.

It didn't help that all this walking had made her sore—her back ached, her legs throbbed, her very *bones* seemed to radiate waves of pain. It sucked the energy right out of her. She could practically hear Leelee's voice: *You're sick, Kayla. You shouldn't have strayed so far.*

With a follow-up bonus question: *How are you going to get home?*

She put her back against a tree and slid down to a sitting position, her elbows resting on her knees.

Here, the forest was quiet. The occasional rustle of leaves as a squirrel darted from tree to tree. A wind came along and shook the evergreens. Above, the oaks and maples were already starting to bud and uncurl the year's new leaves.

She closed her eyes. For just a moment.

And when she opened them again, the sky was dimming. The horizon brightening, like a distant fire on the far side of the forest.

How long had she sat here, sleeping? How many hours, lost?

Sundown. That wasn't good. The living dead were bad news any time of the day or night, but they seemed to become more active at night, more directed. During the day they might not even notice as you passed by, provided you weren't within fifty feet or so and didn't make much noise. One time, middle of the day, she saw one rotter just blankly orbiting a lamppost. Slack-jawed and murmuring.

At night, though, they stirred up more. Kayla didn't know why and wasn't sure it really mattered much; her father said he figured the sun either charged them up like batteries or instead maybe sucked the energy from them. Whatever it was, night-time wasn't a good time to be out amongst them.

She had to get back to the camper.

She stood, her bones aching. Her blood rushed to her head—'orthostatic hypotension,' Leelee told her, also known as the common *head rush*. Took a moment to orient herself. From which way had she come?

Had to be that way, she thought. Past the fallen log.

She hurried in that direction, her muscles sore, her back throbbing from sitting in one position for so long. Everything about this disease tried to sap her strength, nibbling away at her. Sometimes she found herself wishing the cancer would kill her, like it was supposed to have over three years ago.

Kayla pushed through the forest, stepping over thorny tangles and big boulders that looked like turtle humps, the shadows of the trees stretching longer and longer until they began to disappear with the coming of evening. Kayla called out her father's name, feeling panic and uncertainty: had she come this way before? Everything here looked like everything else. That tree looked like that other tree. This rock looked like that rock. She stepped over a muddy gully that she was sure she didn't step over on the way here.

Where were they? She was afraid to cry out—too much noise would bring *them* down upon her head, but even then it was as if her thought arrived too loudly...

Because behind her, a branch snapped.

She spun, hoping to see her father or Leelee coming through the trees, but she was not so lucky.

The rotter's face suffered the undead version of Bell's Palsy—half of the flesh drooped, like a piece of bologna thrown against the wall. Once, this zombie was a park ranger—he still wore the outfit, though it had long given way to tears in the fabric. The name-patch was so soaked through by the creature's fluids—pink and yellow and red—that it was no longer legible.

Kayla didn't bother screaming. She just turned and ran, no longer cautious, no longer caring about the branches or thorn-whips.

As she ran, she realized that she was no longer alone.

Other corpses shambled through the underbrush. They came in from all sides—dozens of them now. Kayla didn't bother to get a good look.

Instead she just picked up the pace and bolted through the trees like a spooked animal.

As the sun dropped behind the horizon, leaving the forest cast in the muddy tones of deepening twilight, Kayla heard gunshots in the distance.

Then her foot caught on a root and she tumbled forward, her head thumping dully against the hard earth.

As she rolled over, foul hands reached down for her, a palm that smelled of bile covering her face. The finger wormed into her mouth and she tasted bitterness and rot: the flavor of a spoonful of spoiled meat on her tongue. She tried to scream, but the hands held her down, covering her eyes.

Teeth sank into the meat just past her collarbone.

Blood wetted her shirt as the zombie hissed.

A terrible thought crossed through her mind:

I am infected.

PART TWO
PROTECTOR

CHAPTER TEN

Feeding Frenzy

AND LIKE THAT, the pressure atop her was gone.

The zombie made a sound like one she'd never heard before: a kind of guttural bark, a chuffing belch. She clamped her hand to her bleeding collar and scooted back against a tree—the rotter who had bitten her, another park ranger (this one female, her scalp peeled back like the skin of a grape), stood there wearing a look more dumbfounded than usual.

The zombie began choking. Its foul tongue thrust out, stabbing at the air. It clawed at nothing. The sounds that emerged became more and more strangled—*grrk, gkkkt, kkkkkllllkkk.*

Then its eyes popped. Like hot eggs jumping out of their shells. From the eye sockets ran fresh blood—not black, but red—and with each rivulet came a curling wisp of steam or smoke.

The zombie dropped, dead. Or, at least, deader than before.

Suddenly, Kayla found herself yanked upward violently. She cried out as she was thrown over someone's shoulder—her face pressed into said someone's jacket—and she smelled leather and blood.

"Don't scream," Coburn hissed. "Just shut up and keep your arms and legs inside the vehicle, unless you want them broken off."

And then he began to run.

But he ran fast. Faster than fast. Branches whipped at her arms, cutting into them, drawing blood. She tucked them tight. She remembered once, way back when, seeing a nature video in school where they put a camera on some kind of hawk or falcon and recorded its flight through a tight forest—this was like that, the world rushing past, the trees nothing but blurry shadows.

Like *that*, Coburn emerged from the forest with her on his back.

She smelled gunpowder and rot. As if to punctuate the odor: a rifle shot split the air. Someone—Cecelia?—screamed.

Coburn dumped Kayla on the ground and then disappeared. Kayla propped herself up on her arms and legs, trying dearly not to vomit. And that was when she saw just how badly things had gone in her absence.

Night had fallen.

The rotters were everywhere.

They had surrounded the Winnebago.

Her father stood in the open doorway, firing off rifle rounds. Abner leaned out of the passenger side window in the cab, desperately swinging with a camping hatchet. Cecelia was at the window, screaming her fool head off even though she wasn't in immediate danger.

Leelee, though, *was* in danger.

The nurse stood up on a picnic table with can of hairspray and a lighter—an easy homespun flamethrower that didn't always do much to kill the undead but did a good job of keeping them at bay. She flicked the lighter, hit the button and set off plumes of chemical fire, like dragon's breath. The rotters swatted at it the way you might at a cloud of mosquitoes. A few of them actually caught fire.

And then the fire died down to a limp, sputtering spray, a few glowing yellow drops falling to the earth before dying out completely.

The zombies swarmed her, pulling her down.

Kayla's heart sank as Leelee's body fell beneath the horde.

But before she knew what was happening, Leelee surged back out of the zombie throng—this time, buoyed by the hands of Coburn the vampire. He threw her back up onto the picnic table, stepped up and then stepped *down* hard onto the picnic bench, catching the see-sawing bench board in his hand.

Then he started swinging that bench like a baseball bat.

Zombie skulls caved in. Some heads bent at the neck at wrong angles. Others twisted around. A few launched off the shoulders, freed by the mighty strikes.

Coburn began to carve a path through the horde. He swung the bench—easily five feet long—before him in great, swooping reaper-like arcs. Leelee fell in behind him and when the board finally shattered, he stabbed the broken shard into some fat rotter's pumpkin head and then went ahead and just used his hands. He grabbed skulls and smashed them together. He ripped faces clean from their skulls. He punched straight through mushy brains.

And when he looked to Kayla and waved her on, she felt what was certainly an unhealthy surge of happiness—*he came back to us, he will be our protector, thank you God Almighty for we are saved.*

It was almost enough to make her forget about the hunk of meat the zombie had bitten out of her shoulder.

She ducked a lurching zombie—as the rotter closed in, his head spun around and a spray of loose, decaying teeth peppered her cheeks like shotgun pellets.

Kayla darted in and clung to his side and she felt his arm around her. She felt Leelee's hand grab her own and then on the ground she saw the small terrier from before, making deft figure-eights around the vampire's feet... and for just a moment, all felt right in the world— even as black blood and zombie teeth rained down upon them.

Her father stood at the door and pulled her inside. The dog leapt in after her, and then Leelee followed.

Then she heard the sound.

It was an awful cry—a keening wail, a banshee's scream. It was like nothing she'd ever heard. It cut to the bone. It sang in her marrow and she was sure then that if she ever slept again *that sound* would be what haunted her dreams.

Coburn pushed her the rest of the way inside. His eyes were wide, like he'd just seen a ghost—and the fact that a vampire, a *bloodsucking monster*, seemed rattled was not a good sign. He gritted his teeth and snapped his fingers.

"We need to go, and we need to go *now*."

CHAPTER ELEVEN
Fresh Mutation

THE RV BOUNCED and bucked like a fat horse, barreling out of Towhee Park—rotters fell beneath the vehicle, and the Winnebago hit each one like a pus-caked speed-bump.

Gil yelled to Ebbie, who was driving: "Damnit, Ebbie! What'd I tell you about driving into those sonofabitches?"

"Sorry, *sorry*," Ebbie said, wincing.

Coburn peered out the back window of the RV, moving aside dusty, moth-eaten curtains. At first, all he saw in the darkness were the throngs of shifting, stumbling dead—moving in to fill the vehicle's wake like a swarm of ants. But then, there it was: a flash of pink, a body moving faster than the others, moving with greater purpose and direction.

It was her. The *hausfrau*. The pink bathrobe. From before.

Except she had… changed.

Her neck was elongated. Her limbs, too—and now her arms dead-ended in something that looked altogether less *human*, more *animal*. In the moonlight he could see a mouthful of curved, needle teeth. Fangs.

Kayla snuck up beside him, looking ashen.

"We're not supposed to hit the zombies with the 'Bago," she said, explaining what her father was going on about. "Did that one time and one got caught in the back wheel well. Grinded him up good. Screwed up the tire, and we were out of commission for a couple days. Now we have a policy: no rotter roadkill."

Coburn smelled the stink coming off her shoulder. Above the collarbone her shirt was stained red. Had none of the others seen yet? Gil was up there leaning out the window, taking shots with the rifle. Ebbie was driving. Leelee sat up in the passenger seat. And Cecelia, well, she was hunkered down crying at the piss-poor piece of laminated particle-board that passed for the dining room table.

"You got bit," he said. He wondered then what he was feeling. Not sadness. He wasn't even sure if he was capable of grief anymore. And yet something nagged at him—some dark, unseen tentacle tickling at his dead heart. Was this guilt? Seriously? Now, of all times? Couldn't be.

She shrugged, swooning. Her eyes unfocused for a moment. "I think so." Was this it for her? Was the bacteria racing through her veins, killing off the good tissue in order to animate the dead stuff?

"That, uhh, fucking sucks," he said, and the words felt stupid coming out of his mouth. Empathy was not his strong suit.

"What are you looking at?"

What did it matter? He moved aside, let her see.

Kayla looked out there and she started to say something, but didn't finish. Instead she remained staring out that back window, mouth forming a fearful 'oh.' Finally she looked at the vampire, wide-eyed, and said, "It's gaining on us."

Coburn shouldered the girl aside and took another look.

He wished he hadn't.

She hit the back of the RV like a bull—soon as Coburn looked, there came the *hausfrau*, hurtling bodily through the air, arms and talons outstretched. And now she'd clamped onto the back of the vehicle, her face at the window. Needled teeth gnashing. Blood-filled eyes wide and without pupils.

Gil ducked back inside the vehicle. "What the hell was that?"

A hard butt of her head cracked the back glass.

Coburn imagined what would happen if she came in here—she wasn't like the others. Soon as that freak of nature tore her way into this giant tin can, it'd be like a tiger let loose inside a daycare center. She'd tear these idiots to pieces. And if that happened, where did that leave him? Kayla's description of the relationship between cattle and shepherd was apt, was it not? Coyote comes sniffing around the herd, you shoot that motherfucker before he gets a taste for hamburger.

The vampire pushed past Gil, but snatched the rifle out of his hands.

"Hey!" Gil protested, but it was too late.

The back window shattered inward. The beast pushed in up to her shoulders, her one arm inside, swiping at air—the claws left ragged marks across the paneled RV interior. But by this time Coburn had already crawled outside through the busted door (which now banged against the side of the vehicle), the rifle slung over his shoulder.

The air was cold. The RV shot down a dark back road lined with needles of blue pine. Coburn swung himself to the top of the vehicle and jacked a shell into the .30-30.

Sure enough, she'd pushed half her body in through the back window—frankly, the only reason the beast probably couldn't get her whole ass through that space was because the pink bathrobe was plush (if filthy), and bunched up around her waist. Coburn took aim and fired.

Her back left foot came off easy as shooting a tin can off a fence. The bone splintered and the dead corpse-foot—the toes now topped with hook-like owl talons—spiraled off into darkness, thudding against the asphalt.

The vampire stomped on the RV roof. Just to let her know who it was that just blew her goddamn foot off.

It got her attention.

She shimmied backwards out of the hole just as a shotgun blast took a hunk out of her shoulder, leaving a gaping hole of ragged meat. The beast didn't seem to care—she hung there at the back window, staring up at Coburn with those gummy red eyes, shrieking like some kind of hell-bat.

Coburn brought the rifle to his shoulder to take aim—but by the time he had cocked the lever and put another shell in the chamber, she leapt.

She moved fast. Faster than anybody that he had ever seen—except for himself, and the one who made him.

Before he knew what hit him, she already had him on his back. Only thing separating the two of them was the rifle. It didn't last long; she broke it in half, Coburn's hands now holding one useless rifle part each.

The beast lifted her head back.

Her mouth opened, curved teeth gleaming wet with saliva, tongue lashing, spraying a froth of curdled pus.

She bit down on his chest. Those teeth tore clean through the leather. He felt her tongue—rough like the wrong end of a cheese grater—stick deep into the wound. *The bitch is drinking my blood*, he thought.

Then he realized: in his hands, a broken gun. Metal. Wood. Not the original weapon, but still a weapon.

He brought each up against her head in turn, pushing blood to his limbs, *urging* them to beat her with as much strength as he could muster. The stock clubbed her in the ear. The barrel bludgeoned her in the back of the head. It was just enough to get her to pull her head away from the bite—it should've popped her head like a tick but mostly just served to piss her off.

She howled in rage.

And when she did, Coburn tucked his feet up and planted his boots on her chest. Then he kicked as hard as was humanly—or, rather, *inhumanly*—possible.

The bitch-beast launched off the side of the RV, disappearing into the pine trees with a crash and crackle of breaking branches.

Groaning, Coburn stood on wobbly legs and pitched the broken rifle parts into the darkness. He looked ahead and saw that the road was dark and empty. Then he tucked his legs back in through the side window and slid back into the vehicle with the rest of the fresh meat.

CHAPTER TWELVE

Sharing and Caring

THE ONE-FOOTED *HAUSFRAU* crawled free from the forest, with ragged vents like rotting gills torn in her flesh by the tree. Awareness bloomed inside of her. She could smell her prey fading fast, but the scent lingered like a thread of sweet perfume, sweet as befouled meat, sweet as fresh blood and dead flesh and cloying corpse-breath.

Inside, a pair of new—or, rather, old—emotions rose, two snakes twining around one another. In her mind's eye she pictured the face of the one whose blood she took, and she was filled with a warm flush. She wanted him near her. She wanted his blood in her mouth. She wanted to hold him as mother and lover, her foul tongue in his ear, her wretched claws stroking his cheek.

And then she wanted to tear his ear off. And rip the skin free from his face. And crack his skull like a clam on a rock and eat what waited within.

She loved him so.

And she hated him dearly.

The blood inside her now was warm and empowering. The *hausfrau* rolled on her back, her mouth opening so wide that the jaw crackled and crunched. She looked down at her leg which now dead-ended in a putrid stump, bone shards jutting from the ruined meat like pins from a pincushion. It was then that instinct took hold, and she wished dearly for the foot to come back—within her, the blood began to stir, began to *move*, a slow and sluggish parade that felt like a hot rush through her body's tangled channels.

The bone shards twitched. The meat around them swelled, then retreated.

With a sharp twist of pain, the bones shifted suddenly, clacking together—and, before her eyes, they began to merge: osseous crystals growing like coral until becoming one. Around the knitting bone, clumps of flesh rolled and stretched. Blisters rose and popped. Pus spattered against asphalt.

It wasn't long before she could wiggle her new toes.

Toes that dead-ended in curved talons. Talons that would help her run, climb, and rend meat from bone.

The *hausfrau* stood, feeling the warm blood oozing around inside her body. She still had some left.

Around her, the moans of the lost and dispirited dead. Her rotting compatriots, each without the responsiveness and understanding she had recently come to know. They milled around, attracted by the commotion of the now-past RV, but uncertain what it even meant—they were operating on the simplest of urges, like moths drawn by flame.

The blood inside her demanded to be free.

One of the zombies stood near her, looking down at her with only the barest glimmer of curiosity—the park ranger outfit with the soaked-through nametag hung loose in some parts, where the flesh had retracted, and fit tight in others where the body had bloated with the gases of decay. Half his face seemed utterly unresponsive, disconnected from the other side.

She chose him.

The *hausfrau* moved fast. Her claws wrapped around the back of his head, twisting it hard toward her. She shoved him to the ground and as he moaned, she felt a squirming clot of blood come up out of her own throat and belch forth—a black slurry poured into his open mouth. Just to make sure, she held his unstable jaw open with her hand.

Later, when he stood up, his eyes flush with red, his tongue tasting the air, he looked at the gathered throng of undead.

He was no longer one of them. He was apart from them. He was *above* them.

Like her.

She had no more to give; if she did, she would've given it to others. But that was okay. She wasn't alone now. And her prey was still out there, and the blood was inside him.

Together, the two creatures moved to hunt.

COBURN SWUNG BACK inside the vehicle, and found himself face-to-face with the wide-mouth barrel of a twelve-gauge shotgun. Gil's face was tight with rage and his finger hovered right over the trigger.

"My daughter," he said, voice shaking. "She got bit."

The vampire craned his neck, felt the flesh and bone at his shoulder begin to knit—he moved to scratch it because *good goddamn* it always itched so bad whenever he had to heal up, but when he went to move his hand, the shotgun barrel pressed tight against his face. Almost up his nose, actually.

"Just notice that, did you?" he asked Gil.

"Did you do it?"

"Did I do what? Bite her? Ugh. No. I can smell whatever disease she has, and let me tell you, that does not make her all that appetizing."

Gil's jaw tightened. Tears burned hot at the edges of his eyes. Coburn tried to imagine what the man was feeling now—the certainty that his daughter was infected, that she was going to die, that all of life was hopeless. He thought for a moment about staring deep into the man's eyes and twisting the knobs and pulling the levers behind the old man's gaze, forcing him to fight against himself as he tilted the shotgun back, back, back... until the barrel rested under his own chin.

But something stopped him. Again, a little nagging pang, a *nibble* of perhaps not guilt but rather, the memory of guilt.

It was really fucking irritating, that feeling.

"You sonofabitch," Gil said. From down near his feet, the terrier growled, teeth bared.

"The dog's right, Gil. You're mad at me, but why? She became zombie chow," Coburn said. "Not my fault, *Dad*. Where the hell were you when some undead fuckwipe thought she looked like a tasty treat?"

Behind Gil, the nurse—Leelee, was it? What kind of name was that?—tended to the girl, who lay across a cock-eyed pull-out couch. Kayla didn't look good. Sweat beaded on her brow. Her eyes rolled around in the sockets.

"I'm fine," Kayla said, though it was clear how wrong she was.

"Shh," Leelee said, wiping a damp sponge across the girl's brow.

"This is all *your* fault," Gil hissed at the vampire. "It was talking about you that made her run off half-cocked in the first place."

"Sure," Coburn said. "Let's blame the blood-sucking monster." He paused, shrugged. "Well, okay, a lot of the time that's actually a good idea. This time, not so much, old man."

Cecelia came up behind Gil, once again became the devil on his shoulder, her wild-eyed hateful face staring stakes right through the vampire's heart.

"This is awfully familiar," Coburn said. "Didn't we do this last night? With the gun and the threatening and the bullshit? If I remember correctly, that didn't go so well for anybody. You really think you got the jump on me?"

Gil blinked back tears. "Damn right I do. Not a half-inch between this gun barrel and your head. You willing to take that risk?"

"He saved me," Leelee said, looking up from Kayla's tomb-white face. "That has to count for something. He didn't have to."

"He only saved you so he could use you like a snack, later. Ain't that right, *vampire*?"

Coburn didn't say anything. He didn't see any reason to lie.

"Kayla wants him to stay," Leelee protested.

Gil barked back: "Kayla's a kid. A sick girl. She doesn't get a say."

"You're very angry, Gil," the vampire said. "Your daughter's over there, only hours from becoming one of those moaning, mumbling mule-kicked assholes, and you won't throw the girl a bone and let her pet vampire stay the night?"

Gil pulled the trigger.

Or, rather, tried to.

Coburn knew it was coming. It wasn't so much a precognitive thing as it was a preternatural sense of everything that went on around him. That simple, tiny act—the motor mechanism of a finger tightening around a trigger—was preceded by a number of little clues. Gil's eyes narrowing. His heart beating faster. His jawline tightening, the tendons in his arm drawing taut. As if upon pulling the trigger he knew that it was going to make a big boom and a messy result, and his body flinched before it happened.

But the vampire couldn't have that. The girl had convinced him of a good thing, and he wasn't going to let some cranky old fucker ruin it. Fuck it, he hoped it wouldn't come to this—*this* being messy and all—but he couldn't have this old man shooting him in the face, either.

Gil struggled to pull the trigger and couldn't. He also couldn't look away from the vampire's unswerving gaze.

"Shoot him!" Cecelia said.

"I'm... trying," Gil said through clenched teeth.

"It's like *this*," Coburn said, smiling. "The real story here isn't how this is my fault but rather, how you're a *bad Daddy*. First, you're obviously not very nice. Second, you're totally kidding yourself if you think this cradle-robbed brat cares anything for you besides the fact you're the silverback with the guns and the food—" At this, Cecelia bristled, screaming at him to shut up, but he did no such thing. "Third, you want to blame me but *really*, the fact your daughter's dead meat—I mean that literally, *dead meat*—is because you let her out of your sight. You could've tagged me last night, if you were fast enough. If you were *strong* enough. But you're not. You're old. Which makes you slow. And weak. I can't imagine how that feels. Probably pretty shitty. So shitty, in fact, that I wonder if it's me you really want to shoot right now."

As if on cue, Gil struggled against himself—but the man's puppet strings were tight in the monster's grip. Gil tilted the gun back, back, back...

"Oh, my God," Leelee said, suddenly. She wasn't even talking about the whole situation with the shotgun. The nurse made a sound somewhere beneath a stifled sob and a laugh, looking down at Kayla. The wet sponge fell out of her hand. "She's healing. *She's healing.*"

Coburn decided to end the charade, snatching the shotgun out of Gil's hands and pushing the old man and the girl aside. He stood over Leelee and, sure enough, the bite on the girl's shoulder was healing up.

Before their eyes.

The purple striations and red tendrils of infection retreated. The flesh slowly rebuilt itself. Scabs dried up and tumbled away like rust off metal.

Coburn knew how it went, because he'd seen it enough times with his own flesh. Even now, his own shoulder—like hers—was healing up.

Except she wasn't dead. Kayla was very much alive.

Well. This was new. Quite the curious wrinkle, actually.

"I think she's going to be okay," Leelee said.

Ebbie peered back from the driver's seat. He laughed, ebullient.

Inside, Coburn's dead heart shuddered. It did that whenever he felt a moment of pleasure—breaking an enemy's neck, guzzling the blood of a difficult victim, eating fine food or drinking a rare wine. But this had none of the earmarks of such an occasion, and it felt odd. He decided to ignore it, and tamp that feeling down. It was of no use to him in this situation.

Coburn instead brushed a sweaty lock of hair away from the girl's forehead. Her eyes stopped rotating in their sockets and she found his gaze.

"Hey, vampire," she said.

"That's me."

"Thanks for saving me."

"I'd say you saved yourself."

He stepped away then and let Gil reach his daughter. The man bent over her, holding her. Her weak arms hugged him right back.

Leelee smiled at the vampire. Cecelia just scowled. At him, maybe. Or maybe at the fact that her lover's irritating daughter wouldn't be tap-step-shuffling off this mortal coil and that chapped her ass. He hoped it was a mixture of both.

Now that everybody was feeling warm and fuzzy about this sudden turn of events, it seemed like a good time to set the agenda.

Coburn cleared his throat, thumped the butt of the shotgun against the floor of the RV. All eyes fell upon him.

"The vampire has the floor," he said, winking. "Okay. Now that the girl isn't going to immediately expire and try to eat all our brains, I'll tell you how this is going to go. The girl convinced me of her plan. I was skeptical at first, but hell with it, she's right. The world's shit the bed and I need food. Further, it's increasingly clear that you weak-kneed blood-bags are going to get yourself nibbled to death by zombies if you don't have someone like me watching over you. So, that said, here's the scoop: you're my herd. I'm your shepherd. But we're not friends. I'm a higher being. An *ascended creature*. You're the dumb cattle. I'm the smart—and if I may say, handsome—cowboy. I'm with you for the duration. Don't like it? Don't care. You talk back to me, I will break your fingers. You try to run from me, I will break your legs. You try to hurt me"— and with this, he looked right at Gil—"then I will hurt something or someone you love. Kayla invited me to join your little posse, and I accepted. That means I'm not going anywhere except where all you cats and kittens are going."

"You're a monster," Gil said, but his words were toothless, without the fire behind them that he'd previously stoked.

Coburn shrugged. "And water is wet, old man."

The vampire scooped up his rat terrier. Creampuff licked his hand, the little dummy. He headed toward the back of the RV. "During the day, the main bedroom is mine. When she's up for it, send the girl back." He saw them all tense up. "Don't give me those looks, I don't mean what you think. She's going to be the liaison between you dumb animals and me, your ever-charming keeper."

He whistled as he closed the accordion door behind him.

CHAPTER THIRTEEN

Special K

ADMITTEDLY, THESE QUARTERS were not up to his usual standards.

His Manhattan apartment was, for all its luxury, small as a coffin, admittedly—but this 'room,' if it could be called that, was basically a doll's bedroom. His Fluevog-clad feet hung over the edge. Sure, he was a tall, lanky sort, but even still—this bedroom made him feel like a giant. And not in a good way.

Plus? Paneled walls? Did someone really think paneling was a good idea inside a recreational vehicle? This was not high-class travel. This was not, 'I'll put on a suit and a fedora and sip a dirty vodka martini while we fly the friendly skies.' This was more like, 'This city bus smells like dead hobo.'

Well, whatever. It was what it was. And what it *was* was the relative extinction of the human race.

The accordion door pulled open. Kayla poked her head in.

"Hey," she said, looking wobbly. He waved her in with the curl of a finger. She entered, closed the door with a rattle.

For the last couple hours, they'd been murmuring about him and what to do. Did they really think he couldn't hear them? If he concentrated real hard he could hear a koala bear fart all the way around the world. He heard the clank of cans and the crisp *tk-tk-tk* of the can-opener. He heard their sloppy eating. He heard Leelee defend him, heard Cecelia call for his *drawing and quartering* time and time again. He heard Ebbie, of all people, say that this was better than what they had before, and given that 'better' apparently included getting ambushed and blood-sucked while trying to take a piss, that was really saying something. Gil kept mostly mum on the subject, saying little more than, "We'll deal with it when we need to deal with it." That was perhaps the most concerning reaction of them all. Cecelia was an empty threat, but Gil, he was the *sit-and-let-it-simmer* type. Coburn decided he couldn't lose sight of that.

Kayla, meanwhile, didn't say a word for him or against him. All he heard from her were weak little mouse noises as she supped— well, slurped really, the way humans ate food was always somewhat disgusting to Coburn—on some broth.

She came into the room and stayed at its margins.

"You can sit down," he said, patting the bed. It was like patting a granite slab—*thud thud thud*. She shook her head. "No, really. Sit down or you're going to fall down." She was still gray-faced, the capillaries in her eyes half-burst.

The girl hesitantly came and sat next to him.

"What?" he asked. "You scared of me still?"

"You said some pretty rough stuff out there."

He waved it off. "The sheeple gotta know what they're up against."

"Still. You didn't need to threaten them like that."

"You kidding me?" He laughed. "Sweet little girl, what did you think you were getting, exactly? You asked a *wolf* to protect the *sheep*. I'm equal parts *serial killer* and *demon from Hell*. I'm not, uhh—" He tried to think of something opposite of that, some polar example.

"Big Bird?"

"What the fuck is a Big Bird?"

"You never saw Sesame Street?"

"That in Queens?"

She wrinkled her nose, gave him a look like a cute-but-constipated rabbit. "No, it's a TV show for kids."

"If wasn't on before sunrise, then I didn't watch it. Besides, New York City? Greatest city in the world. I didn't spend my nights watching the idiot box. I spent it *out there*, on the streets, in the clubs. Eating, drinking, dancing."

"Drinking blood, you mean."

"I can drink more than blood. I can drink anything you can drink. Gimme a shot of bourbon and I'm in heaven. Thing is, I don't need it like you do. Not like I gotta hydrate or anything. I can eat a steak and have a glass of Petit Verdot, but it doesn't do shit for me nutritionally speaking. Milk, in this case, does not 'do a body good.' It's all about the red stuff. Can't go without it."

She was quiet for a little while, obviously noodling this. Or maybe she was just dizzy and trying to get her balance. He looked over and saw that, despite the blood-stained shirt, the wound had completely healed up. A scar was left in its place: an archipelago of puckered skin like pink leather bunched up together and clumsily stitched. That was interesting. He didn't scar. But she did.

He was about to ask her about it, but she spoke first.

"How long you been a vampire?"

"Fifty years, give or take a few."

"What were you like before? Did you have a family? A job?"

That was a fun question. Even in her asking it, shadows scurried away from the light of scrutiny—his mind searched for answers but they were fast to move, like rats or roaches. "I don't know."

"What do you mean?"

"I mean, this thing that I am, when you become it, it hollows you out. Like a spoon scraping the last curls of ice cream from the carton. Whoever I was before, I'm not that now. It replaces you. Remakes you in its image."

"That's sad."

"Says you. Way I see it, human life is an endless line of dominoes toppling from one tragedy to the next. Not me, sweetheart. I just keep on going. Happy as a pig in the proverbial shit."

Again with the scrunching of the nose. "So you have, like, superpowers?"

"No, no, no, this is *give and take* time. Enough about me. Time to talk about *you*. You suffer what should've been a life-and-soul-ending bite—instead, the wound heals up nice and tight. Well, not *nice*—that's a pretty gnarly scar you got."

"It is ugly, isn't it?"

"Chicks dig scars."

She just stared at him, grossed out.

"*So*," he said, persisting. "The fuck is your deal?"

"I'm sick."

"I know you're sick. I can smell it on you like nicotine on wallpaper. What flavor of sickness are you, exactly?"

"Cancer," she said. "Multiple myeloma."

"Multiple what? C'mon, I'm not a doctor. Explain."

Kayla sighed. "I have tumors inside my bones. In the bone marrow, actually. Makes it hard for my body to make new blood cells, I guess, which in turn makes me anemic, which *in turn* makes sure I get sick a lot. Colds, flus, whatever. Sometimes my hands and feet go numb. My back hurts a lot. It hurts in my actual bones, which, I gotta say, really freakin' hurts. It's like the way a cold wind makes a winter day a lot worse. Let's see. What else? My kidneys might fail. My bones break easily. It's a lot of fun."

"Sounds like it's the tits." He took another inhale—the miasma of death hung about her like a perfume. "So, how long you have?"

"I'm living on borrowed time. They figured I wouldn't make it long, six months, maybe a year. It's been three years now."

"So is that why everyone thought you were special? Because you're the little cancer girl who wouldn't die?"

She hesitated. "Not exactly."

"So what is it?"

Kayla stayed quiet.

"Listen," he said matter-of-factly, "I can make you tell me same way I made your Daddy stick that shotgun up under his chin. I'd much rather you tell me of your own free will because, frankly, I'm lazy."

"It's my blood."

"Your blood."

"It's…"

"Go on, goddamnit. Spill."

"It heals people. Well. Not of like, regular diseases or injuries or anything. But, like, it stops those bit by the zombies from turning."

"So why'd everybody act all surprised that you healed up before?"

"Because I never got bit before now. So I guess they didn't know. Guess they thought the miracle girl just got un-miracled."

He cocked an eyebrow and smirked. "Uh-huh. Sure. And how'd you figure all this out? Bunch of half-zombies were sitting around, sipping on glasses of Kayla-juice for breakfast?"

"I... gave Leelee a little of my blood."

"You just gave it to her?"

Kayla stared off at a distant point as if the wood paneling were a wide open sky. "She got bit about a year back. On the hand. We were in the grocery store salvaging some canned goods and the store was closed up pretty good so we didn't think any had gotten in there. But one came up out of a busted freezer case like it was his coffin and, well. He got her.

"Later that night she was sleeping and we were all saying our final words and I had this vision of myself pricking my finger with the belt punch in my Swiss Army Knife, and putting my bloody finger in her mouth so she could nurse on it the way a baby sucks at a nipple and... next thing I knew, I was really doing it. Everyone looked at me like I'd lost my mind and I thought maybe I really had. Daddy pulled me away and wouldn't even talk to me. But by the next morning, Leelee's fever had broke. The bite mark on her hand didn't heal, but it never became infected. And she never changed."

"Huh," Coburn said. "That's pretty fucking weird."

"Shut up! You're a vampire."

"I know. And that's how I know it's weird, because I'm a vampire. Saying that this is weird." He shrugged. "Well. More things in Heaven and Earth, Horatio, blah blah blah."

"Okay. I guess. Whatever." She didn't look happy. In fact, she looked downright uncomfortable.

"Ain't this some fascinating shit? I mean, here you are, a girl who should by all rights be in the ground, talking to a dude who should similarly be six feet under somewhere. And yet we keep on living. So to speak." Each, he thought, with our own special blood disease. Good times.

"I should go."

"Uh-huh. Before you go, I got a job for you. Your first official task as *Liaison For The Wolf, To The Sheep.*"

"What's that?"

"Tell your Pop, I'm not sleeping here during the day. Tell him I don't trust him well enough. You guys can drop me off before sun-up somewhere I can catch my Z's, and then before night falls, just park the RV and I'll catch up."

"We can get pretty far during the day."

He winked. "So can I, pretty little cancer princess." As she stood to leave, he grabbed her arm. She winced—even that caused her some pain. "One more thing. Tomorrow night, when I catch up? I'll want to feed." The bitch in the pink robe took a lot out of him. "So, you better find me some food, otherwise I might take it out of the fat man again. Or maybe your Dad's bratty ho-bag. Oh! And I'm going to leave Creampuff with you. He better be well-fed. If ever I see him starting to look extra-scrawny, I'll break your Daddy's neck."

Kayla could not hide her horror.

"Toodles," he said, waggling his fingers at her.

This might actually work out, he thought.

CHAPTER FOURTEEN

Pretty Little Girlies

A THUNDEROUS DRUM *of horse's hooves, the world trembling under their trampling gallop, cups rattling in the cabinets, tickets burning hot in his pocket, plates clattering together louder and louder until—*
Whack.

Kayla slapped him awake.

"Wake up, dummy," she said.

Coburn blinked, tried to catch her hand before she slapped him again, but somehow his coordination wasn't working—her open palm connected again and left him reeling. In his nose: the smell of sour booze. Like Southern Comfort. Mixed with bad bile.

Two hazy frames of vision merged together until they formed a single picture, and there he saw Kayla standing over him—he was, after all, laying across a kitchen table—and she had her hair pulled behind her in a pony tail and sported a dress as blue as a robin's egg, as blue as—

—corpse-flesh—

He shook his head and stood up off the table.

"We're late," she said.

"Let me guess, for a very important date." It occurred to him then that it was his mouth that tasted like sweet liquor and bile. Jesus Christ on an ice cream cake, was he hungry. He staggered past the girl and went to the kitchen—appliances all in avocado green or mustard yellow (*harvest gold*, they called it, wasn't that right?) and he threw open the fridge to see if there was any blood in there and there wasn't—it was empty but for a pair of roaches wrestling with one another over a crusted marble of old food, food that looked like a dung ball.

"Hey, *vampire*," Kayla said again, this time louder, meaner. "Those roaches are fighting over you, you dumb piece of crap, you dried-up nugget of somebody else's shit. Look at me when I'm talking to you—"

Coburn did look, and he wished he hadn't.

Blood trickled from her eyes and from her nose, and when she opened her mouth to speak once more, all that came out was a bubbling slurry of blood and—bits of lung? Swatches of esophageal tissue? The mess poured down the front of her dress, and he felt around on the countertop to find a towel but nothing was there and he couldn't take his eyes off of her, and then a handful of words came bubbling up through that black blood:

"You couldn't protect me," she said, each word framed by a muddy burp of gore, and then he saw her: Kayla standing in the kitchen doorway *behind* herself, two Kaylas, one with the pony tail and the bloody dress and the other girl with the dirty white t-shirt and torn-up jeans from the RV.

That Kayla, the *second* Kayla, looked over at her blood-drooling doppelganger and then met Coburn's eyes and asked:

"What's happening? What does this mean?"

And then again with the rumbling, the vibrating, the thunderous tumble of horse hooves, a stampede, the cabinet doors juddering against the wood, a glass tumbling out and shattering, a hard and sudden crack across the windowpane looking out over a gravel driveway—

CHAPTER FIFTEEN

Wakey Wakey, Blood and Bakey

A SHOTGUN BARREL prodded him in the shoulder.

"Sun's down," came a voice. Gil's voice. "That means you get up."

Coburn cocked one eye, didn't see any sunlight coming in anywhere. Not that it mattered: when night came, he knew it in his blood. With the advent of day, he felt sluggish, his limbs going stiff like the start of rigor mortis, almost like he was more than half-dead. But at night, his body came alive—well, so to speak—once more.

He sat up on the toilet. They'd dropped him off at a rest stop come morning, then gone to park the RV somewhere. Didn't see any of the moaning dead out and about, which made sense seeing as how they were between towns and most of what was out here on the turnpike was just trees and asphalt. What was it that people said? Pennsylvania: Philadelphia on one end, Pittsburgh on the other, and nothing but backwoods-nowhere-Kentucky in between. Pennsyltucky.

Sleeping in a rest-stop bathroom—curled up in the stall like a dead bug—was not his ideal configuration, and part of him wished he'd just sucked it up and stayed in the RV. But now, with the shotgun barrel once more pointed in his general direction, he remembered why he hadn't.

"I'm up," he said, winking, licking a fang.

"Mm-hnn," Gil said. The shotgun didn't swerve.

"We gonna do this again? Really? Third time's the charm?"

Gil snorted, pulled the gun away, and then headed outside into the rain. Coburn followed and, sure enough, the air was crisp—wet and sharp like a cold bite into a raw apple, with rain speckling his face and loops of fog drifting close to the highway puddles.

The old man didn't say a word as he stepped inside the RV. Coburn followed after, and soon as he set foot inside, the rat terrier came over and fell in line behind him like a good little soldier.

"Creampuff," Coburn said, greeting the dog.

The dog didn't pant or smile or do any of that doofy cute dog bullshit, but instead just looked up at him with fond, glassy eyes. This dumb little idiot had no idea that, if Coburn got even a *wee bit peckish*, he'd break him open like a bone and suck the marrow out. Least, that was what the vampire told himself as he scooped up the dog in his arms.

"I'm surprised," Coburn said. "Didn't expect you to actually come pick me up. I figured on the first night you'd make a run for it, and I'd have to come find you. Glad you didn't. Shit, that would've been tedious."

Gil set the shotgun down. "Kayla made clear the consequences last night." He nodded toward the front of the vehicle. "I'm driving first stretch. Ebbie's going to tell you the plan."

"The plan?"

"You said you were hungry."

Coburn smiled. "I'm always hungry."

"Girls are still asleep. Kayla in the back bunk, Cecelia in the master. Leelee's awake and with me up in the front."

EBBIE SAT DOWN on the couch. It didn't sag or bow, because it already looked like it had a space for him—a concave dip that fit his body in various configurations. Coburn eyed him up.

"Let me guess. This is where you sleep?"

"How'd you guess?"

"I have psychic powers," Coburn lied.

Ebbie gazed at him in awe. His lips held an ill-contained smile. "Psychic powers! Wow. Just, wow. That must be amazing. Being what you are and all."

"It *is* incredibly amazing," he acknowledged, half-telling the truth, half peppering it with what he felt was his trademark sardonicism. "I am the luckiest boy in all of Mayberry. Fuck, fat man, it's like a twenty-four-hour party for me. Well, *twelve*-hour party, I guess, seeing as how half the time I'd get burned to a greasy patch of ash if I hung out in the daylight. At least, that's what I figure would happen. Not like I've ever gone through with it."

"You don't know what would happen? For real?"

"For real, Abner. By the way, I'm not calling you 'Ebbie,' because Ebbie sounds like a made-up name. It's a name you'd give to a guinea pig or the name a child would have for his retarded grandmother." He made a cranky baby voice: "Ebbie! Juice cup! Ebbie!" For added effect, he waggled his arms like the uncoordinated grabby-hands of a needy toddler.

Ebbie smiled. "It's actually what my baby brother called me when he was, well, a baby." The smile faded fast, though. His gaze turned down into his lap and Coburn knew that look: he had exploited his victims' grief many a time. It wasn't hard to follow the trail of tears: here was Ebbie and here was *not* a baby brother. Which meant that kid was probably an *amuse-bouche* for some zombie fuckwit out there. The fat man's eyes slowly refocused and the smile returned, though now it was strained, forced, not really real. "Don't you people gather in clans or families or something like that?"

"'*You people?*'"

"Vampires. You know. Haemophages."

"Haemo-who now?"

"Well, I just figured that would be the, ahh, scientific name for what you are? *Haemo*, for blood, and *phage*, for eat. Blood-eater."

Coburn frowned. "No, you can just call me 'vampire.' Or, 'hey, asshole.' And no, we do not gather in... *clans* or tribes or some shit. In fact, there's no *we* at all. It's just *me*."

"You don't know any other of your kind?"

"Nope." It wasn't a lie, either. Coburn had never met another of, in Abner's words, *you people*. Well, okay, that might not be entirely true: someone made him what he was. It was not an accident or a disease or a curse from God; his first memory as a hollowed-out, replaced-by-the-demon-of-blood-hunger vampire dude was a dark shape—a man, he believed—walking away and standing in a doorframe before finally turning and leaving. Forever. Coburn followed a set of bloody boot-prints for a while, but after 20 feet or so the tracks dried up. And that was the only thing he knew of another like him. Once in a while in the city he caught a smell of something—something familiar, something sinister, a little like blood and a lot like death—but then it was gone again, more a ghost than anything.

"Wow. So that means—"

Coburn felt the RV grumble to life and start to move, and he used that as a chance to interrupt Ebbie. "Listen. Abner. I don't really want to talk about this, and while I'm happy you feel *so comfortable* around me despite the fact our first introduction had me using you like a ham sandwich, what I really want is for you to tell me about whatever plan you hairless monkeys have concocted. You picking up what I'm laying down, fat boy?"

The man looked stung. It was what it was. Coburn wasn't here to protect their feelings, he was here to protect the food supply.

Abner, now quiet and meek like a wounded mouse, pulled out a road atlas and flipped it open to the Pennsylvania map. He opened a red plastic cup, the kind that must've once contained the plastic toys known as a Barrel of Monkeys, and upended it. Pieces from a different toy—the pewter game pieces and green plastic houses of Monopoly—spilled out.

With pudgy fingers, Ebbie began to move most of the pieces to the margins of the map, but then moved the Scotty dog game piece to the East end of the state.

"This is us," he said, tapping the dog on the map to drive the point home. "We've been in and around this area for a long time. But we've been wanting to go West because we keep hearing that out West is where society's started to rebuild. The plague didn't hit them like it did here, so they had fewer zombies and had a chance to mobilize. But there's a problem."

He took a number of the little green houses and started plunking them down at the West end of the map, each at the mouth of various highways and interstates.

"This is what we call the Cannibal Nation."

"A *nation*. Of cannibals." Coburn almost laughed. "So you're saying that a bunch of man-eater motherfuckers have organized. Like a political party. Or like the Boy Scouts."

"I dunno what you'd call it, I just know that they got smart about it. They figured out that the East Coast had a whole lot of people. And that it was like a plague zone: lots of rotters making fast work of a big population—New York, Philadelphia, DC, Baltimore, Boston. It's the megalopolis of the Eastern seaboard. Lot of people trying to migrate West to get to the safe zone, to be with the rest of humanity. The cannibals know that it's like a cattle chute, though, and so they set up their camps along those roads and wait for people to come through. Sometimes they lure them in, other times they just attack like a kicked-over hive of killer bees. They're preying on the dream. The dream of going West."

Something about this smelled goofy. Maybe it was that these idiots didn't know how to think like predators, and that was one thing Coburn knew very well. He knew how to mess with people's heads. How to plant ideas to get them to do what he wanted. He'd tell a couple of club chicks about some new VIP lounge, he'd even make up some tickets with a bullshit address on them—oh, that sweet smell of exclusivity—and they'd come-a-running. There'd be no club. Just him. Waiting in the darkness of the warehouse or walk-up or whatever it was. Fangs out.

Like a roach motel—they check in, but they don't check out.

"It's probably bullshit," Coburn said. "C'mon, Abner. Use your goddamn head. These cannibals? They set up the story. About the safe zone and going West and all that garbage. The myth of Western expansion died with the gold rush, there's no magic white tower in Wichita or Minneapolis. Those places are dead, just like here. You were sold on a lie." A cold realization struck him: "And that means that *I* was sold on a lie, too."

He stood up and set Creampuff down.

He didn't like being lied to. Didn't like being duped.

It was all bullshit.

He was going to kill them all. Right now. There were no pockets of humanity Out West. They got sold on a rumor, and now they were dragging him along toward some mythical Wizard of Oz Shangri-La fol de rol. If the so-called Cannibal Nation really existed, then that *right there* was his food supply. He could graze off those man-eating idiots for months, even years.

It was time to wet his fangs.

Abner had no idea what was coming. He just stared up at the vampire, his plump, cherubic face a mask of innocence and naiveté. Coburn was going to rip that face off its mooring and throw it to the dog.

"It's real," Abner asserted, as Coburn's fangs crept out over his lower lip. "We met some people who'd been there."

The vampire hesitated. He wanted to drink, but still: "...You did? You met people who've seen this with their own eyes?"

"Yeah. About three months back. They called themselves missionaries. They said it was their job to go back into the infested states, find the lost sheep and steer them Westward—to put them on a 'pilgrimage,' that's what they called it."

Coburn sat back down. Still suspicious. He pushed the fangs back with his tongue. "Uh-huh. And you're sure these weren't just a bunch of cannibal assholes pretending to be some kind of holy travelers? How do you know?"

"If it was a lie it sure was a convoluted one." Ebbie shrugged. "They told us how they snuck back through the woods and didn't use the roads, they told us to do the same—"

"And why didn't you?"

"We'd lose the RV, and it's kind of been our home."

"Uh-huh. Go on."

"They told us about how they had set up farms and had livestock and crops growing and even had power in some places, and they said that they were bringing in new folks every day and they had about ten thousand people now and that they belonged to this group, this group that had set all this up, these folks called the Sons of Man—"

At this, Coburn felt the blood drain from his face and move fast toward his dead heart—there the surge of blood gave the crumpled muscle a little kick and the heart shuddered once, twice, and then gave a third spasm before once more going inert.

"The Sons of Man," he said, hands balling into fists, his nails biting hard into the flesh of his palms. "Shit. *Shit.*"

And then it all came back to him.

CHAPTER SIXTEEN

The Sons of Man

HE THRUST UP his middle finger, a fuck-you flagpole flying the colors of the I-Don't-Give-A-Shit nation. Coburn licked blood off his teeth. The camping hatchet—sharpened to a paper-thin edge—swept through the air and lopped the finger off at the base. A boot kicked him in the chest. Footsteps fleeing. Struggling to get up, get out. It was then that the bombs went off—boom, boom, boom, boom.

COBURN ONCE HEARD about something called 'chaos theory,' which sounded pretty cool and was, at least until you got into the math. At its core, it went a little like this: a butterfly flaps its wings over here, and halfway across the world a typhoon hits. The tiniest motion could, over time, have tremendous and unexpected results. A butterfly was one thing, but a human? A living human with emotions and obsessions and opposable thumbs? Well. That was a whole other bag of tricks, wasn't it?

Human beings were dumb, but persistent. They just wouldn't leave shit alone. Everything was a hangnail and they couldn't stop obsessively nibbling at it, picking at it, not until a thread of skin pulled like a rip-cord all the way down to the fucking elbow.

So it was that whenever Coburn acted like a vampire—the monster being *monstrous*—it was a pebble pitched in the pond, a butterfly fluttering his stupid little wings. He drank from some club girl and left her dizzy in a bathroom? He killed some gang-banger thug and drained the body and left it on a garbage scow? He moved too fast in front of witnesses, leaving them wondering what they just saw? Each of these things: an opportunistic hangnail. A loose thread that, when pulled, might unravel the whole of the sweater.

Once a human got a look at the other side, there always came the chance that they wouldn't—*couldn't*—let it go.

Most of the time, fuck it, didn't matter. About ten years back, some girl came sniffing around Coburn's hot spots looking for her fiancé. Some douche-rag Wall Street moneyman, some cocky rich prick in a tailored suit. Frankly, Coburn barely remembered killing him. He wasn't one to linger, after all.

Of course, just because Coburn didn't give a rat's ass didn't mean she felt the same way. This was her fiancé. And now he was gone. Void like that needs to be filled. And there it was: the hangnail. Pick, pick, pick.

Night in, night out, he saw her asking questions. Bartenders. Bouncers. Doormen. Dancers. Strippers. She even came up to him one time, flashed a photo, and that was when he remembered killing the dumb fuck. The suit gave Coburn lip for bumping into him and spilling his whisky, and that's something you just don't do. You don't look into the monster's eyes and call him a—what was it? A low-class worm? Maggot? Something like that? Watch where you're going, you blah blah blah? No. That flag won't fly.

So Coburn found his driver. Broke his neck. Drained him dry. Then waited for Mister Moneybags with the pomade hair and the shiny watch to show up, which he did—some blonde on his arm. The vampire killed him in front of her, then put the voodoo to her, convinced her to get the hell out and forget what she saw.

The suit's blood tasted like the good life. Unctuous, like foie gras. Coppery, like a mouthful of pennies. Sweet, like diabetes.

So when the woman came, flashed a photo, Coburn almost laughed. He told her, no, nope, sorry, no idea.

But she just wouldn't let it go. Kept asking around until someone—Coburn still didn't know who or he would've ripped them a dozen new assholes—said that, sure enough, the suit got into an altercation with *him*. Described him to the nines: the boots, the jacket, the crooked nose.

Few nights later, she found Coburn in an alley and thrust a pawn-shop .38 snubnose in his face with a trembling hand. Said she'd been asking around and *she* heard that he was a real bad dude. Said she needed answers right then, right there, or she'd put a bullet in him.

He let her. Just to make her feel better. It wasn't that he felt bad, but hey, that night he was feeling particularly magnanimous. She got in a good shot, too. Hit him right in the side of the neck. Had he been alive, it would've been a kill-shot, would have left him bleeding out in the oil-slick puddles next to the dumpster that stank of rancid curry.

Instead, he put an end to such foolishness and mayhem.

Her mind twisted easily. His voice, soothing. His eyes, mesmerizing. He found out that her name was Caitlin. Wasn't hard to sell her on the story that her affianced fuck-stick boyfriend had run off with some anorexic high-dollar escort. Eyes watery, lip trembling, snot bubbling up out of her nose, he could see that he hooked her. She bought it. Game over, goodbye.

Or so he thought.

Who knows what it was that put Caitlin back on the path? Bad dreams, maybe? His mesmerism left cracks and holes—hairline fractures and pin-pricks only, but enough to let a little light back in—and that might've been what set her off. Hell, maybe it was just that she loved her dickhead fiancé *oh so much* that she couldn't let him go. It was love, which is to say, it was obsession.

Caitlin was smart this time. She didn't just come back to see him, didn't just follow the same dark trail of blood-soaked breadcrumbs. No, Caitlin looked for help. She found the Sons of Man, which is when the Sons of Man found Coburn.

Bunch of fucking Jersey asshole do-goodniks—handful of amateur hour monster-hunters led by some plumber named Benjamin Brickert. Janitors and car mechanics and volunteer firemen. Not quite a dozen of them. All of them *thought* they had brushes with the supernatural, and hell, maybe they did: ghostly interventions and Jersey Devil sightings and demonic possessions. They weren't a bunch of eggheads, though. They were church-going boys and girls, all of them: god-fearing greaseballs who didn't want to study and find evidence of the supernatural so much as they wanted to *destroy* it.

Caitlin probably found their number on Craigslist; that was where Coburn saw it, but for all he knew those dipshits put up flyers. Whatever it was that she told them, it put them on his trail.

And for the next three years, they fucked with him.

He'd be putting the swerve on some slag in the club and there they'd be, telling her that he was some kind of monster—or, when that wording failed, rapist—and unless she wanted to end up on the back of a milk carton, she'd better hit the bricks. Of course, nobody ended up on the back of milk cartons anymore, did they? Assholes.

They tried following him to his condo. They tried calling him out and engaging him in fights. Coburn managed to get one of them alone—some chubby plumber-type who thought to cave his head in with a pipe wrench—and he broke the dope's neck and siphoned him dry. Problem was, it was almost dawn, so he stashed the body in a manhole. Next night, what should Coburn find there but the red-and-blue coruscating cop lights and a bunch of yellow caution tape?

So *that* put the cops on the area. Turns out, an 'anonymous tip' led them to the manhole. Again, the Sons of Man getting in his business.

That was the turning point. That was when they became more aggressive.

It was a month later when they got him.

They set him up. Put some bird on the wire for him to find: he was at a bar not far from the fashion district and *she* came up to *him*—not too skinny, which meant she had a lot of blood in her. Red hair and green eyes: nothing wrong with that. A little drunk (always a good sign). Said she was a fashion student here but wasn't getting along and didn't know anybody and blah blah blah, he tuned out. All he knew and cared about was that she clung to him all night, a little too needy. But 'needy' was right in his wheelhouse.

She said, "Want to go get high?"

No, of course he didn't, but he lied. "Let's do it."

Girl knew a place nearby.

A theater. Bit broken down. Opened once or twice a year for an art installation or a showing of some classic Hitchcock.

Uh-huh. Whatever. Get her inside, he thought. Drain her but don't kill her. Leave her. Another wonderful night as a mean-ass fang-banger-motherfucker would draw to a warm, pleasant close.

It was a trap.

They were there. Every last sonofabitch Son of Man they could rally. It was a gauntlet: they came out of the shadows, with Brickert at its end. He should've heard them, should've *smelled* them, but all he could see was the pulsing vein at the crook of the girl's neck, all he could smell was her heavy perfume. A tire iron cracked him in the head. Put him down. Boot on his hand. Boots in his ribs. A crowbar. A baseball bat.

Even still, he got up. He wasn't a chump. He pushed blood to his limbs. Coburn moved fast. Became the vampire, not the victim. Hooked his finger into a coat-hook and ripped some lanky fuck's throat out. Kicked out with one of his Fluevogs, turned a guy's knee inside out. The redhead tried to run, but he grabbed her by the hair—no way she was getting off scot-free—and that was when the Taser hit him.

Fucking Tasers, man. He had no idea. Never been hit with one before. Problem is, even being the living dead, Coburn's tissue is still moist. Still *conductive*. And everything still seems to operate by electric impulse. The Taser clipped him in the back of the neck—damningly good shot, turned out it was Brickert who held the weapon—and his whole world lit on fire and his limbs seized up. Felt like he was falling into day-sleep.

Next thing he knew, Brickert with his black goatee and his bright blue eyes was setting Coburn against a row of theater seats. Duct-taping him there. The rest of the Sons were hurrying out of the building. Brickert smiled at him with a mouth full of yellow teeth, and Coburn saw a crucifix tattoo creeping up the man's neck.

"Us blue-collar types have to watch out for one another," the man said, picking up a camping hatchet, running his thumb along the blade.

Coburn tried to muster a response, but it came out as a slurry of word garbage.

"You monsters have it too good," the man growled. "This is for Sully." Then he spat in the vampire's eye.

Coburn flipped him off.

Brickert moved fast with the camping hatchet, cutting off his finger. Coburn watched the middle digit pirouette through the air. Almost comical. As if to add insult to injury, Brickert bent down, snatched up the finger. Some kind of trophy, probably.

Then the fucking finger-thief ran. Just as Coburn started to feel his limbs come back to life, everything lit up—bombs went off around the room. The floor collapsed. A row of seats rushed toward him. He tumbled into darkness. Saw the bright flash of fire before everything went black.

Shit.

CHAPTER SEVENTEEN

One Drop of Blood at a Time

"SHIT," COBURN SAID, teeth gritted so hard he thought they might crack. "We're not going west just to hang with those assholes, I'll tell you that. Bunch of backwoods Pine Barren types and greasy Eye-talian meatballs. No. Hell no. Triple chocolate *no*."

"We're not going for them," came a voice behind him. Kayla. Rubbing sleep out of her eyes. "We want to go past that. Past their territory."

Ebbie nodded. "It's true."

"Say that again?" Coburn asked.

"Stories say there's a lab out on the West Coast," Kayla said. "Downtown Los Angeles. They're working on a cure for the plague. Or a vaccine, since I guess you can't really cure the dead. That's where we're headed."

"Los Angeles."

"Mm-hmm," she said. "We even have an address."

"And where'd you come by this story? And this address?"

Ebbie chimed in: "From one of the missionaries. The pilgrims we told you about?"

Coburn growled low and slow. He didn't trust any of this.

Besides, Los Angeles? Likely just another city chock full of the dead. Like he didn't have a hard enough time getting out of New York City's hell-canyons, the streets stuffed with dead meat? This deal was looking to be a real pisser. Inside his dead flesh, the veins and arteries tightened; that was the hunger coming for him. Anxiety lurked like rats in the wall. He felt suddenly like a tiger shoved in a terrarium. He pushed those feelings back down into the darkness. Sometimes Coburn had to remember: if he played his cards right, he could be doing this for a very long time. Forever, really. He didn't age. Didn't get sick. Just needed blood.

One step in front of the other.

One drop of blood at a time.

"How soon till I get to eat?" he growled.

Ebbie stammered, looked at his wrist where no watch sat, then looked at the wall where a clock hung crooked against the warped paneling: "Three hours."

"Fine," Coburn said, heading toward the back. "Call me when it's time."

"Don't you want to know the plan?" Ebbie called after.

Coburn gave Abner the middle finger—the same one that he lost before the shit hit the fan—and stormed into the back bedroom.

CECELIA LAY ASLEEP on the bed. Face down. Purple-pantied ass thrust upward. Snoring. Coburn sniffed the air, smelled sex. Saw a box of rubbers on the nightstand, probably expired, but what the hell. On the one hand, he had to give it to the old man because, well, *she* was giving it to the old man. On the other hand, she only had her hand around his knob because it was the control lever that made the robot do what she wanted. Cecelia was in control; least, that was how Coburn figured it.

Then again, Coburn thought, maybe that was all human relationships. He really couldn't remember. Maybe all men were puppets and all women were whores. Or maybe it was the other way around. Or maybe everybody was a whore and a puppet at the same time. What the hell did he know?

What he *did* know was, he wanted the room. He grabbed her by the ankle, dragged her off the bed. By the time Cecelia realized what was happening, she started to grab for the sheets but it was too late: she hit the floor with a *whump*.

"Hey! Goddamnit!" she cried out, turned over and tried to kick at him. He slapped away her feet.

"Get out."

"No! You get out."

"Get out or I will tear off your legs."

Cecelia scrabbled to her feet, got up in his face.

"I'm not afraid of you," she hissed.

"You should be."

"I'm not. I've seen you talk a lot, but I haven't seen you do shit. Big tough man. Big scary vampire." Her breath stank of cigarettes. And Gil. She smiled. Licked her lips. Got closer. Cecelia thrust out her tongue and waggled it at him. "Big *sexy* vampire."

"Wanna know something?" he asked.

"Tell me."

"I can take all the blood I've stolen, and I can push it right into my cock. Make the damn thing hard as rebar. I could crack a cement block with it, so you can only imagine what I could do to you."

Her eyes flashed. The sound that came out of her throat—almost a laugh—was throaty, breathy, wild like an animal. "I don't want to just imagine it."

She thrust out her tongue, licked his chin.

He grabbed it, pinched it betwixt thumb and forefinger.

"I could rip this off," he said. "Quick jerk of my arm and this pink meat will come out at the root." She squealed, tried to get away, swatting at him with her fists. "Don't move and you won't lose it. Now listen to me: I don't like you. I don't know what's wrong with you, but you're a brat. And that's saying something, coming from me, because I am a Grade-A sonofabitch. Were you molested by an uncle? Used up by the football team? Or is it just in your DNA? Were you always this way? Don't know. Don't give a fuck. But you're mean. A real abuser. So I'm going to let go of your tongue now and you're going to leave the room. Nod gently if you understand what I'm saying."

At first, nothing but hate daggers coming from her eyes.

But then, slowly, surely, a little nod.

He let go of her tongue. She pulled it back into her mouth, a snake into its hole. She looked shaken up. Eyes wet. Good. She needed that if she was going to survive out here. Maybe he did some good today. But it didn't matter.

Coburn grabbed her by the shoulder, threw open the accordion door, and shoved her out.

LATER, KAYLA APPEARED at the door.

"We're almost there," she said.

"Good," Coburn answered. "Because I need to eat."

"Your dreams..." she started, but didn't finish.

"What about them?"

"Why was I in your dreams? The fake me. The *not real* me."

He stood up, popping his knuckles, flicking his fangs with his tongue to get them to come out and play. "I don't know what you're talking about."

"In the kitchen. In your dreams. I visited you. I didn't mean to, but... she was there. I was there. Some other me. What was that about?"

Coburn came up on her and snarled.

"You get the hell out of my skull. That door's locked. It's marked 'private.' You hear me? Stay. Out." He pushed past her. "Now let's get my belly filled."

WELCOME TO SUBURBAN *Hell*, Coburn thought. Outside, a low fog clung to the ground. The motor home slowly wound its way through forgotten cars and long-dead bodies, passing by the ghostly wrecks of Burger King and KFC, past mortgage huts and check-cashing shacks, each building rising up out of the darkness like a shipwreck. Here and there, the living dead shuffled about—the passing headlights providing a stimulus, and their response was agitation and desperation. They began following the vehicle in a groaning mummy shuffle, but they were slow and stupid and it was too late—the motor home kept on going.

Ebbie came up next to him and peered out.

"Creepy," Ebbie said. "Don't you think?"

The vampire shrugged. "Suburbs have always looked this way to me."

"Oh. Well. The Wal-Mart is ahead by a mile. That's where... they are. They've got a couple spike strips dragged across the road, like the cops use in high-speed chases? To blow tires? Plan is for you to distract them inside—"

"And to feed, Abner. Don't forget about that part, unless you want me to order another meal at the Abnersblood Diner again."

"—and feed, I was just about to say that, yes, absolutely." He cleared his throat. Coburn could smell his nervous sweat. "While you... feed... we'll clear the road and drive past, and wait on the other side of the highway, away from any rotters. You'll find us a half-mile down or so."

"And before that?"

"We'll be circling in town here."

"Good. Let me out, then."

Up in the front, Gil hit the brakes. The RV lurched forward. Ebbie almost tumbled into Coburn, and the vampire gave him a foul look.

"Here we are," Ebbie said, smiling sheepishly. "It's three hours to sun-up, and—"

"Whatever."

"How will we know when it's safe to come through?"

"I'll send a sign."

"What sign?"

"Goddamn with the questions." Coburn didn't know what sign he would use, but that didn't stop his bravado. "You'll know it when you see it."

"One more thing—"

"No more things. Time's wasting."

The vampire threw open the door. He petted Creampuff's head, told the dog to stay put, then descended into the destroyed strip-mall purgatory of Lawson Heights.

CHAPTER EIGHTEEN
The Cannibal Abattoir
of Lawson Heights

HE WALKED, BOOTS crunching on broken asphalt. The motor home rambled away, its tail-lights diffusing in the low-hung fog, looking like dragon's eyes as it retreated back into its cave.

The zombies jogged after it, but it didn't matter.

Soon enough, however, they noticed *him*.

Over there, a strip mall—pet store, bank, Korean nail place, Mexican restaurant. Over there, a *different* strip mall—Radio Shack, vitamin store, Gamestop, another Korean nail place. Cut between them a strip of gray macadam, many of the cars still sitting like grave markers along the way. He mused that it must've happened fast, the zombie apocalypse—people didn't even have time to get home and board up their houses.

Funny, he thought. The zombies here weren't really all that out of place, were they? Zombie shoppers. Zombie consumers. Isn't that what zombies did? *Consume*? He felt proud of himself for putting that together (having never seen any zombie movies before), even as he winged a hunk of broken highway into the head of an approaching zombie, knocking the fucker's head back on his neck like a Pez dispenser made of rotten meat.

"Welcome to America," he said to the horde of approaching rotters. "Bad news. Don't have time to buy what you're selling or sell you what you're buying. Don't want your Blu-Ray player, and you don't want my delicious cookies laced with high fructose corn syrup and weed-killer. But thanks for stopping by!"

He leapt up onto the shoulders of an approaching zombie—a jowly cop whose nose and ears had long rotted off (or were perhaps bitten off by another of his grotesque cohorts) and sprang over the throng into darkness. Not wanting to give them time to track him, he lit a fire to the blood within his body and moved so fast the zombies didn't even know what happened.

THE WAL-MART ROSE out of the dark and the fog: it looked more like a prison than a shopping Mecca. And not a modern prison, either, but something out of antiquity: torchlight flickered behind boarded-up windows, and along the top of the store, rusted burn barrels glowed, one every ten feet or so.

Coburn saw movement up there—sentries.

Sure enough, the highway here cozied up nice and tight to the store. Once upon a time, Coburn knew you could tell what a town or village was like by looking at its highest building. The steeple of a church above all else? Then they were God-fearing folk. The top floor of a bank building? Then they loved money above all else. Over time, height stopped mattering—what mattered became how close a building sat to the major arteries. Like a tumor, redirecting blood-flow to itself. When that building was a Wal-Mart, you knew that the most important thing to these people was the ability to shop until they dropped. The zombie apocalypse should've changed all that, but then again, maybe not.

Just past the entrance into the lot, he could see the faint moonlight caught along the metal teeth of the spike strips laid down on the road. A pair of them, just to be sure. Past *those*, he could see the blown-tire wrecks of a dozen or more cars. They weren't blocking the way entirely, but the passage was pretty narrow. The RV was going to have a helluva time squeezing through there. No time to think about that now.

The vampire eased along, wondering—where are all the zombies? He figured once they got a taste of a place like this, saw that it was home to a squirming gaggle of hot-blooded living humans, they'd be all over it like diabetics on a Whitman Sampler. *This one's filled with brain cream.*

But then, as if to answer his question, he saw a lone zombie came shuffle-jogging up, the busted-out soles of his shoes dragging behind each foot. He could smell the rank stink, and it was overpowering enough that he almost didn't see what was coming next: a thin red beam of light drifted across the lot—a wayward laser looking for a home. It found the zombie, crept up his leg, his chest, then centered on his head.

Bang. Shot from a rifle blew most of what was inside the zombie's skull about ten feet back, leaving the rotter's head an empty 'O,' faceless and devoid of life. The rotter dropped like a suit off a hanger.

The gunshot echoed out, the sound crawling over the highway and the trees the way thunder does.

The sentries were snipers. Good shots, too.

That wouldn't do. They found him, they'd go for his head. They went for his head, well, he didn't *know* that it would be his end, but he damn sure knew that he liked having a brain. Didn't seem like a good idea to let it fall out of his skull.

Coburn figured, okay, better sidle up against the building.

He darted low, creeping through the fog.

One problem, though.

He found another way they kept the horde out:

A moat.

They'd dug a goddamn *moat* around the Wal-Mart. This really was starting to feel medieval. The trench was a good six feet out from the store and 15 feet deep—the massive gutter wasn't filled with water, though. The walls and ground were lined with refuse: bent nails, rebar, broken glass. Wooden spikes thrust up out of the bottom of the trench and stuck out of the walls at various angles.

The moat worked. Coburn knew it worked because even now a half-dozen zombies moaned and gurgled down there in the trench. One was caught on a wooden spike, trying to pull herself away in what was clearly a futile effort. Another rolled around in broken glass, his face a cut up mess, a shard thrusting up out of his right eye. They must clean the thing from time to time because these rotters were fairly recent, he figured.

The moat worked because zombies were dumb. They didn't seem the type to stop and think, *Hey, look, a moat.* They just kept on walking, moving ineluctably forward like floodwater.

Coburn wasn't an idiot.

He crouched, took a hard jump, leapt to the other side of the moat. He only had a couple feet of clearance—part of a busted-up sidewalk—but it was enough.

Palms flat against the building, he wondered: just go right in the front? They were probably expecting that. Lone human travelers probably came up that way hoping to find help, thinking they'd found human civilization—and then once in the door someone probably came up from behind, hit them with a mallet, then dragged them in the back to become Thanksgiving dinner.

Nah, he figured. Better to go around back, find a way in there.

BACK OF THE store was buttoned up tighter than the Pope's asshole. Bay doors at the loading dock were shut, locked at the bottom. Side door, too, was locked. The moat extended back here, but was further out—and they'd built a drawbridge out of pallets, garbage cans, and plastic storage bins.

Coburn's first impulse was to go in hard and fast, making as much noise as he could—rip open the bay door like the top of a tuna can, waltz in like one of God's avenging angels. But as he knelt down by the door, he heard it—

On the other side, a rumbling snore.

Someone was just inside. Sleeping.

Coburn chuckled. This was going to be easy. "Kitty wanna come out and play?" he said, tickling and tapping against the bay door, then knocking louder and louder. "I am rap, rap, rapping on your chamber door, motherfucker."

Sure enough, the snores cut short.

Feet shuffled. Chair legs stuttered against concrete.

On the other side, the fumbling of a lock.

Finally, the bay gate cranked open, ascending upward like a garage door.

The man who stepped out was tall, reedy, but with a pooching belly, almost as if he were three months pregnant. It strained his too-tight sweat-stained wife-beater. He looked about like Coburn expected some wild-eyed cannibal asshole to look: big bushy beard knotted with dried skin and gobbets of puckered meat, hollow cheekbones, mouth full of rotten teeth whose decay was so strong Coburn could smell it.

Man came out, sawed-off double barrel shotgun thrust up.

"Who's out here?" the man said, his voice a gravel-choked smoker's growl.

Coburn came up from the side, reached out and grabbed the man's throat, then squeezed like he was trying to wring water from a tough sponge. His trachea collapsed like a Styrofoam cup. Problem was, soon as the man's throat closed, his bowels opened and his finger tightened, he squeezed off a round—one of the shotgun barrels blurted out a clumsy, aimless shot.

The stink of shit and expended gunpowder hung in the air.

Well, Coburn thought, guess that's it for the quiet entrance.

He bit down on the cannibal's neck, guzzled a belly full of blood, then threw the malodorous hick down like a puppet whose strings just got cut. In a perfect world, Coburn could've been done for the night. His veins were fat with stolen blood. It would be no big thing to leave the body, disappear into the woods, then come back night after night, picking off stragglers like a huntsman spider.

But he had to create a distraction.

Besides, eventually they'd figure him out and mount a proper defense.

Plus, it was going to be fun killing all these hill-fuck man-eaters.

Coburn smiled, hummed the first couple bars of 'Dueling Banjos,' then sauntered inside the Wal-Mart, ready to gorge.

FIRST THING HE noticed: the flies.

Thick, fat flies filled the air, pinballing into one another, hovering about his head, looking for a draught of his blood. On a different night, he'd let one have a taste—mosquitoes and flies thought to bite him like any other human, but his body put stolen blood through its paces, transubstantiating it into a potent slurry. Skeeter or horsefly (or a rat, if he was brave) got a taste of that, it was too much. Killed the critters on contact: mosquitoes and flies would take a drink, then... *pop*. Like a tick under a match flame.

The smell hit him next: meat and blood.

Past the reloading dock, the inventory warehouse had been repurposed into an abattoir. The floor red with dried blood. Massive hunks of meat—some hanging and drying out on hooks, others in barrels of foul brine. Rusty saw in the corner. Gore-caked card tables.

He crept through the dangling meat. At first glance, could've been hogs or beef, but he knew better. A lingering glance showed the leg stumps that cut off mid-thigh, the arms chopped at the bicep.

A half-dozen humans hanging here, swinging gently, collecting flies.

They were doing a pretty solid business. That was good news for him. Meant people were still out there. People filled up with all that lovely blood.

It was then that he heard footsteps coming from within the store itself, fast approaching the loose double-doors connecting the store proper with this back warehouse area.

Coburn leapt, clambering up one of the bodies, and further up the chain the body hung on. As two figures entered the abattoir, Coburn was already up in the metal rafters, looking down.

Flashlight beams cut an arc through the room. A pair of them.

Man and a woman. He, younger—late teens, early twenties, head shorn. She, older, more haggard, her ratty hair gone to dirty dreads. There was a certain meanness to both their features, a familial resemblance. His elder sister? His young mother? Did it matter?

He held a machete. She, on the other hand, had a nice graphite crossbow—something she probably plucked right off the shelves here—and, upon thinking about it, it was a pretty elegant weapon in terms of dispatching human beings. No exit wound. Clean puncture. Didn't ruin the meat.

Fact that she had the crossbow and he had the machete was telling. Maybe she was his mother.

"Charlie?" she hissed, flashing the beam this way and that. "*Charlie.*"

Charlie must've been the bearded yokel whose throat he'd crushed.

Oh well.

Soon as the two were beneath him, he dropped down—

Right between them.

The boy reacted first, swinging wildly with the machete. Bad move. Coburn tilted his body at the hips and the machete arced through empty air—but it still found a target.

The blade buried itself in the woman's neck. She didn't even scream, she was so shocked.

"Sue!" the boy cried out, suddenly unsure if he should wrench the blade free or keep it there. Instead he just let go of it and backpedaled.

It was the wrong move. Not that there were any *right* moves.

As Sue staggered in a circle, blood welling up around the machete, Coburn snatched the crossbow from her grip, then fired an arrow. He'd never used a crossbow before, and actually wasn't really all that fond of guns, but having the blood within him gave him preternatural skill. He wasn't one to miss. Mostly, he used it to win dart games and pool.

The crossbow bolt hit the man in the eye. His arms pinwheeled as he fell backward, dead.

The woman—Sue—stared at him, wide-eyed and full of fear.

"What... what are you?" she asked.

"I'm Batman."

Her eyes went wider: full moons, each.

"I'm just kidding," he said, then twisted her neck until it broke.

COBURN HAD NEVER been inside a Wal-Mart. Never had much cause to go find one; the city didn't have room for any, and why the hell would he ever need a wheelbarrow full of diapers, a ten-pound package of boneless chicken breasts, or a lime green Margarita machine?

Still, he had to admit—the cannibals of Lawson Heights had gone to great lengths to match Coburn's vision of what the inside of a Wal-Mart looked like. The shelves had been stripped bare and battered to Hell, as if some super-important Christmas toy release had come and gone and an army of Super-Moms had ripped through the store, buying everything up like an all-consuming void. Didn't hurt that many of the shelves were lined with piles of bones both human and animal. Torches flickered atop endcaps. Freezer cases were bashed open. Graffiti everywhere—spray-painted pictures of skulls, middle-fingers, dicks, tits, and encouraging messages such as 'Fuk You,' and 'I Eat Yor Skin.' Floor torn up. Lights torn down. Trash blew through open aisles, piled up in corners.

Yep. In Coburn's mind, this was Wal-Mart in a nutshell.

He silently stalked the aisles like a wolf roaming through the rows of a cornfield, sniffing out prey. And oh, could he smell them. It wasn't just the stench of body sweat. It was the rancid odor of human meat. With every breath they gave it off. Blood under their tongue. Long pork between their teeth. *Eau de cannibal.*

Guilt was rarely a factor in Coburn's eating habits. (Rarely? More like *never.*) But sometimes, killing folks gave him pleasure. Felt like he was excising a cancerous tumor from the world—a pedophile, a crooked cop, a gaggle of cannibals? Made Coburn feel like an all-round Boy Scout, doing good deeds with his mighty fangs. Was there a badge for this? Something he could sew on the sleeve of his jacket?

Someone stepped into the aisle next to him. He couldn't see the person—a shelf separated them—but he could hear him. A man, probably. Heavy boots. No effort to be quiet.

In the back of the store, he heard voices: they'd discovered the bodies. Well, the *new* ones, at least.

Coburn leapt up atop a shelving unit, perched there like a crow.

A man walked beneath him. Burly fucker. Long chin beard, hair in a greasy top-knot, no shirt on. Coburn could see the gobbets and curls of meat dried in his chest hair. It wasn't a good look. So he killed him.

That death came easy enough. He planted his feet on the fool's shoulders, crouching down like he had atop the shelf, then put his hands in the man's mouth. Grabbing his upper and lower jaws, he pulled like he was ripping open a bag of potato chips. Human Pac-Man.

The man dropped a weapon: an AR-15 semi-auto. Coburn caught it before it clattered to the floor, moving fast.

He wasn't a big fan of guns, really. Wasn't much point to them. They weren't subtle. A vampire favored subtlety, unless he wanted to bring the world to his door, wondering why he'd got a bloodless body in his jet tub. You fired a gun, it drew attention—okay, not *much* attention, in New York City, but it at least merited a phone call from someone.

Coburn didn't like drawing attention.

Now, though, that was the goal. He'd told Gil and the others to watch for his sign, and truth be told, he was just being blustery, but now, with a machine gun in his hands, he saw a way. Worse came to worse he could just start shooting out windows, but those torches gave him a pretty good idea. Torches meant fuel—you couldn't just swaddle a stick in an old rag and light it on fire. The fire needed something to keep it going—gas, maybe, or motor oil. Something good and flammable.

That meant the cannibals had fuel.

Which further meant he was going to blow some shit up. Ideally by shooting it. The *rat-a-tat* of a machine gun? A bloom of unholy fire?

That would get Gil's attention.

Now, he just needed to find the fuel source. Gas cans? Tanks of propane or kerosene? It had to be around here somewhere. He lifted his nose like a dog scenting prey on the wind.

The vampire wound his way through the store—as he did, a woman came out from behind a pile of ruined tires, screaming and running at him. In her hand? An old classic: a board with a bunch of nails sticking out of it. She swung. He ducked, jacked her in the face with the butt of the AR-15 (it was not yet time to earn unwanted attention) and drove her nose up into her brain.

The smell of her blood trickling from her smashed nostrils made him hungry. *Refocus*, he thought—there would be time enough to feed.

It was then that he caught the odor.

Kerosene.

That was what they were using. It was the sharp, acrid tang of kerosene. It was... drifting down from above? He tilted his head, lifted his nose.

Was it on the roof?

He heard the *squeak* too late.

The creaky squeak came from behind him—and just as he pivoted heel-to-toe with the rifle, the world roared with a bark from an autoloader shotgun.

It took Coburn's right leg off at the knee. It was the leg on which he pivoted and now, quite literally, he didn't have a leg to stand on.

He tumbled to the ground, taken totally by surprise. He'd been first dizzied by the scent of blood and then so consumed with searching out the invisible threads of kerosene vapor that he never heard the old man coming up behind him.

The old dude—his chin whiskers and head buzzed to salty nubs—rolled up in a wheel chair, a Remington 1100 shotgun sitting in his lap.

"Interloper," the old man hissed. His voice carried a distinct Southern twang—a guttural West Virginian accent.

Coburn went to bring the rifle up to dispatch the old sonofabitch, but a boot stepped down hard on it. Two men—one short and fat, the other tall and thin with a scoliosis bend in his back—snatched the gun away and then started to pick him up under the arms.

The old man leered. "You're invited to dinner."

Coburn got the joke, ha-ha, he was supposed to be dinner, but really, fuck that right in the ear. He still had one good leg and two dummies supporting him. He shot out with a hard kick—but the old man was just far enough away that his boot snapped against nothing.

Boom.

The shotgun slug took off Coburn's good leg right below the knee. The half-leg pirouetted through the air, clanging into a shelf.

Coburn's first thought was, *I like those boots.*

His second was, *I'm going to need new legs, stat.*

"Wyatt, Stevie, get him into the carrier." The old man gestured behind him, and sure enough, Coburn saw that behind the old cannibal lurked a pet carrier—a dog kennel big enough for a German Shepherd.

"You motherfuckers," he growled through gritted teeth, as Wyatt and Stevie carried him over to the kennel. He wasn't going to go easily—he knew he had a choice here, which was to concentrate for a minute and put all his energy into growing a new pair of legs, or, instead, make short work of these monkeys without worrying about the legs.

He decided, for now, hell with the legs.

The vampire didn't know which one was Wyatt, which one was Stevie, but the way they were carrying him, they had his arms around the back of their necks while they carried him around the trunk. Didn't give him a whole lot of leverage, but his arms were pretty well-placed—

He cinched up his right arm and started choking the short, fat one— then he leaned over and took a bite out of his neck, or, at least, *tried* to. All he managed was to get hold of the cannibal's rubbery ear, but that would have to be good enough. Coburn jerked his head and ripped the ear clean off.

Short, fat cannibal—Stevie? Wyatt? Styatt? Weevie?—screamed.

Then Coburn pulled tight on the other arm, bringing the back-bent cannibal's own head around until it *thwacked* hard into the other one's skull. All three of them dropped to the ground in a heap.

Coburn "stood up" on his two uneven stump-legs, triumphant, resplendent, fangs out, tongue tasting the air moments before he intended to thrust his face downward and feast upon one of the two chuckleheads...

But the old man in the wheelchair had other ideas.

Gone was the shotgun. In its place: the AR-15 that Coburn had dropped.

The old man licked his lips, then began firing.

CHAPTER NINETEEN

Ambrosia, the Queen

BEING A VAMPIRE had its perks. Endless life (provided he followed the rules). No conscience to worry him (provided he tamped it down into a deep dark hole). He could run fast, jump high, and twist people's brains like a nipple held betwixt thumb and forefinger. He could even survive, when, say, shot in the chest a dozen times by a .223 Armalite Model 15 assault rifle.

But one thing a vampire could not do: betray the laws of physics.

Normally, bullets didn't cause him much worry. They didn't *feel* great, and getting punched in the trunk with a high-velocity rifle round was certainly *distracting*, but even still, it wasn't a game-ender. Not like he had internal organs anybody could hurt. Perforate his spleen? Puncture his lung? Explode his heart? Eh. Whatever. He wasn't using them. They were just dusty meat inside his dead body anyhow.

But his bones.

He needed those. They were his support system. If one part of his body held particular importance, it was his skeleton.

Disrupt the skeleton—with perhaps a shotgun slug to the kneecaps or rifle-rounds to the bones that held his arms together—and things got a lot more difficult. Especially since healing for him was not immediate: bones took a while to knit or regrow. Like slow osseous crystals forming from a bed of salt and calcium.

But even *that* was not Coburn's biggest problem.

His problem right now? The dog kennel.

Soon as the old man—whose name, as it turned out, was simply 'Grandpaw'—finished hole-punching Coburn's body with rifle rounds, the other two cannibals shoved Coburn's broken, legless body into the pet carrier. Though, not before the taller, stooped-over cannibal stripped him of his leather jacket—now perforated with holes—and put it on.

It was barely big enough. His leg stumps thrust up against the back of the kennel, and that was again a cruel reminder that he could not violate the laws of physics. Much as he wanted, without room to grow his legs, they would not grow. No legs meant he couldn't dismantle this thing.

And his blood was swiftly leaving his body through the many holes and two stumps. Given that blood was a necessity when it came time to *heal up*, it meant he couldn't heal his arms, couldn't tear the door off this carrier, couldn't do squat. He tried to *will* his body to retain the blood, to harness it and channel it—but it wasn't happening. With every moment, a darker shadow of desperation drifted over him.

Wyatt and Stevie—the tall one who stole his jacket was Wyatt, the earless buttplug was Stevie—hooked the carrier up to a chain, then started dragging it across the busted-up tile floor of the Wal-Mart. Grandpaw wheeled alongside as Coburn struggled to make something, *anything*, happen.

"Shit," Grandpaw said, peering in through the side holes. The word came out as *shee-yit*. "You still alive in there? After all that? You must be some goddamn *miracle food*. Ambrosia might make you a meal all for herself."

Coburn tried to curse the old man out, but all that came out was a ragged whisper and a mouthful of blood. A bullet must've clipped him in the throat.

Grandpaw had one thing right:

Shit.

* * *

THEY HEARD GUNFIRE. A couple *booms*, then several *pop, pop, pops*.

"Was that it?" Ebbie asked. "Was that the signal?"

"I don't know," Leelee answered.

Kayla nursed on a juice box, nervously chewing the straw. "I bet that was it. I bet that was the signal. He said we'd know."

"But we don't know," Ebbie said. Leelee looked to her with eyes uncertain, eyes lost and wandering.

They'd been orbiting a strip mall parking lot for the last hour, leading a small but growing band of the undead around in circles. It was like herding cats with a laser pointer. But once the gunfire started off in the distance, about half of them broke away from the pack and started staggering off toward the Wal-Mart. That was how they were: creatures of stimulus and response.

"I think it could've been it," Kayla insisted.

Gil came up behind them in the front of the mobile home. Jaw tight as he chewed on sunflower seeds. "That wasn't it. We need a bigger opening than that. That distraction wasn't more than a couple mouse farts." He spit seed hulls into a paper cup. "We wait."

"But—" Kayla started.

"I said, *we wait.*"

"BRING ME THE meat."

He pressed his face against the cage of the carrier, and his first thought was, *That body must contain blood in the gallon, not the pint.*

Ambrosia, the Cannibal Queen of the Man-Eating Wal-Mart, was easily eight hundred pounds. She did not *sit* so much as *allow her fat to sprawl out* across a dais made from shipping pallets, six-packs of soda, and various repurposed ottomans. Her 'throne room' was framed by a niche of flat-screen televisions (this was, after all, the electronics department). While none of the televisions had electricity, on each was painted a garish and frankly amateurish portrait of Ambrosia in greasy colors.

Incense burned—ghostly serpents of scented smoke coiled around her head. But it did little to mask the smell: Ambrosia's stink was wretched. Had Coburn tears in his head, his eyes would be leaking.

The odor was some mind-boggling combination of rotten onions, rancid lunchmeat and sweat-soaked gym socks.

Basically, she smelled like human garbage.

Wyatt and Stevie dragged the vampire kennel up to the edge of the dais, then lifted it up with a groan and placed it before their fleshy mistress.

Ambrosia struggled, grunting as she leaned over her own prodigious flesh, and stared into the kennel. Coburn bit at the grate like a rabid animal. It didn't work. His strength was swiftly waning.

Next to him, he heard the squeaks of Grandpaw's wheelchair.

"Ooooh. He's feisty," Ambrosia said, chuckling. Her words and chortles sounded like someone had stuffed her throat with pudding. Gargling, gurgling. And her breath could've choked a hyena.

"Shot him plenty of times," Grandpaw said, sucking air through his teeth. "But there he is, still kicking like that battery bunny what used to be on TV."

"I want him for breakfast." She licked her rubbery lips.

"You want him raw?"

"*Sashimi*," she corrected. "We must strive to be civilized, Grandpaw. We are creatures of the world."

"'Course, what was I thinking?" In his voice, Coburn could hear the man's dismissal—he didn't give one whit about this woman or what she was saying, but put up with it because clearly she was the one with the power. Was it just her size that convinced others? How the hell was she so damn big? Coburn decided to ask.

"How—" he started, his voice croaking. He pushed past vocal cords that felt like broken glass: "How the hell are you... so... fucking... *fat*?"

"My breakfast speaks!" Ambrosia said, her voice a high-pitched twitter. She clapped her hands together, hands that were actually quite small, like doll's hands. "My dear, I have a most undesirable metabolic disorder." She studied his face, saw it wrinkle up in disbelief. "I'm just kidding! Human meat is wonderfully complex and fatty." She leaned in and whispered, as if confiding a secret: "I eat a lot of people. And soon I'm going to eat you, little rabbit."

She pulled back from the cage.

"I want most of him cooked," she declared, as if ordering a chef to do her bidding. "Take him to the roof and roast him over the spit. But.

But! I would like a raw preparation of sashimi to precede my meal. Also, if any of his back-fat remains, I require a lardon of man-bacon."

Ambrosia flapped her little hand in a wave of dismissal. Her arm-fat shook with the motion, like a sandbag full of gelatin.

As the cage withdrew, Grandpaw wheeled up and presented her with something. Coburn saw that it was one of his feet.

"An appetizer if'n you want it," the old man said.

She took it like a buttery cob of hot corn, shucked the boot and rolled back the pant leg—

Then took a big wet bite.

As the pet carrier rounded an endcap away from the electronics department, away from Ambrosia's throne room, he could hear the moans of delight, the smacking of her lips, the pleasurable sighs blown through her nostrils as she chowed down on the vampire's flesh.

He hoped he tasted good, at least.

CHAPTER TWENTY

The Spit

WYATT AND STEVIE slammed the pet carrier down onto the roof after using a pulley-and-pallet to haul it up there. They slid the pet carrier in place between two other carriers, both similarly-sized but different in design—both were wire mesh, more 'cage-like' than Coburn's own kennel. Then they went back inside.

Even with the blood having mostly fled his body, the vampire could feel his skin tingle. It wasn't long until sun-up. The edge of the sky beyond the Wal-Mart's roof was growing slowly stained with purple, like a cloth mopping up wine.

Once the sun came up, they wouldn't need to cook him. The rays of dawn would do that for them—the world becoming one big microwave oven.

He looked around, took quick stock of his surroundings.

Sentries manned the roof. Four of them, by the look of it. Each armed. Each squirrely, jacked up on something by the look and the smell of them. Trucker meth, maybe. Or just cranked-up cold meds.

Over toward the AC unit was a big oven and spit made out of cement blocks and wood. The spit was a truck axle. A pot-bellied, sallowchested cannibal in an apron stained with yellow fat and red blood upended a bag of charcoal briquettes below the rusted axle.

Beyond that? The stockpile Coburn needed: tanks of fuel. Kerosene containers, but gas cans, too.

Coburn was not the only meat on the menu—the two cages he sat sandwiched between were occupied. To his left, some Charlie Manson wannabe picking at his skin like it might be run through with ants and worms. To his right, a clean-cut kid in a too-white t-shirt and jeans— maybe 16 or 17 years old. A ginger. Freckles and everything. Smelled like soap.

He didn't have long. He felt his body going weak from the blood loss and knew that with the coming of morning everything would begin to stiffen up—so that meant this was a *now-or-never* situation.

Coburn pressed his face against the side of his carrier. Holes peppered the hard plastic, presumably so a dog could stare out, and that was exactly what Coburn did, lined up both eyes with two holes and stared into the cage of the teen boy.

Kids were dumb. He was counting on that.

He pretended to have something in his mouth and spoke accordingly.

"Hey, you," he said to the kid. "I gah the key. In mah mouf. Can use it to opeh your cage."

The boy, though, didn't say a peep and instead shied away.

Fine. Wasn't taking the bait.

"I want the key," whispered Charlie Manson. "Gimme the key. Come on. I'll do it. I'll let you out, legless dude. I'll let us all out."

Good. *Someone* was taking the bait.

"Here," Coburn said. "I nee you to puh you toh—" He tried again. "You *tongue* fru the hole. Stig it out! Hurry! Fas!"

Charlie scooted over to the edge, and then Coburn saw that he was basically just skin and bones—hollow cheeks, the two bones of his wrists clear beneath the skin like a pair of rotten broomsticks.

Manson-esque stuck his tongue out, pressing his face hard against the side of the cage. His pink tongue thrust through the side of his cage and into Coburn's, but only by a couple of millimeters. It wasn't enough for Coburn's plan—of course, Coburn didn't have a key. What he *needed* was blood, and this dummy's tongue was going to be a blood spigot once Coburn had enough on which to clamp down with his fangs.

The tongue kept waggling, like an earthworm just poking out of the hole.

"'Imme uh key! 'Imme uh key!" Manson-esque chanted.

"Moh closer! Moh closer!" Coburn hissed back.

Manson squashed his face hard as he could so that one of his eyes was bugging out against the metal mesh.

The tongue came all the way through.

And Bingo was his name-oh.

But then Manson-esque muttered, "Shit!" and sucked his tongue back in his mouth, retreating to the back of his cage. Coburn dropped the pretence of having something in his mouth.

"Hey! Get the fuck back here."

"Shh!" Manson exhorted, but it was too late. Suddenly Coburn's kennel rattled with the butt of one of the sentries' rifles.

"Shut the fuck up, you dumb mong—" The sentry stopped and peered into the cage. "Jesus, Cookie, this hunk of meat really doesn't have legs."

The 'chef' (apparently named Cookie) mumbled in assent while sharpening his knives against a cement block. "I'm told that Grandpaw blew the legs off with that Remington of his. Fuck it. Best meat is on the trunk anyhow. Get him out of the cage and bring him over."

In the distance, the sky brightened at its margins, from purple to red with the barest fringe of orange.

The sun was almost here.

As two sentries opened the cage and reached in to grab hold of him, the vampire realized that this was well and truly his last shot.

The hands hauled him free—he had no strength, had no legs, didn't have a snow-cone's chance in Hell to make any dramatic moves. But one wrist strayed awfully close to his mouth...

He bit down. Fangs crunched through tendon.

His mouth, flush with blood.

The world brightened. Came alive. His flesh tingled, his leg stumps burned. A hot rush of giddiness swept inside him: feeding was, in its own way, like the human orgasm. Longer he waited, the stronger the sensation. Positively Tantric.

It was that moment that represented a somewhat critical divide for Coburn—a branching of paths, a choice made unexpectedly. A small voice, a *loud whisper*, rang out inside his head.

Everything came to this point.

At the horizon's edge, the sun slid upwards, rising, rising.

The sky, brightening.

Coburn wrenched himself free from the man's wrist.

The man's rifle clattered to the ground. The world moved in slow-motion. Cookie came at him with a meat cleaver. The other sentry scrambled for his own rifle, bringing it clumsily up against his shoulder.

Coburn, a legless, pale freak, grabbed the rifle.

And he made his choice.

He jacked the bolt back, threw a round into the chamber and fired—it flew true and found its intended home.

The kerosene tank went *ping!* as the bullet struck it, and then a half-second later, exploded. A mushroom cloud of black smoke and demonic flame belched up into the morning sky just as the sun crested the horizon—

Cookie was thrown to the ground, the meat cleaver clattering away—

The sentry fired his own rifle, striking Coburn in the chest.

The sun's kiss began to smolder the vampire's skin—it blistered fast, pig-tail curls of smoke rising from his suppurating flesh.

He caught flame.

He screamed.

And that was when he knew it was all over.

CHAPTER TWENTY-ONE

This Way to the Great Egress

"THERE." GIL POINTED out the window. Sure enough, above the Wal-Mart fire blossomed—a mushrooming cloud brighter than the coming sunrise. From the fire came a belch of black smoke. "That's our window. Ebbie, drive."

By now, even Cecelia came out to see. She'd been in hiding ever since Coburn kicked her out of the bedroom. Not that a Winnebago like this offered any actual hiding space—mostly she'd just curled up away from everyone, moping and refusing to rise. Gil had tried to comfort her, but it was never his strong suit, and so she retreated, chastened and unsure.

Now, though, she stood shoulder to shoulder with Kayla. "Looks like your boyfriend did good."

"He's not my—" Kayla shook her head, gave up. "Whatever, Cecelia."

Ebbie gunned the RV. The mobile home rocked on its axis any time they careened around highway debris or forgotten cars. He drove up over a median. He took a short-cut through a parking lot. Kayla braced herself against what passed for the kitchen cabinets; she almost fell into Cecelia, who gave her an *eat shit* look.

And then, there it stood—up on their right, the Wal-Mart. Zombies already starting to gather at its periphery. Dozens here already, and more on the way. Shambling toward the store. Tumbling into the moat.

Gil slapped Ebbie on the shoulder. "There! There. The spike strips. Stop here, stop here!" The RV lurched forward as Ebbie hit the brakes. The cabinet doors opened—plastic cups and plates tumbled out over Kayla.

Gil flagged Leelee and together they hurried outside. It had been agreed earlier that they were the two who could move the fastest. Gil was the oldest, but in good shape. Leelee, too, was lean, muscled—she used to run marathons.

Kayla crawled up into the passenger seat and watched as the two of them raced out and began dragging the first strip back. Must've been heavier than it looked, because they were struggling to pull it in. It folded up like an accordion but it was slow going.

And the zombies were starting to take notice.

Most of them were focused on the Wal-Mart. The boom, the fire, the smoke—and now, the screaming—drew them to it the way a porch light drew moths, but a handful of them had peeled away and were staggering not toward the RV but rather toward the two specimens of fresh meat that stood out in the open, dicking around with a recalcitrant spike-strip.

Kayla rolled down the window and screamed for her father. He looked up and she pointed toward the approaching rotters.

He felt at his hip. No gun waited there.

Kayla grabbed Cecelia and tapped Ebbie on the shoulder. "Get the guns! We need to start shooting."

"No!" Cecelia protested. "That'll draw them toward us."

"We need to save Dad and Leelee," Kayla said, opening up an overhead bin and pulling out guns—she thrust a shotgun into Ebbie's hands and *tried* to give Cecelia a pistol, but she waved it away.

"I can't shoot," she said.

"You and Dad went out shooting just last week!"

Cecelia looked horrified and… was that shame in her eyes? "We… didn't end up doing any shooting."

"Gross," Kayla said, pushing past her and fumbling with the gun.

She pulled back the action, which was always harder than it looked in the movies, and threw open the RV door.

Ahead of her, Ebbie leaned out the passenger side window, stuffing through as much of his profuse bulk as he could to get a clean shot.

Kayla squinted one eye and stared down the barrel. She wasn't a great shot, but Gil had taught her well enough.

Together, she and Ebbie began firing.

Her shots hit, but they didn't hit true. She clipped a zombie nurse in the leg, and while it staggered the monster, the bitch kept on coming, now dragging her ruined foot. She hit another in the hip, and a third in the neck.

No headshots.

Ebbie, on the other hand, was downright surgical with that shotgun. He always had been and, curiously, he credited it to video games. Gil credited it to him having such a big body, as the big boy was able to anchor himself and steady his shots without much effort. Unlike Kayla, whose frame had all the strength and stability of a wind-swept napkin.

With Ebbie shooting, heads erupted like kicked pumpkins.

Gil and Leelee finally pulled one of the spike strips across just as the zombie nurse came up behind them, mouth like a snake ready to swallow a rabbit—threads of mucusy blood connecting her lower jaw to her upper.

She leapt onto Gil.

And then her head exploded as Ebbie took her out.

Dazed but not down, Gil waved Leelee on to the next spike strip. By now, the other zombies had noticed the RV—and worse, Kayla saw movement on the roof as one of the cannibals peered over to see what all the ruckus was about.

The man had a rifle. He took aim. Kayla screamed for Ebbie.

The cannibal took his shot and the side mirror spun away from the vehicle, the round hitting only inches from Ebbie's head. He pulled himself back inside. Kayla, too, swung the door shut just as a rifle bullet punched a hole in it.

The worst thing about the zombie apocalypse is the people, Kayla mused.

She scurried up to the front as she heard another *crack* of the rifle and the ricochet whine of the bullet hitting somewhere near the wheel well. He was aiming for the tires. If he hit even one tire...

"Ebbie!" she said, panting. "Just drive!"

"But they haven't pulled back the second spike strip yet!"

"Then drive backwards, I dunno! It's harder to hit a moving target!"

Ebbie hauled himself back into the driver's seat, and threw the RV into reverse, the tires squealing and kicking up loose asphalt.

Kayla peered out one of the side windows—

Just as a rotter's face appeared. Mouth wide. Foul slug tongue licking the glass. Kayla yelped and hit the floor. Then the window shattered as a bullet drilled a hole from the back of the zombie's head all the way to the front of his forehead and through the glass. The monster fell away and tumbled under one of the tires; the RV hit it like a speedbump. Kayla screamed, "Ebbie! Now go forward! Go, go, go!"

Ebbie did as commanded. Again the RV lurched. Again tires squealed and broken asphalt complained beneath them.

Suddenly, Ebbie was, well, ebullient. "They did it! They got it!"

The RV skidded to a halt. Outside, Kayla saw that the shooter up top of the Wal-Mart had changed his targets—now he was taking down zombies. The moat had filled up in places and some zombies were crawling over one another and coming up on the other side. If it kept going like that, they'd soon be overrun.

Coburn, she thought. She knew he'd make it out of there okay. He had to. Even though the sun was up, he still managed to send the signal. It was because of him they were free.

When her Daddy and Leelee came tumbling inside the RV and Ebbie once more jammed on the accelerator, Kayla felt a swell of pride and triumph—it had been a long time since she felt that way, felt full of hope and promise and possibility.

It would be short-lived.

Kayla threw her arms around her father's neck. He stroked her hair and kissed her forehead.

"The vampire did good, Daddy," she said, twinkling.

But he didn't say anything.

"We'll pull over soon?" she asked. "You told him about a half-mile.

I don't know when he'll make it, but I think we're good—the cannibals have their hands full with the zombies, and the zombies have their meal for the day I figure..."

Gil sighed and shook his head. "We're not stopping, little girl."

"Wait. What?" Kayla's heart sank.

Ebbie looked back, too, a quizzical look on his face. "Yeah, what?"

"Keep on driving," Gil said. "We're not stopping for anything. Not until we need gas."

"But Coburn—" she started.

"Is a godforsaken monster," Gil finished. "We're not playing this game anymore. Besides, he ain't coming out of there. He's up against cannibals and surrounded by the living dead. The fact it's daylight only complicates issues."

Kayla felt tears at the corners of her eyes. Her cheeks reddened, became hot. Her hands formed fists and she pounded at his chest. Hard.

"Leelee!" Kayla said. "Tell him he can't do this. Ebbie! Ebbie, please."

"Yeah, Gil, I don't know about this," Ebbie said, protesting.

"Ebbie," Gil growled. "You keep on driving. You pull this vehicle over and you're going to have to deal with me. I saved your life before but I am just as happy to toss you back out there into the world like chum for sharks."

Kayla sneered. "*You're* the monster here."

"Kayla..."

"No!" she said, pushing away from him. Cecelia replaced her at his side, looping her hand around his hip and pulling him close.

Cecelia kissed his neck and said, "Good job, baby."

CHAPTER TWENTY-TWO
Food of the Gods

IT WAS IF he were underwater. Words, warped. Sounds, distorted—*echo, echo, echo*. Womb-like. The rush of blood. The dull thudding of a heartbeat. Not his own, surely. *Your heart is a piece of dead meat, like a fatty gobbet of beef.*

Time had no meaning.

It stretched, taffy-like, and collapsed upon itself again and again.

Meanwhile, shadows flitted in the deeper dark. A tall silhouette stood always in his peripheral. The shadow flashed glinty fangs. Leaned as if in a doorway.

Beyond him, crying. The wails of a little girl. Calling for her Daddy. *Kayla?* he thought.

He heard the roar of flames—both real and imagined. Gunshots, too. *Echo, echo, echo.* Movement. Fabric against fabric. Leather against flesh. A sound like ice cracking all around, tiny fractures ever-crackling. With it, the smell of char. The smell of gunsmoke. The fetid stink of human sweat and spoiled meat.

Voices swam with him here in the tenebrous depths like fat eels just under the surface of black water.

"...looks like he done cooked himself..."

"...still see the whites of his eyes... his teeth, too..."

"...just keep the monsters at bay, I still haven't had my breakfast, which is now, regrettably, going to be my dinner..."

But then, an unexpected visitor. A tongue worming into his mouth. And with it?

Blood.

AMBROSIA WOULD NEVER abandon the Wal-Mart, because this was her temple. She was the queen of this place—no, she was its *goddess*. She refused to acknowledge the deeper reality: they couldn't get her out of here if they tried. Ambrosia—real name Martha Cason-Jones—came here on a flatbed truck and would have to leave here on one. She'd lost a little weight since coming here, she knew, maybe even as much as a hundred pounds. But that still put her at, what, six hundred? Seven?

Uh-uh, no way. She wasn't going anywhere.

Still. It was hard not feeling like she was losing control here. Up top, the sentries on the roof were picking off the zombies all around, but the gunfire was only drawing more of them. The moat was no longer working like it was supposed to—damn thing had piled so high with rotter bodies that the monstrosities were just clambering over their fallen, spike-stuck brethren. So they poured gas down from above and lit it on fire. Zombie bodies burned pretty well, and in fact, because they kept bumbling into one another, the fire spread—though it didn't kill them, either. They just kept flailing around, blinded by the light, limbs ruined by fire.

Of course, they'd spent all their remaining gas lighting those fires.

Because *someone* had decided to break free of his doggy kennel and start shooting up the place. Ambrosia looked down at the plate of food in front of her—the 'plate' was really just the lid flap from a piece of luggage and the food was the scorched head and torso of their most recent visitor, interloper, and victim. His arms were mostly burned to brittle sticks. His leg stumps looked like charred elbows. Only things left unblackened were his teeth and his eyes.

Ambrosia belched, took her knife and fork and cut another wedge of meat from his mid-section. It wasn't bacon, but hell with it, she didn't care. This was delicious. Far tastier than any meat she'd ever consumed—and, by this point, Lord knew she'd eaten a lot of so-called 'long pork' or 'pink pig.' But this? Exquisite. It wasn't the fat—frankly, he didn't have much fat on him. And the meat by now was long cold. But every once in a while she'd get into a sweet pocket, and the pink juices ran like she was squeezing a fresh steak in between her hands. Bloody and delicious. The one good thing about the fire on the roof was that it had cooked the meat just right: charred on the outside, rare on the inside.

Cookie, the Chef, said it wasn't the explosion that got him, though—he said the body just caught fire all on its own. "Spontaneous convection," he said, even though he meant combustion. Cookie was a meth-head—as it turned out, making meth once the world ended was a lot easier when you had no competition for supplies and no cops kicking down your trailer door—so anything that came out of his mouth was more than a little dubious.

Still, in some places the char was a little challenging.

She wiped her greasy hands on her mammoth cleavage, licked her lips, and then saw a precious gem—like a pearl hidden in the ugly labial folds of an oyster.

The tongue.

The tongue wasn't burned. It was pink, perfect, untouched by fire.

She felt herself salivate.

Ambrosia knew she deserved a taste. She deserved everything. The whole world. This place was her kingdom because it was what the universe owed her. Grandpaw—her actual grandfather—made that dream possible. With his mind and her girth they were a pair of easy, natural leaders. Plus, why would anyone rebel against such a wondrous system? They were fed, weren't they?

She took her fork and knife and poked around the corpse's mouth the way a dentist might, but when she tried cutting into the tongue she really couldn't get a good *angle* on the whole affair.

"We're losing it all," Grandpaw said, wheeling up. He looked haggard. Long day of fighting off zombies—and punishing the men for letting a goddamned *camper* full of fresh meat go driving past—and now night was coming, which meant the zombies would start to get riled up again like a kicked-over hive of killer bees. "They're on all sides. And they keep coming."

Ambrosia snarled at him: no words, just a brutish, animalistic sound. Its intent was clear: *I am eating.*

"It's all falling apart," he said, turning his chair and wheeling away. "It's all going away..."

Ahhh. Alone again.

So. Fork and knife not working.

"Let us try a more direct route," Ambrosia said, lifting the corpse's face to her own. She cracked back the jaw like she was busting open a crab claw, exposing the sweet meat—*the tongue*—within.

Then she sucked the tongue into her own mouth and started to chew. The cannibal's French kiss, she thought, and felt a bubble of giddiness rise inside her.

The tongue was tough—not unusual, really. No fat on the tongue. All meat and muscle. Were you to cook it, you'd cook it long and low and slow, but now she did not have that luxury. She bit down hard—

And in the process, bit into her own cheek.

She tasted blood.

The tongue between her teeth—not hers, but his—wiggled.

Her eyes went wide. Did she just feel what she thought she felt? Wasn't possible. Or maybe it was. Corpses sometimes moved after death. Didn't nails and hair continue to grow? Or was that just a myth?

An odd thought struck her: *he didn't die very easily, did he?* Grandpaw shot off his legs. Shot him in the chest. And still he lived. Hell, he didn't just live—he got out of his crate and bit somebody and stole a sentry's gun.

That, in retrospect, seemed strange.

Teeth clamped down on her tongue. She screamed. The fangs sank deep. Blood filled her mouth—but then was vacuumed away, sucked into the carcass cradled at her bosom. The corpse made hungry, happy noises.

*   *   *

THIS, THEN, WAS how the vampire imagined it:

What lurked before him was a massive puffed pastry, its pillowy dough filled with a salty-sweet umami karate kick from its unctuous blood filling. He was like a little boy and this meal awaiting him was like a bean bag chair—no! Something even bigger, like a moon bounce full of coppery icing, like a piñata one could shatter and live within.

He was going to eat his way through.

And that was precisely what he did. He had no arms, so he chewed like a worm boring to the heart of an apple. First, her tongue—then, his head stuffed into her bulging cheeks, he drank deeper, chewing downward until he felt her ragged face-flesh flapping at his shoulders. Her screams long-dead, Coburn wormed his way into what must've looked like some kind of bizarre reverse birth—

What remained of his body disappeared within her hulking flesh.

She was still alive, of course, flailing about—but where could she go? Her legs had long atrophied beneath her.

It was hard to say when she died.

And it was hard to determine how long it took him to feed—and feed, *and feed* some more. For a while, all was quiet. Her booming canned ham of a heart eventually shuddered one last shudder and then gave out like an old motor.

In the distance, gunshots. Zombie moans. Cannibal screams.

Ambrosia's stomach—hidden beneath a 'shirt' made from diaphanous bedsheets—rippled. Like water disturbed by fish feeding beneath.

Then, another ripple—this one, stronger. The flesh tented.

Finally, a bone erupted. A sharpened rib, actually, broken from within.

It was enough of a hole. Coburn stuck his fingers in the fleshy tear, got his hands around the skin, then tore it open.

He emerged, the reverse birth itself reversed, emptying out of her midsection like the contents of a shark's stomach after having its belly cut open.

Coburn slid down off the dais, naked as the day he was born. He had new legs. Fresh flesh. Real arms.

Everything was back.

He sat up, and saw Grandpaw sitting there in his chair, a shotgun across his lap. The old man's hands shook as he looked beyond the vampire to the woman, a mound of flesh who in places looked less like a human and more like a microwave-exploded hot dog.

"Ambrosia," the old man said, his voice a hoarse whimper.

Then he turned his gaze, now hateful, toward Coburn.

"You," the old man hissed.

"Me," Coburn said, grinning, his teeth slick with blood. Hell, *all* of him slick with blood.

"It's not possible. You aren't human."

"Nope."

"You'll pay for this."

Coburn laughed. "Fuck you, you old man-eater."

The old man thought he had the drop again. Thought he was *fast*. He grabbed for the shotgun but his hands found nothing. Coburn stood, leaving the man weeping. Somewhere toward the front of the store, Coburn heard the windows shattering, boards splintering. Bodies tumbled inside like so many sacks of dirt. He couldn't see them yet—too many aisles, too much store between them—but they'd be here soon enough.

"They're coming for you, Grandpaw."

"Go to Hell."

"Not today."

And then, for giggles, Coburn swung the shotgun like a hard-slicing golf club into the side of the wheelchair. The wheel dented in hard, giving the chair a mean front lean. The old man tried to wheel away, but now couldn't.

Coburn chuckled, then wandered off in search of some clothes.

WYATT SAT HUDDLED up against a display case that once must've held fishing rods or pen-knives or something. He had a pistol held in a prayer grip, his hands shaking as the moans of the dead come ever closer.

And then suddenly, all went topsy-turvy. He felt himself lifted up across the counter, hard and heavy hands wrestling with him as the leather jacket he'd stolen from the vampire was pulled over his head. All was dark until it wasn't. And when once more he could see, he found himself deposited onto his butt-bone.

Standing there, on legs he shouldn't have, was the vampire.

Naked and unabashed.

He shook the jacket at Wyatt.

"This is mine, you goddamn yokel."

"The zombies—" Wyatt started to say.

But then the vampire kicked in his kneecap. Pain exploded up and down his leg.

"Enjoy being one of 'em," the vampire said, slipping on the jacket. Coburn wandered off, whistling.

THE MOON ROSE above the Wal-Mart, bandied in rheumy clouds. Coburn wrestled with Cookie's torn-up jeans, since the 'chef' had about the same build as him. The vampire had figured he'd have to fight for them, but found instead that Cookie had taken his own life: a small two-shot derringer under the chin. Bullet never exited. Probably just ricocheted around up there like one of those motorcyclists riding in the circle cages at the circus. Scrambled brains so he'd never turn into one of the hungry undead.

The others, the sentries, well. Those assholes, he had to kill. Four of them, their bodies laying draped across sandbags and the AC unit. He didn't bother taking a nibble from any of them: Ambrosia's blood had filled him to the brim. Every time he took a step he expected to hear a spongy *squish squish squish*.

As Coburn was tugging on Cookie's jeans (not the underpants—he didn't want that man's soiled boxers, and decided instead to go commando), he looked over and saw the trio of dog kennels.

The Charlie Manson wannabe was dead. All-day-dead. Burned up probably when Coburn ignited the explosion with the AR-15.

But the teen boy remained alive. Hunkered in the back of his cage, eyes as big as the moon above.

"I must be getting soft," Coburn said as he plodded over in bare feet (Cookie's shoes were too damn small) and twisted the lock off the cage.

Then he went to each of the sentries, looking for something to put on his feet. Nothing. Nada. Boots too big. Sneakers too small.

He missed his Fluevogs. They had to be around somewhere.

But already the store was flooded with the hungry dead. Shit, though, those boots were worth it, weren't they?

An answer came howling across the parking lot. Somewhere—not close, but not too far—came the banshee's wail of that bitch in the pink bathrobe. The one who had tasted Coburn's blood. With it came a second howl: not hers, but the keening of another. *Two of them?*

The boots weren't worth it.

He had to get the fuck out of here. Fast. But how? He looked out across the parking lot: more and more rotters staggered out of the darkness, heading toward what was now the center of their universe: the Wal-Mart. Could he just jump it? Take a long run and leap and hope he landed strong and could clear the horde?

Then, from behind him: a snapping of fingers. Coburn turned to see the teen boy waving him over. The kid pointed to a ladder down.

Coburn walked over, sneering. "Don't snap at me, kid. I'm not your kept monkey."

The boy gestured again toward the ladder.

"Use your words."

The kid just stared.

"Let me guess, Ginger. You can't talk."

The boy shrugged.

"Fine. Talking's overrated anyway. What is it you want to show me?"

Just then, another pair of howls. Closer, this time.

Coburn felt the hot blood in his dead body go suddenly cold. He peered over the edge of the Wal-Mart roof, saw that the ladder led to a concrete pad. A ratty looking lime green dirt-bike sat down there.

"Sorry, Ginger, I don't drive."

The boy mimed riding a bike. Or, in this case, driving a dirt bike.

"*You* can drive it?" Coburn asked.

The kid nodded.

Coburn looked out over the sea of rotters.

Before he slid down the ladder, he looked to the kid and poked him in the chest, hard. "If you crash us, Ginger, I'm going to eat your heart."

CHAPTER TWENTY-THREE

Abandonment Issues

THIS, TO GRANDPAW, was a fact: zombies were fucking stupid. Dumber than the average possum because, hell, even a possum knew he had to go scare up his own food. Rotters were like water, just moving to fill in the gaps. Sure, they had basic *responses* down—big noise or bright flash meant 'stagger on over in the hopes of catching a meal'—but beyond that, the living dead didn't possess the capability of higher thought. It was why the moat worked. Mostly.

Grandpaw once heard a story about a town out West, Colorado somewhere, where they kept a headless chicken alive for a year and a half. Was in all the record books. Story was that the chicken killer's cleaver missed a reasonable nub of the brain-stem (like the tip of a man's pinky), taking the head but not that critical bundle of nerves. It was enough to keep the chicken running around, scratching the dirt, being a dummy. The chicken's keepers fed the bird with an eyedropper, squeezing nutrients into the chicken's neck stump.

That, then, was how Grandpaw thought of zombies: each one a headless chicken, only thing remaining being that final bundle of nerves that just wouldn't quit. It was why he knew that he was going to make it through this alive.

Because he was hiding in the men's restroom.

Grandpaw had abandoned the destroyed wheelchair and dragged his way to the bathroom—while his legs were for shit, he'd used the wheelchair long enough to build up some pretty good arm muscles over the years.

The others here at the Wal-Mart were all dead. Ambrosia—well, Martha—was gone, that sweet girl. Sure, she was a megalomaniacal brat who weighed as much as a subcompact car, but she was *his* megalomaniacal brat. His granddaughter couldn't have lasted long in this world, anyway. If the zombies didn't get her, her heart would've given out. If her heart didn't give out, eventually the cannibals she *trained* to eat human meat would've gone through a dry spell and realized, oh hey, that chick is made of enough meat to keep us fed for weeks. And they would've killed her and cooked her up and tanned blankets from her skin.

Grandpaw, though, he was a survivor. Survived Viet Nam. Survived a car accident in the late 'eighties. Survived a bout of prostate cancer that hit him hard at the turn of the millennium. And he survived into the end of the world when the dead began to get up and shuffle around like a bunch of mule-kicked ninnies. Hell, he survived whatever the hell it was that ate its way out of Ambrosia's body—that man was no man. Couldn't be killed. Like something out of a movie. Maybe he was some kind of robot? Grandpaw didn't know, didn't care.

All he knew was, he survived all that, and he'd survive here, too. In this bathroom. The door was locked. The stall was locked. He had a little bundle of jerky—strips of 'long pork' dried and braided. The zombies would come. They'd clean the place out. And then they'd move on, like locusts. That was when Grandpaw would emerge.

Eventually, the door to the bathroom rattled on its hinges. That was them. The rotters. Just testing things out. They'd do this, then move on. He wondered, did their disease-eaten brains contain the barest ghost of a memory? Like, they realized somewhere, *this is a door*, but they couldn't remember exactly how to work the damn thing?

But then came a sound that wasn't right, wasn't right at all.

Sounded like—well, not a wolf howling. Not really. Maybe if you took a woman's scream and merged it with a wolf's howl, that might've been almost right, but it would be missing a certain *shrieking-bat-out-of-Hell* factor.

Grandpaw's bowels turned to ice water.

Then: other noises.

The moans of the dead. And the sounds of a scuffle. Not just a scuffle, but a knock-down-drag-out fight. Sounded like whole shelves were being toppled. Then came another one of those pterodactyl hell-shrieks. Closer. Just outside the door.

As if on cue, the restroom door was ripped from its hinges. Grandpaw didn't see it—he was, after all, hidden in one of the stalls—but he knew what he heard.

Then: footsteps. Wet. Hard toenails clicking on tile.

Two sets of feet—foul, filthy, the flesh cracked and blistered—appeared outside the stall. Grandpaw couldn't get a real good look since it was dark in here, but he knew this wasn't right, wasn't right at all. First the one man ripped his big fat granddaughter in half and now a pair of rotters found him locked away in the men's shitter?

The last cogent thought that went through Grandpaw's head was: *the world is home to more monsters than I imagined.* Then the stall door shoved inward off its hinges, crushing his head. His last sensation was being dragged outside. He was pretty sure he saw a flash of pink fabric, which didn't make much sense at all.

THE DIRT BIKE idled nearby, the teen that Coburn had christened 'Ginger' sitting on top of it, the moonlight above highlighting the confused look on his face.

"They were supposed to be here," the vampire growled, pacing the side of the highway in his bare feet. They'd driven up the highway by a half-mile, not seen anything, then kept going. Kept going for another two miles, and still, nothing. Coburn could smell the exhaust, though, from the RV. And it didn't stop here. Didn't stop anywhere. It just kept on going.

He tried to excuse it. *They must've been attacked by zombies.* But that didn't make a lick of sense. Weren't any rotters out here. Saw a few on the way here, but those were dragging their putrescent asses toward the Wal-Mart.

Which meant only one thing: the herd had abandoned the shepherd.

"I've been through some shit over the last several nights," he said, lips in a twisted sneer, fangs out. "Woke up. Ate a deer. Found myself in the zombie apocalypse. Fell off a building. Got chewed up by some zombie bitch in an ugly bathrobe. Got shot by an old man and then taken in by his sickly daughter. Got chewed up *again* by the same bitch-in-a-bathrobe except *now* said bitch is some kind of undead demon, then got shot by a totally *different* old man—those old men sure love their rifles—before I got burned up by the sun and had to eat my way out of a morbidly obese cannibal queen. But you know what, Ginger? This hurts worst of all."

Coburn didn't—or wouldn't, or maybe even *couldn't*—articulate the truth behind this sentiment. It wasn't just that his pre-apocalyptic existence had been full of endless pleasurable meals where he felt like the King of New York and now he was just another hungry wastrel in the ruined vista of God-fucked America. It wasn't just that he'd been through the grinder.

It was that moment back on the roof of the Wal-Mart.

Gun in his hand. Mouth full of blood.

He'd picked up a gun. He could've turned that weapon on his captors. But he didn't. His first thought—his only thought—was to shoot the fuel tanks and send up a bloom of mighty fire to serve as a signal to his herd. To his *people*.

That was a choice he made. It was a choice based on—well, he told himself it was based on a sense of pragmatism, but that wasn't it at all. He'd made a choice because he wanted those people to be safe. He wanted *Kayla* above all others to be safe, to get the signal, to get through the cannibal's roadblock.

It was the first time he'd ever cared about someone more than he cared about himself. Coburn hadn't even realized this was something he was capable of feeling, much less *willing* to feel. And that was the key word, wasn't it? *Willing.* Up until now, he'd enjoyed pretty much ultimate control over his feelings. He jerked the strings, and his emotions (or what remained of them) did a dance.

But this thing he felt for the others, for the girl, wasn't under his control.

He put himself out there.

And now they left his ass hanging out in the wind. Pants down, waiting for the zombies to come eat his bowels for brunch.

He wasn't supposed to feel this way. He didn't even want to feel the way he did for the dog, for Creampuff—

Goddamnit.

Goddamnit.

"Goddamnit!" he snarled. Ginger blinked. Incredulous, he explained: "They took my dog, Ginger. They stole my terrier." He popped each of his knuckles. "They didn't just abandon me after *I* got them through, after *I* kept them alive. They rubbed salt on the wound while they pissed in my eyes. I can't believe they stole my dog."

Coburn grabbed the kid by his too-clean shirt and shook him like a baby. "Listen. You're going to drive me to go get Creampuff, my terrier. And then you're going to watch as I break bad on the people who abandoned me. I'm going to hurt them. I'm going to hurt them *so good*. And then I'm going to eat one of them, for good measure." Ginger's eyes went wide. "I'm a vampire, kid. Can't you see the fangs? Weren't you weirded out that I had no legs and now, ta-da, legs?"

The boy just shrugged. *He must be retarded*, Coburn thought. Whatever. Kid could drive a dirt-bike and right now, that was all that mattered.

Coburn realized his mistake was that he'd started to care about the herd. Shepherd doesn't have emotions about his cows. They're just that: cattle. A cow's just a very advanced *meat-containment unit*, and that was how he had to think of these humans again: as bags of blood that went astray. Fine. It was time, then, to find those dumb animals and lasso their duplicitous disloyal necks until they went where he wanted and did what he said.

"Let's go rope some calves," Coburn said.

* * *

CUT TO:

The RV, overturned.

Couple zombies underneath, still thrashing—well, sluggishly shifting, perhaps. Their soft decayed heads thumping dully against the macadam. Coburn stepped off the bike. Told Ginger to kill the engine.

He and the boy had been riding the highway now for a handful of hours, zipping through defunct towns, passing by zombies that groped at the air ten, twenty feet away, as if that would somehow matter. Coburn scented the Winnebago like a hound and had the boy turn the bike off Lincoln Highway and down to Route 70—in the distance, Coburn could make out the shadowy hills and buildings of Pittsburgh, and no way was he going to brave wading into the middle of a city again. That way, the streets were surely choked with the living dead, like rats and roaches in the walls of a ruined building. Thankfully, the RV didn't go that way, which meant he didn't have to, either.

But now, here it was, laying on its side like a dead, beached whale.

Hollow. Gutted. Nobody inside.

Two rotters jogged up—literally a pair of joggers in full jogger regalia, tracksuits with the line running top to bottom, shoulder to ankle—and Coburn grabbed for both and smashed their heads together. They fell, unmoving.

Beyond them, though, lay other zombies. Dead. Extra dead. *For real* dead. Shot in the head so as never to move again.

Two there. Five over there. Another half-dozen in a clumsy circle.

Somebody'd made short work of these undead.

He sniffed the air. Smelled blood. Not sure whose, though—he cursed himself, wished he had taken a moment to become acquainted with the scent of each human's blood, because right now he couldn't differentiate Gil from Ebbie, Leelee from Cecelia. But he also smelled their sweat and desperation. And mingled in there, the odor of a rat terrier named Creampuff.

Coburn put together a picture of what happened.

Looked like they were driving along, maybe even at a good clip since the highway here wasn't gummed up with too many broken cars. Then... something happened. Zombies, probably. Came out of nowhere. Smart money said Ebbie was driving and Ebbie knew the rules that Gil put forth: *thou shalt not make roadkill of the living dead lest they get all wedged up under the tires.*

And so big boy panicked. Cut the wheel hard.

Overestimated. RV wobbled. Maybe he cut the wheel back the other way. Again, too hard, too far. And with that, the RV tipped, hit, skidded.

Loud sound. Fast movement. The zombies came, then.

Gil or someone shot a handful and they fled, knowing that more would come.

"They got away," Coburn said to Ginger, who stood there straddling the bike. "But the fools didn't take the highway. They left it. Went over the guardrail here. Hightailed it into the woods, near as I can tell. Stupid, stupid, stupid. Out there in the dark, they could get lost, ambushed. They might be out there right now, wandering in circles. Or maybe the whole lot of them turned to the stumbling, mumbling dead."

Other problem was, the sun wasn't long away. Half-hour, no more. The hairs on his neck stood to attention.

And then a little voice inside him spoke up, a mean little voice, the voice of the bully, the addict, the monster:

Cut bait and run.

There it was. The solution.

Fuck 'em. Fuck 'em right in the ear. The cattle had wandered too far astray and disappeared into the badlands and best thing a shepherd could do was say *hasta la vista* and move on to greener pastures. Besides, Coburn wasn't a shepherd. He wasn't a protector. He was a predator. Deciding to become that other thing was shoving a square peg in a circle hole, like cramming the fat end of a Louisville slugger up some poor fucker's poop-chute. An uncomfortable fit all around.

"I'm done with this," he said, smiling, laughing. Snapped his fingers. Did a little Michael Jackson twirl. "No more protecting the food supply."

Ginger looked worried. As he should.

Eat him, that monster's voice said, louder now than before. Almost back to the volume it had been before this had all begun. *Grab that mute moron, break his back over the dirt-bike and drain him dry.*

Coburn grinned, sauntered over to the boy.

Ginger's face wore a mask of concern, but he wasn't yet frightened—no pheromones of fear, no stink of scaredy-sweat. Kid really was stupid.

With a flick of his tongue, Coburn pushed his fangs to the fore.

Feast, the voice said.

Instead, Coburn pushed the kid.

"Go," he said, not believing the words coming out of his mouth. "Go, get the hell out of here, drive that dirt-bike so far I never have to see you again."

Ginger shook his head.

Coburn slapped him in the face. "I said, *go*."

Again, Ginger shook his head. The vampire grabbed the kid and kneed him in the gut once, twice, then thrice for good measure. The boy made a sound—no words, but an audible groan. Then came the stink of fear. Sweat, not piss, but whatever: the fright-fueled uncertainty was growing.

"I'll count to three," Coburn said. "You're not gone by the time I finish, I will rip you apart and do a step-dance on your entrails."

The boy nodded. Slow, hesitant, but a nod just the same.

"One," Coburn said.

Ginger stepped back, revved the dirt-bike.

"Two."

But before the vampire could get to *three*, Ginger gave it gas and the dirt-bike launched forward. Coburn watched it disappear, heard the Doppler sound of the engine's mosquito whine fade until finally, he could hear it no more.

You're an asshole, the voice inside him said. The monster, ever-mocking.

"Yeah, I know, sue me." But the voice was right. He'd let a perfectly good meal go in the same moment he decided to relinquish his attention on his *other* food source. It was like he wanted to give up the ghost or something.

He actually thought about it. Thought about staying out here while the sun came up, see how far it could burn him down. Would it burn him to cinders this time? On the roof of the Wal-Mart, he presumed he lived—or, rather, 'lived'—because they brought him inside before his crispy ass could turn to ash. Or maybe he just had it wrong. Maybe the sun didn't kill him. Maybe it just turned him into the vampiric equivalent of a house fire—but he didn't think so. He figured that the sun would get him eventually. The damn thing was like the eye of God, ever-vigilant and forever punishing.

But for now, Coburn decided that this morning would not be the one where he met his maker. Still, though. As he crawled inside the RV to get his daysleep, he came to realize that seeing the sun those mornings before was something he hadn't done in a long, long time. The sunrise sure was beautiful. Even if it would turn him into a greasy soot-stain.

Perchance to Dream

THE VAMPIRE FELT his heart thudding dully in his chest. A red roar of sound in his ears. A feeling of tightness in his chest and neck: *the pressure of blood, the fullness of an overworked circulatory system.*

You're human again, he thought.

Which meant this was a dream. A daydream.

"I'm dreaming too often," he said to no one, his voice quiet, soft, no echo. He got louder, shouting into the void: "I don't dream! I die during the day. I want that back. I want to shut it all out."

Somewhere, everywhere, a girl crying.

"Shut up. Shut up *shut up* shut up."

Sweat beaded on his brow. It trickled into his mouth. Salty and sweet. His pits, damp. His palms, slick. Human, indeed.

"Hell with this," he said. "I'm walking out of here. This dream has to have an end. I'll find it. Every dream ends."

And with that, a door appeared. A red door. Old. Paint faded. Above it, hanging in the darkness as if by fishing wire, a window. Across the panes of that window? Streaks of blood. Wet. Flies dotting the red, hungry, buzzing.

Seeing that, his heart kicked in his chest like a bucking mule. Adrenalin cut through the fog. Was this what being alive felt like? This constant pressure? The jerking up and down like on a puppet's strings? Feeling alive felt uncertain. It was not a pleasurable memory.

Well. He'd asked for an end to the dream, and here was a door.

He opened it.

And walked into an old farmhouse. Floorboards creaking underneath dusty runner rugs. Country décor: wooden chickens on the wall, an Amish hex over a wooden stove, iron heating grates, borders with mallard ducks. It smelled of must and mold. The air felt heavy.

Kayla stepped out into the hallway.

"You're here," she said. Smiling. Wiping away tears.

But for this moment, Coburn didn't care. He wanted to see past her. Something in that room. Flies buzzed over her head.

"What's in that room?"

"You don't want to see," she said.

"I do want to see. Get the hell out of my way."

Kayla stood in front of the door. "Coburn. I swear. You don't want to see this. Not now." Her eyes were puffy. Cheeks wet.

He bent down, got nose to nose with her, and showed his teeth. With his tongue he went to flick forth his fangs—but all that he had was a pair of regular old human canine teeth. Good for chewing steak. Not so good for perforating necks or wrists.

"I don't need to listen to you," he hissed. "You left me." He tried to see over her shoulder, but she waved her hand in the way.

"It wasn't me. It was my father."

"*Gil.*" The name dripped off Coburn's lips like so much bile.

"He thought he was doing the right thing."

"Well, he didn't. Because now I'm gone. And you're... God knows where, and only God cares."

She held up her hands as if to offer a clumsy *ta-da*. "We're here, Coburn. Here in this farmhouse."

He tried to see past her again, but somehow, couldn't. Didn't make any sense. Kayla wasn't a big girl. He was a tall dude. But somehow, every time he peered past her, something moved in the way—her hair, her hand, a shadow.

"I can't see into the *goddamn room*," he seethed. "Move!"

"We're here," she said, ignoring his pleas. "It's not far from the highway. Not even a mile. You can find it."

"I don't believe you. Just another lie. Besides, this is *my* dream."

"And your dream is telling you to find us. It let me in. You let me in."

"Go to Hell."

"Help us. Help me."

Coburn looked around. "You don't need my help. Perfectly nice farmhouse. Love the chickens. Now fuck off and move."

"We're surrounded," Kayla said, her voice cracking. Fresh tears ran. "Leelee got bit and I gave her some of my blood but I feel weak. And now outside they're everywhere. I don't know why. I don't know where they came from. Hundreds of them. Maybe more. The house is weak. They're going to get in eventually. Got the windows boarded up but it won't hold. We don't have much food. Don't have any water. We're dead before dawn."

"So die already."

Her hands trembled, like she wanted to hit him. "You're an awful person."

"Not a person, sweetheart," he offered her his winning smile, but it was devoid of mirth and contained a tight thread of anger tucked between his clenched teeth. "Can't say it enough. Not human. Not alive. Total monster. Go to Hell."

"Please..." she said, a spit bubble blowing on her lip.

Coburn sensed opportunity. It was as if the dream *shifted* somehow— as if Kayla had been in control all along and had relinquished (or, rather, *lost*) some of that control. It came back to him, fell back to his hands, and he picked her up and moved her aside and then Coburn saw what was in that room.

His heart stopped beating. He felt it die, puckering and shriveling into the peach pit it should've been. The tightness at his chest loosened. The pressure at his neck, his jawline, his temples—it faded like a dying man giving up one last breath, one final exhalation where his life left in a single sigh.

This was how it felt to no longer be alive. To be alive was an awful sensation, Coburn had thought before—and, in many ways, it was.

But he had forgotten how truly wretched it was to feel dead. To have nothing inside.

He blinked, turned away from the room. Couldn't unsee that.

Kayla crumpled to the floor, crying. Coburn offered her his hand. Helped her up and said, "Hold out as long as you can. I'll find you. Farmhouse got a driveway?"

She nodded. "But it's full of *them*."

"I'll figure something out."

And then he awoke.

CHAPTER TWENTY-FIVE
The Blood is the Life

COBURN KICKED OPEN the RV door, gazed up into a clear night full of stars, and emerged into the darkness.

The vampire smelled him before he saw him.

Ginger sat on the overturned front-end of the RV, his legs dangling over the side. When Coburn emerged, the kid offered a game little wave and a goofy smile.

"I hate you," Coburn said.

The boy said nothing, but at least the smile died on the vine. The vampire had to take solace in small victories at this point.

Eat him, the monster's voice said again. Coburn ignored it.

"Get up," Coburn said. "Go on. Shoo, off the bumper." The boy looked stung. "No, I'm not going to threaten you or chase you off but I need you to stop sitting on the goddamn Winnebago."

Hesitantly, the kid hopped off.

Coburn stood on the highway. Underneath the RV, the trio of zombies still lay pinned, groaning, moaning, rotting fingers grabbing handfuls of loose stone to no effect. One by one, the vampire went to each and crushed their heads with his bare feet. It was like making wine, if wine were made with spoiled brains instead of grapes. He shook the gore off his feet and then assumed a Sumo pose.

"Here," he said to the boy. "Check this shit out."

Swift and sudden strength was one of the vampire's tricks—the blood churned in his veins when he willed it to, and like Moses commanded the red seas to split he could push the blood to any part of his body he wanted. Push it to his tongue, he could lick the paint off a wall. To his jaw, he could bite a spoon in half. Move it to his hands or arms, he could snap necks like they were a bundle of cheap Chinese chopsticks.

This, though, was a feat perhaps beyond him.

Still, the vampire was nothing if not overconfident.

The blood inside him moved to his arms. The skin grew warm, then hot as his body burned through the blood. He squatted down and squeezed his hands underneath the RV.

What was it they said? Lift with your legs, not your back? Or was it the other way around? Whatever. He willed blood into both legs and back.

Then he *lifted*.

The RV moved a couple inches—and then it felt as if his leg tendons were going to snap like angry piano strings. His body trembled. His spine bowed.

Coburn moved more blood to his extremities. His brow felt hot, now.

His bones felt like they were cracking—and then he *heard* them crack. Like hairline fractures across the surface of a frozen pond.

But the RV moved again—two feet now instead of two inches.

Then, three feet.

Four.

And he stopped.

His legs were shaking so bad it felt like he was standing on a fault line as plate tectonics shouldered against one another. Felt like the DTs. Felt like Parkinson's. His hands were bending back.

Coburn did a kind of shuffle—scuffing his feet forward until he could get more of his body underneath. Then it was time for *more blood*. He felt his body growing hollow. Hungry. He tapped into a deep well, moving deep into the final reserves of Ambrosia's blood:

like a mosquito who stuck his drinking straw into the jugular vein of a coked-up rodeo bull, there he found power.

He gave it his all.

He fell to the ground.

The RV shot forth, landed on all four wheels, gently rocking back and forth before finally staying still.

Ginger stood staring. Mouth agape.

"Told you I was the shit," Coburn said, his voice hoarse. His body felt like a bridge embankment that had been hit by a tanker truck. Cracked and half-collapsed. He healed what he could.

Tried to ignore how fucking hungry he was now.

He pointed to the RV. "You can drive this thing?"

Ginger shrugged, but gave a weak nod.

"Good. Shove the dirt bike inside."

WASN'T HARD TO find the farmhouse. Coburn thought it might be, given the fact they were driving and not tracking the scent through the woods—but the rotters made it easy. The RV drove along a steady trickle of zombies all heading in one direction, like a bunch of stoned groupies stumbling toward Woodstock.

The farmhouse—a two-storey stone job with a slate roof and a big red barn next to it—sat down in the cradle of a misty valley.

And *Sweet Jesus on a carousel* were there a lot of zombies.

Maybe there weren't any more than he'd seen at Wal-Mart, and it just looked worse because the farmhouse was comparatively *so small*. Or maybe they really did outnumber that other horde. Why did so many show? With more on the way? Were they smelling the blood the same way he did? Drop a Taco Bell chalupa on the floor in the middle of a thousand starving men and they'll all come hungry.

He told Ginger to park away from the farmhouse—"Don't go down the driveway. Keep moving down the road." Some of the zombies noticed their passing and grabbed at the Winnebago like they actually had a chance. But then, seeing the opportunity fleeing, they continued to head down toward the house.

You asshole, the voice inside said. *Don't do this. Fuck those people. They're just food. You wouldn't wade into a swimming pool filled with sharks to get a bowl of rice. Let them rot with the rotters.*

The voice was right.

Even still.

He remembered what he saw in that room in the dream. The dead girl on the floor. Her throat torn open. Her pigtails stuck to the gummy, coagulating blood which had crept along the lines between floorboards. It was the same girl from the other dream—the one who looked like Kayla but wasn't. He didn't know who she was, but he knew that to see her dead killed him inside, killed everything he was and had been. Emptied him out and stripped him bare.

Because of *that*, he had to do *this*. He didn't understand why, not really. But the vampire mind is as much about instinct as anything, and this was something he felt in the labyrinth that was his long-dead guts.

Coburn rooted around the Winnebago, found some things he needed. A lighter, check. An old t-shirt of Kayla's, check. No guns, as it looked like they took every last one, but he did find a camping machete that would have to do.

Finally, duct tape. God's own miracle.

He patted the seat on the dirt bike, and then let Ginger in on the plan.

THE ATTIC WINDOW was waxy, a film of dust and age smeared across the warped glass that wouldn't come entirely clean no matter how many times Kayla wiped her shirt across it. She lay on the floor, staring out, petting the rat terrier behind the head. The dog stared vigilantly, sometimes growling low.

Out there, in the moonlight, she saw their death.

The meadow surrounding the old farmhouse looked like an undulating sea—heads and shoulders of the hungry dead jostling against one another, surging toward the house. Downstairs came the loud bangs of their hands echoing against shuttered, boarded windows, slapping against the stone, shouldering against the door again and again. The danger of the undead menace was not that they were monsters, but rather that they were a kind of environmental hazard, the way that a hurricane or flood was. Go unprepared and the floods would come and sweep you away, drown you in the dark, make you one with the waters.

This attic, Kayla thought, might be their very last stand.

And what a last stand it was. Cobwebs everywhere. And junk, too. The couple that had lived here before—an older couple whom they'd found embracing in a clawfoot bathtub on the second floor, an empty pill bottle laying on the cracked tile—were maybe not hoarders, exactly, but they certainly used the attic as a dumping ground for all manner of forgotten antiques. Old photos, flea market paintings, a rocking horse, a child's wagon, boxes of paperback books, chairs, you name it, it was up here. Atop everything, a thick rime of dust. It was aggravating Ebbie's allergies; he kept sneezing again and again at the far end of the attic, blowing his nose into some Christmas wrapping paper.

Cecelia sat on a rocking chair in a corner, a handgun in her lap. Gil paced in front of her, thinking. Kayla could see him chewing over their options, but she could also see that he wasn't coming up with anything good.

Not far from Kayla, sitting under a blanket between a stack of boxes of old photographs and a busted-up gumball machine, sat Leelee, pale and sweating and looking worse for wear. Soon as they all emerged from the overturned RV, she'd stepped down and hadn't seen that the vehicle had pinned a trio of zombies underneath; one of them found an opportune target in the meat of Leelee's ankle and took a good bite out of her Achilles' tendon.

She'd screamed, and it had been enough to signal the other zombies.

When the rotters started coming, they'd fled. *Over the hills and through the woods to grandmother's house we go,* Kayla thought. *Except grandmother and grandfather are both long-dead in a tub downstairs, and now grandmother's house might as well be our tomb. Oops.* Kayla had given Leelee some of her blood, and it seemed to be helping. But while the blood seemed like it would fight off the undead infection, it still wouldn't fix her ragged tendon. Leelee wasn't hopeful that she'd ever walk right again, not without a hospital or real medical attention.

"She needs a doctor," Kayla said.

"I'm fine," Leelee said.

"Daddy, we need to do something."

Gil worried at his lip. "I'm thinking."

"Think harder."

"Girl," Cecelia spat. "Leave your Daddy alone. He needs to think through this and doesn't need you nattering in his ear like a chipmunk. Leelee needs medical attention; well, we need a good way out of here. And Ebbie needs a Benadryl and a cheeseburger, probably."

"Hey," Ebbie protested, sniffling.

"Besides," Cecelia added, "*she* is our doctor. Not like they're out there growing on trees."

"I'm not a doctor," Leelee said.

"Whatever. A nurse, then."

Leelee shrugged. "I'm not even a nurse."

"She's a veterinarian," Kayla said. She guessed Cecelia never knew that. Never had reason to, she figured, but it seemed strange Daddy hadn't told her the truth. Was he withholding anything else?

"A vet?" Cecelia was incredulous. "All this time we've been getting our medical advice from someone trained in taking the rectal temperature of golden retrievers? You're kidding me."

"Sorry," Leelee said, lowering her gaze. "I thought you knew."

"Leelee, no!" Kayla said, standing up. Downstairs, the zombies had grown louder, more insistent—boards creaking, groaning, shuddering. "Don't feel that way. Cecelia, don't you dare diminish what she does. You see someone better qualified in this room? Are *you* qualified, Cecelia? Heck, are you qualified to do anything except sleep with my Dad and be a big ol' B-I-T-C-H?"

"Kayla," Gil admonished with a growl.

"Oh, don't you dare, Daddy. Don't you pretend like you don't have any dirt on you. It was you that put us here. You made us leave the vampire behind. *You* led us into the woods and to this farmhouse. You're supposed to be the one we look to! You're supposed to be the one *I* look to. How can we count on you to do anything for us when half the time you act like a horny teenager with Cecelia pulling on your—" She felt a blush rising to her cheeks. "Well, your you-know-what."

Gil wasn't one who liked to be backed into a corner. When he was, he reacted like a pit bull, hunkering down and baring his teeth.

That didn't happen this time. Instead, he just looked crushed and crestfallen. His words were soft: "It is my fault."

Cecelia reached for him. "Baby, no."

"No, she's right." He pulled away—gently, but surely. "I made choices. Choices that led us here."

"Gil, don't you listen to that little girl. She is just being a poison pill." Cecelia shot Kayla the look of a kicked dog, the gaze bundling up her disgust and hate and sadness in one septic little package. She leaned forward in the rocking chair. "Daughters don't always know to *respect* their fathers, which means that someone should step in and give them a good smack across the face—"

"Cecelia!" Gil barked. "You watch your goddamn mouth. That's my daughter you're talking about, and I won't have you speak that way to me, and most certainly not to her. This isn't the time for your petty nonsense."

Cecelia's jaw dropped. He'd never spoken to her like this, least not as far as Kayla had ever witnessed. She collapsed back in the rocker and muttered, "Stupid old man."

"We need to think," Gil said. "Think of a plan."

"It's hopeless," Ebbie moaned.

"Can't be hopeless. Think. *Think.*"

The terrier's persistent growl turned deeper. Wasn't long before Creampuff began barking in earnest. Something caught Kayla's eye out the window. A flicker of light, moving.

She pressed her face against the glass and saw something wholly unexpected: what looked to be some kind of motorcycle was bounding down the meadow hill toward the zombies gathered in the valley.

And, far as she could see, the bike was on fire.

THE DIRT BIKE gunned its way down the hill and hit the crowd of zombies just like Coburn had planned. Hit them hard, hit them fast. The bike was light, and soon as the front tire hit the first rotter the whole thing flipped up in the air.

It exploded. Better timing than he had anticipated.

It wasn't *much* of an explosion, granted. Wasn't nearly as impressive as the mushroom cloud that bloomed atop the cannibal Wal-Mart, but it didn't have to be: it just had to have enough *flash* and *pop* to get the zombies' attention.

And boy, did it.

From up here, it looked like a colony of ants had discovered a fallen spoonful of ice cream not far from the anthill. The zombies responded to this new stimulus the only way they knew how: to surge and swarm, driven by the most basic paramecium-level curiosity.

Coburn had stuck the t-shirt in the tank, got it wet with gas, lit it, then got the bike running with Ginger's help. The accelerators were already duct-taped and the cycle shot off like a horse with a dart in its ass. Just in time to blow up, cascading flame down upon a dozen rotters and drawing the rest.

But it wouldn't last. Soon they'd return their attention to the farmhouse and bog down the RV. Hence, phase two of the plan.

Machete in hand, Coburn ran screaming and cackling toward the zombie throng. It caught their attention.

They surged away from the burning bike and came toward him. As intended. Whenever one got close, he chopped with the machete, taking off hands and bisecting heads. Soon as he felt he had their attention, he took off running, away from the farmhouse, away from the RV. Most importantly, away from the driveway. Hopefully Ginger would do his part next.

THE RV WOULDN'T start.

They'd killed the engine because the vampire—Danny couldn't believe he was dealing with a bonafide vampire but what else was to be expected with the world gone to Hell in a handbasket during the zombie apocalypse, and by this point he figured that werewolves and mummies were real, too—*because the vampire* had said it would draw the rotters.

And now the engine just turned over. And over. *And over.*

He didn't really know how to drive this thing, didn't know if it took any special training. Seemed like driving a car, and he'd long been driving cars even before he was supposed to—on the farm, it was important to know how to drive the tractor, drive the four-wheeler, drive the pick-up.

Heck, it was that pick-up he tried driving to the Wal-Mart. His parents had long succumbed to the plague, leaving him all alone on a farm whose fields had gone fallow without the attention needed. He used up everything that was in the root cellar and was running low on canned or jarred food, so he thought, hell with it, why not take a trip to Wal-Mart? He washed up by pumping water into a pail, used a little soap and shampoo, and headed out to the store wondering if he'd find anybody there. Well, he found people, all right. They seemed to find him potentially delicious.

Then the vampire—holy crap, a vampire!—showed up and everything went batshit. And now they were staging some kind of rescue?

And the RV wouldn't start?

He wasn't half the mechanic his Daddy was, but he was trying to noodle what might be stopping the darn thing from getting going when two things happened.

First, the RV rumbled to life.

Second, the headlights kicked on and illuminated the road in front of him. A road filled with zombies.

They'd found him. Maybe they smelled the exhaust or could somehow sniff out his shampoo. Right now it didn't much matter *how* they found him, but they did. And they began swarming the RV.

Danny—who by now was almost thinking of himself as 'Ginger'—gritted his teeth, closed his eyes, and punched the accelerator.

Turned out, it was impossible to lead a throng of zombies on a merry chase. They were just too damn slow; every time Coburn turned around, they were playing catch-up, staggering through the woods, tripping on fallen branches, disappearing into the carpet of fog. It was like leading a herd of old people.

Coburn, feeling cocky, danced up to the wall of oncoming rotters and took a swipe here, a hack there—the machete cleaved faces and separated limbs from the bodies. Drop a leg, the zombie falls and the others just walk over him. Drop an arm and they continue to try to use it, grabbing with the phantom limb that got left in the fog ten feet back. They hissed and groaned, expelling gases, baring teeth like rotten kernels of corn.

Being cocky was often Coburn's downfall.

The mists were thick. So, too, the trees. He didn't anticipate the nature of the undead swarm, that they tried to fill in any empty spaces.

And so it was that they flanked him. They probably didn't *mean* to flank him, exactly. Big strategists, they were not. They came up behind him because it was their way, to occupy emptiness, to surround any potential prey, to make it their own and make it like *them*.

He heard the branch snap behind him. He wheeled with the machete, cut halfway through the spongy neck of a dead dude in a tattered ski jacket, the head still connected to the body by a rubbery swatch of dead flesh. The zombie pirouetted drunkenly before falling to the mossy earth.

And from behind him, the undead surged.

One grabbed his free arm and before he could shake the fucker off, the rotter bit down between his thumb and forefinger. Another pulled him backward, got teeth in his neck. A third bit his arm, but instead got a mouthful of leather jacket.

This isn't happening again, the vampire thought. He snapped his head back, exploding—literally—one zombie's nose. He jerked his arm, sending the hand-biter back into the throng. The one gnawing on his jacket got the machete—the blade bit between his cheeks popped the top of his head off the way you might slice a Champagne cork off with the swipe of a saber.

For a half-second, Coburn felt a surge of ass-kicking triumph— the zombies that had been surging suddenly backed away, moaning, flailing. *Fuck you, rotters—that's right, behold my awesomeness, gaze upon my rampant ass-kickery.*

But that didn't feel right. Zombies, as discovered, didn't exactly have a great deal of self-awareness. They could barely put one foot in front of the other.

Something else was at work.

Then Coburn saw.

The two that had bitten him had fallen to the ground. Were thrashing about in the mist. The one wearing a mud-and-blood greased rain-slick rose above the mist, mouth wrenching open, the tongue elongating, the gray meat flapping about like a whipping possum's tail. The other, a woman in a barely-there house dress with both tits out (one rotten and ruptured like a stepped-on bag of dogshit), began clawing at the earth in earnest, frenzying and keening. Coburn heard the bones snapping in her hands. Fingers tightened to arthritic claws. Her nails began growing to tapered, jagged points.

The zombies were afraid, all right. They just weren't afraid of *him*.

Rainslick and Rupture-Tit both pivoted their heads toward him at the same time. He saw a mad glint, but worse, he saw in there a glimmer of intelligence. Same spark he'd seen in the eyes of the bathrobed beast.

It was time to go. He hoped like hell that Ginger was on the stick with this plan, because there was now no margin for error.

THE ZOMBIE SMEARED his face across the RV's windshield. It left a tar-like streak of blood and rot that reminded Ginger—or, Danny, rather—of squished spinach. Another rotter joined the zombie at the fore, and Danny couldn't see anything. He'd made it onto the driveway, gravel popping beneath the RV's tires, but with rotters climbing over every square inch of the RV, he couldn't see how far down the driveway he'd come or how close to the house he was.

The first zombie at the windshield hissed. Opened his mouth, tried to bite the glass. Danny squeezed his eyes shut, slammed the brakes. That rotter went flying, but the other one held on just barely, using a now-busted windshield wiper as a lifeline.

The zombie reared his head back, triumphant.

And his head exploded. Danny about wet himself.

Suddenly, the sound of gunfire erupted. A zombie at Danny's side window tumbled away. Another came rolling down the front, sans head, before spinning into the mist and out of sight.

That was when Danny saw them. Midway up the driveway came a handful of survivors: an older man and a young teen girl with a middle-aged black woman between them, and trailing after, a fat guy carrying a little dog and another woman who, in Danny's eyes, matched what a prostitute might look like. Not that he'd ever seen a prostitute back on the farm.

They disappeared around the side. The Winnebago door flung open and they came piling in. The teen girl hurried to the front.

"I knew you'd come," she said, panting, but then she got a good look at Danny. Her face scrunched up and she cocked her head like a dog who just got asked a math problem. Danny still thought she was pretty. "Who the hell are you?"

Danny just smiled and shrugged.

"Who cares?" Gil said. "Get us the hell out of here, boy."

Danny gave a thumbs-up and threw the RV in reverse.

GIL JUST WANTED to do right by his daughter. Of course, he wanted to get laid, too. He didn't mean for it to be that way. For the last several months he'd felt like a teen boy again, in ways good and bad. He liked getting the attention of a pretty girl. He didn't so much like the effect she had on him, but he'd convinced himself that the world had gone and ruined itself and in times like these you did what you had to do to feel a little pleasure, to keep yourself going.

Fact was, he'd kept himself going for all the wrong reasons.

Kayla was his purpose. Not Cecelia. Cecelia was prettier than a blue sky in May, but she had a mean streak, too. He figured time would take that out of her; Lord knew that when he was a young buck he was brimming with piss and vinegar, too, and even some of that still sloshed around his head, his heart, his guts. But these days he'd found new focus, and not necessarily a good one. Cecelia was a part of that. Here he was, just shy of sixty years old and he was putting the pipe to a girl not much older than his own daughter.

Shame filled him.

He positioned himself by the RV's door as the red-headed kid reversed up the driveway. Gil saw a trio of rotten bastards shuffling up. Took 'em out with a few shots.

This was his job, he knew. Protecting his people. Protecting his *daughter*. He'd lost sight of that. So when something *thumped* hard against the back of the RV, he leaned out, lifted the shotgun to his shoulders and took aim toward the tail end of the Winnebago.

He didn't see anything.

Maybe they hit a zombie. Still, nothing went under the tires. Could be that the rotter spun away from the other side—they were about as sharp as a bowling pin and half as graceful, after all.

Above him: a fast shadow moving. A blur.

Feet kicked him hard in the chest, bounced him on his ass and punched the air right out of his lungs. With the wind knocked out of him, he gasped for breath.

The vampire Coburn stood above him. Grinning.

"Well, shit," the monster said, tossing aside a machete. The terrier ran up to him and sat down by Coburn's side. "Didn't think I'd see you again, Gil."

Finally, Gil caught a thread of air, pulled it into his chest.

The vampire offered a hand. "Get up, old man."

Gil took the hand, was pulled forcefully to his feet.

Coburn held onto Gil's hand like he was shaking it.

"You left me," Coburn said.

"I know. And for that, I'm sorry. It… it was a mistake. I've made a few."

The vampire's grin spread. Gil didn't like that look.

But what Coburn said surprised him: "It's okay, Gil."

"It is?"

"Sure." The vampire tightened his grip, shook the old man's hand.

"Thanks," Gil said.

Coburn winked. Then broke two of Gil's fingers.

He gripped them hard and twisted back. The *snap* was a sound Gil would never forget. The pain was hot, electric, it lanced up Gil's arm, re-routing at the elbow and shooting all the way up his neck and into his head. His eyes watered as he fell to his knees. The vampire's smile fell away.

"That's me being nice," the vampire said. Behind him, Kayla gasped, ran to her father. "Remember, I told you that you if dicked with me, I'd kill one of you. You'll note that not only are none of you dead, but me and Ginger here, we saved your lives. Even still, I can't let such treachery lie. You left me for dead—for *double* dead—and worse, you stole my goddamn dog. You were due worse. But I figured I had room in my wretched heart for a little mercy."

"You sonofabitch," Kayla said.

"It's okay," Gil said, pulling her close with his good hand. "Vampire's right. I deserve worse."

Cecelia said nothing. Ebbie just stared, shell-shocked. Leelee lay over on the bed, drifting in and out of consciousness.

"Daddy—"

"Shh," he said, stroking her hair. "It's okay."

"Damn right it's okay," Coburn said, chuckling. "None of us are dead. Well. None of us beside me, anyway. And we got the old RV back. Frankly, you assholes should be throwing me a parade instead of staring at me like I'm Frankenstein's monster. I didn't drown a little girl or anything." He plopped down on the edge of the kitchen pull-out table. "Somebody get me a map. It's time to chart a new course. Need to move you moo-cows to the West Coast, I hear."

His laugh was dark and deep and it filled the air.

PART THREE
PREY

CHAPTER TWENTY-SIX

The Herd Moves West

THEY WERE BEING hunted.

Down Route 70 'til it turned into Route 44, through Indiana, Illinois, across Missouri, and finally into Oklahoma, they always felt that pressure at their backs. They never saw their predators, but Coburn knew who they were. Those rotters who had supped on his blood became different, somehow. Like his blood turned a dark key and unlocked something inside of them.

Sometimes, if the wind was right or if the road was flat, they'd hear it: a chorus of their cries carried long across the distance. It chilled even Coburn's already cold marrow—the sound they made wasn't animal, wasn't human, but was somewhere in-between. It was the sound of the Devil on the hunt, the keening wail of a vengeful banshee driven by a terrible and unpredictable hunger.

The awful calls twined together, but if you listened hard enough, you could pull them apart and hear the four separate threads: a fearsome foursome out there wandering the highways and the hills, the long tracts of dead towns and empty forests.

Nobody knew what to call them: super-zombies? The uber-dead?

The rotters, squared? Nothing sounded right. All the names seemed twee.

Mostly, they just thought of them as, well, Them.

Closest they came to seeing them was just a week back—they'd been traveling now for a month, winding their way low and slow through the highways, avoiding towns and cities wherever possible. But then, not far from Joplin, Missouri, they heard those keening wails rise up like a hurricane wind carrying with it a handful of ghosts, and this time it was closer than before.

Then—a bloom of fire and a distant *whump* shook the earth. Sky lit up before dying back to dark.

"We passed a gas station back there," Ebbie said. "You think..."

Coburn nodded. "I don't think. I know."

"But why? Why would they do that? Why take out a gas station?"

"Because," he said. "They want to fuck with us. It's what I'd do."

COBURN WAS HUNGRY.

Out here, they'd found that, as expected, the dead weren't as numerous, which made sense from a population standpoint: the entire state of Missouri had half the population of New York City. Fewer living folk made fewer dead folk. Of course, that also meant fewer survivors. Fewer survivors meant less blood.

To reiterate: Coburn was hungry.

He'd taken to supping off Ebbie, but that sonofabitch's blood was so buttery-delicious that it took all his will not to crawl into the man's gutty-works the way he had done with Ambrosia the Cannibal Queen. Plus, whenever he drank a little from Ebbie, Creampuff got it in his head to growl and bite at Abner's pant-legs, sometimes nipping at any exposed flesh whenever the sock slipped down. That was just embarrassing for everybody involved.

During the day, Coburn slept in the RV. Seemed like the hunger made his dreams worse. Heightened them, sharpening his daytime visions to a dagger's point. Damn if he didn't have some rough dreams. Dreams of dead little girls. Dreams of starving. Dreams of the floor falling out from under him, of his middle finger cut off and spiraling down in the darkness, of a house on fire under a fat full moon.

Hunger made him more irritable, too. Sharpened to a brittle edge. Anxiety nibbled at him. Like piranhas biting. Back in the city, before waking up into the zombiepocalypse, he had everything he wanted. Having your wants filled up did a lot to curb worry. But out here, worry was suddenly all he had. Worry about whether or not he'd get fed. Worry over whether or not Gil would suddenly grow a pair of balls and come at him while he slept. Worry about Them: the monstrosities who were seeking his blood above all others'. Coburn didn't think the humans in his herd understood that, yet, and he damn sure wasn't going to tell them. The herd didn't need to know that the wolves wanted a taste of the shepherd, not the sheep.

Worst of all, hunger gave volume to the awful voice inside him. It was a bullhorn for the monster's monologue. In his head, a constant chatter encouraging any and all manner of atrocities.

At the very least, he was able to convince them to ditch the plan of heading through Sons of Man territory. *He* figured, go south. Curve low toward Mexico, maybe down what remained of old Route 66, take that path toward Los Angeles. No need to go messing with his old enemies, much as he'd love to be the maggot in their soup.

Still. Hunger. Fear. Dreams. Worry.

A bad combination.

KAYLA WAS SCARED.

Nothing was going right anymore. Not since that night in the farmhouse. Their rescue and respite was anything but.

Coburn had changed. Up until that night when he broke her Daddy's fingers, she'd thought that in him was a glimmer of something good, a tiny portion of his humanity left intact. She'd felt close, like she was unlocking something, but turned out all she was doing was uncorking a bottle filled with bile and blood and shadows darker than what had been there before. His dreams were no longer accessible to her; she tried to reach him in the space between sleep, but whenever she reached for him a wall slammed down. And when that wall slammed down, the dream turned into a nightmare.

The same nightmare.

A series of images played out: a fire in the desert, blood dotted across sandstone, the howls and gibbers of their hunters, city streets choked with the dead and the skies darkened by flies, hands reaching for her and pulling her apart.

One morning—late morning, when she would try to sleep and reach the vampire's own day-dreams—she awoke from that nightmare and found herself feverish and sick to her stomach. Worse, her left hand was numb, it wouldn't move. Leelee told her that it was the cancer. Getting into the bone marrow. Destroying the bone. But the numbness was more than that. That meant it was in her spine. Little tumors putting pressure on her nerves. Numbness. Paralysis. Soon it could—*would*, Leelee said—get worse.

After all this time, she was dying.

She tried to tell Coburn, but he didn't want to hear it. Didn't even want to talk about it. He was mean, too. What did she expect? She'd invited the monster into their life and now she wanted him to be her friend? Kayla reminded herself that she'd known the deal going into it.

Nobody seemed the same. Her father remained present, but distant. Like he was retreating from the world. Cecelia tried to talk to him, but he didn't want any of it. And that only made her meaner, too. Like it was somehow Kayla's fault.

Maybe it was.

The only upside was Danny. Danny, who Coburn still called 'Ginger,' was the one shining thing in her life. He couldn't speak, he wrote for them, explaining. That was how he communicated: jotting notes down on paper. He wasn't deaf. He could hear okay. He wrote down on the paper that his muteness was due to an 'iodine deficiency.' She didn't know why that would happen, but it didn't bother her. He let her talk most of the time, which was fine by her.

Of course, he was also really cute.

When she was with him, she didn't feel scared. They'd take a break when the RV would pull over during the day, somewhere that Ebbie couldn't see any zombies, and she and Danny would walk the dog, spend a little time together.

Whenever they were apart, though, the fear came back.

It was never gone for long.

DANNY WAS IN love.

Or, at least, that was what it felt like. He'd never been in love before. Whenever he was with Kayla—whenever he even saw her sleeping on the RV floor in a sleeping bag while he uncanned some food for breakfast—he got this happy tightness in his stomach. And everything seemed more alive. More awake.

It was either love or a stomach bug, he figured.

He preferred love.

GIL WAS LOST.

Not physically lost, no, but spiritually, emotionally, mentally. Inside his head was a labyrinth built out of shame and failure, and he wandered it nightly—but at the center of this maze was not a minotaur. It was Gil. Gil was both the wanderer of the labyrinth and the monster at its heart.

The days and nights passed in a way that made him feel like they had no borders—they oozed together like runny eggs in a hot skillet.

The pain of his fingers had never properly subsided, and it always nagged at him: with every heartbeat the pain radiated, a dull, drumming throb. Leelee had set them as best as she could, but that night back then at the farmhouse she was sick, feverish, on the verge of falling over into the void and becoming one of the starving dead—yes, Kayla's gift had saved her, but that night when she set his fingers in a makeshift splint using some duct tape and a wooden spoon, the job was only so good and his fingers still felt crooked.

It amazed him how critical those two fingers are. Especially in a zombie apocalypse. Those two fingers helped him use a gun: the middle finger beneath the trigger guard and the doubly important index finger—to *pull* the trigger. Without them, it felt like he might as well have had his legs chopped off.

Of course, almost everyone around him was a cripple, these days. Leelee limped, still. Always would, she figured. Danny couldn't talk. Ebbie had actually lost a dozen or so pounds, but he was still north of three hundred and would never run a sprint in record time. Cecelia was, well, an emotional cripple. And finally, his daughter—her left hand, numb, moving towards paralyzed.

Only one who wasn't broken in some way was the vampire. Even though Gil knew it was absurd, he couldn't help but imagine that the vampire had done this to all of them, not just him—like he was a vampire that drank more than blood. He drank their luck, maybe. Their spirit. Stole Danny's voice. Robbed Kayla of her hand. It didn't make sense but it didn't have to. Monsters were real. Who knew what they could do?

Gil pictured how miners used to hobble slaves, chaining them up or breaking their feet so they couldn't go far. Wasn't this like that? Coburn keeping his 'herd' nearby so they couldn't stray?

That was Gil's fault, he knew. First bad decision was letting the vampire stay. Second bad decision was trying to get away.

Yes, indeed, Coburn saved them.

But sometimes, Gil thought, maybe being saved was worse than dying. Especially in a world like this.

The only glimmer of hope he had was for his daughter. He knew she was special. She could see things in her dreams sometimes. And then her blood—that was special, too. But it didn't stop her being sick. That sickness was getting worse. Cancer was an insidious thing, a monster, like Coburn, that moved in and wouldn't move back out again.

Sometimes, Gil thought, *you just gotta cut the cancer out to be rid of it.*

EBBIE WAS WORRIED.

He was so worried, he could hardly eat. And there *was* food out there to be had. Sure, you'd think it's the end of the world, all the food's probably used up or spoiled outright, but this zombie thing happened fast. Lot of food left in the stores. No, you wouldn't find a bag of spinach or a box of frozen hamburgers, and no matter how far you drove you'd never come across an operational KFC, but in stores and houses you could still find canned goods, bags of candy, sodas, even cereal. Amazing how good cereal tasted after two years. Must've been all that high fructose corn syrup, he thought. Which didn't really help his diabetes, but the end of the world meant he didn't have much time to think about his blood sugar levels, thank you very much.

What had him worried—well, besides everything else that was awful about the broken, zombie-infested planet—was the Winnebago.

This old beast had been with Gil and them since before they even picked him and Cecelia up. But the engine was starting to knock. Sometimes it sputtered.

Thing was, the RV—a 1994 Winnebago Itasca Suncruiser—was diesel, which, according to Gil, was a good thing since diesel fuel didn't 'expire' like other gas. Ebbie didn't even realize that gas expired in the first place, but the addition of ethanol cut its shelf life down to ninety days or so. Which explained why they couldn't just go snatching up any car on the road even though they had gas in 'em: they wouldn't even start.

Diesel was harder to find, but they managed: the highway was home to enough diesel vehicles (any time they caught sight of one of those little Volkswagen hatchbacks it was like playing a game of Punch Buggy, except *this* game had a lot higher stakes to it).

Still, Gil said that maybe this batch of diesel was no good. Maybe it had water in it. Or microbes. That could happen, he explained, but he explained it in a way like he just didn't care. Like he'd given up the ghost.

That had Ebbie worried, too.

Gil went on to say that it might be that the filter or fuel injector was gummed up—this was, after all, a decades-old motor home with 115,000 miles on it. At this point it was like an old dog. Everybody knew it wouldn't last forever, but they really didn't want to think about putting the beast to sleep.

Along the way they'd been keeping their eyes out for something new—but not only had they not found anything, smaller vehicles just wouldn't accommodate them all anyway. Back in Indiana, about ten miles south of Indianapolis, they found a motor home dealer. Lot full of RVs of all shapes and sizes.

And not one of them diesel.

Soon as the 'Bago died, Ebbie didn't know what they'd do. He couldn't walk long distances. He was too big. And then he really would have to worry about his diabetes. Walking made him sweat like a pig. They had bottled water, but not enough to keep him conscious.

Of course, walking had another issue: Them. Behind them, the monsters followed. They couldn't catch up, Coburn said, because the RV was fast enough—while they were fast, too, they weren't machines.

But once they started walking, well.

The monsters would surely catch up.

CECELIA WAS PISSED.

Fuck all these assholes. Fuck 'em right in the eye. They treated her like a pariah, now. She got food last. Water last. Always had to hold her piss until Ebbie deigned to stop. That dipshit kid who faked being mute got better attention than she did. It just wasn't right.

The tables, they had to turn. Only way that was going to happen was if she made them turn. Her mother always told her, "Cecelia, you want something in this life, you have to go out and get it yourself. Nobody's going to give you shit, girl. The only way you get the cookie is if you reach in the jar and take it."

Then the woman would suck her Parliament cigarette down to a sizzling nub and hand Cecelia—young as age twelve—a sip of her Gallo wine.

She was going to get Gil back.

She was going to show him how to teach his uppity bitch daughter what's what.

Then she was going to send that vampire to Hell.

LEELEE BELIEVED.

It was hard not to. She'd always been something of an agnostic, forever leaving room for God (or Buddha or the Goddess or whatever name the power of the divine had) in her life, but it was never something she thought too much about. Such an idea remained firmly abstract, outside her grasp, beyond any practical meaning in her life.

That had changed.

The dead walked. They had a vampire with them. They survived impossible situations. All those things were by themselves fantastic and strange and ostensibly served as proof of *something* beyond mortal ken.

Really, though, it was all about Kayla.

Kayla. The girl who should've been dead. The girl who dreamed. The girl whose blood was a curative for the rotten and wretched plague that destroyed... well, at least most of America, if not the rest of the world.

Leelee knew that she herself should be dead. It was just that simple. She should be dead, taken over by whatever parasite, virus or bacteria it was that not only undoes rigor mortis but forces the dead to get up, stumble around and hunger for flesh.

But a draught of Kayla's blood had the power to change that.

Which meant it had the power to change the world. Just as it could reverse the zombie plague in a person, it could reverse the sickness that plagued the human condition.

Kayla could cure the world. Kayla wasn't God—or Buddha, *or* the Goddess—but in her shimmered a spark of the divine.

That was what Leelee believed. And it gave her hope.

THE HUNTERS HUNTED.

Four of them stalked the wasteland.

They had changed. And the changes kept on coming, every night a new evolution. Long, curved claws like a vampire's fangs but serrated on the inside. Legs broken, twice-jointed so that they could move and run faster. Their rotten skin tightened up—where it split, scabs formed and hardened like chitinous nodules, like hard caps of porous volcanic bone.

Their tongues elongated, narrowed, hollowed. All the easier to drink. Their teeth multiplied: rows upon rows growing in their widening mouths.

They were learning, too.

The Bitch Beast in the bathrobe—now just a tattered pink scrap draped over her neck and shoulders—was the one who learned things first, and then she taught the others: Ranger, Rain-Slick, Rupture-Tit.

They learned how to lure prey. Bitch Beast made a sound like a wounded fawn, and soon a doe came out of the woods.

They learned how to hold weapons. Ranger had a hunk of conduit. Rupture-Tit cradled a fire ax against her ruined breast. Bitch Beast and Rain-Slick preferred tooth-and-claw.

They learned how to taunt their enemies. Ranger found a lighter. Bitch Beast tore a gas pump off, left a trail of it. They set fire to the gas, let it ripple like a swiftly-squirming snake toward the pump, then— *boom*. A warning to their target, the one whose blood sated them like nothing else. A warning that said in a burst of fire and a dull roar, *we are coming for you.*

But most of all, they learned how to lead.

Before, they viewed those other staggering undead as lesser beings— which remained true. But, just like the fire ax or the lighter, that did not mean they could not be used. The zombies wanted to follow them. Once, Bitch Beast demanded they tear the undead limb from limb if only because it satisfied her need to destroy. Now, though, she gathered them to her. The others did the same.

They followed behind. Slowly, but surely. A growing, staggering mass of bodies—as single-minded and stupid as a plague of locusts, but infinitely more destructive. The four hunters had a kind of grim, awful gravity now. They pulled horror behind them in a rippling, putrid wave of undead bodies.

It was a beautiful thing.

And so they hunted.

CHAPTER TWENTY-SEVEN

Get Your Kicks

THE WAY THE Winnebago died was far from spectacular. It did not put on a show. There came few moments of suspense where they wondered, *will it make it? Could we get just... a little bit... further?* Instead, it just gave three good shudders like a dog ridding itself of fleas, then died with gas still in the tank. Ebbie tried the key, but the old Suncruiser wouldn't turn over.

They emptied out of the RV. The sun had set not long before. A sign nearby told them they were in or near a town called Erick, Oklahoma, but far as anybody could see on the map or with their eyes, the town wasn't so much a town as it was an intersection of highways.

Outside, a deep purple eventide band hung low across the horizon. The sky flashed with faraway lightning. It was good and warm right now, the heat rising up off the highway even in spring. But that would change. Daytime saw temperatures in the low eighties— hot enough to cook a frog on the road if he sat there too long— but at night, that same frog would freeze where he stood as the temperature plummeted into the low thirties.

Moaning nearby alerted them to a pair of rotters jogging up—well, not jogging, really, but maybe more 'drunkenly lurching.' Zombies so often seemed to be leaning forward when they walked, as if their movement was ever the product of almost falling face-down, their legs moving just in time to stop that from happening. Coburn didn't bother wasting any ammo. He met them halfway to the 'Bago and bashed their skulls in with the butt of a shotgun.

"Nice job, Ebbie," Cecelia said, casting eye-daggers in his direction.

"I'm sorry."

"Not his fault, Cecelia," Gil said, but Coburn noticed the old man's vim and vigor—his *cantankerousness*, one might say—was gone. As if the vampire had broken his spirit the same time he broke those two fingers. Coburn was mostly pretty pleased with that, and the monstrous part of him was particularly tickled. Still, another part of him couldn't help but worry. Gil was an asshole, but made of tough stuff. Couldn't have him wilting like a pissed-on daisy. Needed his head in the game. Kayla went up to her father and rubbed his shoulder. Danny just stood around like he was ready to stick his thumb up his ass.

"Listen up, moo-cows!" Coburn called out, clapping his hands. "We're going to have to hit the bricks, do some walking. Looking ahead, seems like there's a town up a ways. How far on foot, Gil?"

Gil perked up, looking surprised anybody was asking him anything. "Uh. Well. Erick the town you're talking about?"

"See any other towns around here, old man?"

"I'd guess about two, three hours."

Ebbie went pale. "...Leelee can't walk that far."

"Leelee," Coburn repeated, cocking an eyebrow. "You sure you're talking about *her*, Abner?"

"Hey!" Ebbie protested.

"I can do it," Leelee said.

Coburn frowned. "No, Leelee, you can't. Ebbie's right, even if he was talking about himself more than he was talking about you. That foot of yours is still fucked three ways from Sunday and that makes you a bit of a gimp."

"Coburn the vampire," Kayla said through gritted teeth, stomping up to him and sticking her finger into his chest. Way she said it like that reminded him of how parents sometimes talked to their children, saying the whole name and all. Good for her. She, like Gil, had lost something over the last several weeks. Maybe if she was getting her stones back, so too would her lame duck Daddy. "You be nice. It's hard enough out here without you being mean to everyone. Don't you think you're leaving Leelee behind, neither." She thrust her lip out, pouting. "I need a cigarette."

Cecelia, probably just to be a jerk, lit one up and blew a jet of smoke in the girl's direction.

"As I was *saying*," Coburn continued. "We need to walk but Leelee's limp is going to put us too far behind. That means I'm carrying her the whole way."

"What about me?" Ebbie asked.

"What about you? You walk like the rest of us."

"But I've got diabetes."

"And I'm dead."

"But I'm... not in great shape."

"Now's a good time to start exercising, then. Listen, Abner. You need to decide which you like more: *eating*, or *getting eaten*. If it's the latter, hey, no worries, just roll over here and die. But by the looks of you, I'd say you're a champion eater. And if you want to keep that going for you, you're going to have to move your big fucking body from Point A to Point Z because I'm not carrying you. Even my mystical vampire voodoo has limits."

Ebbie's face sank, but still, he nodded.

"We're going to need supplies," Gil said.

"True. So go get 'em. You've got fifteen minutes, my ugly little sheeples. Go forth and scavenge. Canned goods, ammo, guns, whatever you can carry without falling on your asses. If you have jackets and blankets, bring those. Because I suspect it's going to get cold tonight."

He clapped his hands again and the monkeys did their dance.

THEY WALKED. OUT here, wasn't much to see. Scrub. Dirt. A few scattered trees. Highway here was a busted-up ribbon of concrete. Few cars. Few bodies. The occasional zombie looking lost and separated from his cronies.

The moon above was just a bitten-off fingernail. More light seemed to come from the stars, of which there were many—more than Kayla had ever seen. The sky possessed an infinity of them, it seemed. A million, billion little pinpricks through a black blanket, so many points of light shining through.

It was beautiful, really.

Too bad she was having trouble appreciating it. It was her own fault, but now it was too late to say anything. She told everyone she was a big girl, could handle her share of the load but the fact was, she couldn't. Her bones ached. Her left hand still wasn't working right, and in fact seemed to have gotten worse. She had a bag slung over her shoulder full of canned goods and a backpack full of clothes and ammo, and even that felt like her spine was going to snap in half—she half-imagined one of the vertebrae shooting off and hitting someone in the head.

Tears lined the corners of her eyes and her jaw was set so tight the tendons in her neck were starting to feel hot. But she refused to complain. Refused to give into it and show them—the vampire especially, who she had come to resent—her weakness. Her show of faux-strength seemed to be working because nobody, not even her own father, noted her pain.

Nobody, it turned out, except Danny.

Suddenly, her load was lightened—Danny snuck up behind her and scooped the canned food bag right off her shoulder. It lightened not only the physical burden but the emotional one, too. A weird, bubbly laugh rose up out of her. But then she saw Danny was carrying too much already. A gun bag. An ammo bag. And now the food bag. She reached to reclaim it.

He caught her wrist—not hard, but with a gentle twist put her hand back at her side, then smiled. He shook his head and tapped his chest.

"You sure?" she asked.

He nodded.

Gil shot them both a look, but said nothing.

They kept walking.

* * *

IT BOTHERED COBURN that he hadn't heard from their friends, the howling keening hell-banshees. It wasn't that he *wanted* them on his trail, but somehow, the not-knowing made it worse. Stranger still, he knew they were out there. It was more than just a hunch, moving beyond his normal sense of pervasive paranoia. Rather, it was as if he could *feel* them back there. Like an indelicate scratching at the back of his brain, the desperation of an animal who wanted to be let in.

They came to the town of Erick around midnight after about three hours' walking. Wasn't much of a town, really. Not quite flyspeck, but it looked like a modern version of a dustbowl Okie town out of something written by Steinbeck. It was good they got there when they did, though. Not only was the temperature really starting to bottom out, but Ebbie looked like he was going to shit his pants and fall over, dead.

Erick wasn't much of a planned community, that was for sure. Everything just kind of sprawled out. Two small houses next to a corner bank made of crumbling brick. Across the street, a rancher next to the Brandin' Iron Motor Lodge. Dead lawns. Leaning fences. The long-decayed corpse of a dog chained up to a flagpole outside a half-collapsed house, the American flag atop it looking like it had been half-eaten by moths.

To Coburn's eyes, this was a town that gave itself up long before the zombie apocalypse swept across the country. Somewhere in the last twenty years this town just gave out one last rattling cough as its lungs collapsed.

Thing was, it was quiet here. As the cliché went: too quiet.

"No rotters," Coburn said. He sniffed the air. Couldn't find any on the wind, either. He smelled death, but not *the zombie* kind of death. Zombies were like spoiled meat, but in there was the stink of real human fluids: blood, shit, bile. This wasn't that. Something about the situation bothered him. It was like with the hunters: he could see they weren't here, but they were out there *somewhere*. This felt tweaked. Off-kilter. Some part of the puzzle was missing, and Coburn didn't care much for puzzles. He was a simple man with simple, almost reptilian needs.

Cecelia asked: "What the hell is a Thug Low?"

Everyone turned, wondering what the hell she was talking about. She pointed to a sign out front of what must've been some kind of pre-school. It was one of those signs with the letters you could rearrange. But instead of saying something like SEE YOU IN THE FALL or BAKE SALE NEXT WEEK, it said something nobody really understood:

THUGLOW AINT UR BITCH.

Below those letters, someone had spray-painted what looked to be a king's crown with three diadems.

"Anybody know what that means?" Gil asked.

Coburn shrugged. "Guess whoever or whatever Thuglow is, he ain't our bitch. Good to know. Let's keep walking. Keep an eye out for supplies and places where I can crash during the day. And stay frosty. I have a bad feeling."

THE TOWN WAS stripped of supplies. In fact, it wasn't just stripped of supplies: it was stripped of everything. Furniture was gone. Boards were ripped up out of floors. Pipes were pulled out of walls. Not a single canned item in the general store, and not one pistol, rifle or shotgun to be found. Wasn't even any ammo, and that was one thing they usually found a lot of—the zombie plague had hit fast and swift. Despite appearances and assumptions otherwise (and despite the propaganda of the NRA), Americans for the most part had long lost their love of firearms, but those that hadn't were usually sitting on huge stored-up surpluses of ammunition. That left a lot of bullets to be scavenged.

But not here.

As they walked, Gil pointed out a sign. A commemorative historical plaque. "Look at that. Commemorating the Mother Road."

"Mother Road?" Ebbie asked.

"Route 66," Gil said. "The quintessential American highway. Motor lodges and hamburger joints and little towns with big drive-in theaters. It was the main route from Chicago to Los Angeles. The second major Westward expansion in American history. Route 66 birthed a whole ecosystem. Towns sprung up just to support it. Then came the age of the superhighway. Pulled most of the traffic away from 66, which pulled most of the traffic from all those towns and businesses. It was like rerouting arteries away from the heart. After a while, a lot of what lay along the old Route 66 just shriveled up and died."

Gil had kind of a sad look. Coburn couldn't smell nostalgia, but if he could, he figured it would be coming off the old man in strong waves. Probably would smell like old shoes and bad cologne, the vampire imagined.

"You ever plan on traveling West," Gil said—or, rather, sang a little. "Travel my way, the highway's the best. Get your kicks. On Route 66." He cleared his throat. "Song by Bobby Troup. Late 'forties, early 'fifties. Before my time, really." He looked to Kayla. "Your grandfather used to sing it."

Coburn spoke up. "Enough reminiscing. We best keep moving."

THEY FOUND MORE graffiti.

On the side of an old meat market: 66 STATES FUCK YO MUTHA.

Spraypainted on a tattered banner hanging across the top of the street: YOU BEST BE DOWN WIT DA CLOWN.

Then, on a mailbox, someone had written a handful of phrases in a metallic Sharpie:

THUGLOW IS KING

NUTT IN UR PINK EYE

SATAN'S CAROUSEL

THUGLOW SHANK YOU VATO

And, finally, PUSSY PUSSY PUSSY PUSSY PUSSY.

Kayla blanched. "Ew."

Danny patted her on the shoulder and she melted into him.

COBURN WAS ABOUT to say something making fun of the names around here—after all, the street they were on was named after someone named 'Sheb Wooley,' which didn't even sound like a real name. It sounded like someone's made-up idea of what corn-pone in-bred hick fucks called each other, but, no, this was real.

But he never got the chance.

Because they found the rotters.

They were piled up in the center of town, at the intersection of Sheb Wooley Avenue and Roger Miller Boulevard. Hundreds of them. Chopped into chunks—legs, heads, arms, torsos—and stacked like cords of firewood. They weren't fresh. The flies had long given up and moved on. These parts and pieces were desiccated, leathery, like dried-up rolls of rotten leather.

"Oh my god," Ebbie said, covering his mouth even though the stink was mostly gone. It registered with Coburn, but mostly, the odor was stale.

"Someone did this," Gil said.

Coburn gave him a look. "You think? Here I figured the zombies just disassembled themselves."

It was Kayla's turn to shoot a look, this time at him. He smiled at her like a crass asshole and winked, but she turned away, clearly disgusted. He refused to acknowledge that it stung a little.

"Wherever we set up shop," Cecelia said, nose wrinkled, "it better not be anywhere near these bodies. This is nasty."

"We're not setting up shop," Coburn said.

Kayla: "What?"

"I don't like it. Someone owns this town. They took all the food, all the guns. They even stripped the pipes out of the walls. I haven't even seen a single automobile in this place. They killed every last rotter in a five mile radius, from the looks of it. Whoever these dipshit psychopaths are, they've claimed this rat-fuck ghost town and I don't feel like being around when they come back. Plus, they can't spell for shit, and I don't trust folks who can't spell. My assumption is they're far likelier to swing through here during the day." He grabbed the map from Gil. "Look at the map, here. Another three hour walk will take us into Texola. That's where we're headed. We'll camp there."

CHAPTER TWENTY-EIGHT

Welcome to the Wall

THE SIGN READ:

WELCOME TO THE 66 STATES

PLEASE WIPE UR DICK

The words were cobbled together out of pieces of broken signs, each letter a different font and a different size than the one next to it. Like a ransom note writ large. Coburn and his 'herd' stood beneath it, highlighting it in the combined halo cast by their flashlights.

"Looks like it goes on for miles," Kayla said.

"Cuts right across the highway," Leelee said. "Pretty impressive."

"Impressive?" Coburn asked. "'Please wipe your dick' is impressive? You people are easily stirred."

They never got to Texola.

A mile before they got there, they found that they weren't *going* to get there—at least, not easily. Because a wall cut the highway in half like a giant cleaver blade smashing down across it. The wall wasn't just one wall type: it was dozens of different barriers welded together and held up by posts pounded into the dry earth. Over here, a thick-gauge chain-link. Over there, heavy corrugated metal. Between them, thick green metal poles as big as a man's arm.

It didn't stop there. Atop it sat coils of barbed and razor wire, and behind it, on the far side, the wall was further bolstered by...

Well, junk.

Wrecked cars. Old washing machines. Busted furniture. Mounds of debris, stacks of worthless shit. Coburn knew now why someone had gone through a town like Erick and stripped it of everything that wasn't nailed down (and then some). It was clumsy. It was ugly. It was like something out of Mad Max. But, the vampire had to admit, it looked not only intimidating, but functional.

All told, the wall was ten to fifteen feet high. Made even taller by barbed wire.

Gil shined his light up and down the length of it. "Looks like some of it could be the border fence. The one they were putting up between us and Mexico. One that never got finished."

"Here, look," Leelee said, pointing up above the highway. "This part of the fence isn't just a fence. It's a gate." And sure enough, the fence here had a break in it—it wasn't on hinges, but rather on a track embedded in the dirt. Almost the way a sliding patio door works: unhook it and pull it across the track. At first that didn't seem to explain how to get through because behind the gate anybody would still have to move a handful of junker cars. But when they looked deeper, they saw it worked the same way. Those cars had been hollowed out and made light, and they too were on tracks. Explained why Coburn caught a whiff of what may have been WD-40: as long as the tracks were lubricated, seemed like they'd be able to slide out across pretty easy.

"The Sixty-Six States," Kayla said. "I don't get it. Country only has fifty states. Guess they can't spell *and* they can't count."

Gil grunted. "It's not a count. It's like I said, this is the old Route 66. Cuts right through."

"The Sons of Man must have territory a lot farther south than we thought," Ebbie added.

"No," Coburn said. "I don't think this is them. Those assholes weren't exactly a brain trust of intellectuals, but this seems somehow beneath even the Sons. Plus, doesn't look anything like what the stories say. This isn't the product of a functional society. Then again, two years is a long time, and nobody said the stories can't be—"

Suddenly, floodlights clicked on and blinded Coburn into silence. A voice came over a loudspeaker, and they heard the mechanized roar of a vehicle fast approaching.

THE CARS WHEELED back, grinding across the tracks with the sound of what could've been wheels or gears turning. The gate, too, began moving—it was not automated, but Kayla also couldn't see anybody making the motion happen. It occurred, as if by magic.

Creampuff started growling.

When the gate was retracted, more lights blinded them and Kayla shielded her eyes: a Humvee came bounding across the cracked asphalt and skidded to a halt, blocking the opening.

Kayla's jaw dropped.

She hadn't expected this. In a million years she never would've imagined that the men bolting free of the Humvee, automatic weapons in hand, would be dressed like clowns. But not straight-up circus clowns—no red nose and nuclear-green afro wig. White face paint. Blood circles around their mouths, black paint around their eyes. All smudged, flaking off, exposing patches of stubble and skin.

Three of them stepped out. Three grim-faced, pissed-off clowns.

Kayla looked to Coburn—

Except he was nowhere to be found.

The lead of the trio, a pear-shaped pig with white-blonde dreadlocks sticking out of his do-rag like the legs of a squashed albino tarantula, stepped into the fore, gun up, barking at them. Literally. Barking at them like a dog.

"*Ruh ruh ruh*," he barked. "Back up, bitches. I *said* BTFU or I'll peel your scalp with a shit-storm of lead."

They did as told, putting their hands up.

"Drop the fucking bags. Drop 'em!"

They dropped everything they were carrying as the two other

Goth-clowns—one built like an inverted triangle, the other a reedy old man whose graying goat-beard was similarly gummed up with greasepaint—stepped in behind the pig-nosed, pear-shaped leader.

"What the figgity-fuck do we have here?" Pig-Nose asked. "Looks like we got a handful of terrorists wantin' to do some assassination with a bunch of bombs and shit."

Gil stepped forward, holding up his splinted hand. "Listen, fella, we're not here to cause any kind of—"

Pig-Nose thrust the gun barrel hard against Gil's face, the end of the rifle actually entering his mouth and scraping up against his gums.

"Did I say to talk, you old bastard? I didn't say shit. You keep flapping them lips and I promise you, dude, I will split your motherfucking wig. You gonna step to me? You feel like steppin'?"

"No," Gil said, pulling gently away from the rifle. He slowly spit a bloody loogey off to the side. "I'm not... stepping."

"Good. Now whatchoo got in those bags?"

Gil didn't say anything.

"I said, what's in the damn bags?"

"I can talk now?"

Pig-Nose looked wounded. "Yes! Yes I told you to fucking talk. I asked you a question, didn't I? You some kind of retard?"

"Supplies!" Kayla blurted out. She couldn't stand seeing her father put in harm's way again. "We have food. Guns. Ammo. Some clothing."

Pig-Nose pointed the rifle at her. Her guts turned to water. "No bombs?"

"No bombs," Gil said, hands still up.

"No bombs," she confirmed with a peep.

Pig-Nose whistled, gestured to the two lugs behind him. "Dope Fiend. Jester. Go get that shit and bring those bags to the car."

As they moved to grab the bags, Kayla saw movement behind them, by the gate. A shadow eased along the edge of the fence. It was Coburn. The tight knot in her stomach started to loosen, because if anybody could handle these oh-my-god-they're-actually-clowns, it'd be him.

He held up a finger to his lips, noting that she was watching him.

She nodded.

And then he disappeared through the gate and was gone.

That bastard. Again her bowels tightened.

"Hey!" she yelled out, before she even realized what was coming out of her mouth. Pig-Nose came up, puffing out his chest like a dumpy-assed rooster, and pointed the gun at her heart.

"What are you yelling about, you little slag-a-muffin? Huh? *Huh?*"

"Hey now," Gil said, protesting. The old man—who must've been Jester, because he wore a ratty jester's cap with tinkly rusty bells on it—shoved him backward. "She's just a girl, now. She doesn't mean any harm."

"I..." Kayla said, searching for words. "I just didn't know you were going to take our stuff."

Pig-Nose chuffed. Might've been a laugh, she didn't know. "You bet your sweet cupcake ass we're taking your stuff. That's the payment for passage into the 66 States. You don't get to see the King if you don't tithe to the King. That's the law. One of the *only* laws here, you feel me?"

"The... King?" she asked.

"Hell *yes* the King," he said. "King Brutha Thuglow. The leader of these here glorious fiefdoms. The keeper of Satan's Carnival. And a straight-up psychopathic *ninja*. In fact, he needs to meet your asses to make sure you can stay here, that you not some kind of *terrorist*. So get your poop-chutes into that Humvee. It's time meet the King."

CHAPTER TWENTY-NINE

The King and His Castle

OUT THERE IN the desert, Kayla watched as two motorbikes chased each other in the distance. Their mosquito whine barely heard, headlights obscured by the occasional bloom of dust.

None of this sat well with her. She felt like this was a detour, a terrible move away from their intended destination. Pig-Nose—who introduced himself as 'Lieutenant Necro-Loco,' or, just 'Loco'—said they were headed southeast, which meant technically they were losing ground. Going backward. And they'd been driving for an hour already.

Coburn was nowhere to be found. He'd ditched them, she knew. Revenge for when they'd done the same to him. He was a callous creature, and she could easily imagine what was going through his head: hungry, he surely figured that his own herd was worthless. Five—well, six now with Danny—troublemakers who didn't want him around. The breadth and depth of the 66 States, however, surely was home to any number of human beings. Human beings filled to the brim with so much blood. Why slum it with Kayla and the others? What did he care if they made it to Los Angeles? The answer: he didn't.

And now he was gone.

Fine. Whatever. Good riddance. He got them this far, and they got him here, too. The deal was done. Close enough for horseshoes and hand grenades, anyway. Of course, he left his dumb little dog—the terrier kept climbing up over Kayla's lap and whining out the window, sniffing the glass like the vampire was out there, somewhere. The stupid little animal missed his master.

Danny seemed to sense her apprehension. He reached over and held her hand. She leaned her head on his shoulder. In the seat behind them sat the old Jester and the beefy Dope Fiend. They didn't have their guns up anymore, but she knew that they still had them pointed at their backs through the Humvee seats. Ebbie sat back there with them since there wasn't room in the middle row. Gil sat up front with Loco. Loco either didn't consider the old man with the broken fingers a threat, or he'd relaxed somewhat.

"You said we're heading to..." Gil started, let his words drift off.

"The Castle," Loco said. "Home of Satan's Carousel."

Gil tensed. "And Satan's Carousel is a... an actual merry-go-round."

"No, dumbass. Satan's Carousel isn't a *thing*. It's a state of fucking mind, vato. It's our existence. It's our attitude. Brutha Thuglow is the essence of Satan's Carousel, he's the dude who carries the flame of chaos and entropy. That makes him, like, the epicenter and shit."

"Right," Gil said. Kayla knew that tone. It was him being patronizing, but Loco clearly didn't pick up on it. "Is the Castle a real thing?"

"Yo, man. Yeah. It's an old Air Force base."

As if on cue, the Humvee passed a rag-tag trio standing next to a junkyard Dodge pick-up truck that was more a skeleton of a vehicle than an actual vehicle. One of the three—a skinny girl, totally topless, her ribs showing—hoisted a rocket launcher on her shoulder.

She fired a rocket-propelled grenade. The RPG whistled through the air like a bottle rocket, struck an old school bus out there in the dark of the desert. The bus lifted up from the back end, then came smashing back down again. The ground rumbled and the sound was loud enough to leave Kayla's ears ringing. She turned around, looked out the back window, saw them hopping up and down, high-fiving, the shooter's breasts bouncing.

"Jeez," Ebbie said. He met Kayla's eyes. He looked scared. More so than usual.

"So I'm guessing there's still armament there," Gil said.

"Fuck yes," Loco said.

"I suspect that's how you deal with the rotters."

"Rotters? You mean the boogies?"

"The boogies."

"Boogiemen, yeah. Fence keeps 'em out, mostly. But we got dudes along the fence too. Take 'em out with some M-16s. We send out hunting parties, too. Chop them bitches up and fuck the corpses." Loco paused, his voice got kind of quiet. "We don't really fuck the corpses, though."

"That's real good to know."

FRIENDSHIP, OKLAHOMA. HOME of the Altus Air Force Base.

Across the street from the airbase? A drive-in movie theater. Playing a zombie flick at 4AM in the morning. Kayla didn't know what film it was, all she knew was that as they passed, she could see something—a splinter? a nail?—go into some girl's wide-open eye. It made her cringe and sent her sour stomach even further south. Nobody sat in cars, but they sat on blankets and fold-up chairs next to sputtering burn barrels.

Loco turned the Humvee into the airbase proper.

Kayla had never been on a military base before, but she used to live not far from one—Navy, not Air Force. They always looked clean, utilitarian. Frankly, a little boring. Brick, square buildings. Everything at sharp, plain angles.

This was that, but it was a space subverted.

They passed rows of on-base housing—little one or two bedrooms, all brown, all nearly identical. But each had been ruined. Not by the zombies, but by those who had colonized this place. Graffiti on the walls, shrubs torn up, home-made Halloween decorations (lots of scarecrows and clowns) on the lawns, broken windows, more burn barrels. One house had a couple in full-body greasepaint humping on the front sidewalk like a couple of dogs. Kayla thought that was pretty gross, too, in some ways a lot grosser than the splinter in the girl's eyeball.

The good news was, Danny must've felt the same way, because he stared outside with a look that suggested he was watching a car wreck happen before his very eyes.

Further down the way—past a circle drive with an old WWII bomber propped up in the center like some kind of decoration, a bomber that had been tagged with even more elaborate images—they passed by a series of concrete administration buildings. Same effect here: broken windows, spraypaint, toilet-paper in the trees, furniture on the lawn. Outside one, somebody had set up a half-deflated moon bounce. *This place looks like a frat party gone nuclear*, she thought.

Then the Humvee went through a chain link gate and suddenly they were on an airstrip, whizzing past transports and tankers, past trucks and cars. They passed a helipad with a big clunky olive green chopper sitting in the middle. On the side, spraypainted in purple, was a big crown. Three diadems, like the symbol they'd seen way back in Erick.

Up ahead: big hangars. One after the other.

But Kayla knew that only one of them was their destination, and it was easy to see which. For starters, the damn thing was covered in neon signs, and it was lit up like a city bar at Christmas. Beer signs. Hotel signs. Open signs. Carnival signs. All stuck up around the hangar—either bolted to the side or stuck on poles—with neither rhyme nor reason. The black cables coming off them looked like bundles of black licorice. Then, the front of the hangar was closed off with a giant patchwork of fabric: bedsheets, towels, tarps, all stitched together to make a mostly red-and-purple motley curtain. Like a show awaited them inside.

Loco gunned the Humvee, and instead of braking and easing to a stop like most people would, he instead accelerated toward the bunker.

"What are we doing?" Kayla whispered to Danny. He shrugged, looking worried.

"Slow down!" Ebbie said.

Loco grinned, licked his lips.

"Loco," Gil said, "you might think about—"

Loco engaged both brakes—yanked up on the parking brake and slammed his foot down at the same time. The Humvee skidded, its back end sliding like the ass-end of a dog running on oiled linoleum.

Smoke drifted as rubber burned. The Humvee stopped.

Loco hooted. "God*damn* but that feels like a fucking meth enema. Lets you know you're still alive. Now everybody get the fuck out of Dickbucket."

Kayla, assuming that *Dickbucket* was the name Loco had given to the Humvee, got out of the vehicle. She heard the *chug chug* chug of a nearby generator, which explained the neon. Instantly she felt a not-too-gentle shove from the beefy 'roid-head, Dope Fiend.

"Move, bitch," the thick-necked freak mumbled.

"Hey, okay," she said, scowling. "Chill."

Danny stepped up to Dope Fiend and shoved his finger in the muscled freak's face. The look on Dope Fiend's face said that he wasn't happy—the skin tightened and his tendons corded, and he made a grimace like he was straining to take a really hard shit. Kayla knew what was coming, knew that he was going to cock back one of those log-jam fists and with it push Danny's face to the back of his head, but then next thing she knew Loco was there, slapping Dope Fiend hard in the face with an open palm.

"Goddamnit, Dope Fiend, you about to be in the presence of the King of 66. Why you gotta be such a cranky nug?"

Dope Fiend looked like he was going to cry.

"Whatever," Loco said. He made a little fanfare by forming a trumpet with his two chubby hands. "You are about to meet the Joker, the Monster, the motherfucking Mix Master. You are about to be in the presence of the Killer Carny, the Psychopathic Supa-Villain, the Clown Prince of Strangling Scrubs. It is time to behold the first rider of Satan's Carousel, the liberator of Hell's Highway, the King of the 66 States: King Brutha Thuglow!"

Loco whipped back the curtain, almost tripping as he did so.

Smoke—green and greasy—gusted from the open curtain.

Loco ushered them inside.

They were greeted by an even deeper haze of smoke and the sound of...

A pinball machine? Bells, beeps, clangs, fake screams, the familiar *dun-dun-dun-dun* from the Jaws soundtrack.

The hangar was pimped out. In the center, a big circle bed with black velvet sheets. Two naked girls lay slumbering across one another, asses up, their bodies forming a kind of pink, fleshy 'X' across the fabric. In the back, a hot-tub. Up front, a bar made with studded leather. Kayla was too young to know what bong-water smelled like and further, what a sex swing was, but if she *were* to know those things, she would've detected their presence immediately.

A blow-up Frankenstein hung out against the back wall. In fact, the whole place had kind of a ''seventies pimp meets a haunted house' feel—a shelf of chalices lay draped in faux cobwebs, a series of foam graves lay across the floor forming a kind of obstacle course, a series of warped mirrors hung from above.

And in the back of this massive hangar stood what must've been the King of the 66 States, King Brutha Thuglow.

He was not what Kayla expected. By the looks on everyone's faces, nobody expected this.

Thuglow was tall, and he stood hunched over a Jaws 3 pinball machine. He was shirtless, and so skinny that it looked like you could've reached out and gotten your fingers most of the way around one of his rib-bones. For pants he wore a baggy pair of zebra-striped chef-pants. His hair was long and thin, an aged rockstar mane that went down to the middle of his back.

He turned to face them—Kayla saw that his face was so lean it was gaunt, the cheekbones standing out like hard granite edges. It gave him a skeletal look, but he was certainly a *happy* skeleton. His grin of yellowed teeth stretched from ear to ear, and his eyes were pinched, watery, bloodshot.

"Oh, shit!" he said, laughing so hard he coughed. "We got guests?"

Loco hurried over and held up his M-16, then knelt by Thuglow like a knight offering his sword. Thuglow didn't even seem to see him and kept walking.

They all stood around, not sure what to do.

Thuglow sauntered up, threw his arms wide and embraced as many of them as he could. Kayla noted that his hair reeked of skunky smoke.

"Pinball," he said, shaking his head. "What a fucked-up game. Am I right? No matter how long you play, man, result is always the same. You lose. This isn't Pac-Man or Asteroids. You never win that shit.

Maybe you play for ten minutes. Maybe you play for ten hours. But you never win." He headed over to a card table, reached down beneath it and pulled out a purple glass bong. With a lighter he sparked the flame, took a gurgling hit, exhaled a dragon's plume of smoke—one jet from each nostril. When next he spoke, his words were more growly, and he coughed a little. "It's like life, I guess. Nobody gets off this carousel alive."

Gil stepped forward. "Listen, uhh, Thuglow—"

"*King* Thuglow," Loco corrected, raising his gun but not pointing it (yet).

"King Thuglow," Gil continued, "we're just—"

"You cannibals?" Thuglow asked.

They all looked at one another. "No."

"You got any diseases that you know about? AIDS? Gonorrhea? Sexual shit? Some kind of, I dunno, *space flu?*"

More shared looks—this time, even more confused and concerned. They all shook their heads.

"And nobody here is a boogieman."

He was seriously asking if any of them were zombies.

"No," Gil said. "None of us are boogiemen." He pointed then to Leelee. "In fact, one of us has some medical training and would probably know if we were boogiemen or had some kind of disease."

"Sweet!" Thuglow said, again laughing so hard he hacked. The lanky stoner wiped tears from his eyes, and Kayla was having a hard time believing he was king of anything but his own deluded imagination. "Hey, man, you guys want a bong hit? Or I can fix you a cocktail or something."

Gil answered for the group. "No. Listen, King—"

"Cool. Here, check this shit out." Thuglow went over to the wall, and pulled down a bundle of wrapped cloth from a metal shelf. He unswaddled it and revealed a cheap, flea-market katana. He started doing action movie poses with the Samurai blade. "I'm like the king of ninjas over here."

"*Listen*," Gil said firmly—he'd clearly had enough. The politeness in his voice had gone ragged. "This is all well and good but we're just passing through, heading on out to the West Coast. Los Angeles. If we could just get a place to stay for the night, maybe we could discuss or negotiate transportation or food..."

"The West Coast?" Thuglow asked. "Pshh. Why? We got everything you could ever want here in the 66 States, man."

"That's for us to know."

"Let me guess. You heard the CDC has some lab set up out there. Military dudes and scientists and shit. Trying to cure this thing. I heard that, too. Way I figure it, it's total bullshit."

He sliced the katana through the air at some invisible enemies. Imaginary boogiemen, Kayla wagered. "Same way those jizz-bags to the north are full of shit, too. Sons of Man utopia. *Whatever.* They got everything they need, why do they keep sending guys down here try to negotiate with us? Trying to buy up our jet fuel supplies? Trying to convince us to cede territory? Buncha richy-rich red-in-the-necks. They come at us, we'll run at them with the hatchet, bro." He cut a hard arc downward— the blade's tip hit the floor of the hangar and snapped off, clanging off to the side. It woke the two naked girls in the bed. They looked around, but closed their eyes and went back to sleep. "Shit! Shit. Aw, man. Anyway. My bet is that out West? You ain't gonna find nothing but a limp dick."

"No, not the CDC. And we'd like to find out for ourselves."

Thuglow came back with just the katana handle and part of the still-attached shattered blade in hand. "Nn-nn. Uh-uh. Nope. Sorry, old timer. But the 66 States isn't inclined to let such healthy folks go. It's like that old poster with Uncle Sam pointing all up in your grill and shit, and he's all like, *I Want You For The US Army*? This is that. I want you for the Kingdom of the 66 States."

"Excuse me?"

Thuglow seemed to be thinking. He began pointing to them one by one, down the line.

To Gil: "You look smart. You can rock the motor pool."

To Leelee: "You got medical training. So you can do doctor shit."

To Ebbie: "Man, you are a big dude. We got a gladiator circuit round here, figure I'll send your meaty ass down to Abilene to fight in the arena."

And finally, to Cecelia and Kayla: "And you two will make good whores."

Uh-oh.

CHAPTER THIRTY

Mojo Rising

KAYLA SAT ON the bed, trembling. Morning light, bright and white, came in through the blinds of the motel room, hurting her eyes.

As they said in the military, things had gone AWOL. SNAFU. FUBAR. The idiot 'King' of the 66 States sentenced them all to roles—and soon as he told Kayla and Cecelia what *they* were going to be doing, Gil moved faster than an old man should. He snatched up the glass bong and cracked it over Thuglow's head—he screamed, backpedaling with shards of glass stuck in his head, the air filled with the sudden skunky stink of the spilled water. Loco, Dope Fiend and Jester were suddenly knocking Gil to the ground, kicking him and pistoning their rifle butts into his curled-up body.

Chaos reigned. Kayla and Cecelia attacked back, both singling out the muscle-head, Dope Fiend. Loco raised his rifle but found himself hoisted off the ground by a charging Ebbie. The wiry Jester started to get into the fight, but Danny stepped in his way, fists balled up. They had no chance, of course—Ebbie wasn't anything close to a gladiator, and with Kayla's cancer in play she and Cecelia had the combined upper body strength of a wilted daisy. Danny put up the best fight of the bunch and turned out to be quite the scrapper, but even still, he got dropped, his lip split and bleeding, a gun thrust up against his throat.

Didn't matter anyway—eventually the hangar filled with the chatter of machine-gun fire. Ears ringing, Kayla rolled over and saw that King Thuglow stood there, a small submachine gun in his grip, gunsmoke climbing up out of the barrel like a pair of snakes wrestling.

Thuglow looked like he was crying. Like he just didn't get it.

"You don't appreciate me, man," he said, blowing a snot bubble and wiping tears away with the back of his scrawny arm. "I thought I was doing you cats a favor, but this is how you repay me? My hair stinks! I got glass in my head!"

Then he swept his arm—"Take 'em away, Loco"—and turned to pout.

And now, here they were. In a place called the Friendship Motor Lodge. The sign out front made up in the motif of a giant teepee, for some reason. It was draped with tinsel and toilet paper. The power lines around it were hung with bloody sneakers, baby dolls hung together with makeshift nooses, and other morbid accoutrements.

They'd been separated. Ebbie, Gil and Leelee were off somewhere. Kayla and Cecelia were here in a room done up in a mid-century-modern meets the desert look. Thuglow had decided to take the dog, Creampuff. And Coburn...

...well, he was gone.

"I hope Gil's all right," Cecelia said. The face she wore was either sincere in its worry or a very convincing mask. Not that Kayla was in a real good position to know. "Those motherfuckers."

"Daddy's tough. He got beat up pretty good but..." She couldn't finish it. He *did* get beat up pretty good. His face looked like a horror show, bruised and bloody and one eye already swelling shut.

"It wouldn't be so bad, you know."

"What wouldn't be so bad?"

"Being... you know. Whores."

"Ew. Cecelia. *Ew.*"

Cecelia knelt down in front of her. Desperate for something, all of a sudden.

"The word *whore*, it doesn't mean what you think it means. Way back when, the Romans or Greeks or whoever, they didn't mean that word in a bad way like we do now. It meant something different. Whore meant to desire, or be desired. There's nothing wrong with that. Is there?"

Kayla paled. "You used to be a damn hooker, didn't you?"

"What?" Cecelia said, suddenly incredulous. But she couldn't keep it up. "We preferred to be called escorts."

"Oh, god, Cecelia!" Kayla said, suddenly grossed-out. She stood up from the bed and started pacing by the window, squinting in the bright daylight. "That is nasty. And you and my Dad? That's gross. Was he paying you? Is that how you saw this whole thing? As a business transaction? Just... ew."

"It's not gross," Cecelia said. "It's the way men and women are. Men do nice things for women so they can sleep with them. It's just biology. Being an escort just cuts out the middle-man. A guy doesn't need to buy me drinks or a meal. He just... has to buy me."

"That is cynical as... well, that's cynical as *hell*, Cecelia." Kayla wasn't used to using curse words like that, but it felt right.

"That's why Danny is being nice to you."

Kayla's jaw dropped. What was worse was that Cecelia wasn't saying it out of malice—when she was being mean, her face twisted up like a fox who just caught a whiff of some possum shit or something. This wasn't malice. She was being sincere.

"You shut up about Danny," Kayla said. "Danny's just a nice boy, is all. He doesn't have that kind of poison in his head. We haven't even kissed yet! And I don't know if we're gonna. I don't know if it's like that. He probably doesn't even feel that way. I don't know if *I* feel that way. I just know..." Her words drifted off. "I just know that I hope he's okay."

"I hope Gil's okay."

Kayla plopped back down on the bed. "I'm tired. I need a cigarette."

"Me too."

Locusts sang.

Somewhere above, two crows circled, complaining to one another.

A rattler crawled across the hot broken macadam, accompanied by serpents made of dust, creeping along as the wind blew.

And then, the locusts quieted. The crows shut up and took wing away. The rattler hurried off, found somewhere else to be.

Loco had left the I-40 gate last night in the Humvee, taking Dope Fiend and Jester with him. That left Big Money Jigalo—AKA Pete Sorvin—as the one guard at this gate, which wasn't that big of a deal. They didn't see humans all that often, and mostly the zombies stayed away because there wasn't much out here for them. Thuglow's crew had cleared out Erick and all the surrounding towns.

Still. Pete—er, 'Big Money'—liked having his rifle handy. A Ruger Mini-14 with a long-looking Leupold scope on it and chambered for .223 Remington. Any zombies thought of hiking it up the highway, they'd find their skulls evacuated by a bumblebee made of hot lead.

Killing zombies was one of the only things that gave Pete much happiness anymore. Everything else was gone. His wife. His boy. Swept away by the zombie horde. Turned into... well, God didn't even know. Only the Devil had a clue.

Pete didn't much like the other survivors here. Bunch of lunatics, they were. Taking their dopey names. Dressing like clowns and like the jokers in a deck of cards. All because of, what? Some white rap group the King liked? They gave everybody dumb names—'Skull Hustla.' 'Pimp Killa Z.' And him, 'Big Money Jigalo.' He didn't have any money. He damn sure wasn't a jigalo. The name didn't make any sense. It was like they picked it out of a hat.

In this way, the apocalypse was a lot crazier than Pete imagined it would be.

But that was okay. He had his rifle.

He leaned up against the top of the fence, laying atop an old beater Oldsmobile, and pressed his eye against the scope.

Heat vapors rose up off the highway like the sizzle off a hot pan. Way those vapors worked was, they distorted things a good bit, and sometimes in there you'd think you saw a zombie when really it wasn't anything at all.

So when he saw the four dark shapes come up at the horizon's edge, heading down the highway, at first he thought, *this can't be real.* They didn't look right. Taller than they should've been, maybe. Longer arms, too. And necks he could see. He caught a flash of pink fabric.

But they kept coming. They weren't a mirage.

And behind them, Hell's own army followed.

They rose up from the horizon's edge like the first dark wave of a coming tide, a black tide, a *dead* tide—zombies. And not just a handful of them, either, but dozens. Maybe hundreds. They just kept coming, following behind the four like an ineluctable force. Pete felt his hands shaking. Remembered seeing his Mary—with their son Owen in her arms—swept beneath a crowd of zombies a fraction of this size. He lined up a shot. Cranked the magnification.

The four in the front weren't like the others at all.

Their mouths, bigger. Filled with tiny teeth. Hands curled with claws. He let one of their wretched faces fill the scope.

Thumbed off the safety.

Took a deep breath.

Steady.

Just before he pulled the trigger, he was sure the thing looked right at him. The monster hit the ground just in time for the bullet to sail over its head, clipping one of the zombies in the back in the neck. A jet of black blood arced up and that zombie dropped.

"Shit!" he said, moving the rifle to rediscover his target in the scope. The monster was nowhere to be found. Neither were the other three.

He pulled his gaze away from the rifle, and with his bare gaze he could see them: they were loping like animals, like wolves launched straight out of Satan's womb, and they were headed toward the fence.

It all happened so fast.

The one draped in scraps of pink launched herself up over the fence like it wasn't but a knee-high hurdle. Pete stood, staggered backward, tried to get off a shot—but this wasn't a shotgun and that wasn't a clay pigeon.

She struck him in the chest. It felt like he was hit by a bull. Launched him off the Oldsmobile and down to the ground, to the dust.

He tried to get his rifle between them, either to shoot her or to shoot himself, but she tossed it away. Then she buried her face in the crook of his neck and began to chew. Everything felt wet, hot, cold, electric.

The other three hit the gate like sharks headbutting a diver cage.

As Pete's life drained away, he saw the front fence denting, bowing, crashing inwards. The cars behind it jumped the tracks as the hunters struck them again and again, pushing them back with the groan of metal.

The way was open.

Hell's army was here. The 66 States were breached.

Pete saw blood in darkness.

GIL STOOD IN the motel room bathroom, looking at himself in the mirror. He looked about as good as a shovel full of road-kill. His left eye was shut behind two swollen lumps competing for attention. Half his face looked like a roadmap of broken capillaries. In his palm he held two bloody teeth.

He upended them into the sink with a clatter.

He hadn't felt more alive in a long time.

Seemed strange, really. Even he couldn't quite justify it. All things considered, they were pretty well screwed. Held captive by a kingdom full of mad-men in greasepaint. His daughter on the path to prostitution. His other friends—they were that, he reminded himself—held against the wall for their own strange fates. He *had* been resigned to the motor pool, which sounded fairly benign, but apparently attacking that dope-smoking dickweed who called himself 'King' was frowned upon, and about an hour ago they'd come in to tell him that his sentence was set: they'd drag him out into the firing range, stick a grenade in his mouth, and a bunch of stoned clown-faced fuck-wits would take shots at him until one of them managed to blow him to pieces like a scarecrow with dynamite up its ass.

So, no, things weren't looking so hot.

And yet: he felt good.

Maybe it was the beating. Pain had a way of clarifying things. Probably a brain-thing. Adrenalin. Dopamine. Endorphins. Something. He'd been in a fight before. Hell, he'd been in dozens of fights. As a younger man—and, frankly, sometimes as an older one—he had quite a temper. Anybody said something to him he didn't like, he'd make sure to give them a good whipping. Sometimes he took the whipping instead, but way he figured it, he'd won more than he lost.

Really, though, it came back to something Leelee said to him. As they were being dragged into the Friendship Motel, as Kayla and Cecelia were thrown into their room and Leelee was being moved into hers, she bent over and said something to him, something that stuck with him.

"Your daughter is special," she said. "She is protected. Fight for her and she will be free."

Fight for her and she will be free.

"Okay," Gil said now, to his busted jack-o-lantern face in the mirror.

He knew he couldn't go out the window: they'd been smart enough to bolt wrought iron bars (really, old garden gates) against the frames.

They weren't *that* smart, though. They'd left the trappings of the motel in place. Like, say, the bedside lamp. It didn't work—the motel didn't have power, not like Thuglow's hangar did. But the lamp didn't need to work.

He grabbed it. Pulled the cord taut.

He cleared his throat, sauntered over to the motel room door, then pounded on it and yelled out in his best tortured voice:

"Oh shit. *Oh shit.* I think something's broken inside me! I'm hemorrhaging. Help! *Help.*"

He stood to the side of the door. Out there, he knew, stood two guards: his favorite buddies, Dope Fiend and Jester.

The older fellow, Jester, was first through the door. He caught the lamp right under his chin and he went down like a stack of teacups. Dope Fiend—the human wall—was close behind but slow to react. Probably, Gil figured, because he was dumb as a wrench.

With the cord pulled taut, Gil stepped in behind the muscle-bound freak and pulled against his throat.

It didn't go as planned.

Dope Fiend started whirling around, carrying Gil with him—suddenly Kayla's father felt like he was stuck on the back of a mechanical bull, smashed into the door, into a closet, into a bedside table.

Gil couldn't hold on. He hit the ground hard on his butt. He reached for Jester's fallen rifle, but Dope Fiend was already firing his own—the bullets stitched across the floor and juggled the other machine gun out of Gil's reach.

He saw no choice: as the room filled with machine-gun fire, Gil bolted out of the room, catching a face full of splinters as bullets chewed through the doorframe.

THEY TRIED TO play nice.

They sent an emissary to talk diplomacy, trade, to make a *deal*. That emissary—Tom Fichter—came back after having been beaten with phonebooks. They branded a symbol in the meat of his ass: a three-pointed crown.

Fucking animals. Or clowns.

It was time to do something about it. Benjamin Brickert stared out at one of the northern gates of Thuglow's territory. The Route 54 entrance, coming down out of Goodwell, Oklahoma, with the gate preceding Texhoma. It was the easiest way in—come down out of their own territory in Kansas and hit them from the top. No need to come in from the side. Here, he figured Thuglow would've been better protected, figuring that Brickert and his people would stage an attack one day—but, nope, not really. Not much defense at all, and easy enough to remove. Thuglow wasn't any kind of strategist. Just an idiot king idling time.

His ears were ringing from the shot. He snapped his fingers, told Shonda to hand him the glasses. Benjamin pressed the binoculars to his face, saw in the distance the dead man hanging half-out of a repurposed lifeguard station. Something red dripped from his skull. A crow had already alighted on his chin, was starting to pick at the meat.

Brickert gave the thumbs-up to his sharpshooter: Carlos Gonzalez. Carlos twiddled a toothpick with his tongue and winked. Then he hopped off the top of the moving truck, the Remington 700 slung over his shoulder.

"Chain her up," Brickert whooped, turning his finger in a circle, telling everyone to *move, move, move*. At his back waited a small invasion force: pick-up trucks with DIY-mounted armament, armor-plated Cadillacs, a few moving trucks (to reap any loose bounty), and a shitload of the Sons of Man. Capable men. Men who knew what it was to shoot straight, take a life, and thank God for the privilege of being alive.

These were hard times. But they were good times, too.

The men moved heavy gauge chains, looped them around the gate leading into Thuglow's bullshit kingdom. Shonda—Brickert's own second-in-command, a tough woman built like a mailbox filled with bricks—went over and supervised. Chains were connected to the back of one of the pick-ups: the diesel (all the vehicles were diesel, as they had to be) gunned it, kicking up a dragon's plume of dust.

The tires spun at first. But then the gate started to bend and buckle, making a sound like a submarine about to be crushed by the pressure of the sea.

Then: the truck leapt forth like a bull with a burr in its ass, bringing the gate with it. Some of his soldiers hurried through the gate, clambering up over the remaining roadblock. They found the crank-wheel that moved the cars and moved the mechanism aside with the grinding clamor of metal on metal.

Brickert snorted, spat into the dust, gazed out over the long ribbon of highway ahead of them. Noontime sun high above, baking the macadam. Up in Kansas, the sky was blue as his daughter's eyes, but here, the sky had taken on a bleached, bleary quality. Like someone had taken the whole canvas and dunked it quick in a tub of bleach.

South was Thuglow's kingdom, then. Brickert pretended like this was a course of action he did not want to take. He had to offer that to his people, to project that sense of *gravitas*, in order to be a real leader to them. Real leaders did not delight in the conquering of their neighbors: they acted as if it were a burden, a regret, a terrible choice but the *best* terrible choice.

It was a lie. Brickert wanted to drive this mobile invasion force right up Thuglow's bony stoner ass. He was a polluted human, impure of thought and body. Not to mention a fucking moron. The Sons of Man took their territory and made something of it: they had working farms. Running water. Electricity in some places. It was clean. Safe. *Sane.* Sure, it was necessary for folks to make sacrifices. The laws were strict. Disease was not tolerated. Dissent was punished swiftly: there came a time for opposing opinions, for a little bit of revolution, but now was not that time, not as they were just getting a foot-hold on civilization's rebirth.

But Thuglow? Chaos reigned in the '66 States.' Thing was, they had resources. They had Altus AFB. They had jet fuel. They had a helicopter. And that was just one part of the territory. Abilene? Amarillo? Austin? They had taken those cities but now were squandering what they found. That was how the country fell apart in the first place: mankind had long-forgotten that yes, he was the master of nature, but being its master did not mean being its abuser. Humanity didn't give a fuck. Trees? Cut them down. Fossil fuels? Burn through it all. Hell with clean skies. Piss in the clean water. The natural world meant nothing.

And when the natural world failed, the supernatural took hold.

That was how Brickert saw it. You tore enough vents in nature's fabric with careless claws, eventually something would come through. Something sent by God to punish you, or by the Devil to ruin you. They saw it first with the monsters hidden in the shadows: vampires, spirits, the Jersey Devil, the blind troglodytes they found in the tunnels beneath Manhattan.

But those were just the initial wave. Those monsters were only a warning.

And mankind did not pay attention. Did not see the signs.

And so, the zombies came. An emblem of man's own selfish subversions. Just as man ruined nature and turned it to his will, the zombies ruined man, and made man just like them. It was a second, deeper subversion: a subversion of life, of free will. Zombies were rotten flesh and lizard brains and not much else. They took and they took and they took, never giving anything back. They were, in that way, a perfect expression of man's worst instincts.

Thuglow was a zombie. Or close enough. Zoned out on drugs. Ready to take, never to give back. That meant he had to go.

That meant the 66 States were now the property of the Sons of Man.

"We ready?" Shonda asked him. Brickert blinked, wondering how long he'd been standing there. All the vehicles—all two-dozen of them—were sitting, engines rumbling. He nodded, and hopped in the back of a Chevy Silverado with an old Vietnam-era .50 cal bolted into the back.

Brickert manned the gun, and whistled for the invasion to begin.

* * *

A MOTOR LODGE wasn't like some motels or hotels—its doors opened right to the parking lot. They were a staple of old highway travel. You'd park. Go get your keys. Then walk right from your car to the door of your room. Easy-peasy, Japaneezy. No hassle. Good privacy.

Gil burst out of his room as machine gun bullets gnawed at the frame, darting left out of the door. Across the street was an old Applebee's, and down the way was a handful of fast food joints and gas stations. But it was all open. Nowhere to run, nowhere to hide—soon as he bolted for the highway, Dope Fiend would be emerging into the light like the goddamned Terminator, and it wouldn't matter how bad a shot he was with that thing. You let fly with enough bullets, *one* of them is going to hit home.

For a split-second, Gil knew that this was it. It was all over. His escape had failed. Dope Fiend was going to run him through the wringer.

But then he looked back on all the fights he'd ever fought: in bars, in alleys, at work. It was a myth that men fought with honor. Honor was for the boxing ring, but when it came time to teach another man a lesson or, even more importantly, just stay alive, you fought however you had to fight. Not like a punch to the face was particularly honorable: you hit the nose, the eyes teared up and stopped your opponent from seeing. Hitting them in the gut wasn't much different from hitting them in the nuts: pain shot through their middle, they doubled over, they groaned.

You fought how you fought. You fought to win.

And sometimes, that meant using your environment.

DOPE FIEND WAS going to kill that old man.

Dope Fiend was built like an M1 Abrams tank. He wasn't no pussy. What, he stuck a steroid needle in his ass-meat every couple of days just to let some scrawny old cocksucker get away from him? Oh, hell no.

Dope Fiend was good at beating the shit out of people. Shooting them, not so much, but that was why he had Little Kim, here. His M-16. Fully fucking auto.

Dope Fiend stepped out of the hotel room. Jaw muscles so tight, he could've bitten through a steel girder. And just for a lark, he did some kegel exercises, too—keeping his pubococcygeus muscle nice and tight so he could hold in his orgasms and really give the whores the what-for.

Dope Fiend looked around for the old man.

Dope Fiend found him.

A half-second before Gil smashed him in the head with a tricycle.

GIL HAD NO idea why a tricycle was sitting there in the parking lot. He didn't know that life here in the 66 States grew tedious, and that these clowns—in many cases, literal, actual clowns—resorted increasingly to dumb, Jackass-style stunts to keep themselves from keeling over dead from boredom. Had Gil known this, that would've explained why the tricycle had a faint dusting of black carbonization over the frame, and why it smelled a little like burnt vinyl and kerosene: just a few days before, one of Thuglow's idiot soldiers lit the thing on fire and tried to ride it around the parking lot for as long as he could—some insane variant of rodeo, staying on the bucking beast as long as you could. Except, instead of a thrashing bronco it was a fiery tricycle.

That soldier—'The Beava Smasha'—now was laid up in an infected hospital bed with third-degree burns up and down his ass and legs. He wasn't expected to live. Darwinism had proven its mettle yet again.

Gil didn't know any of that.

What he also didn't know—but was swift to realize—was that a tricycle was basically a tangle of metal with lots of empty air. That meant, instead of just hitting Dope Fiend in the head, his head actually tangled inside the tricycle, trapping him within the metal frame.

Dope Fiend cried out, fired the gun. Recoil juggled the gun upwards, bullets tossing through open air. The muscle-head was like a giant ape with his head in a bucket, crying out and trying desperately to shake his cranium free from his tricycle prison.

Gil stepped aside, kicked the inside of the man's leg. The knee popped—it didn't break, but it didn't have to. Dope Fiend went down.

And so did the gun. It clattered free of his grip.

"Please," Dope Fiend said.

Gil picked up the gun and shot the man. Blood blossomed across Dope Fiend's chest, but still he didn't fall. He looked up at Gil and spat at him.

"Fuck you," Dope Fiend hissed, spraying blood and froth.

One more bullet to the head, and Dope Fiend dropped.

It was time to rescue his daughter, his friends.

HE JUST DIDN'T get it, man. "I'm a good leader," Thuglow said to Babette, who stood behind him, her breasts pressing into his shoulder blades. She reached over his shoulder and, with two pairs of tweezers, delicately picked purple bong glass out of his head.

Outside, evening had fallen. He'd stayed in the hangar all day, totally bummed out. He'd got his back-up bong. Smoked some vicious medicinal marijuana from California he'd been saving for just such an occasion (so much better than this Texas ditchweed he'd been using). Eventually Loco had come back, told him their new 'guests' were lined up at the Friendship Motel on the far side of the base. Then Loco had asked him if he wanted to, uhh, you know, pick the broken glass shards out of his face? "Oh, damn," Thuglow had told him. "I forgot about that."

Loco asked him if he wanted one of the nurses. Thuglow told him to get one of the whores instead. Steadier hands, he told him with a wink, but really, the King's heart wasn't in it.

Times like this, he didn't feel much like King Brutha Thuglow of the 66 States.

He felt like Johnny Ludlow, of Tulsa, Oklahoma. He felt like the 30-year-old who was still living in his parents' basement. Or the helicopter pilot who lost his license because he was stoned. Or the guy who put crazy Youtube videos on the Internet of him rapping or ramping a BMX bike off a Gamestop roof or playing pranks on his other 30-year-old-and-probably-still-living-at-home buddies.

Out here, though, he commanded respect. Turned out, the world was home to any number of miscreants and deviants looking for a guy who could lead them. No, he wasn't a leader by choice—mostly, he was just dumb enough to forge ahead, no matter the consequences. But to others, that looked like the real deal. And before too long he had a whole host of other weirdos and cast-offs who followed behind him like he had some kind of nutso gravity.

And somewhere in that, Brutha Thuglow was born.

Most of the time, he *felt* like the King. He could have whatever he wanted. Guns. Ditchweed. A threesome.

But then along came a handful of people who broke a bong over his head, covered him in skunk-water and made him feel less like Brutha Thuglow, King of the 66 States, and more like poor Johnny Ludlow, King of a Big Pile of Dogshit.

"It's hard out there for a pimp," he said, forlorn.

Equally forlorn was the dog he'd stolen, some squirmy little terrier who sat leashed over in the corner with a piece of clothesline from one of the residences. The animal's jaws were muzzled with a belt because, what a surprise, the dog was a biter. Just another hunk of crap on the steaming pile of feculence that Thuglow felt was his life: what the hell was he going to do with a dog? Why did he steal it?

Babette licked the back of his neck just like he liked.

It made him feel a little better.

Well, a whole lot better, really.

He turned around—she still hadn't gotten the last piece of bong glass out of his forehead, but hell with it, it was time to feel like a king and fuck his queen, or at least the queen of *right now*—so he pulled the tweezers out of her hand and dropped them to the floor. His spidery fingers snaked along the small of her back and he reached in and started kissing her neck...

And then he looked up.

Emerging from the shadows: a pair of eyes and the whitest teeth he'd ever seen. Not just teeth, though: *fangs*.

"You took my dog," Coburn said, grinning.

THE GIRL SHRIEKED and came at him with her painted nails out, but Coburn wasn't going to be put in his place by some trollop with an amateurish above-the-ass tattoo that looked like an evil clown's wicked grin— or would do if it hadn't been drawn by some shaky-handed meth addict. He caught her by both wrists, spun her around, then gave her a little eyeball-to-eyeball voodoo.

"You go now," he said, patting her on the head. Her lips moistened with saliva. Her empty stare came complete with a numb, game nod. And then the girl tottered off like a scurrying mouse.

Coburn turned around to find Thuglow whimpering, clumsily trying to thumb .44 shells into a big ol' hand cannon—Smith & Wesson Model 29a, by the looks of it. The vampire didn't have to do much. He just stomped his foot and said 'boo' and the King fumbled the shells. They hit the hangar floor with a metallic tinkle and went rolling away.

Then he grabbed the gun and smacked Thuglow in the face.

"Settle down, your highness," Coburn said, a growly chuckle in his throat. "I'm not going to eat you."

It was true. He had no intention of eating this buffoon. Sure, the blood would give him a bit of a 'contact buzz' for maybe ten, fifteen minutes, but that wasn't what he was looking for. Plus, he was full. Blessedly, blissfully full.

Last night, when the three assholes in the Humvee came up, guns out, Coburn slipped into the shadows and crawled under the vehicle when nobody was looking. And it was there he dangled—the bottom of his jacket scraping hard against shattered macadam—as they headed southwest to the airbase. He had to admit, he was starting to feel some deep worry that they were going to be driving too long, that he'd be under the Humvee when the sun started to come up, which meant at some point he'd drop out from underneath the vehicle like a burnt hot dog that got stuck to the underside of the grill.

But then they pulled into the base, and Coburn saw his opportunity. As they passed by rows of brick homes once used to house airmen, the vampire relaxed his fingers and slackened his legs and...

He hit the ground hard as the Humvee kept on going.

At that point, he knew he had maybe an hour, maybe two, before the sun came up. His skin wasn't tingling yet; the hairs on the back of his neck hadn't shot up like prairie dogs at the hole. These houses, people lived here. He could smell them. *Boy*, could he smell them. Booze. Coffee. Pot. The acrid cat-piss tang of methamphetamines. And... greasepaint.

Coburn didn't know what was up with all this clown makeup. Best he figured was that the apocalypse had really done a number on people's heads, scrambled their brains like eggs, made it seem that dressing up like Gothy ghetto clown-pimps was a fine idea, indeed.

Normally, he'd be more discerning with his food. But this wasn't the time to play the picky gastronome, was it?

At first, he thought about just kicking down one of these doors and marching inside like he owned the place—feeding with the aggressive gusto of a man ripping the top off a package of Cheetos and shoving his whole head inside like it was some kind of gratuitous feed-bag. But last thing he needed was to draw undue attention at this wee hour of the morning, so it seemed as if a bit more *subtlety* was in order.

He found an unlocked window and slipped inside.

Found some shallow-chested shorn-skull jerkoff with purple lipstick, cerulean-blue eyeshadow and a DIY tattoo across his gut that turned his belly button into the Eye of Sauron. Jerkoff had his eyes closed and lay on a ratty mattress surrounded by empty Pabst Blue Ribbon cans and scented candles—if Coburn had the smell right, it was 'mulberry.' Pair of headphones sat snug against Jerkoff's ears, thudding some kind of erratic bass. The house here didn't have power, but he obviously had batteries for his MP3 player.

On the walls were posters of some white-boy rap duo that Coburn had never heard of, probably the same shit that was pumping into Jerkoff's ears through the headphones. Appropriately, the white boys on the poster were dressed like, you guessed it, clowns.

Coburn clucked his tongue. What the hell was wrong with people?

Next to the mattress sat a sawed-off shotgun. He'd painted it green and purple, like it was something used by one of the Batman villains.

The vampire didn't want any big booms to draw attention, so he kicked away the gun, then let his fangs slide to the fore of his mouth.

It was time to feed.

But then, her voice. Kayla's voice. Not real, not even really her, but it came up out of his mind the same way his monster voice sometimes did—the angel on his shoulder instead of his devil, speaking in the voice of a teenage girl with a sort-of-Southern drawl.

You can't just kill him. Take enough, leave him and go.

Shut up, he thought.

Coburn! You be nice.

Shut up shut up shut up shut up. Not cool. Not at all cool. He wanted to kill this chump. Jerkoff was full of blood, blood he wanted in his body right now. And he deserved it! If only for that dick-brained tattoo.

Still. Something prevented him from doing the deed.

Coburn left Jerkoff and wandered around the house. The living room wasn't much of a living room: furniture had been overturned and broken apart. The rug was scorched in places. The TV had been hollowed out and, in its center, a pair of plastic baby dolls were arranged in a lascivious 69 position.

He didn't know what he was looking for, but roved about just the same, eyes peeled.

He went to the kitchen. Flies buzzed around a stack of empty MREs—Meals Ready to Eat, the self-heating rations of the military—and in the ceiling was stuck a bunch of silverware, as if Jerkoff lay on the floor, bored, throwing forks and knives (and probably spoons, the dumb-ass) to see if he could get them to stick in the drywall.

Nothing here, either.

Goddamnit.

And then, the bathroom.

Truth was, Coburn expected a horror-show. The rest of the house looked like a toilet, so that meant the toilet probably looked like some awful hybrid of a backstreet abortion clinic and a sewage treatment plant. But that wasn't what it was. It was clean. Smelled a little of bleach. Jerkoff liked to be comfortable when he did his business. Handsoap. Nice towels.

And reading material.

Coburn didn't need to look too long at it to know what it was. Soon as he caught a look of a little girl's crying face—she couldn't have been more than ten, this girl—the vampire figured out what Jerkoff was into.

Justification, achieved. Kayla's voice inside went to the monster's voice: *Destroy him. Wear his ribcage like a hat. Beat him to death with his own legs.*

Coburn didn't do any of that. Instead, he stomped into the room, threw a hard knee onto Jerkoff's chest, then bent down and buried his fangs into the dumb fucker's neck like he was cradling a baby to burp. He drank, and drank, and drank some more until Jerkoff shuddered, gasped, went still, then went cold.

Then just to be sure, Coburn broke the pedophile's neck.

With the sun coming up, he went down into the basement and slept.

And with the sun going down, he decided it was high-time to find his herd. Once more, his nose was essential—as the empurpled evening sky darkened, he found the trail of Humvee exhaust, the stink of Cecelia's perfume, the poochy odor of Creampuff. That led him here. To the domain of King Brutha Thuglow.

Who now sat on his knees, blubbering.

"Don't kill me, man," Thuglow whimpered. "I've had a really bad day."

"Tell me about it," the vampire said.

"I know, right? Life sucks."

"*No.* I mean, tell me about it or I rip your jaw off and use it like a boomerang."

"Oh. *Oh.* Uh. These people came? Led by this old dude? And we were gettin' along okay and shit and I was like, *welcome to my kingdom, I'd like to invite you stay and I will give you these jobs to perform*, and the old man was like, *fuck you, clown, I don't respect the King's laws* and next thing I know he's breaking my goddamn bong over my fuckin' head and shit." Thuglow wiped a string of snot from his nose. "I thought I was being magnificent and whatever, giving them a place and a purpose."

"Magnanimous. Not magnificent."

"Oh. Okay."

"So it was an old man. Let me guess: the others were a big ol' heavyset guy, a black lady with a broken foot, a... I dunno, a trashy brat, and a teen girl who looked too skinny for her own good."

Thuglow nodded. "That's them, man. You got a beef with them, too?"

"Not *quite.*"

"Oh, shit. They were your peeps?"

"They are, at that. My herd, actually. That dog belongs to me, too."

The King's face fell. "You're here to hurt me, then."

"Not yet. Not if you help me."

"Help you."

"That's right. I want to find them. I want your help in doing so. Then I want you to grant us safe passage through this insane tract of land you call your 'kingdom.' And while we're at it, we'll want our stuff back. Plus a little extra. Like, say, a pair of airman boots because goddamnit if I'm not tired of walking around in my bare feet."

Thuglow's eyes went wide. "I can do that. It's just…"

"It's just what."

"I don't know if your people are still here."

Coburn hoisted Thuglow up under the armpits, threw him against some metal shelving. The King yelped in pain.

"Explain," Coburn said, hunkering down and baring his fangs.

"I sent them to the motel for… processing. The old man, I sentenced to death. They were supposed to do it at sundown."

Coburn didn't much like Gil. They were two alpha dogs snarling and tussling over who got to control the pack. Even still, he respected the old bastard. And even more importantly, Gil was the girl's father. Coburn still didn't get what it was about the girl that made him think so fondly of her, but for now he didn't have time to pick that apart.

The vampire reached for Thuglow. Planned to snap his neck. But the King cried out: "Wait! Wait. I can call. It may not be done yet. My posse… sometimes, y'know, they're a little slow to get going. I just need my radio."

Coburn stalked over, grabbed a two-way off a nearby card table.

He tossed it to Thuglow. "This one?"

The King nodded, then hit the radio button.

"Dope Fiend. Come in, dude. You read me? Dope Fiend. This is your King speaking." Nothing. "Dude. *Dude.* Please please please."

Coburn snarled.

"Hold up! Hold up. Let me try Loco." He dialed another frequency. His voice was more panicked, now. "Loco, come in, Loco, shit, man, come on, this is Thuglow, bro. Do you read me?"

A burst of noise came out of the radio. It was Loco's voice—Coburn recognized it from the night prior—but the words were indecipherable, what with all the machine gun fire in the background. Way Coburn heard it, he was pretty sure Loco was yelling. Or maybe 'screaming' was a better word for it.

Then the radio cut out.

Thuglow stared at the radio like it had just grown a dick.

"No, no, no no no," he protested as Coburn stalked toward him, hissing, and Thuglow knew full well that whatever it was that came next, it wasn't going to be pretty and it was likely to involve giving his hangar a new paint-job, with the *paint* being gallons of his own bodily fluids.

But then, outside:

Distant machine gun fire.

And worse, a sound that Coburn knew too well. A chorus of banshee wails—four of them threaded together, a terrible harmony born of Hell's own misery.

They were here. The super-zombies. The uber-rotters. The four hunters.

"What the fuck was that?" Thuglow said.

"New plan," Coburn snarled, heading over to unmuzzle and unleash Creampuff from the corner. "Got a vehicle around here?"

"*What the fuck was that?*" Thuglow asked again. Coburn smacked him.

"Vehicle! Moron! Do. You. Have. One?"

"Uh, a, a, a golf cart. Behind the hangar."

Coburn grabbed Thuglow by the neck, forced him to stand. "Good. Hope you got the keys handy, because we need to take a ride."

CHAPTER THIRTY-ONE

Satan's Carousel

BRICKERT STOOD ATOP the pick-up cab, legs apart, shoulders back, the binoculars up against his eyes. It was hard to make out what was going on down there, but he damn sure knew it wasn't good. The bright flashes and staccato pops of machine gun fire. The screams of men dying. The *whumpf* of a grenade going off. And the howls of something terrible, something that to Benjamin sounded altogether *ancient*.

Someone lit a flare, god only knew why. It lit up the sky bright red, red the color of blood, red the color of Hell's fire. And in that light Brickert saw the mass of bodies: a veritable tide of zombies. Hundreds of them. Now swarming an overturned Humvee the way army ants carpeted their prey, mandibles clicking and dissecting with unerring precision.

Shonda popped her head out of the cab. "Doesn't look good from down here, Ben. It look any better up there?"

"No," he said, sucking air between his teeth. "It does not."

"The 66 States are lost," she said. "Just wasn't us that took 'em."

He said nothing.

She made it even clearer: "We need to turn around. Head back."

"No." That word, heavy as a lead weight. "Altus AFB has weapons, but that's not what makes them special. They hosted operations. Airlifting, but even more importantly, refueling. They've got jet fuel. And I want it."

"Ben—"

"The zombies make our job harder in one way, but easier, too. Thuglow and his paint-faced mutants will be occupied by this threat and they won't even see us coming. We must view this as an opportunity. For now, we go around the threat. Head southwest, then cut in hard to the east."

Shonda said no more. No reason to. He'd laid down the word and the law and that was that. Sure, some folks wore those WWJD bracelets, but someone like Shonda had to be worried more about WWBD: What Would Ben Do?

He hopped back down off the top of the pick-up and went back to mounting the gun in the truck bed. He whistled, and the convoy began to move.

GIL FELT A tight knot in his gut like a bundle of snakes. They should've been long gone by now. Once he shot Dope Fiend and took his keys, it seemed like an easy course to chart: free the others, find a vehicle, and high-tail it the hell away from what seemed to be the center of that lunatic Thuglow's self-described kingdom. Kayla had hugged him and cried, and Cecelia came up and gave him a kiss on his busted-up bruised-as-hell cheek, and everybody was laughing and crying and feeling like they got a reprieve. Danny had shaken his hand but then gravitated right to Kayla, and that made her happy—which, to his surprise, made Gil happy, too.

Ebbie wanted to know why they needed a vehicle, and for Gil, that answer was easy: outside the base was nothing. Crossing that dustbowl would not be an easy journey, and he didn't feel like recreating *The Grapes of Wrath*. Besides, with him being all beat to shit and Leelee still (and likely forever) limping, they needed to get a ride.

Easier said than done, as it turned out. Base had plenty of vehicles lurking around, but most of them were junkers. Any time they found an old Jeep or a Humvee, it wasn't gassed up—it was as if these clowns were treating them like single-use items, like a road flare or a juice box. Run out of gas? Leave it where it died. Pretty astounding that these clueless apes managed to hold onto a whole Air Force base with that kind of attitude.

As the sun fell, and they crossed the base on foot looking for something, *anything*, to get them out of Dodge, he found what he thought was the holy grail: a garage. With a fueling station on the side.

"There has to be a working ride in there, Daddy," Kayla said, and he smiled and said yes, yes there probably was, little girl, and she held his hand and he held hers and for a moment, everything felt like it was finally coming together.

Then the garage became like a hive of bees that got kicked over. The doors rolled open. Thuglow's 'soldiers' swarmed into the garage wearing ill-fitting body armor and carrying armament. The Humvees all revved up and started ejecting from the garage like popped zits, one after the other—hell, two drivers managed to smack into each other and treat it like it was nothing.

The vehicles all sped away. Gil's heart fell, and then as he heard the discordant howls of the hunters in the distance, his guts rose to meet his wilting heart and he thought he might throw up the contents of his stomach (which at this point wasn't much more than a shallow pit of acid).

Cecelia's face wore a grim mask. "Oh, god. Is that what I think it is?"

"I suspect so," Gil said. "I don't think running is going to do much good. I think it's time to hide."

THE FIRST ZOMBIES had started to trickle in. And the howls had come again, and this time, they were much closer: somewhere on the base. Out there. In the darkness. Coburn wasn't one to be afraid of the dark; after all, that would be like a great white shark being afraid of the ocean. Even still, he heard that sound, and the blood inside his body went chill and he felt a shiver grapple up his spine. The dog felt it too, tucked in his football grip: from Creampuff's throat came a long, low whine.

The golf-cart—really a decked-out urban camo four-man transport with ruggedized tires and all-wheel-drive—whizzed down the main avenue that cut through the heart of Altus AFB. Thuglow drove, but he sure wasn't keeping much focus. Two zombies held down a girl, chewing into her still-kicking legs like they were a pair of boneless chicken wings. In the distance, machine gun fire and the screams of men dying, swiftly followed by the sound of an explosion. A dead man lay in the streets. Zombies clawed at windows. They began emerging from the shadows on all sides; the avenue was still open, but for how long?

"It's all falling to shit, man," Thuglow said, wide-eyed, barely watching the road. Coburn could see it on the man's face: he was watching his kingdom crushed like a child's wagon under the tires of an 18-wheeler. "Game over."

Coburn was about to smack Thuglow's head hard enough to either knock some sense into it or knock his brain out of it (both represented a certain improvement), but then, down the way about a quarter-mile, the avenue lit up with headlights and the growl of engines as a convoy of trucks and cars came rounding the corner at breakneck speed.

"Those aren't our trucks," Thuglow said, and then, from the back of one of the trucks, a heavy caliber gun opened fire. Bright starburst flashes from the barrel: a guttural *chug chug chug* of bullets. Lead bumblebees dug into the street around them. One of the golf-cart's tires popped. Bullets punched into the front of the vehicle, started taking off the roof in a way that called to mind invisible rats chewing ever-swiftly. A bullet clipped Thuglow's arm, sending up a spray of blood, and another popped a hole in the back of his seat's headrest where he'd been a fraction of a second before. Coburn, seeing that Thuglow was like a deer in headlights, had already grabbed him and was yanking him out of the cart and dragging him bodily toward an austere brick admin building.

Coburn carried Thuglow and the dog around the side of the building in a small alley, and threw the stoner behind an oversized metal dumpster on which one of the King's cronies had spray-painted a pair of cartoon breasts and, above that, the word Tɪᴛs.

By now, the golf-cart—still in sight, about fifty yards off—had turned into a smoking wreck of bullet-riddled junk. The truck convoy barreled up to it, brakes squealing and gravel crunching under tires.

The vampire and the King of the 66 States ducked behind the dumpster.

"They shot me, man," Thuglow said, pulling his hand away from his arm and seeing the palm wet with red. "I'm feeling dizzy."

"That's because you're high as a Jewish holiday," Coburn growled. "You got shot in the arm. Man up, Jennifer."

"Am I going to die?"

"You are if you don't shut that bear-trap you call a mouth."

Then, Thuglow did the unthinkable—he stuck his head out from behind the dumpster. Instantly the machine gun barked bullets, and they *spanged* against the side of the metal trash-bin. Coburn grabbed the King by a fistful of hair and reeled him back in before one of those .50 cals ejected his brain a half-mile outside his skull. "Fuckface! What are you doing?"

"We're invaded," Thuglow said, shaking his head, looking genuinely sad. "I never thought they had the stones. Shoulda known. Shoulda known, bro. They sent that guy and we fucked with him, fucked with him real good, oh, hell."

"Invaded? Guy? What guy? Who's here?"

But Thuglow wasn't answering. He had checked out. His brow heavy with sadness and regret, head shaking like he didn't want to believe any of this, like he just wanted to go back to his hangar, roll a joint, and play pinball forever.

Which meant Coburn had to get a look on his own.

He wished he hadn't.

The sign painted on the door of the lead pick-up was a symbol he'd seen before, though back then he'd seen it stitched on a patch on the shoulders of denim jackets and sports jerseys like they were fucking Boy Scouts earning badges for killing vampires. A hand spread open, palm out, and in the center of the hand, a blazing sun. *The Sons of Man.* Goddamnit.

And there, manning the .50 caliber bolted into the truck bed was the man himself, Benjamin Brickert.

Coburn tucked his head back behind the dumpster just as a flock of bullets tore the corner of the trash-bin to frayed metal ribbons.

Now, the question: did Brickert see him?

The answer came fast. He heard Brickert yell out, "Not our target. Don't waste any more ammo. Go, go, go!" Engines revved, and the convoy of vehicles moved on, disappearing down the street toward the hangars and airstrip.

Brickert didn't see him. Or, at least, didn't identify him. Such was the joy of having a vampire's night-vision: what Coburn could see, others often could not. That also meant Brickert hadn't identified King Brutha Thuglow, either.

Small favors.

"I gotta get to my chopper, man," Thuglow said. "I gotta bail. It's over. The whole thing is over."

"Chopper. What chopper?"

"I got a Bell Twin-Huey UH-1N."

"Yeah. Great. You're telling me you can actually fly that thing?"

"Shit yeah. I can smoke a blunt, drink a box of wine and *still* thread a needle with that bitch. I used to be a pilot." He stared off at a distant point, maudlin. "Once."

"Where's the helicopter now?"

"Back near the hangars. Just off the first airstrip."

Wonderful. Exactly where Brickert was going, by the looks of it. Still, an airlift out of this place? He didn't know dick about helicopters, but he knew one could get them a lot further than hoofing it.

"Needs fuel," Thuglow added. "I... kinda forgot to refuel last time."

"Jesus Christ. Fine. You go and do that. Don't fuck it up." He handed him the dog, who growled. "Take Creampuff with you. You hurt him, I hurt you. Play nice, you two."

"Where are you going?"

"I'm going to find my herd."

KAYLA REMEMBERED HOW it was when the plague first took hold of the nation, and not long after, the world. She remembered long nights in her bedroom, holding a stuffed pink bear that was almost as big as the real thing and staving off nosebleeds with a box of Kleenex. It was bad enough that she'd only recently received the diagnosis of multiple myeloma— in effect, a death sentence. But now the rest of the world had its own walk down death row, and a much faster walk it was, too. At the time of diagnosis, they told her she had six months, *maybe* nine, but suddenly the world was going to Hell—or rather, Hell had come to the world—and just like *that* her six predicted months became a whole lot less.

It was the sounds outside their house in Raleigh, North Carolina, that told her the gig was up, that life in America was officially a thing of the past. Outside, she heard people screaming. Cars smashing into one another. Single rifle pops and later, the chatter of machine gun bullets—those accompanied by squelches from radios, police sirens, even helicopters overhead.

And in the distance, explosions. Gas mains, her father had said, but even she knew it was something far worse. The military were 'quarantining' in their own special way: with munitions, armament and big scary bombs.

This, now, was like that. They'd holed up here in the mess hall, a long building that had been subverted by Thuglow's crew and turned into something that looked more *carnival* than *cafeteria*. Outside, bullets and bombs, the screams of men, the moans of the dead. And worse: the dissonant howls of the hunters that followed them here. But even in that, Kayla found a small modicum of hope: she believed that the hunters were not hunting them but, rather, Coburn. And if they were here, that might mean *he* was here, too.

It was a strange place to be, mentally: she'd written him off and put him aside as traitor to them all. And yet, was that fair? He'd always come through for them. He helped them get through the cannibal roadblock. He'd found them at the farmhouse. Why had she lost faith so quickly?

She wanted to believe. In no small part because Leelee believed. The veterinarian-turned-nurse had changed in these last days—maybe even weeks. Leelee showed bright eyes and a small smile. Like she knew something nobody else knew. Like she believed—no, *knew*—that things were going to work out just fine even if she was the only person who knew it. The look in her eyes, puckish, almost playful, said, *I am the only sane person in this room.*

Occasionally Leelee would reach over, stroke her hair, offer her a tissue. Because now, like before, her nose was bleeding something fierce.

Danny helped, too. He had his arm around her. He kissed her temple. It felt nice.

Outside, the howls of the hunters grew in intensity and volume. They were closer, now. Everyone tensed. Hands seeking weapons. Just in case.

Just then: a sound above. Someone—*something*—on the roof. Crawling.

This is it, she thought. In the roof was a square of dirty plexiglass that served as a skylight: it had long been covered in dust and debris. A shadow appeared at the skylight, darker than the night beyond it. Gil settled in next to Kayla, gun in hand, taking careful aim—

A hand swept across the skylight, wiping a path through the greasy dust.

Coburn's face pressed against the glass. Nose and lips smushed.

The smushed lips twisted into a grin. Kayla couldn't help but smile herself.

"Is that...?" Gil asked. She nodded and eased the weapon down; the skylight lock popped and it swung open.

The vampire dropped down from the darkness.

"Hey now, brown cows," he said, dusting himself off.

Kayla hurried to meet him but then stopped, mustered courage and spite, then stuck her chin out and crossed her arms.

"You *left* us," she said.

His smile faded. "Did not."

"Did too."

"Did *not*."

"Then where *were* you?"

"Under the Humvee. Sun was coming up. Didn't think it'd be a real hot idea if those clowns caught a whiff that a vampire was among them." He paused. "Though, thinking about it, those loons probably would've thought I was cool. Wouldn't have been hard to depose that dope Thuglow and become the vampire king of Route 66. Well, fuck it. Roads not taken and all that."

"Oh," Kayla said. A pang of guilt struck her. She didn't believe. Didn't have faith in their shepherd. Leelee had faith. Why couldn't she? "You were here all along." Gil and Danny came up beside her. Her two men. Cecelia and Ebbie stayed back, uncertain.

"True that," the vampire said. "But if we don't move soon, we're going to end up as either zombie chow or prisoners of the Sons of Man."

The Sons of Man? Kayla was about to ask, but Coburn must've seen the look on her face: "I have no goddamn idea. They just showed up like a bunch of cowboys, shooting the place up. No time to worry about it. We got a helicopter ride waiting for us. Down by the hangar, Thuglow is fueling it up as we—"

A second shadow dropped down from the window, dangling there— Kayla saw a flash of pink as the hunter snatched up the vampire and drew him back up through the skylight. And just like *that*, he was gone.

THE BITCH BEAST slammed Coburn down on the mess hall roof, his body denting the aluminum. Above her, heat lightning flashed purple between clouds, and Coburn saw the horror of what she had become. The hunter—or huntress, as if sex mattered at this point—had changed since last he saw her up close. Flesh vented with ragged tears, eyes bulging and red with blood, layers of teeth like little needles bristling in her distended jaw. Everything was stretched, torn, toughened. She pinned him with claws, opening her mouth and ululating with a pair of serpent's tongues that seemed to battle for supremacy.

Below, Coburn heard a *pop* as a rifle went off—the bullet came up through his chest and into hers. It hurt him. It annoyed her. Even still, it was enough of a distraction for her to loosen her grip on him, and quick as he could manage he rolled over on his belly and looked down through the skylight.

Gil stood below, smoking rifle in his hand. Coburn grunted, waved them on—"Go, go, go! Back to the hangar! To the helipad!"—just before the Bitch Beast dragged him back by the ankles, lifting him up in the air, and slammed him back down onto the roof. The whole mess hall swayed like a drunken sailor, and for half a second Coburn thought the damn building was going to collapse.

It didn't.

Yet.

That changed when he tried to scramble away on his hands and knees, and the Bitch Beast leapt up in the air like a fucking crackaddled jungle tiger and hit him hard, claws-down. The roof couldn't handle the stress. It buckled. And with her claws in his back and her mouth closing on his neck, he felt the whole thing give away in a clamor of tenting metal.

THUGLOW'S HANDS FUMBLED with the keys as he unlocked the gun box he'd left on the helipad. The hose from the fuel truck was already in place, gurgling fuel into the belly of the chopper, and now Thuglow was popping his gun box and emptying weapons into the Twin Huey. Into the chopper he chucked a .45 ACP, an AR-15, a replica of a ninja short sword called a *wakizashi*, a switchblade, a camping hatchet, a hairspray can with a lighter duct-taped to it (*homemade flamethrower for the motherfucking win*, he thought), and a pair of grenades.

He tried to calm himself, tried to see this as a kind of Zen activity—focus on the grenades' waffle-pattern, feel the cool metal of the pistol, imagine doing kick-ass ninja flips with the *wakizashi*. It wasn't working. All around him were the sounds of his kingdom being dismantled—ripped asunder by the hands of the dead and shot to shit by Benjamin Brickert and his self-righteous asshole brigade.

Not far off, he heard terrible shrieks and wails, and a sound like a car forever crashing into another car: the tearing of metal, the shattering of glass.

He had no idea what was going on. Part of him thought, *this is just some kind of flashback. Too much LSD in the desert. None of this is real. This is a nightmare.*

But he couldn't convince himself.

The little dog, who stood at his feet staring holes through him like suddenly he'd try something funny and the dog would have to tear his nuts off, turned from him and started growling. The hackles on the terrier's back bristled.

"Oh shit," he said, fumbling for the pistol. He raised the gun, then realized he forgot to jack the action, and suddenly he was trying to pull back the action but it was awfully stubborn and his hands were slick with sweat—

A hand shot out of the darkness and snatched the gun from his hand.

Then a fist cold-cocked him.

Thuglow tasted blood. He blinked back tears. A man moved over to him, picked him up, and as the tears cleared, he saw his opponent.

"You sonofabitch," Gil said. The old man's face looked like it had been run over by a motorcycle. "You mess with me and my family again, next time I'll do more than break your druggie-device over your fool head."

Thuglow smiled meekly and nodded. "It's cool, man. It's cool."

COBURN STOOD, SHOULDERING off a strip of corrugated metal, just in time to see the Bitch Beast come at him like a freight train. The vampire felt instinct take over, felt the monster inside him kick open the cage door. Blood fueled his limbs, burning hot and bright inside his body, like his heart was a fist of burning coal pumping lava to every extremity.

He stepped to the side as she tore past—but he wasn't content to let her come back around. The bitch had to go. It was time. That meant, he figured, taking out the head. And that meant getting behind her.

As she passed, he hooked his arm out, caught her neck, and leapt up onto her back like a cackling monkey. He covered her eyes with the flat of his hand and blinded her as she bolted forward—straight into a telephone pole. Coburn planted his feet on the ground, slamming her head into the pole again and again—and, just as she was dizzy and howling, threw her down onto her back.

The concrete cracked as her skull hit.

It was time to end this.

He leapt upon her with the ferocity of a coke-addled puma.

She squirmed beneath him, twisting like a snake. Her claws embedded through his jacket into his side but he wasn't having any of it. The rage was in him, red and wet. Fingers curled. His fist cocked. The hand felt hot and swollen as he channeled all the blood he could muster into that limb, turning it into a weapon, an instrument, a fucking *sledgehammer*.

Coburn began hitting her. Not fist-down—not like a punch. But like the way you'd pound on a door, wanting to be let in. He *did* want to be let in. He wanted to get inside her head. Not in a psycho-babble *what-are-you-thinking* way, but in an *open-your-skull-to-turn-your-*

brain-to-treacle way. He smashed in her nose. He shattered the teeth in her mouth. He popped her forehead so hard the skin ripped, black blood bubbled out, the bone pulverized as the concrete beneath her had done.

He felt her skull give.

One more hit, and she was done.

But he didn't see the other three coming.

He'd grown so focused on her that he didn't realize—she was just the first out of the gate, the front line of the attack. The other three hunters came swiftly out of the shadows, loping like wolves. Ranger hit him like a bull, and the world went end-over-end as he rolled into the street. Rupture-Tit grabbed him by the arm and flipped him over— the bone snapped, the ligaments tore—as he crashed into the street, bones and asphalt both cracking. Rain-Slick struggled to get a taste, clawing past the other two to get at him.

And before he knew it, he was pinned to the earth, face up, nose to nose with the Bitch Beast. With ragged claw she dug deep into the meat of his chest and raked downward, leaving behind four fleshy furrows that burned like fire.

Then she receded into shadow as her progeny surrounded him.

And behind them all, a tide of zombies incoming.

The hunters howled, for they had taken their prey.

LEELEE FELT IT in her gut. A tightness. An *itch*. She knew.

"Almost ready to rock," Thuglow said, giving a thumbs-up from on the helipad. Gil stood behind him with the rifle, just in case. Cecelia stood behind him, rubbing the small of his back in gentle circles.

Kayla paced, chewing on her thumbnail while Danny and Ebbie watched, helpless. All of them—except maybe Thuglow—were tense, concentrating elsewhere. They heard the shrieks of the hunters. Heard the sounds of metal tearing, asphalt cracking. The predators had found the vampire.

Leelee knew it in her gut, in her heart, in every fiber.

She went to Kayla and held her hands, then kissed her cheek.

Fact was, Kayla was a special girl. So special, in fact, that a true monster—a blood-hungry thief-of-life, a *vampire* who had committed endless sins and depravities to support his own selfish solipsistic needs—had put all that aside to save her. Time and time again. He had his logic. Calling them moo-cows. Calling them his 'herd.' But Leelee knew that it was a show. A way to puff out his chest like a proud rooster and strut around like *it wasn't no thang*, like none of this invalidated the power of who he was and what he'd done.

But the fact was, his monstrousness would not persevere. It wasn't clear if there was any good in him. It perhaps didn't matter. What mattered was that Kayla *was* good, *was* special, so much so that the vampire fought to save her again and again. Despite what he was. Despite what he'd done. Or maybe because of those things—on that point, Leelee was a bit fuzzy.

On everything else, though, she was clear as Waterford crystal.

She believed things in her heart differently now than she had before. Before, all the world's questions were given over to a kind of shrugging agnosticism—belief was only so useful in the face of facts, of data. Now, though, things were different. The impossible was possible. And Leelee believed beyond the margins of all doubt.

Or maybe it was faith, not belief. Maybe the difference there was that belief was something you suspected, while faith was something you *knew* even without having the facts to back it up.

This, then, was what she knew: The vampire would not make it. Not this time. Some part of him had made those other monsters and now, as the saying went, the chickens had come home to roost. They would tear him apart. And his role in all this would be done.

But she also knew that if he was done, so were they. Not now. But eventually. They still needed him and now he was lost to them.

Unless one of them paid him back for all he'd done.

He'd come for them plenty of times. Now it was her turn to go to him.

The others weren't paying attention. They were occupied with one another, and with the distant sounds of their keeper, their shepherd, being trounced and torn asunder by the hunters that found him.

When nobody was looking, Leelee reached into the helicopter and pilfered both grenades off the seat. Thuglow was crawling into the cockpit and starting to power up the chopper. That meant it was time.

It was dark. They'd never see her leave.

With one grenade in each hand, she sneaked away into the night, ready to do what needed to be done to save the monster.

THE KING WAS not in his castle. Not that he needed to be. Thuglow was, as his name suggested, just a low-class thug. A thug who had taken—or, rather, been given—power that he did not deserve. He was meaningless in the grand scheme of things, but that didn't mean Brickert didn't want to drag the fool back to Kansas and hold him up before the free council and hang him by the neck in front of all.

Shonda kicked over a pinball machine. The glass broke. A silver pinball rolled out and drifted across the hangar.

"What a mess," she said. "It's like a frat-house in here."

Benjamin wrinkled his nose. Smelled like body odor and bong-water in here. He scratched his beard. "He's not here. The rat found a hole. He'll turn up. Meanwhile, we need to start rounding up some tanker trucks and capturing the fuel—after that, we can do a more thorough check, but the fuel is the—"

Somewhere outside, the whine of an engine, the slow-but-certain whirr of rotors. Brickert's sphincter tightened.

"Is that a goddamn helicopter?"

THEY PINNED HIM against the street. Ranger knelt by his wrist, his twin tongues frolicking in the rent flesh. Rupture-Tit hunkered down by his foot, the pant-leg rolled up as her teeth bit open his skin and drank the blood with surprising delicacy, like a Doberman gently chewing open a roll of Lifesavers candy. Rain-Slick lay on the asphalt, belly down, playfully gnawing at the meat of his neck, not so much drinking as *playing*, lapping at it hungrily, giddily.

All the while, his chest burned where the Bitch had marked him.

The Beast watched. A proud mother, perhaps. Waiting for her lessers to feed before she filled her own belly. Whenever the surging tide of zombies tried to get close, she roved and roamed, hissing and clawing at the air to keep them back. And by god, they listened.

Everything Coburn had was fading fast. Blood and energy ebbing.

The hunters were strong. Stronger than he could have ever imagined.

Given that they came from him, he was almost proud. Almost. He wasn't like the Bitch Beast, though, who seemed to be a very good mother. He was a certifiably bad daddy, because he hoped these rotten children of his would catch fire and die.

He had no idea how close his desires hewed to reality.

Maybe twenty feet away, he heard a sound—almost like a full can of soda hitting the asphalt. Zombies turned toward it, moaning. The hunters had little interest.

They had little interest, at least, until it exploded.

The ground shook and a half-dozen undead hit the street, torn to rotten ribbons by hot, angry shrapnel. *That* got everybody's attention. The hunters did not want to share their kill. They did not want to be attacked while feeding. Each leapt free from their prize, snarling, spitting, crouching low to the ground, claws clicking on the macadam.

Coburn, weary, lifted his head, tried to summon his strength.

That was when he saw Leelee. She marched forward despite her limp, chin held high. They always said that pregnant women had a kind of *glow* about them, and Coburn didn't think she was pregnant, but she damn sure had that glow.

Her hands were clutched to her chest. Almost as if she were praying.

The zombies did not go near her. It was like she'd been marked. Marked for *Them*, for the four hunters.

Her eyes met his. In her face: an eerie look of peace. Like a lake whose waters sat completely undisturbed.

The hunters moved toward her. Slow at first, but then with greater speed.

The Bitch Beast strode on two legs. The others loped on all four.

Coburn's hearing picked up a faint sound—a *ting* noise, like a bullet casing hitting the street—but when Leelee smiled and opened her hands a little he knew that the sound was from a grenade's pin being loosed and dropped.

The hunters leapt for her. Unaware. Unrealizing.

Leelee closed her eyes.

The grenade went off.

*   *   *

THEY HEARD THE *whumpf* of the first grenade go off in the distance. Kayla stopped pacing, turned. It was then she knew.

"Where's Leelee?" she asked, but her voice was drowned out in the rising noise of the whirring rotors. All around them, dust and papers and debris swept around as the blades of the chopper gained momentum.

This time she yelled it: "*Where's Leelee?*" But just then: the second grenade detonated.

Suddenly it was chaos.

"We got company!" Thuglow yelled, pointing at headlights growing brighter, fast approaching from the other end of the airstrip. Gil turned, raised his weapon and started firing. Bullets responded in kind, stitching across the ground and coughing up chips of concrete. Gil danced out of the way and leapt into the chopper, waving everyone else in. He helped Kayla in with a hand, and together they started getting everyone on board.

Everyone but Leelee and Coburn.

Thuglow pulled himself into the cockpit with his one good arm. Danny held Kayla close. Between them, Creampuff growled and barked, a steady stream of canine invectives.

Kayla yelled, "We have to wait! For Leelee! For Coburn!" But again her voice was drowned out. Her father tried to hand her a head-set to protect her from the noise but suddenly the helicopter lurched upward like a drunken pelican, and the head-set fell from his hands and went out the open door.

The headlights brightened. Bullets thunked into the side of the helicopter.

Thuglow was screaming something, but Kayla couldn't hear what.

Someone sat down next to her hard, pushing her into Danny. Creampuff scrambled over her lap, and when she turned to see who had shoved her...

Coburn was sitting next to her. He looked like he'd been run through a grain thresher. Neck torn open. Hand in tatters. Foot looking like a pound of ground beef.

Kayla mouthed a word: "Leelee?"

He just shook his head.

* * *

CREAMPUFF SNUGGLED INTO his lap. For a moment, things felt right. A tiny moment in time where all felt okay. Kayla to his right. Dog in his lap.

But it was fast swept away by the undercurrent of imagery that played out in his head. Leelee. Beatific. Happy. At peace. And then erased in a flash, the grenade taking out her legs and ruining her face and without warning she was just a piece of meat and so were the monsters with which she'd surrounded herself.

Coburn had seen lots of bad shit. He'd been the engineer of most of it. He'd seen blood and horror aplenty and it didn't mean squat. To him, the human population of the world comprised nothing but meat-puppets and blood-bags: people to manipulate and motherfuckers to eat. And that was that and never would it be different. Or so he thought.

And then Leelee went and blew herself up.

For him.

That was the part that needled him. That stuck in his mind like a blade. Somebody did something... well, to call it *nice* was the understatement of the year, wasn't it? Like saying 'the ocean is pretty big' or 'Hitler had some issues.' Leelee *died* to save his very existence. He didn't have to twist her mind to do it. He didn't have to threaten her. She destroyed herself so that he could live.

Or, whatever you called the rough approximation of 'life' he possessed.

She was crazy, said the monster's voice inside of him.

But that wasn't it at all. It may have been true; he had no idea and didn't care to speculate on the state of her sanity.

Coburn leaned out of the chopper, feeling the air rush through his hair with rough fingers. The ground began to move away from them as lead thunked into the metal hull of the chopper.

Out there, in a pickup truck, he saw him.

Benjamin Brickert. Long beard. Hollow eyes. Eyes that met his own. Eyes that flashed recognition and echoed rage.

Coburn gave him the finger.

CHAPTER THIRTY-TWO

The End Begins Again

THAT FUCKING VAMPIRE.

Brickert felt the air sucked out of him. He couldn't catch a breath. His temples pounded. His heart felt like it was ready to kick its way out of his chest.

That motherfucking piece-of-shit vampire.

Coburn was supposed to be dead and crispy, crushed by the collapsed floor of that old theater in New York. That was years ago. And now? He was here?

It didn't seem possible. For a moment, Brickert seriously entertained the notion that he had died years ago and that this was Hell. To see that clown-king fleeing in a Twin Huey chopper was one thing. To see that God-forsaken vampire up there with him felt like it was designed to punish him personally.

Brickert manned the .50 cal and again lifted it skyward.

He put the vampire in his sights.

And then he moved the gun to the left. He fired a fusillade of .50 rounds into the ass-end of the chopper. He prayed that those bullets did their job, and it wasn't long before he saw that they did. Out of a trio of holes in the back, fluid sprayed even as the chopper lifted up and gained distance, pressing forward like an eager hummingbird. The bitch was leaking fuel.

Brickert finally found his breath and sucked in a lungful.

"No," he said, grinning. "Fuck *you*, vampire."

THE BITCH BEAST lifted her broken body, rising up out of the carcasses of her brothers, her sisters, her children—what they were she had no name for, no deep understanding, she only realized that once they had been connected, but now they were scraps of meat perforated by searing shards of angry metal.

She, too, had been torn ragged. But they had taken it head-on. Their heads and faces hung on shoulders only barely, turned to pulp and splinters of bone.

They were gone from this world.

She, however, was not. But she needed sustenance, and feeling no more loyalty toward her ruined companions, she knelt down and began to eat of their flesh and drink of their black blood. A glorious and wretched sacrament.

THE SUN WAS coming up, soon.

Coburn could feel it.

So when the warning began going off in the helicopter—an insistent beeping that they could hear even over the chopper's rotors—the vampire did not know what the hell was going on.

But he learned soon enough. Thuglow leaned over the seat, pale, sweaty, and he mouthed a phrase that nobody else could hear but Coburn.

We're leaking fuel.

Shit.

PART FOUR

PENITENT

CHAPTER THIRTY-THREE

Down in the Dark

AFTER A CERTAIN point, it all went away.

Coburn remembered giving Brickert the finger. He recalled the helicopter rising and with it, a deep and thriving hunger deep within him, a hunger for blood and the realization that he was surrounded by blood on all sides, blood in pink skin, blood pushed by pulsing drum beats, blood sticky and wet.

He remembered the fuel alarm. Remembered going down—not a crash landing, not really, but definitely a controlled accelerated descent down into what Thuglow said was Texas but what looked to Coburn like the fucking moon (a wide open expanse, no plants, no trees, just ground cracked and pale like dry skin).

Coburn remembered the sun. A bright liquid lava line at the edge of forever, and then it was all blankets as they swaddled him like some big bloodsucking baby, then dimness, then darkness, then everything went still.

It was then that it all went away.

It was then that he woke up here. In a kitchen. With Rebecca.

Rebecca. With her pig-tails. And the freckles on the bridge of her nose.

And a too-big-for-her men's flannel robe—his robe—so big, then, that she almost disappeared inside of it.

"You like my robe?" she asked. "It's yours. You let me wear it."

"You look like Kayla," he said, his hand inadvertently touching a highball glass of Scotch made cool by a trio of ice cubes gently drifting within.

"Actually," Rebecca said, "*she* looks like me. Isn't that how it works? The someone after is the one who looks like the someone before."

He nodded and smiled. "Yeah. Yeah, I guess that's it."

"So. What are we doing here?"

"I don't know." He lifted the Scotch to his lips. It tasted like blood.

"You remember my name, at least."

"Is that a good thing?"

She smiled. "No, probably not."

The room swiftly brightened: the bulbs in the fixture in the ceiling and above the sink hummed and glowed white hot, blinding him, the humming turning to buzzing, and then as fast as it had come, they dimmed once more.

Someone stood behind Rebecca.

A tall man. Standing in darkness. He emerged from shadow.

Blonde hair slicked back and pressed to his pale scalp. Nose, smashed flat to the left. The upper lip, sneering to the right thanks to a puckered scar from what might've been a cleft lip. He grinned. His teeth were smeared with red, like he'd been eating raspberries.

"Hi, John," Blondie said.

Coburn winced like he'd been stuck with a needle. John. *John.* "John?"

"John Wesley Coburn. We've met before."

"Have we? You know... my name. So what's yours?"

"That, you don't know. That you may never know. I'm still out there, though. Passed through the bowels of life and out on the other fucking side, pushed out like a kidney stone through a tight pisser." Blondie smiled, came up behind Rebecca, started playing with one of her pigtails. Coburn wanted to launch himself across the table, rip his head off. But he couldn't.

"How do I know you're still out there?"

"Easy." The word came not from Blondie but from Rebecca, who was leaning into Blondie's touch like it pleased her. "Because you're still around."

"I don't follow."

"It's one of those old immutable laws," Blondie said, making a face that might've been a grin, might've been a sneer. "Kill the maker and you kill the monsters he made."

"You're my maker."

"Could be, rabbit. Could be."

"The one who turned me into a—"

But then the lights brightened again, everything lost behind a searing white curtain. The ground shook this time. Coburn's—*John's*—body seized tight. But then, like before, it passed.

Rebecca and Blondie were gone. He heard sounds coming from the living room. Coburn grabbed the Scotch. Heard the ice clink around the perimeter of the glass. He stepped into the living room. Saw Rebecca lying on her belly, the robe splayed out like a blanket, her face bathed in the black-and-white glow of the television. Looked like Ed Sullivan. But his face was different: the grin too wide, the eyes black like tar. Every time Ed spoke, flies poured from his mouth.

Rilly big shoe.

The window by Rebecca gently shook, then slid open with nary a sound. A shadow slid into the room, almost liquid, and it became a person: formlessness found shape. Blondie stood behind her.

Coburn tried to move, tried to cry out, but couldn't.

Blondie eased behind her. She popped something into her mouth: rock candy on a wooden stick. Her head bopped left and right. Pigtails bouncing.

The vampire struck. He moved fast, like a praying mantis, his hands around her neck, his fingers ripping open her throat, a gush of red blood on the shag—

"No."

A voice in Coburn's ear. Rebecca was gone. So was Blondie. The blood, however, remained. The TV continued to flicker, now gone to static.

Blondie stood behind him, now. Hands on his shoulders.

"You don't get away that easily," Blondie whispered into his ear.

"Is this how you remember it? Is this what you find when you start moving dirt? You're hiding behind a stalking horse, John. Let's keep moving dirt. Let's try this again."

The world lit up. Bright. White. Hot.

The flash receded like a nuclear tide.

There, again: Rebecca by the TV. Rock candy. The window opened. Liquid shadow turns to Blondie.

A new wrinkle: Coburn was there, too. He could see himself. Sitting at the back of the room in a recliner. Reading a newspaper whose words are gibberish, letters shifting like nervous ants, the corners of the pages wet with red (*what's black and white and red all over—a newspaper*).

Things moved differently this time. Blondie walked not to Rebecca but to the Coburn in the chair—to John Wesley Coburn. Gently, Blondie pulled down the newspaper with an index finger. John Wesley looked shocked, but only for a moment. Blondie's gaze met John Wesley's gaze. Blondie murmured something: hushed, like a prayer.

And then it all leapt forth in terrible fast-forward. Blondie dragged John Wesley off the chair. Bit him. Arc of blood. Rebecca screaming. She ran at him. Beating at Blondie's back. He threw her across the room. Into the TV. John Wesley thrashed on the ground. Blondie tore open his own throat with a twist of his thumb and forefinger, the way you might uncap a cola, then pressed John Wesley's face to his neck.

Fast-forward again. Rebecca sat bound to a kitchen chair. Clothesline pulled taut across her mouth, pulling back her cheeks. Blondie's hand rested gently on John Wesley's back. Blondie pushed him forward.

John Wesley didn't look right. Eyes unfocused. His own neck wound already healed up. When he opened his mouth, two fangs flicked forward. He wasn't John Wesley anymore. *That* was the difference. Now he was Coburn. Just Coburn. Life lost. Identity gone but for a name. The girl in front of him not his daughter, not really, not his blood so much as merely full of blood.

Rebecca screamed.

Coburn tore out her throat and drank.

Again, the world lit up. Bulbs popped, rained sparks. Floorboards groaned as nails bent. Everything white, wiped out, tabula rasa.

*   *   *

A LOW SOUND keened across the open expanse as the moon sat pregnant above, the stars twinkling, and for just a moment, Coburn thought: *it's them, it's the hunters, they're back from the dead again and they're coming to make me pay for what I've done.* But then he realized, it was just the wind.

He smelled blood. Tasted it, too. About ten feet away, the Twin Huey helicopter sat on its haunches, the uneven and rocky ground giving it a crooked look. The rotor above gently turned, moved by the wind.

The front window lay shattered. A hand draped out. Blood, thickened like syrup, collected at the fingertips, drops hanging there but never falling.

A cold feeling ran through Coburn. He felt full. He'd fed.

Oh no.

Coburn found Danny first. He lay draped across a rock like a sacrifice. His throat, torn out. Not far away, Cecelia. Her head had been bashed in. Hair matted with blood and brains. Coburn looked to his hands, saw the fingers and palms flecked with dried blood that flaked away like old paint.

Ebbie was face-down toward the front-end of the chopper. Both wrists, opened. Blood pooling out across dead earth.

The hand sticking out of the helicopter was Thuglow's. In his neck, a gaping hole. In death his head had fallen onto his shoulder; the blood drizzled down his arm and to his fingers.

On the far side of the chopper Coburn found Gil, Kayla and Creampuff. Arranged like a loving father and daughter, with their little terrier. Gil's arm had been draped across Kayla's shoulder. Her head, tilted gently so she rested on her father. The terrier, curled up and sleeping in their lap.

But the scene was imperfect. Gil's mouth was stretched open in a horrible smile, his tongue missing. Creampuff's head was turned too far inward, the neck plainly broken—his body thin, ribs exposed, drained of blood.

And Kayla. Her throat torn out. Like Rebecca's.

Coburn collapsed onto his knees. Inside him, the monster's voice chuckled, then the chuckle rose to a manic cackle, a breathless, riotous laugh that went on and on—above him, the moon looked too bright, the stars seemed to shift and swim, leaving trails of light. He felt the grim humming and buzzing in his own heart as the earth split open and swallowed him whole.

CHAPTER THIRTY-FOUR
Blood Drive

Voices bubbled up out of the darkness. Incomprehensible at first. Like hearing them underwater. But soon, they became clear—

"—coming out of it." A man's voice. Deep. Bass. "I'm almost impressed."

A woman's voice: "Nobody can take that much voltage."

"The Devil has many powers." That voice, he recognized.

Benjamin Brickert.

Coburn opened his eyes. The world swam in and out of focus. Someone—a woman, thick, tough, broad shoulders—shined a bright flashlight into his face.

Beyond her stood two other men. One a gone-to-pasture biker-looking dude in a leather vest. A bit of gut showing from beneath a dusty white wife-beater. Next to him? Brickert. Older. Leaner. Gaunt. Gone was the well-fed whatever-he-was—plumber, brick-layer, dick-sucker, Coburn never knew. His black goatee had gone to a full beard and was now shot through with gray.

"The vampire awakens," Brickert said.

"Fuck you," Coburn said, his words slurring.

"Fuck me? Sure. You want to flip me off again? First time you gave me the bird, I cut off your finger. And boy, didn't that turn out real interesting. Second time you flipped me off, I shot down your chopper. But I guess you can't show me all that piss and vinegar with your hands bound up behind your back."

Coburn tried to move: it was true. His hands were bound up. Tight. Maybe with zip-ties, he didn't know. His feet—barefoot, since he'd never found a goddamn shoe to fit him in the 66 States—were sitting in a tub of water. Not far away, he saw a couple car batteries, wires, alligator clips. They'd been electrocuting him. Brickert learned that trick long ago.

He sat in an alcove made of boxes. The ground bucked and bounced beneath him, beneath everyone. They were in a truck. A moving truck, by the looks of it.

"Do what you want," Coburn said. He shut his eyes, found a cascade of images behind the lids: his daughter Rebecca dead on the floor, Leelee blowing herself to pieces, Kayla sitting propped up with her father and the dog. Plus, a whole host of corpses with Coburn's name on it: dead on bed, dead in tubs, dead in shallow graves. All that blood. His eyes shot open. "I deserve all of it."

Brickert laughed. A genuine laugh. He wiped tears from his eyes.

"I killed them," Coburn said. "I killed them all."

"Who's that?" Brickert asked.

"My daughter, Rebecca. Kayla. Gil. The whole lot of them."

Brickert and Shonda shared a look. "You did, at that. That was a messy scene. You're one mean mother, Coburn."

Brickert backed up. "Redbone," he said to the biker-type. "Let's hit the bloodsucker again. Light him up like Christmas."

Redbone did as told. Came over, got Coburn in the neck with alligator clips. Coburn's world lit up as his body seized. Redbone yanked the clips, bringing a bit of the vampire's flesh with them.

"Shonda," Brickert said to the woman. "Did I ever tell you the story of how me and the vampire met? How he gave me the middle finger, and I chopped that finger off and took it away?"

She nodded. "You did. But good stories like that one, I'll listen to again and again."

"That finger of yours," Brickert said, "wasn't something I meant to take. But it happened and in that moment before I hurried away and the bombs went off, I had what some people call an epiphany. So I snatched up the finger. Bombs went boom. And I thought you were really for-real dead.

"That finger. I wrapped it up nice and tight. Put it on ice and dropped it in a cooler, then took it down the next morning to a friend of mine who worked for a little lab that got a bunch of freelance work from Big Pharma. I gave your finger to my buddy, and, hell, I guess I had some bullshit science-fiction idea in my head that he'd be able to, I dunno, *clone* you or something. That way, we'd be able to find your weaknesses. See what makes you tick-tock, Mister Clock. Like I said: bullshit.

"But my buddy—who belonged to our group and so he was excited to have vampire tissue under his microscope—said he could do experiments at the cellular level. Said your dead cells came back to life, or almost, at least, when put in the presence of red blood cells or blood plasma. He said the mitochondria, which looked inert, would suddenly swell up and go crazy soon as red blood cells even got *near* to them.

"My friend gets this idea. Decides to... I don't know the correct term here, so forgive me, but he decides to 'infuse' the vampire DNA into a simple bacteria. Bacterium? Whatever. Interesting thing: it kills the bacterium. Or seems to, at least. Bacteria stops moving. Cell structures rupture. Mitochondria shrivel up to nothing. And yet—suddenly, the bacterium started to move again. And when put in the presence of other non-infected bacteria, it infects them, and the same thing happens there: pseudo-death, then revivification."

Brickert walked behind Coburn, now. Hiding in the shadows offered by the alcove of boxes. "Now, maybe you know where this story is going, maybe you don't, but like people used to say on the Internet when there *was* an Internet: *spoiler warning*, this is how the zombie apocalypse was born."

"You're a shitty liar," Coburn said. But it was just bravado: Brickert wasn't lying, was he?

"My buddy was the first to get infected. Be honest with you, I don't know how it happened. I wasn't there. None of us were. Maybe he didn't follow procedure like he was supposed to. He always was a little sloppy. Or maybe someone else fucked up. All I know is that lab was ground zero for the infection. And I know that the first zombie I put in the ground was my friend. From that point, it was all over after a couple days. Nobody knew it was coming. Nobody but us. This was the kind of thing we prepared for."

Coburn almost laughed. What a horrible thing to discover, so horrible it was absurd. His middle finger. The progenitor of the zombie apocalypse. A little *fuck-you-attitude* can really change everything. "So when you say you should thank me, you're being sarcastic, that right?"

"What?" Brickert said. "No, no, Coburn. I mean it. Thank you. *Thank you.* When a thing's a little bit broke, you can do a patch-up job to fix it. Table leans a little, you put something under the leg to set it straight again. When a thing's a *whole lot* broke, well. Table has a crack down the middle, only thing you can do is put something better in place. Sometimes, you fix something, you first have to destroy it. That's what happened. The world was getting too awful for its own good, Coburn. It's like before, when God sent the deluge to drown out the iniquities of man."

"Does that mean that God sent me, then?"

Another laugh. "Maybe He did. Mysterious ways and all that." Brickert mussed up Coburn's hair—a crass, almost fatherly gesture. "Jeez, Coburn. This has been a real bad night for you. Chopper crashed. Killed your friends. Realized that you killed most of the known world just by flipping it the bird. There's an old myth that vampires can't see themselves in mirrors. It's not true, obviously, as I'm sure you know. At least, it's not true in the technical sense. But you look a little deeper, maybe it is true. Maybe the vampire isn't supposed to see what he really is, because then what does he become? What happens when the monster sees himself in the mirror for the first time?" He got right up in Coburn's face, unafraid. "Now you see yourself? That right? Bet you don't like what you see, vampire. Bet you don't like the Devil staring back."

Coburn could've moved. Could've lurched forward, bit him right in the face, got a taste of blood. But he didn't have it in him. He hated Brickert. But that hate had a softer edge than he expected. Almost like his heart just wasn't in it. The man detested Coburn for what he was: a monster. It was certainly earned.

He was, after all, the creature that killed the world.

CHAPTER THIRTY-FIVE

Putrid Frequencies

DOWN IN THE dark once more. They tortured him with electricity. They beat him. They cut on him. When day came they shoved him in a box; sometimes they pulled his hand and held it out the door, let it burn up, let it char to a stump that looked like a marshmallow held too long over the campfire. Mostly, though, Coburn drifted down in the murky depths of his own mind. Horrors and nightmares waited down there. Faces swimming up: Kayla, Blondie, Rebecca. A distant dog—the yips and yaps of a rat terrier—barking. The darkness turned red as blood before clouding back to squid-ink black.

Somewhere down there, a thread. Down below everything else, it flicked and twitched like loose fabric from a fraying sweater hanging out to dry in a hard wind—and when Coburn reached for it, he discovered that it was familiar.

It was pink.

He pulled on it, and he felt the darkness swivel toward him. Like a pair of wolf's eyes noticing its prey.

There she was: the Bitch Beast. Not bodily. He couldn't even see her. But he could *feel* her. Searching for him. At first he didn't understand, but then the connection, which felt so intimate, like a coil of intestine shared between two bodies, became clear.

She's mine. I made her. Then, to her: *I made you.*

In the darkness, she howled in protest.

He could feel her anger. It rose up like bile in a thermometer. Her scorn, her hatred, her hunger. The ragged wound she left him across his chest suddenly felt like it caught fire, like someone had upended a pot of scalding water there—her rage made manifest, her mark on his skin alive with pain. She wanted to tear him apart the way her own brothers and sisters had been torn asunder. He saw in her mind, saw her eating the other hunters, gaining their power and then sharing it with others in turn: tilting back zombie heads, vomiting black blood and dead flesh into their mouths, making more of them, giving of herself as much as she could give.

Coburn could feel them, too—though not as completely. They were hard to grasp, like seed motes floating through the air, evading touch.

But the Bitch Beast, she was as bright as a bonfire.

Her desperation was laid bare like a bone stripped of meat. When he had fled, she had lost the trail: Coburn's scent had been on the ground before, but now it was in the air, dispersed, and when the time came for her to hunt him she was unable to find the trail. She did not know of the thread.

Not before now.

Coburn looked at what had become of everything. He'd sown so many seeds of horror. And now, the worst of it all lived in his dead heart. Guilt. Shame. Grief. These were not things he understood, and now that he was feeling them it was like being burned for the first time—it was a child's first comprehension of pain, and that made it a thousand times worse. He could not dull the sensation. It throbbed, as alive as anything, certainly more alive than he.

Everything was lost.

And so Coburn reached and grabbed a hold of that pink thread that tied around the Bitch Beast's primitive mind like a string around a pinky finger, and he pulled on it hard. He told her:

Here I am. You want me, you come and get me. You can have me. You can have my blood. You can tear me and the rest of the world to pieces.

She howled in response. Not a howl of rage, but a howl of desire, of celebration, a signal that the hunt was back on.

CHAPTER THIRTY-SIX
City of the Dead

COBURN AWOKE TO the sound of gunfire. Not steady. Just a few shots: *pop, pop, pop.* He didn't know how long it had been. How long he had been down in the dark with her. Did that just happen? Was it hours ago? Days? Years? As a vampire, that was something he genuinely had to worry about: theoretical eternity made such lapses in time-keeping possible.

He lay on his side in the moving truck, still surrounded by boxes. At his back he heard the clomping boot-steps of someone big: probably Redbone, by the sound of it. Redbone, the fat biker in the too-tight wife-beater, was his constant companion, a steady presence whenever he rose from consciousness.

Coburn tried to crane his neck to see—his hands were still bound behind his back, and his feet were similarly trussed with zip-ties, obliterating any mobility he hoped to have—and as he did, the skin around his neck and jawline cracked. It sounded like a rib of celery bending and snapping.

It was his skin. His whole body was drying out like a corpse under the vigilant eye of the desert sun. He was a man without fluids, a creature without blood: the end of that road was clear. Soon he'd dry out entirely, turn crispy as a Kafka roach, and then be naught but a shattered husk, an exoskeleton on par with the remnant shell of a seventeen-year-old-cicada. It wasn't a total death, but the transformation would still strip him down, his existence turned inert. Just as he had been beneath the collapsed floor of that theater back in Manhattan.

He still managed to crane his head—despite sounds that called to mind someone chewing through crunchy fried chicken—and look at whoever was moving around behind him. Sure enough, it was Redbone. Coburn saw his boots: they were steel-toe workboots, like you might see on a construction site.

"Those look about my size," Coburn croaked.

Redbone looked down at him, grunted.

"I'm just saying. Nice boots."

"Don't get any ideas," Redbone warned. He heaved another car battery up onto one of the boxes, then patted it the way you would a good dog.

Coburn tried to laugh, but what came out sounded like he was gargling glass. "I got ideas, but no way to work 'em. I haven't eaten in forever. Don't suppose you feel like giving me a taste."

"Fuck your mother."

"Guess that's a *no.*" Something tickled at the back of Coburn's mind. A little scratching finger, entreating him forward. His head was too foggy to make much sense of it. He ignored it. Outside, more gunshots popping off. "Hell are we?"

Redbone stared down at him, not sure he should answer, but Coburn could see the acquiescence cross the man's face, an attitude of *eh, fuck it.* "Los Angeles."

"Los Angeles."

"Did I stutter?"

"Might as well have. I thought we were going to Kansas." He noticed then that the truck wasn't even moving anymore. They'd stopped. Again, that tickle at the back of his brain.

"We'll drag you back to Kansas soon enough, vampire. Gonna make an example of you in front of all our people. Let them know that the authority of the Sons of Man is total and complete."

"Uh-huh. But why are we in Los Angeles?"

"Not your business. Curiosity killed the cat, you know."

"And what'd it do to the vampire?"

Redbone grinned. "Got his ass electrocuted." He held up the two alligator clips, tapped them together, got a few sparks arcing. More gunshots outside: these coming faster, more frequent, before cooling off.

The tickle at the back of Coburn's head became more insistent, so much so that it was more like an irritating *flick* or even a swat.

A question suddenly entered his mind:

Why am I hungry?

He shouldn't have been. He'd had a last meal. Kayla, Gil, the others: a blood-gorging orgy. The undead crucible that was his flesh should've been *bloated* with the red stuff. When he'd awoken in the truck with Brickert, and even now, his flesh in places was still disrupted where the hunters took him: neck, wrist, foot. He hadn't healed up properly yet. But why? If he killed those others and guzzled their blood like fruit punch, those wounds should be all closed up.

Further, the ragged wound across his chest—his reward from battling the Bitch Beast—remained open and suppurating.

Frankly, he shouldn't even *be* in this situation if he had consumed such a *grand guignol* meal like that. That chest wound especially should have long healed over. In fact—did he even have the wound when he killed the others?

When he *remembered* killing the others?

Through his veins, an icy blast of realization. No, he didn't.

In his vision, that wound was healed.

Which meant—

They weren't dead. Were they? Kayla. Gil. Ebbie, Cecelia, Creampuff, maybe even Thuglow. That vision of them—it was just that. A vision. A dream. No. A *nightmare.*

Hope, sickly sweet, gurgled in his dead heart.

He was then forced to contemplate the other puzzle piece: Los Angeles.

Why here?

It was where they'd been headed all along. To Los Angeles. To find the lab. To take Kayla, to make her blood part of the cure. Brickert brought them here. He was their escort. He did what Coburn could not: he shepherded them forth, got them to where they needed to go. The vampire had been wrong all along. The Sons of Man weren't trying to hurt them. Well, they were trying to hurt *him*, okay, sure. But their interests were human interests. Not like him. Him with his selfish hungers and callous games. Brickert was doing the right thing.

Of course, it all made sense: the Sons of Man were fighting for people this whole time, weren't they? They were trying to help Kayla. Help her by keeping the monster out of the equation.

Well, shit.

He was about to explain to Redbone just how funny—not funny *ha-ha*, exactly, but funny *ironic*—all of this was, but he didn't get the chance.

Outside, a familiar shriek, a banshee's cry:

The Bitch Beast was here. But not just her. Other monstrous howls rose up after hers: one, then two, then three, and soon there were so many keening all at once that Coburn couldn't even count.

He had summoned her here. And she had brought friends.

HER BODY, AN infinite sacrament. It was a thing she learned, not a thing she realized from the beginning when she was once again gifted with a kind of life on the streets of New York City. Then, and for long after, she believed that to sustain herself, to ease the hunger within, *to create more like her*, it was necessary to have the blood of her maker: the vampire.

But then came the night when her three siblings were eradicated by that weak, limping *human*. That vile act was a secret blessing, for she learned that she was able to eat of their flesh and feel sustained. It helped to heal her. It was like a key turning in a difficult lock, and suddenly it opened to her.

The next night, when she had healed up entirely, she took her claws and ripped a piece of meat off her own body—a pound of flesh in the form of one of her bloated, blistering teats—and fed it to one of her lesser cousins, the stumbling, shambling fools unaware of their own potential for greatness. That zombie—a woman in medical scrubs—

hit the ground writhing, her body shifting, the bones popping, her eyes opening, no longer as a mere rotting thing but as one of the hunters, with long claws and needled teeth.

Her body began to heal the flesh she'd stolen from herself.

She could take her meat. Feed it to others. Make more of herself. And heal the void. The others could do the same.

Her body was therefore infinite. Their potential ranks, innumerable.

It was then that she began to move, to hunt the vampire once more: no longer only to take his blood (for she still desired it, its taste unparalleled in her mouth) but also to punish him and tear him apart. It was as primitive as man's need to blaspheme God, this urge to spit in the face of one's maker.

Ah, but his trail was gone.

Her and her growing army of undead, inhuman hunters roamed without a meaningful direction, but then came the night in the Sonoran that she heard the vampire calling to her in the void of her mind. They were connected. Another thing she had not known but needed to learn.

She no longer needed to scent his trail. Once he pulled that thread and brought her awareness to him, she could suddenly *sense* him out there. Like a fly buzzing in a far-off room.

THE FEVER WAS getting worse. Not like Kayla had a thermometer or anything, but she could tell that it was hitting her a lot harder than it had even a few hours before, when they first rolled into the city. Everything hurt. Her legs trembled. Her spine felt like it was an antenna drawing to it a signal composed only of electric misery.

Inside the building at 1100 Wilshire, she stood propped up between Danny and Gil. Her head felt like a skillet. Her brain, a slow-cooking egg.

Outside, one of the Sons of Man sentries popped off some rounds from one of the .50 calibers bolted to the back of a pick-up truck as Benjamin and Shonda worked to pull the metal gate back down behind the door.

Somewhere up above them, in the top of this tower of glass and steel, waited the GeneTech lab. Or so Kayla hoped. Though the way she was feeling, she didn't even know if she was going to make it up there—the elevators were damn sure out of commission, which meant walking thirty-seven flights. That was a lot of stairs, and Kayla didn't know if she'd have been able to walk them two years ago, much less today.

Brickert had popped the padlock on the door-gate with a pair of heavy gauge bolt cutters, but had nothing to replace it with. "Don't want any rotters taking advantage of the opportunity," he said. Even though they had a semi-circle of Sons of Man vehicles—half the convoy that invaded Altus AFB—protecting the front, it still behooved them, he said, to keep this building locked tight.

He called for a screwdriver, then used that to stick through the hole. It was enough to keep the gate shut. A living human would be able to figure out how to remove the screwdriver, he said. Hell, a monkey could've done it. But a rotter didn't have the presence of mind to consider it, not even by accident.

The lobby of the building was well-kept, for the apocalypse. Most of Los Angeles outside looked like a ghost town, except, of course, for the throngs of zombies they passed, throngs chewed apart by the barking fifty-cal. Whole city was dirty, decrepit. Tattoo parlors and dumpling houses and movie theaters, all broken and sagging like slumped-over corpses. Here, though, the lobby wasn't exactly clean— the beams of their flashlights showed an infinity of dust motes drifting through the air like snow—but nothing had been *ruined*. It looked merely abandoned, which again gave Kayla some small comfort.

She sat down in one of the lobby chairs—a plush red-leather affair— and found herself shaking. Another bout of chills.

"I wish Leelee were here," she said, teeth chattering. Danny petted her head.

"Here," Benjamin said, turning his palm over and shining his flashlight onto it. Three white pills sat in the center. "The last of the aspirin."

He snapped his fingers, flagged Shonda over. She handed him some water without him saying a word. All along Kayla noticed the two of them were in sync. They didn't seem to be lovers or anything. They weren't even all that friendly; their rapport by all accounts was based on respect and honor. But it was a strong bedrock just the same.

Kayla didn't trust either of them.

Everyone else seemed on board but her and Gil. Even Danny gave a non-committal shrug when, a week before, Brickert suggested he help them get out to Los Angeles to find what they were looking for. When his soldiers showed up at their downed helicopter late that morning, there came a sense of uncertainty about what was going to happen. The Sons of Man didn't look like a cozy bunch: they were hard-edged home-brew soldiers, and most of them seemed ready to lock-and-load without a moment's hesitation.

But Brickert had done a lot to allay their fears. He told them he was just an ordinary man trying to make his way, and keep humanity safe. So when the time came that Ebbie spilled their intention—to get to Los Angeles and get a sample of Kayla's blood to the scientists still reportedly working on a cure—Benjamin seemed enlivened. He said that this was good news—'gospel,' he called it—and said that he felt it was his job to carry the ball the rest of the way. Which meant helping them get to the West Coast to complete—again, his words—'God's mission.'

Kayla wasn't so sure. The way he treated Thuglow, for instance. He didn't hit him or say anything—but the way he grabbed him, hoisted him up, it looked like it hurt. And through clenched teeth he sent Thuglow with the other half of the convoy, the half that headed back north toward the Sons' home territory in Kansas. Not that Kayla had any love for the Clown King of Nowheresville, given that he tried to force her into underage prostitution—but even so, he *did* fly them out of there and when she saw Shonda throw him into the back of a covered truck, she had a strong suspicion Thuglow's days could be counted on two hands. Maybe one.

But the way they handled Coburn? That was even more telling. Coburn was asleep, or dead, or whatever happened to him when the sun rose. He slumbered in the shadow of the helicopter, swaddled in a trio of blankets they'd found inside it. Brickert didn't say anything; he and Shonda just loaded the vampire into the one moving truck. Brickert said they'd handle him. Said he could be dangerous, given how hungry he was, said, "We'll take good care of Coburn." It was the look in his eye, though, that got Kayla. A brightness. Excitement. Victory living in the curled up edges of his smile.

All along the way, as the convoy traveled long desert highways through Texas, New Mexico, Arizona, Brickert kept avoiding the subject of the vampire. Whenever she pressed him on it, he said that the vampire 'wasn't doing well,' that whatever he tangled with 'left him pretty broken.' At one point, Brickert tried to persuade her how dangerous it was being buddies with one of the blood-sucking dead, but she balked, got angry, spat on the ground. That was the last he spoke to her about it. For the rest of the trip, he always rode in a different truck.

It was because of all this that Kayla wouldn't tell him the address of the labs. She told him it was in downtown Los Angeles, but that was it. She'd give him the address when they got there. He seemed reticent at first but eventually said okay, stopped pressing her on it.

And now here they were. The fever had been wearing her down for the last day or so. Rubbing her raw, and now she felt like an exposed nerve. Every little blast of air, every footstep, they all reverberated through her, awoke pain deep in her marrow.

"What floor?" Brickert asked as Kayla swallowed the aspirin.

"The thirty-seventh, I think."

"That's a long way up. Can you make it?"

"I can," she lied.

"We can carry you."

"I *said* I can make it," she said, scowling. She stood up, waving away all hands trying to help her. "Let's go, time's wasting."

By the time the screams and wails of the hunters rose up across the streets of downtown Los Angeles, they were already in the echo chamber of the stairwell, unable to hear anything beyond their own feet clomping on the steps.

By the fifteenth floor, Ebbie couldn't do it anymore. He was proud of himself that he made it this far. Dragging several hundred pounds of flesh up the stairwell of an office building was no easy task, but he'd gone a lot further than he figured on. That made him feel pretty damn good, even as he poured buckets of sweat and felt like his legs were about to catch fire. Kayla looked worse—actually, she looked like ten pounds of hell in a two-pound bucket—but she kept on going and that was what gave him confidence.

He sat down on the step, panting, telling everybody to keep going. He told them he'd catch up, take it one floor at a time.

"I'll see you at the top," he told them. He kissed Kayla on the cheek. Cecelia came and gave him a hug, which surprised him. She'd been a lot nicer on the whole since Oklahoma, though. He shook Gil's hand. Danny's, too.

Brickert said, "We'll leave someone with you, just in case." He peeled off one of his soldiers, a smaller guy who looked like he could've come out of the Sopranos: slick-back black hair, an owl's beak nose, dark little eyes. Joey, Ebbie thought his name was.

Ebbie bid them adieu.

He and Joey didn't speak much. Joey just kept watching him. Ebbie talked, instead, just filled the air with chatter. He liked to talk. Especially to new people. Ten, maybe fifteen minutes later, with the sounds of the footsteps above them having receded and stopped, Ebbie heard the loud click and clatter of a door opening, and then the footsteps were gone.

"I think they made it," Ebbie said. "That's good. That's real good."

"Yeah," Joey said, smiling.

"I think I'd like to take a shot at another couple flights?"

"No prob," Joey said. "Let me help you up."

Ebbie started to get up and put out his hand, but Joey didn't take it. He looked up to see why, and found himself staring down the barrel of a small .380 pistol. "I don't understand."

Joey shrugged, then shot Ebbie in the head.

SOMETHING STILL WASN'T right, Coburn thought. And it wasn't just the howls outside, the cacophony of monsters calling to him.

It was something else.

Brickert had thanked him.

He'd said, "the world was getting too awful for its own good, Coburn. It's like before, when God sent the deluge to drown out the iniquities of man."

The zombie pandemic. The resultant apocalypse. Brickert *wanted* those things. Was pleased as punch that they'd happened. So why bring Kayla and the others here where they'd aim for a cure?

Brickert didn't bring them here to cure it. He brought them here to stop the cure.

Outside, the howls came closer and closer. Wouldn't be long before they'd be on top of them, tearing this convoy to pieces.

Coburn had to move.

But his body was dried out. Hands and feet bound. Not enough strength to do shit about any of it. Most he could move was his head.

"What is that?" Redbone asked. He set down the alligator clamps, drew a Glock pistol and snapped back the action.

Think, you stupid motherfucker, think.

Redbone took a step forward.

Nice boots, Coburn had said.

That was it.

No way he was ever going to bite through those things. The leather was tough. Meant to withstand a beating. But he didn't *have* to bite through the leather. This didn't require brute force, but rather just a little finesse.

With a crackle of crisp skin, Coburn moved fast, before Redbone took another step, and he missed his window: he opened his mouth, wrapped it around the shoelace, and jerked his head back. The shoe came untied.

"Boot's untied," Coburn said, hoarse.

It was a natural inclination, a reflex built into children by over-protective parents: *tie your shoes or you'll trip and fall into traffic and then a bear will eat you.* So Redbone, without thinking, muttered a profanity, set down the gun, and bent over at his waist to tie his shoe.

Coburn could practically hear the man's heartbeat drumming in his neck.

The vampire launched himself forward, clamped his mouth on the biker's neck, and began to drink. The sound of the blood filling his body dwarfed Redbone's screams and drowned out the howls of the fast-approaching damned.

*   *   *

THE THIRTY-SEVENTH FLOOR.

Down a hallway lay several doors. The Rush Agency. Gershowitz Insurance. Something called StarPortraits, Inc. And at the end of the hall, on a simple placard, the words: GeneTech Labs, LLC.

The door had no lock, but a keypad and biometric scanner. Above the door hung a small spherical camera no bigger than a golf ball.

As they approached—Brickert, Shonda and three other soldiers flanked by Gil, Danny, Cecelia and Kayla—the camera blinked red, then turned like an eyeball toward them.

"They have power," Brickert said. "But just to their lab. Not to anywhere else in the—" He stopped, looked at Kayla. His face, aghast. He fished in his front pocket for a red paisley handkerchief.

"What?" she asked.

Gil tilted her chin toward him. "Oh, Kayla. Your nose."

She dragged her forearm across it without thinking. It came away wet with a bright smear of red. Panicked, Kayla took the handkerchief and held it up to her nose. Her head suddenly spun. She almost fell, but Danny and Gil caught her.

"Told you we should've helped you up those stairs," Brickert said. Gone was his smile. "Well, can't do anything about it now." He instead turned his attention to the camera. "My name is Benjamin Brickert. I'm the head of Sons of Man, who have settlements across the Kansas territory. We have a girl with us, a girl who—"

Kayla's legs went out from under her. She hit the floor before Gil and Danny could stop her. Next thing she knew, she was on her hands and knees, throwing up—no food, just bile spattering onto the gray berber. Out in the stairwell, she thought she heard something, something that might've been a gunshot, but it was too distant, too hard to tell, and before she could say anything—

A speaker clicked on. A woman's voice, tinny, replied:

"She's sick."

"She's not sick!" Gil said, pushing his way to the door.

"We do not have a cure for the contagion," the woman's voice continued. Her words were hard-edged, but contained a morsel of remorse. "We cannot help the girl. Please remove yourselves from the building."

"It's not the plague," Gil said, pleading. "It's multiple myeloma. She's got cancer. It's a cancer of the plasma—"

"I already know what it is," the voice replied, "and I don't believe you. Please remove yourselves from the building."

"Her blood. Her blood cures the plague. We've come a long way. You have to listen to me."

Kayla looked up from her place on the floor. Her damp hair hung in her face. Her father was impassioned in a way she'd not seen in a very long time. He sounded, in fact, like he was ready to cry. Even more surprising: the fact that Cecelia joined him.

"It's true!" Cecelia added. "It does cure the infection. Maybe you can make some kind of cure from it, some kind of wonder-drug—"

"Some kind of vaccine," Gil said.

"Vaccine, yeah. We came all the way from the East Coast. You wouldn't believe what we've been through." Cecelia started pounding on the door. "Open this goddamn door, you stupid bitch." *That* was the Cecelia Kayla knew.

Brickert shoved her out of the way. "Let's blow it."

He nodded to Shonda, who moved behind Kayla, picked her up and started moving her to one of the side offices. She tried a few doors, found one—the insurance company—that opened.

"*Wait*," Kayla said. "I don't understand, what's happening?"

Shonda pushed her inside. Kayla cried for her father as Shonda followed her inside the office, and slammed the door shut.

"Quit your crying, girl," Shonda said, then pulled a pistol.

COBURN SHOOK LIKE a dog with fleas. Dried skin flaked off him like meaty flecks of dandruff. Redbone lay still on the floor, *deflated* by more than a little. Just because he was pissed, he picked up the car battery and dropped it on the dumb fucker's head. Then he stole his boots.

He had to admit, he felt a little like his old self again. But different, too. Better, even. Like he had a purpose. A real purpose. Turned out, he'd had it for a while now, ever since he'd met the girl, but he'd been pretending that wasn't true.

Now he knew the truth.

With one of his new boots, he kicked open the back door of the truck.

The dark street of downtown Los Angeles awaited. A machine gun nearby chattered bullets. Echoing over the dead city came the discordant calls of the coming hunters. It wasn't long before Coburn saw them: emerging from around the corner across a strip mall, it was like something he'd seen on a nature program, the way that a big pack of wolves ran across an open field, shoulder to shoulder, driven by their persistent need to feed. This was like that, but bigger. Not a pack of wolves but big as a whole goddamn herd of buffalo: dozens of them, maybe hundreds. Not zombies. But *hunters*. Evolved. Mutated. Damned.

Coburn leapt from the back of the truck, bolted toward the building. Saw that while the front doors and windows were all shattered, beyond them a metal gate had been drawn down.

No time for finesse.

He stuck out his shoulder, pushed blood to his legs, then crashed through it.

GIL HAD A gun, and nobody knew it. Well, nobody but Kayla, because he showed it to her not long after he stole it out of one of the trucks. He didn't pull it, not yet, because once he did that, the stakes changed. But he was ready. The weight of the gun was heavy at the base of his spine where it sat tucked in his pants.

"No, no, look," Brickert was saying, pointing to the door. One of the soldiers, a jack-booted thug with an Irish red faux-hawk, tried to go at the door with a crowbar he'd brought, but Ben stopped him. He pointed to marks along the frame and edge of the door. "Bullet holes here. Axe marks here. Someone already tried to get in. This door is fortified. Like I said, we need to blow it."

The other soldiers kept Cecelia, Danny and Gil back against the wall. Faux-hawk dropped a long duffel and from it withdrew a handful of empty shotgun shells that had been shoved together, forming a closed tube, a cap on each end. From each capsule came a little fuse. Together, Faux-hawk and Brickert began duct-taping these shells against the edge of the door, then Faux-hawk unspooled some det cord, cut a length of it, and tied each little bomb fuse to the longer length so it was all connected. Brickert gave it a once-over, offered a satisfactory nod.

"This is wrong," Gil said. "This isn't the way. We blow our way in there, they're going to see us as intruders. They're going to—"

Brickert stomped over, pointed a long-barreled .357 Colt Python at Gil's face. "Shut up, Gil. You're not giving the orders." He turned to Faux-hawk. "Blow it."

Faux-hawk flipped open a Zippo with the American flag on it, struck a flame with a snap of his fingers, then touched the fire to the cord.

The fuse sizzled.

That was when everything really went to shit. Cecelia stepped in between Brickert's gun and Gil and she thrust her chest out and sneered.

"Don't you point your gun at my boyfriend," she said, proud.

Brickert shrugged, then shot her in the heart. Gil screamed. Cecelia dropped. The fuse struck the shotgun shells, each a second after the last, and a series of small deafening pops filled the room: *pop, pop, pop, pop.* The door fell off its hinges as the air filled with what smelled like the acrid stink of burned bleach.

But then Gil was sidestepping, his own .38 snubnose already in his hand, and the revolver was barking bullets as he backpedaled through the stairwell door.

BRICKERT DIDN'T REALLY intend to show his hand so soon. Wasn't supposed to happen like this, but like the saying went, no plan survived contact with the enemy. And Brickert, well. He was forever besieged by enemies.

He'd never planned to help the girl 'save the world' or whatever bullshit illusion she had going on. What mattered was that she lead him to this lab, these people. Brickert planned on putting a stop to this 'cure.'

The world was as it was because God demanded it be this way.

Same as the Flood, same as God tearing down the Tower of Babel. God had a plan and that plan involved plagues—whether it was a plague of locusts or a plague of the dead. It wasn't for man to intervene with his "science." Hell, it was science that got everybody into this mess to begin with.

Besides, if the Sons of Man were able to get hold of that cure for themselves, well, all the better. Just to be sure that it was in the hands of righteous men. Those who deserved the cure would get it. Those that didn't would suffer and die as God had decided.

Simple enough.

Now they'd blown the door, killed the one bitch, and if everything had gone according to plan, Joey'd finished up with the fat fuck. And now that the old man had escaped back down the stairs, Joey would take care of him, too.

Fine. Whatever. His mother used to say, "Shit happens, but shit comes out in the wash."

He checked the door where Shonda and the girl had gone. Still closed. Good. He wanted Kayla kept alive. In the instance that what she said she could do was real, then she'd be a real prize to bring back to Kansas. Actually, Ben had entertained the idea of keeping Gil alive, too, if only to calm her down. That, it seemed, was no longer an option.

Where was the mute kid, though? Tommy? Denny? Danny? Whatever his fucking name was. Ben looked around. Saw Carlos standing there to his left, and over closer to the door stood Ray-Ray with his red shock of an almost-mohawk. "Ray-Ray, lock and load, let's take the lab."

But Ray-Ray staggered forward, itching his stomach like a man who just woke up from a nap. When his hand came away, it came away bloody.

"Old fucker tagged me," Ray-Ray said.

Then he fell forward, faceplanting into the carpet. Bomb smoke whirling around him in artful spirals.

SHONDA HAD THE gun pointed at Kayla. She ordered the girl around the far side of the desk, but when she told her to sit in the chair, Kayla wouldn't.

"You sit in that damn chair," Shonda said. "Don't make me shoot you."

"Go to Hell."

Kayla glanced down to her left and right, looking for something, *anything*, to help her out here. Her nose was bleeding something fierce now, not just down her front but also down the back of her throat. It almost gagged her.

Then her eyes caught something. Sitting in a half-open desk drawer. Outside the door, the gun fired, the bombs went off.

It was enough. Shonda flicked her attention toward the door. Kayla remembered something that Coburn had said long ago:

The blood is the life, baby.

Indeed. Kayla grabbed a silver letter opener from the desk drawer, clambered up over the desk, and just as Shonda was turning back toward her, she spit a lung-gusting spray of her own blood into Shonda's mouth and eyes.

Shonda fired the gun but the bullet went wide, smacking into the drywall—Kayla fell forward into the woman, stabbing her in the chest with the letter opener.

AT FIRST GIL thought the blood on his chest was all Cecelia's, and his mind replayed that horror again and again as her body rocked and fell into him—the poor girl, the poor, sweet girl. A part of him knew she wasn't sweet, not really, but he also knew that the life she led made her the girl she was. He knew that she was starting to change, starting to figure out how to be a person and not a user, not an abuser. And now she was dead, her journey cut unmercifully short.

But when Gil started firing and backed out into the stairwell, he almost collapsed down the steps. He found it hard to get a breath suddenly, and pain radiated out from his shoulder into his arms and neck.

The bullet had gone through Cecelia and struck him in the shoulder. A small part of him thought, *shit, that's poetic*, but it wasn't poetic. It was tragic, was what it was. Plus, his daughter was still in there.

He had to go back in. Had to get her. At any cost. Even his own life.

Gil leaned against the railing, overlooking the steps down. Catching his breath. But then a dark shape ascended the steps.

Joey. The soldier that Ben had left behind.

He smiled at Gil, a sociopathic smirk, then drew sight on his .380.

The sound of his neck breaking echoed through the stairwell. A dark shadow—a blur, really—whirled up beside him like some kind of ghost, and Joey's head spun around on his neck like a cap on a soda bottle.

Joey dropped, but Coburn caught him, then threw the body down the stairs.

Coburn leapt up, caught the railing, and hoisted himself over it next to Gil.

"It all went wrong," Gil croaked.

Coburn nodded, grim. "Then we better go fix it."

KAYLA EMERGED FROM the office, wet with her own blood and Shonda's. The woman lay dead inside the office. She'd fallen on Kayla, choking her, but as she eased forward, she pushed the letter opener deeper into her own chest until it punctured something important. Heart, lungs, didn't matter. Her eyes clouded over and that was that.

Her ears were ringing. Her eyes stung from the smoke in the air. Kayla, as numb and confused as a zombie, stumbled forward, saw Cecelia's body laying still. Sadness rose up in her like a storm. She saw the lab door had been blown off its hinges and shuffled through the doorway.

Ahead of her, a woman screaming. A man yelling. Gunshots.

She stepped through the haze and moved deeper into the lab.

Cubicles to her right. A young man in a black t-shirt lay dead across a desk, a microscope under his unmoving arm.

To her left, open lab space. Tables. Centrifuges. Whiteboards. Glass door. Blood sprayed up on the glass. She could see a pair of feet. Loafers askew. The rest of the body hidden behind a table and chairs.

She staggered ahead, the fog of smoke thinning out.

Ahead stood Ben and one of his fellow soldiers. Ben pointed his gun at the chest of an older woman with graying dark hair and a lab coat.

The gun went off. The bullet bloomed in the woman's chest like a red rose, and she fell over an office chair, dead.

Kayla screamed.

The other soldier—Carlos—saw her, raised his own gun.

His head snapped back as a bullet clipped him in the forehead, taking his brains out the back of his skull.

Kayla turned, dazed, as behind her by about twenty feet came her father and Coburn. It was her father who held up his weapon, the barrel's mouth blowing gunsmoke.

Everything swung into a kind of slow motion. Kayla felt a presence behind her, felt Brickert's forearm closing hard on her throat, drawing her to his chest. His gun barrel pressed against her temple. Coburn and her father came up, skidding to a halt, hands up. Somewhere in the distance, the sound of screams—inhuman screams, the shrieks of the infernal hunters, a sound Kayla had never expected to hear again—rose up from inside the building.

Her heart thumped dully in her ears. The rush of blood. The roar of fear. Brickert was yelling, as were the vampire and her father. She couldn't make the words out: the ringing in her ears made sure of that. Gil put out his hand, let the gun fall around the hook of his trigger finger before finally dropping to the carpet. Coburn hissed, bared his fangs, looked like a bull ready to rip a matador in twain. Cecelia was gone. Ebbie was nowhere to be found, nor was Danny. She imagined that both were no longer among the living.

Then, movement to their right.

She turned to see Danny. He saw her, too. Their eyes met.

He came out from behind two cubicles, bolting toward her and Brickert like a dart thrown from a fast hand.

Brickert turned. The gun barrel left her temple. It found its target.

Danny took the shot in the chest, and he spun heel-to-toe, dropping.

Kayla felt herself scream, but could not hear it.

The distraction was just long enough.

Before she knew what was happening Coburn was pulling her aside, cradling her protectively with one hand, and with the other, grabbing a tuft of Brickert's long beard. He jerked his hand forward, and she saw Brickert's head unmoor from the neck—it still remained attached, but the neck had broken completely. What Kayla had heard referred to as an 'internal decapitation.' The gun fell out of Brickert's hand. Then Coburn and her father were around her, holding her, helping her sit down in a chair.

Coburn picked up the gun that Brickert had dropped and put it into her hand. "Here," he said. "I've got it all figured out."

CHAPTER THIRTY-SEVEN

The Maker of Monsters

COBURN KNEW THEY were coming. The hunters. The damned. He detected it in many ways: the way the building trembled as they came pouring up through the stairway, through the elevator shaft, in the duct-work. He could hear them, too, like a fast-approaching cloud of crows or starlings blotting out the moon. But worst of all was the way he could sense them. Like a deep hungry well of darkness pulling at him. They had terrible gravity, those monsters.

He wrapped Kayla's hand around the gun. He waved Gil over.

"Danny," she said, wiping away tears. She reached for him, almost as if he were there. Coburn could feel the heat radiating off her. The fever was tearing her up. He pulled her gaze back toward him.

"Kayla," he said. "Listen to me. The monsters are coming. There's too many of them. We can't take them on. And there's nowhere for us to go."

"Please, Daddy, Danny, please..."

"I think I know how to make them go away," Coburn said. "But you have to listen to me. Are you listening?"

Gamely, she nodded.

In his head, he replayed a voice from his dream. *"It's one of those old immutable laws,"* Blondie said, *making a face that might've been a grin, might've been a sneer.* *"Kill the maker and you kill the monsters he made."*

Kill the maker.

Kill the monsters.

Easy-peasy lemon-motherfucking-squeezy.

"I need you to shoot me," Coburn said.

"No," Kayla said, eyes tearing up. "What? No!"

"Yes. In the head. Here." He helped her lift the gun, tapped the barrel hard against his forehead. Now the screams of the damned were louder. The floor began to visibly shake, and Coburn could see that even Gil noticed it. The fact they weren't hearing any gunfire outside made it clear that whatever remained of Brickert's convoy had been taken apart in short order. "You need to hit the brain. You hear me? The brain. Destroy the brain, destroy me."

"I can't, don't make me—"

"I can't do it. I won't. It doesn't make sense."

He heard the stairwell door on the thirty-seventh floor crumple inward. Heard the elevator doors banging, then bending, then wrenching out of their mechanics. The duct work below groaned; he could sense it through the floor.

They were almost in.

"I can't do it," he said. "I don't think I'll let myself. I'm a survivor. The monster inside of me wants to live but *by God*, I want it dead. You're a girl of pure heart, as pure as I know, so pure your blood wipes away the stains of evil and can turn a real asshole like me into someone worth having around."

Shrieks filled the lab. They were here.

"Shoot," he said, steadying her hand.

"No," she wept. "Please."

"*Shoot.*"

The damned entered the room. The Bitch Beast at their fore. Claws out. Jaws wide with their needled teeth. The ground shook. The air stank.

"Coburn," she said, tears streaming down her cheeks.

He felt the air move behind him. Gil started shooting.

"Shoot!"

She whispered, "Thank you."

Then she pulled the trigger.

GIL FOUND THE hammer on his gun falling on dry rounds, *click-click-click*, but they kept coming, kept swarming, a room full of rotten, leathery flesh, of glistening mouths and blood-red eyes—

Then the gun went off in Kayla's hand.

Coburn tumbled backwards.

The hunters all felt it at the same time. Some careened into cubicles, others merely fell onto their knees or curled up on their sides. Their flesh began to smolder and pop like the sound of water drops flicked into a pan of boiling oil. It was as if they'd all just taken a hot bath in bubbling acid: their flesh began to blister and erode, black blood erupting like motor oil. They disintegrated with sputters and hisses until all that was left were foul stains and the moldering bones—and teeth, and claws—collapsed atop of them.

Gil went and hugged his daughter and felt the heat coming off her in waves. She cried. So did he. They held each other like that for a while.

Eventually Kayla looked up and put her hand on her father's chest.

"You got shot."

"I'm okay," he said, though he didn't really know how true that was. If the world were back together again, he'd say it wasn't a killing shot. But this was a lab, not a hospital. Infection would set in soon enough. "Are you okay?"

"I don't think so," she said. "I don't feel good."

"We'll get you all taken care of. Get you out of this place come morning. We'll leave the city and..." His voice trailed off. He didn't know what else to say. Gil didn't have a plan. Didn't even know if she was going to be okay.

Kayla smiled, then, a surprising gesture, and one that made him feel a little bit better. She reached up and kissed his brow. "You're a good Daddy."

"Thank you, baby. You're the best daughter."

"I guess we won't ever make a cure, huh?" she asked.

"No," he said. "Not today." *Not ever.*

But then—from across the room, a cough. Gil looked in that direction, saw that a woman with a lab coat lay there, shot in the chest, but there she was, lifting her head up. Blood coming from the corners of her mouth. For a second he thought, *shit, she's turning into a goddamn zombie*, but then she spoke.

"This isn't the lab," she said, spitting up blood onto the floor.

"What?" Gil asked.

"Sorry, this isn't the"—another cough—"*only* lab. Certainly not the main one. Other one's in—" A coughing fit this time, and with it came a deep rattle that made Gil certain she didn't have long before she tap-danced off this mortal coil. "Other one's in San Francisco. In the bay. On one of the ferry boats."

Gil's heart fluttered. They still had a shot. He laughed. Kissed Kayla. "You hear that, baby? They got another lab! This isn't even the *main* one. On a boat! Genius. Just genius."

"Dad. I'm not gonna make it."

"What? Baby, no, shhh, don't say that." He looked to the woman, said, "Doc, tell my daughter that she'll be okay." But it was too late. The woman's chin was to her chest, and she wasn't moving. "You'll be okay. Shhh."

"Okay, Daddy."

"You believe me, little girl?"

"I believe you, Daddy." She tried to stand. "I want to say goodbye to them, if it's okay." He didn't understand at first, but she was looking in the direction of the vampire and Danny. He petted her hair, told her it was okay.

He watched as she crouched by Danny. Pressed her forehead to his. Kissed him on the cheek. The very act damn near broke his heart. Danny was a good kid. Saved their lives more than once. All for nothing. Or maybe it was for something: maybe it was for her, his baby girl.

Then she crawled over to the vampire. Gil decided he wasn't going to watch—he'd seen goodbyes enough for a lifetime. Instead, he stood up, figured he'd go looking around for some kind of medication, *anything*. Antibiotics for him. Ibuprofen for her, to bring her fever down. Any pills he'd had prior were left with the caravan. She needed something now.

Gil went over to a desk, started rooting through drawers. *Lucky day*, he thought with more than a single serving of irony, because there in the drawer he found both a bottle of Tylenol and a bottle of Advil. Both good for dropping fevers.

He turned to his daughter, started to say, "Kayla, I found—"

But his words devolved into a breathless cry.

Kayla knelt over Coburn's body, over his ruined head.

A letter opener stuck awkwardly out of the side of her neck.

And her blood poured into his unmoving mouth.

CHAPTER THIRTY-EIGHT

Metempsychosis, Transubstantiation, and Other Big Words

IT FELT LIKE being pulled backwards through the Devil's asshole. Up through the hot coals that lined his colon. Into the sulfur pit of his stomach. Up an esophagus lined with razor wire and broken glass. And then back out the Devil's own mouth, over his rough tongue, past the blackened teeth.

The bones in his face reknitted.

His tongue popped free from his swollen throat.

His brain reformed, one screaming synapse at a time.

And before he knew what was happening, Coburn was lurching to his feet, staggering drunkenly about. His blood felt hot. His mind felt white, clean, an open expanse like a snow-covered hill or a winter sky. Holy fuck, he felt *good*.

He laughed. Until he saw Kayla. Laying still.

The blood on his lips *tasted* like her. Like the way her hair smelled. Like cotton candy. Like lambs-wool.

And then, before he could say anything or do anything, there stood Gil. Brickert's gun—the Colt Python that ended Coburn the first time out—was in his hand.

"Why?" was all Gil could muster.

Before Coburn could answer, Gil shot the window behind him, then shoved the vampire through the open window.

As he tumbled out, Coburn said words he never expected to say: "Daddy, wait."

Then he fell thirty-seven floors.

HE HIT A BMW. His body folded the car in enough so that both ends lifted up on each side a little bit. The windshields popped with a sound of a cannon going off and rain coming down after.

The car alarm started to go off.

All the bones in his body felt like they'd just been shattered. They felt about as put-together as a bucket of loose LEGO pieces.

A voice inside him said, *Don't worry. We'll get you fixed up right.*

Except, it wasn't the monster's voice. Wasn't his own voice, either. It was hers.

"Kayla?" he asked, but no voice—internal or external—answered.

Inside, he felt his bones start to knit. He didn't even have to do anything about it. No effort at all. That was new.

Then he felt something wet on his cheek. First he thought, *I think I'm crying*, but then he smelled the gamy gust of dog's breath and found himself face-to-muzzle with Creampuff, who seemed awfully happy to see him.

And then he felt it: a warmth on his arm.

The street around him started to brighten.

Morning rose, the sky a kind of nuclear pink, with fingers of orange shot through it. The sun wasn't up, not yet, but it would be soon.

And Coburn decided to meet the sun head-on. He didn't deserve to live. Didn't matter how good he felt. He wasn't going to hang around this endless life anymore with Kayla's death on his hands.

He stood atop the ruined BMW and waited for the sun.

It rose. His skin grew warmer and warmer.

And now the fire comes.

But it never came.

What did come was Kayla's voice again, and this time it spoke at length inside the echo chamber of his skull:

You can't leave this world yet, silly. You've still got work to do. Got bad things to make up for. You have my blood.

It's yours now, forever and ever. Carry it with you. Give it to others. Now you're the cure, Coburn.

Now, Coburn did weep, his cheeks slick with blood.

CHAPTER THIRTY-NINE

I Left My Heart in San Fransico

THE ZOMBIE'S HEAD snapped back, the crossbow bolt going in through the eye and sticking out the back. It coughed up a little black mist when it did so.

"Nice shot," Coburn said.

"Mm," Gil said. He went back over, planted his shoe on the rotter's head, withdrew the bolt. He wore a pair of diving gloves that looked almost like chainmail. Were good in case you got bit by a moray eel or something, but were *also* good to make sure you didn't get bit by some wayward rotter.

The rotters were still around, after all. Coburn's death—his first death, or shit, maybe it was his second—ended the hunters who had been born on his blood. But though the entire zombie epidemic came from his own DNA, even still, it was never a blood-to-blood thing. At least, that was how he figured it.

"Speaking of a nice shot," Coburn said, "that one there would be a pretty nice shot if I had a camera. That's some picturesque shit, pops."

"Don't call me Pops," Gil said. But he agreed just the same. "It is awfully pretty."

Down there, San Francisco lay quiet, shrouded in fog. The spires of the Golden Gate Bridge peaked out of the mist, too. South of the city lay another army of cannibals and a whole lot of zombies; so they'd taken the long way and come at the city from the north.

It started to spit rain. Even still, Coburn could see a little sun up there through the pendulous cloud cover.

The sun didn't bother him much anymore. It itched a little. Maybe that was normal. At this point, normal was meaningless. He was still dead. No heartbeat. Could still do all the things a vampire could do. But he felt stronger. And while his body still sustained itself on the blood of the living, he didn't need to drink as much and the hunger had lost some of its teeth, so to speak.

Convincing Gil of what had happened wasn't easy. Kayla had given herself up because she knew she couldn't make it on her own. Enter Coburn, a vampire whose body was an undead water jug that could carry her blood or her essence or whatever-it-was with him. Gil didn't like that. Shot Coburn a few more times. Hit him, too—the old man knew how to throw a punch.

But then it occurred to him that the vampire was taking punches in the middle of day-time. Stranger still was how sometimes Coburn spoke in the little girl's voice—not a man speaking *like* a little girl, but actually with Kayla's voice.

Gil came around.

Mostly. He still wasn't real excited about it. Didn't help that he was emotionally torn up over the events of that day and physically torn up from the gunshot wound. The resultant infection had run him ragged. They never got around to finding antibiotics. Instead, Coburn gave the old man a little bit of his blood and, overnight, the infection cleared like a storm sliding out to sea.

"Ready to go?" Coburn asked.

"I suppose," Gil said, tucking the crossbow bolt back into the homemade quiver he had hanging at his side. He'd taken to using the crossbow he found in a sporting goods store because, he said, the ammo didn't disappear on you. "Recycling," he'd said. "Good for the planet."

"Let's do it, then." Coburn snapped his fingers. "That means you too, you little sonofabitch."

Creampuff barked, having found himself a squirrel to chew on. He came bounding up, squirrel fur still stuck in his mouth.

Together, the three descended toward the Golden Gate Bridge, heading for the City by the Bay. It was time to fulfill Kayla's mission.

ACKNOWLEDGEMENTS

To Michelle, who lets me be who I need to be and isn't afraid of me being a writer, crazy as we are.

To Tracy, who first put a Robert McCammon
book in my hand.

To McCammon, who made me want to be
a writer and a storyteller.

To Stacia, who gave me a shot and got me out there.

To Coburn, who got in my head and in my blood
and put this book before you.

Bad
Blood

PART ONE
FREAKS

The Conversation: #1

DID YOU THINK it would end like this?

Nah. Not really.

I'm cold.

Me too. But fuck it, I'm always cold.

I'm slipping away. Mouthful by mouthful. Gulp by gulp.

Now we know where you live, I guess. You live in my blood. Not in my head.

Did you doubt? See, I knew you doubted me. I could feel it, JW. All up inside you, squirming like a handful of nightcrawlers.

Doesn't much matter now, does it?

Guess not.

Sweet dreams, little girl.

Oh, but I'm not ready to go to bed just yet. Are you?

CHAPTER ONE

Now You're The Cure, Coburn

COBURN'S GUTS SAT heavy in his hands, spilling out across his forearms like a heap of bloody kielbasa. He jacked his back up against the stairway and kicked both legs out, bracing his boots against the door as a wall of rotten flesh pressed against it. Through the octagonal window at the top of the door he caught glimpses of mouths like wet holes in turned dirt, splintered teeth, eyes the color of diabetic piss. Hands slapped uselessly against the glass—red blisters on gray flesh popped, leaving greasy streaks behind.

Nasty-ass motherfuckers, he thought.

In his head, a voice altogether not his own answered: *Tsk-tsk, such bad language, Coburn. Naughty man.*

Outwardly—and inwardly—he growled, gnashing his teeth so hard he thought they might snap. Turned out that Kayla the ghost girl—having taken up residence inside his skull like it's a fifth-floor walk-up on the Lower East Side of NYC—liked to chat. Chatty in life. Chatty in death (or what passed for it).

He told her to keep quiet.

She listened. For now.

"You don't look good," came a voice from behind him on the stairs.

Gil. Kayla's father. "Bad news when your insides are outside."

"For you, maybe," Coburn said. "For me, it's just a stubbed toe. A bloody nose." Bit of bravado, but it wasn't entirely untrue. Not like he needed his guts for anything. They were dead as every other organ in his body: might even be better if he could rip them out and leave them behind. He'd travel a lot lighter. Move faster. Hell, stitch in a zipper and he'd have a storage compartment. Could keep Creampuff in there, maybe. As if sensing what Coburn was thinking, the rat terrier wriggled at his side, snarling and snapping at the air in the direction of the zombie horde.

Coburn blinked. Looked around. The window afforded them a little sunlight: a fact he still wasn't used to, all this *not burning to a blackened nub* when the sun came up. But all that changed when he took in every last drop of Kayla's blood, didn't it? He hears her laugh inside his head.

Still. It let him see what he was dealing with. Here in San Francisco, all the houses sat crammed together in a dull array of pastels—that one there the color of Pepto Bismol, the one next to it looking like a sun-bleached robin's egg, and this one they were in, looking like the petals off a daffodil.

All the colors made him a bit sick. He felt a pang of nostalgia for New York—the grays, the blacks and browns, all the steel, cement, glass.

This house—a crass mash-up of Victorian and Art Deco—had been split into apartments. A bank of four mailboxes hugged the tin-tile wall to Coburn's right, with an apartment door to the left. The mailboxes were a good size, with lockers big enough to each accommodate packages: Coburn grunted, got his fingertips behind the box and tipped it over with a crash.

He wedged it under the apartment doorknob. Then eased off with his boots.

The rotters surged, but the door *thunked* dully against the fallen mailbox locker. They could not get through. Their frustration came through the door, in gassy hissing and soggy burbling. Rotten fingertips, some worn to the bone, searched around the door margins to no avail.

"Upstairs," Coburn said to Gil. "Go, go, go."

Gil turned, bolted up the steps.

The vampire grabbed his guts in one hand and the terrier in the other and marched up after the old man.

THEY KNEW SAN Francisco was going to be trouble. How could it not be? Be foolish to think that a city that once contained a stone's throw from a million living human beings would not now contain a *nearly equal portion* of undead assholes. They had a plan, and it seemed like a good one.

Might've been the bridge that gave them a false sense of confidence.

They crossed the Golden Gate that morning. Bands of fog thick above their heads, like rain-soaked cotton swallowing the brick-red cables and towers. Ahead of them, the way lay packed with abandoned cars. And not a single rotter in sight.

Creampuff the terrier seemed suspicious. Sniffed the air with a muzzle still bloody from a freshly-killed squirrel only an hour before (a little bit of the squirrel's tail hung from the small dog's chin like a tiny dog beard) and growled.

Gil commented on the absence of undead assholes: "I don't see any dead folk stumbling around. That seem right to you?"

"Sure." The vampire shrugged. "Way I see it, the bridge is basically a really long, really fat tightrope. Whatever zombies get herded onto it end up fumbling and stumbling over to the railing and over the edge into the bay below."

"I read that lots of people kill themselves here."

"Beautiful way to die, if dying's your thing."

"Says the man who can't die."

"Says the man who's already dead." Coburn headed over to the ass-end of a Toyota Corolla. He snapped his fingers at Gil. "Map. C'mon."

Gil set his crossbow down, fished a Rand McNally pocket atlas from his pocket. "You snap at me again, I might shoot one of those fingers off."

"Just bring out the fuckin' map, old man."

Kayla, inside his head, admonished him: *Apologize to Daddy.*

As Gil slapped the map down on the filthy car trunk, Coburn told the girl inside his head no, he won't apologize, she didn't get to make demands—

He knew it was a lie and she called him on it fast. Suddenly the noise level in his head cranked up like someone just spun the volume knob, broke it off, and stabbed him in the eardrum with the shattered plastic. Kayla screamed senselessly inside his mind, a shrieking banshee wail, and behind it all a sub rosa thread of thought that said: *I can do this all day, all night.*

Coburn curled his lip and muttered: "Sorry, old man."

The psychic cacophony stopped.

"I'm not old. I'm barely into my fifties." Gil cocked an eyebrow at him. "Was Kayla that made you apologize, wasn't it?"

The girl's father still wasn't comfortable with the fact that Coburn had drunk the lifeblood of his daughter and that she was now taking up real estate inside the vampire's blood, body and mind. He *believed* it; he just didn't *like* it.

Coburn said nothing. Just grabbed the map and used his finger to trace their route through the city. "Look. We cross the bridge. We go south. Hug the water's edge. Any dumbfuck zombies come after us, we snag a boat or just dive in the water. They don't seem to do so well with the wet stuff. End to end, it's not even six miles. If the lab's on a ferry, it's gotta be operating out of the wharf. There, or somewhere along the piers off the east side. We should be there by the afternoon."

The wind kicked up. It had fangs. It whistled through the bridge cables. Gil didn't say anything; he just stood there staring at Coburn, scratching at his salt-and-pepper beard with an idle hand.

"Can you see her?" Gil finally asked.

"No. I hear her." Coburn thought about it, and clarified: "But I do feel her. She's like a... well. It's like when a TV is on somewhere in the house, and even if the sound is down you can still feel it. A white noise. An indiscernible buzz."

Inside Coburn's head: *Aww, how sweet. Every girl just wants to be thought of as an indiscernible buzz.*

Gil nodded. Satisfied or not, Coburn wasn't sure.

"Let's keep moving," Gil said.

And they did. They trudged south. Found a few rotters stumbling around at the toll gate at the end of the bridge. One woman with no arms staggering around, a rat's nest of bleach-blonde hair gathering flies the way a tree gathers crows. Two men with dark blood-poison striations up their necks—toll booth attendants, one fat and tall, one thin and small, both easy to fell. Coburn shattered their knees with hard kicks, then stepped on their heads like overripe honeydews. Gil dispatched the blonde with the crossbow, the arrow going clean through her eye and out the back of her head.

As they headed south down the 101, the fog thinned and the sun came out and again Coburn felt that old spike of fear and for a half a second it felt like ants were crawling under his skin trying to bite their way free—but then, once more, he realized it was just the warmth of that unfamiliar ball of fire in the sky washing over him. He didn't much care for it.

They left the 101. Got off on Mason. A stretch of wet grass (and the distant bay) to their left. On the other side, whitewashed warehouses and the trees encroaching behind and overtop them. A rotter flopped around on the ground, his legs tangled in the chain and spokes of a bicycle. Coburn kicked its head off.

Seemed like a cakewalk.

The air grew warm.

The sun was out.

What few rotters they found were dumber than hammerstruck calves, and just as easy to dispatch. Even Coburn—not a naturally optimistic creature—started to feel pretty good about their chances. He could feel Kayla growing excited, too. Her voice in his head like a cool glass of sweet tea:

Remember: you're the cure, Coburn.

Things went off the rails as soon as they entered the city proper. They started seeing the tall needle-like masts of boats bobbing there in the water, and the warehouses and trees gave way to the condos and duplexes and single homes.

And to the zombies.

The street ahead lay crowded with them. Jostling together like sluggish fetid molecules, elbow to elbow, shoulder to shoulder, the stench of death pairing with the stink of brine from the bay.

Gil brought the crossbow to his shoulder.

Creampuff bared his teeth.

Watching a horde of zombies figure out you were there was an exercise in patience: they lift their heads, sniff the air with ruined noses, let their rot-clad skulls teeter on mushy necks until *finally* they turn toward you, their prey.

Coburn didn't think to give them the time.

He grabbed Gil, nudged Creampuff with a boot. The vampire pointed to a side street—Baker—and ducked down it. In the distance he could see that the road tilted up sharply, which was unsurprising given how San Francisco basically sat atop an epic hill. This way wasn't clotted with rotters, though it had a dozen or more milling about the street, pawing at one another and gurgling. A few more plodded along the sidewalk, collecting flies.

One zombie—face all but indistinguishable from a plate of raw meat except for the eyes staring out—started jogging toward them. Others caught sight, started coming at them, too.

"*Coburn,*" Gil warned.

"Follow me," he said. The vampire scooped up the terrier and leapt up onto a parked car, helping Gil up after him. Then he hurried along the cars, jumping from one to the next. The zombies were slow, stupid. By the time they lurched forward against the car, Coburn and Gil were already moving onto the next one. The undead were not efficient hunters—they went where the prey *was*, not where the prey was *going*. Yet another difference between the bloodsucker and the rotter.

But they come from you, Kayla said. *Never forget that.*

How could he, with her reminding him like that all the goddamn time.

Of course, it was *true*. They were of his blood. Part of his grim legacy. Flipped the wrong motherfucker the middle finger, which lost him that finger. And that digit went on to spawn the undead menace, the zombipocalypse, the end of the world as they knew it. His *fuck you* to one man became a gigantic *fuck you* to the whole of the human race— and given the fact he needed their blood to survive, kind of a boomerang *fuck you* right back to him.

He was almost proud.

But then, as one zombie stumbled forward like a drunk and cracked its head into the passenger side window of a parked BMW, that pride dissipated like steam.

Coburn called to Gil behind him: "We work our way up to the next street, then we head east. You good?"

"You don't need to worry about me. You just worry about yourself."

"What's that mean?"

"I just mean, you do what you do best: worry about you."

"You saying I'm selfish?"

"What? No." Gil followed Coburn, jumping from a Hyundai to the back of a Dodge pickup and into the truck bed. Coburn was already at the front. "Just go."

"You think I'm a selfish asshole. You think I can't keep your daughter safe."

"Well," Gil growled, "you did a bang-up job back in Los Angeles."

Coburn stopped moving. He spun around on the roof of a Subaru Forester and showed his teeth. "*Hey,* I did my best. Besides, I wasn't the one who led her into that goddamn deathtrap, now was—"

That's the moment everything went pear-shaped.

The vampire had been seeing things on a horizontal playing field. And arguing with Gil, with his backup, made him miss what was coming.

And what was coming fell from above.

Bam!

A zombie tumbled off a roof and landed right on Coburn, knocking the vampire off the Subaru and onto the ground. Creampuff whined and tumbled under the car, claws scrabbling.

The rotter—a dead woman with skin the color and consistency of tar paper—clambered atop him and put all her weight on his chin. Her rotten tooth-stubs sought out his throat, hankering for a taste of his blood. Coburn couldn't let that happen. Last time he let rotters have a sip of his go-go juice it changed them. Turned ordinary zombies from brain-dead stumblers to smart super-predators. A condition they could spread, and that only ended when Coburn killed himself—or tried to, before Kayla brought him back to existence with that magic blood of hers.

Everything seemed to happen at once. Coburn got his hand under her cheek and pushed upward at the same time Creampuff darted out from under the car, snarling and nipping at her. She reared back, and only then did Coburn see that her left arm had no hand—the arm dead-ended at the elbow, which was just a jagged, shattered spur of broken bone.

The zombie plunged that bone right into his belly.

It wasn't an attack. The dumb cooze was trying to *lean* on a hand that wasn't there. And now she was bone-deep in his guts, writhing like an animal caught in a trap. Which, as it turned out, was not all that great for Coburn's interior.

The zombie struggled, wrenching her arm up—

Slicing a ragged tear across Coburn's stomach.

Cool air blew across his exposed guts.

Well, shit.

The zombie saw his undead bowel and thought to dive in the way a porky kid goes at a pie-eating contest, but as she dove forth with zeal and hunger, he grabbed her head and racked it backward until the spine snapped and her dead eyes went deader. Other zombies were already shuffling forward, crossbow bolts sticking out of a few of their heads as they dropped.

Coburn, laying on the street looking up, saw something else.

More zombies. On the roof. Milling about.

Their attention had been gotten.

Coburn grunted, packed his viscera into the cavern of his body and yelled to Gil: "Up, up, up!"

Gil looked up to see the zombies start spilling over the edge, two stories up. He danced out of the way as one slammed hard into the Subaru, rolling off the back end. Another crashed into the boughs of a small tree growing out of the sidewalk, thrashing as it tangled itself in the branches.

They kept falling. One after the other. None of them landing with grace, but all of them getting up afterwards.

And now the zombies from the bottom of the street—the horde—had been alerted. A seething tide of corrupted unlife. Rotten as a tsunami of dead fish.

Coburn backed up to a house—a house the color of daffodils—and shouldered open the door, waving Gil and whistling for Creampuff.

The zombies were coming.

CHAPTER TWO
Blood Light

As Gil used the butt of the crossbow to bust the knob off one of the apartment doors upstairs, Coburn realized he was losing a not insignificant amount of blood. Soaked his jeans. Dribbled over his arms, milked from his exposed intestinal loops. Left a trail of it up the steps.

His hunger was different now that Kayla was nesting in his brain, blood, mind, soul, or wherever it was she *existed*. His need for blood had lost its serrated edge—it was still sharp, just not so jagged, so raw.

But hunger was hunger.

They pushed into the apartment. Nice place. Open concept. Built-in bookshelves, granite countertops, stainless steel appliances, travertine tile in the entryway. And a long-dead man in a leather recliner with a gun in his mouth and a rusty, clumpy peacock tail sprayed on the wall behind him.

A year ago, the sight of even that dried, shitty blood would've had Coburn tearing the pipes out of the walls in the hopes of finding a rat to eat, but now he kept his cool. As Gil orbited the room, Coburn muttered through gritted teeth: "Yeah, I'm going to need to eat something."

"Can't you heal that"—Gil gestured toward the exploded gutty-works—"first?"

"Normally. But turns out, a big hole in your midsection is one way for blood to make the great egress outside your body. And I need the blood to heal up."

"Take my blood."

The reaction inside Coburn was like a tiger with a string of firecrackers shoved up its ass—he damn near leapt across the room to get a taste of the walking blood-bag standing right in front of him. But Kayla's presence—not even her voice, just her *existence*—inside of him cooled his heels.

"I've fed from you... too much already." Pained him to say it, but it was true.

Last time he had a proper non-Gil-flavored meal was three days northeast of the city, where they found a trio of cannibals living out of a dead conversion van outside of Vallejo. They'd been driven mad, could barely speak English—everything was just howls of rage and single syllable words like *hunt, kill, eat*. Almost mistook them for zombies.

They thought to hunt Coburn and Coburn let them.

He ate them up. Drained them dry. They were too skinny. Their blood tasted of ash and madness. And an iron deficiency.

Now, most of their blood was on the ground.

Useless, now. Once again, ash and madness.

"I'll be fine," Gil asserted.

Again Coburn resisted the urge to go hog wild and break open Gil like a fucking Pez dispenser. "I said *no*. I feed off you now, you'll be weak; too weak. Might give you a stroke or tweak your heart. You may die, but I won't be the one to do it. Your daughter would never forgive me."

You got that right, she said.

Gil slumped against the wall, slid to the floor. The crossbow clattering away as Creampuff sat next to him.

Coburn smelled the salty tears before he saw them.

The girl's father was crying.

"Oh, goddamnit," Coburn said, trying again to hold up his guts. The hunger coiled and uncoiled like a rattlesnake in his mind. "We're gonna do this now?"

"I failed her," Gil said. "You were right. I was her protector, and her death is on my hands. Not yours." He sniffed up a snot bubble and his mouth formed a mortified line. "Her. Cecelia. Ebbie. All dead because of me."

"All dead because of Benjamin Brickert, who was the one who led you into that death trap." *And Benjamin Brickert*, Kayla reminded him, *came looking for you, didn't he? Doesn't that make our deaths your fault?* "Shut up!" he barked at her, not meaning to say it out loud, but there it was. He decided to run with it. "I need you to toughen the fuck up, Gil. Your rope's got too much slack in it; your daughter doesn't need a limp snot-slick handkerchief. She needs her father. She's not dead like you think of her being dead. I have her blood. I have the future."

Those words made him sick to say, but there they were anyway.

"I need blood. Can't be yours."

The terrier whined.

"No," Coburn said. "I'd need ten of you."

Creampuff wagged his tail.

"You need to hunt," Gil said, sniffling.

"Assuming anybody's alive in this city may be a fool's errand."

"What happens if you don't get blood?"

Coburn shrugged. "I start to dry up like a dead bug. Though what happens now that I have her up in my noggin remains to be seen."

Remember what you did in New York, Kayla said.

An image flashed in his head—an image he did not put there. Him. On the roof. Scenting for blood. How did she know that?

I have your whole head to wander around. It's all up here. Stuff you remember. Stuff you... don't.

That last part chilled him a little, and he wasn't sure why.

Still. She had it right.

"The roof," he said. "I've got to go to the roof."

HE UNDERSTOOD NOW. Why zombies were up here. People came here to wait out the horror. This house, like many others, was set-up to offer a roof-top patio: chairs, tables, outlets, little BBQ grills. One zombie hadn't realized that all his buddies had bailed on him and was still milling around, a sharp-angled pinstripe suit hanging loose on his desiccated, sun-dried body.

Gil knocked him off the roof. Crashing into the throng of massing zombies below. They accepted him as one of their own.

They were only two stories up, but Coburn could see the rooftops and, in the distance, the city on the hill. The tall buildings, the spired churches, the city of soft-colors and sea-bleached houses. The bay was a grim blue line. Behind them the skeleton of the Golden Gate rose, a crossing of bloody metal bones.

Blood.

Coburn sniffed the air. The perfume of decay rose from below, again mingling with the smell of the sea—salt and fish and sand. Decay, then, from all sides, too, just like in New York. Rotters this way and that way and *all* ways, because that's how the world was, now: home to the decomposing dregs of ex-humanity.

But no life.

No one alive nearby but them.

Weakness sucked the energy from his muscles, the life from his bones.

"Nothing," he said to Gil. "Not a goddamn thing. Maybe we press on. Try to find the ferry. If there are living people there, I can..."

What? came Kayla's voice. *Make nice with them by making one of them a quick snack? I'm sure they won't think that's the least bit rude.*

She was right.

Gil said something in response, but Coburn couldn't hear the old man—Kayla spoke again. More truth from the ghost girl.

You're sniffing for the wrong thing. Try again. Something's out there.

No. Nothing. He still couldn't—

Wait. There.

Not blood. But sweat. Body odor. The human musk—a sign of life.

He didn't understand how she'd smelled it and he hadn't.

You did smell it, you just didn't realize it yet. I'm you and you're me, dude.

"I smell someone," Coburn said, interrupting whatever Gil was saying.

Gil stared at him like he didn't believe it.

"I've got to hunt. I've got to hunt now." Before the scent was lost on the bay-born wind.

"How you plan to do that with all those rotters out there?"

"I go roof to roof. Only five feet between them."

Gil shook his head. "It's all short blocks. You'll hit a street before long."

"Then I hit a street. By then I'll be ahead of the throng. They're slow. Stupid. I'll be fine." He didn't necessarily believe it, but this wasn't the time to tell Gil that.

"What about me?"

"Hunker down. The zombies'll come after me; my blood makes them a little crazy." Coburn cringed as he pushed his guts back in his body, then closed his jacket over the wound and zipped it up snug. "When they're gone? Bug the fuck out of here. Find the lab. And I'll find you."

"I can't do this—"

Coburn didn't let the old man finish.

No time to waste. He bolted forward in a clumsy gallop and leaped from this roof to the next—soon as he hit, the vampire tucked his legs and rolled, barely managing to come back up on his feet.

But he did. Because hunger afforded him little choice.

CHAPTER THREE

The Rat Man

HE HAD HIM, now.

Coburn knew he was on the trail. The man—and it most certainly was a man, that was just a thing that the vampire knew—left his unwashed scent on every street sign and mailbox and curb.

Humans were such dumb apes. They never knew how plainly they were telegraphing their weakness—generally to other stronger humans, apex predators like con-artists, robbers, rapists, but this time to all flavors of the living dead. Broadcasting that signal of frailty and isolation to one lone vampire and a deluge of always-starving zombie motherfuckers.

Hunger was driving Coburn, now. Still not as toothy as it had been, and now with Kayla there he was able to push it longer, harder, faster—but just the same, the edges of his vision were tinged with a rose-red hue. By now he'd normally be feeling like an infinite carpet of insects crawled just beneath his skin, but here the hunger was clear and cleanly sharp like a shard of broken glass.

He moved south through the city. Through the once-hoity-and-also-toity neighborhood of Pacific Heights, now looking like it had been through a riot: sandbags and fallen coils of barbed wire and burned cars stacked together. Then below that, toward gutted restaurants and shattered boutiques (Indian food! Head shop! Turkish coffee! Weird hats! Oaxacan blankets!).

The zombies were thicker, here—an environmental hazard to be dealt with, to be got past, as obtrusive as floodwaters, as empty-headed as a pack of starving dogs. Coburn was singularly-driven. He hurt. He starved. Any zombie that got in his way found its knee popped, neck snapped, head crushed. When the throng got too thick, he clambered up fire escapes, went roof to roof and back down again.

All the while following that trail.

Invisible handprints of sweat.

A gob of spit on the curb.

A swipe of snot across a bent parking meter.

And then, bright as the moon in a dark sky, a dime-sized dollop of blood in the middle of the intersection of that old hippie standby, Haight and Ashbury.

That blood lit up Coburn's brain like a full-tilt pinball machine, bumpers flickering and flippers clicking and lights and klaxons and *an electric surge of raw hunger* coursing through his fingertips and eyeholes—

Wait, Kayla said. *Something's wrong.*

No time for that. No need. Zero interest.

Move, rove, run, hunt.

Coburn, stop.

He felt her somehow reaching through his dried-up veins and tugging on them like puppet-strings, but he had no time for that—the demon within bucked like a scorned hell-steed and Kayla's ghostly grip slipped.

There.

A shape, a form, darting around an overturned dumpster and into an alley.

Moved fast.

Human. Not zombie.

Coburn!

He screamed inside his own head to shut her up as he rounded the corner, found a small man hiding behind a pile of ruptured sandbags in a dingy puddle-soaked alley—Coburn growled and grabbed him and hauled him to his feet. Saw wide scared eyes, the eyes of a rabbit, and long greasy black hair with a kinky dread-twist beard to match, and the man mumbled something but it only came out as a froth of spit bubbles and *who cares just fucking feed—*

Kayla screamed inside his mind.

He bit deep into the dirt-caked neck.

Blood ran hot into Coburn's mouth. Coppery, oily, heavy, sweet—

But then, something else, too. A bitter edge on the back of the tongue. A rising taste of salt; a crass medicinal tang.

Coburn's head suddenly felt like it was doing loops and whorls, a biplane flying barrel rolls inside his skin. Kayla tried to say something, but her voice grew warped, distorted, like he was a little fishie inside an aquarium and she stood on the outside yelling in *whash ish appeming—*

The vampire could not pull away. The blood continued to pump into his mouth. When the rodent-like man pushed Coburn away, Coburn could not resist *that*, either. He felt like a store mannequin, his limbs somehow distant from the rest of him, his brain out there on a tether like a child's birthday balloon.

The rat man whimpered, fumbled clumsily for a square of dirty gauze which he quickly slapped over the neck wound. From behind the sandbag he rescued a roll of black electrical tape and a walkie-talkie.

He wound the tape around the gauze with one hand, and spoke into the walkie with the other.

"He got me. I mean—I got him. I mean, *shit*, ahhh, you know what I mean. Over." The rat man stared at Coburn as the vampire teetered there, trying desperately to will his limbs to respond to his desire to rip out this freak's throat.

The response from the walkie came from with rough voice that sounded like two bricks being rubbed together: "What's he doing? Over."

"He's just standing there. Staring at me. Over."

The rat-man mouthed two words to Coburn: *I'm sorry.*

The gravelly voice: "Good. Bring him to the corner of Page and Masonic. I'll send Flores and Jeepers to help you bring him in. Hurry before the stumblers find you. Don't fuck this up, Fingerman. Over and out."

The rat-man—Fingerman, apparently—looked at Coburn and then shrugged. That's when his face melted. Leaving behind only a grinning skull.

The sky above turned to an eye.

The blood in the vampire's mouth and throat felt suddenly like a bubbling pile of clipped fingernails, chewed calluses, and battery acid.

Fingerman pushed Coburn over, wound electrical tape around his eyes and mouth, and began dragging him.

CHAPTER FOUR

The K-Hole

COBURN'S WORLD, PLUNGED into darkness.

But in the darkness, light flared like a burst of red phosphorus.

He saw faces in those dark spaces, faces lit by crimson light. A prostitute with her neck torn open. A pair of club kids, tongueless, made to kiss with their bloody mouths as Coburn watched. A meter maid, skin gone ashen, a pair of puncture wounds on her bloodless, mortified wrist.

Ebbie's moon face.

Cecelia, laughing.

Together they all whispered his name, his *true* name:

"John Wesley Coburn."

Then:

Kayla. Sitting on the floor. Watching a television whose round full screen flickered static with a black and white image dancing behind the noise—a voice crackling through the hiss: *Rilly big shoe.*

Kayla became Rebecca. Hair into pigtails. Sweet smile.

Then, back to Kayla.

"It's a strange place in here," she said. "Messy."

"How'd you get in here?" he asked, even though he knew the answer:

You stabbed yourself in the neck and made me drink your blood, and now I'm your keeper, your container, your little Coburn. Cure for what ails the world.

"Lots of dead people in your head."

"Not like you, though," he said. "You're really here."

"They're *all* really here, JW. Can I call you that now? I think I will."

He wanted to tell her *no, don't call me that,* but couldn't find the words.

She continued: "Everybody you killed, whose blood you drank, lives in here. Part of them does. Maybe it's biology. Maybe it's the soul. Who knows? I'm stuck, too. Not like I have access to the Internet in here."

Kayla laughed. But it wasn't her laugh. It was Rebecca's laugh.

"My daughter," Coburn said. *If everybody I ever killed is in here...*

"Don't worry about her right now. You gotta bring yourself back from this. You've fallen down the rabbit hole, JW. And you're falling still. It's time now to wake up, you hear? Time to see where you are."

"But Rebecca..."

"Isn't going anywhere. But you are, big guy."

"Wait."

"No time to wait."

"Wait!"

His scream echoed.

His eyes opened behind black tape.

HIS HANDS MOVED. They moved when he told them to. Not fast. Barely functional. Felt like they were somebody else's arms and he was willing them to move with telepathy—there came a delay from when his brain issued the command and when his arms flailed upward like the limbs of a doll. He cried out. His numb fingers found the tape around his eyes. Pried the tape off. No pain. Just bright light that washed out the middle; reality bled in at the edges.

He saw zombies.

Upside-down zombies. Filthy gore-caked faces. Lips ripped away. Dead tongues lolling, tasting the air. About ten, fifteen feet away.

Floating. Flying.

Coburn grunted. Sat up. A cry of alarm erupted at his feet—a fist popped him in the face, knocked his head back down as upside-down zombies continued to lurch forth. The sky was on the ground and asphalt was the sky and—

You're upside-down, Kayla said, *not them. Silly vampire.*

It all began to work itself out.

Coburn dipped his chin to his chest, saw that three humans were dragging him up toward a house on the corner, a house walled away behind sandbags and cars and coils of razor wire. House the color of turned earth, of fresh mulch, of grave dirt.

The three humans looked back at him as they hurriedly dragged him forward by his boots—one of them, the rat-man, Fingerman, yelped. "He's wakin' up! Chee-rist, he's *wakin'* up!"

Another one—a wild-eyed Hispanic-looking motherfucker with fat biceps and a corded neck that looked like the trunk of a sequoia—barked at him: "Go back to sleep! Go the fuck to sleep!" To the third man, a wispy old dude with a Gandalf beard and a cheap pink plastic lei around his neck: "Give him the shot! The shot!"

Gandalf let go of the vampire's boot, coming at Coburn with a syringe full of red. Coburn's mouth tingled—*that's blood,* Kayla told him, *but it's bad blood*—but he had to suppress the hunger. He tried to kick his feet but they were slow to respond, tried to bat at the incoming hippie-wizard but his fist felt like it was swaddled in cotton swabs, and before he knew what was happening the dude's beard was in his eyes and the syringe was squirting blood into his mouth and—

There. The bitter tang. The medicine wrapped in a spoonful of sugar.

Kayla: *They're drugging you.*

"Muhfuh!" Coburn muttered—it sounded better in his head—and once more the darkness found him, again touched by the faces of the dead and tinged by firelight cast through a curtain of blood.

HOURS. DAYS. WEEKS. Years.

Coburn could not say long the parade of the doomed and the dead lasted this time. When he finally awoke, it felt like leaving a too-loud, too-crowded party and walking out onto a balcony or sidewalk where the air is cool and everything is comparatively quiet and the clamor and clatter has been left behind.

That effect did not last.

When Coburn's eyes adjusted, he found himself nailed to a dining room table. Dark cherrywood. The air smelled of—what was that? Hash. The crispy, pungent tang of hashish.

Gandalf stood at Coburn's side. Whistling 'Baby Elephant Walk' as he worked. In this case, *worked* meant *swaddled Coburn's guts with a ribbon of duct tape.* Gandalf wound the tape over the vampire, then under the table, then over the vampire and back under the table.

Above the vampire's head, a water-stained ceiling. Cracks in the plaster like cracks in glass. To the right: a hallway. Toward his feet: a beaded curtain in rainbow colors, with no idea what lay beyond—though he saw figures moving. And smoke vented through the beads. Again: hashish.

Coburn tried to move. He felt weak. His body, still partially unmoored from his brain. The effort to move shot ragged cigarette burns of pain up and down each limb—hundreds of them.

I think they used a whole lotta nails, Kayla said. *Owie.*

"Sonofa…" Coburn growled. "*Bitch.*"

Gandalf, startled, danced away, dropping the duct tape. It rolled away.

"Hey, brother," Gandalf said. Voice throttled by a frequency of fear. "You okay over there?"

"Fucking delightful." Coburn noted that his voice sounded like he'd been smoking cigarettes full of ground-up glass for the duration of his long unlife. "I really enjoy it when some whacked-out moon-units kidnap me off the streets of a zombie-infected city and then nail me to their dinner table."

"Cool," Gandalf said, clearly not sure if it *was* cool.

Coburn helped him with that. "No, it *ain't* cool, you old goaty wizard. Let's make a deal, you and me. You start ripping these nails out and you let me up and I won't kill you. But"—he interrupted Gandalf before the old fool spoke—"if you *don't* let me out, then here's my promise to you: I'm going to kill you first. And I'll make it hurt. I'll bring pain to you that before now was an impossible nightmare.

That's the deal I'm offering. One time. One time *only*."

"I..." Gandalf thought about it. Coburn could see that. The dude stroked his long gray beard with nervous spidery fingers, and then finally he said: "I better go get Minister Masterson."

The willowy old-timer darted through the curtain, the beads clattering against one another. Coburn snarled, yelled after him, but it was too late.

Kayla, of course, had to chime in, *You'd think by now you'd realize: more flies with honey than vinegar, JW.*

The beads whispered against one another once more.

A man came up to the foot of the table. Coburn craned his neck, put his chin to his chest to see.

Tall sonofabitch. Oily crow-black hair pulled back. Scraggly beard. Little teeth behind thin lips. Reached in past a shirtless vest and idly itched a nipple ringed in black hair. The guy had a distinct *Charlie Manson* vibe hanging around him—along with a gauzy haze of hash smoke.

"You must be Coburn," the dude said. He had a familiar voice. Coburn recognized it as the one from the walkie-talkie. Like gravel under a wheelbarrow wheel. "Thanks for stopping by, vampire."

Coburn seethed. "You *know* me?"

"Seems you're a popular motherfucker, motherfucker."

"Masterson, I presume," Coburn said. Upstairs, he heard sounds: footsteps, people moving around. *How many more are there?*

"Presume away."

From behind the so-called Minister came the rat-man, Fingerman. He came up on Masterson's left, clinging to the Minister's hip like a squirrel. On Masterson's right came a reedy love-bombed sylph with pink puckered lips and a diaphanous gown with one wine-glass breast exposed as if she didn't even realize it. She wasn't looking *at* Coburn so much as *through* him.

"Nice place you have here," the vampire growled.

"Thanks, man. It's pretty well-defended. We got a cushy thing going."

"I bet. What'd you dose me with?"

A voice to Coburn's right: "Ketamine, bro."

There stood the thick-necked Hispanic. Looking like some cracked out PTSD Marine.

He was eating something.

Chowing down on it like it was a big old turkey leg.

It was a human foot.

Coburn's first thought was: *oh, of course, I've been captured by a nest of drug culture cannibals*, but then something else became clear: the man wasn't eating a healthy human leg. Nor a cooked one. It was rotten. Skin pocked by red sores. Muscles mushy like the flesh of an overripe pear.

"Ketamine's some bad-ass shit," the Hispanic man said around a mouthful of what looked to be undead meat. He chewed noisily, tongue smacking. "It's like a... a dog anesthetic or something. You give someone a good strong dose of it, they fall into the K-Hole. Total dissociation of body and mind. Great for putting the moves on a girl. Get her all loosey-goosey. Once you get her lubed up with that stuff, she's like putty in your—"

"Flores," Masterson said. "Enough, man. Enough."

"Oh. Right, bro. Right."

"You eat zombies," Coburn said.

Masterson nodded. "We do. Some of us see it as a transubstantiation of the flesh thing. Some of us just figure we've got an easy meat source out there. Free range long pig."

"It's *diseased* meat. Which means you have the disease."

Flores laughed. Masterson shot him a look, then said: "We have ways of keeping ourselves pure. Don't you sweat it, man."

"You and I have very different definitions of purity."

Masterson shrugged. "This is the way. The new way. I'm leading people toward a symbiotic future. Where living man and dead man have a place in each other's worlds. We can feed off of them as they feed off of us. Can't you see the beauty in that? In the cycle of life to death to life again?"

"You're fucking baked."

"Baked on an idea. Baked by the power of our purity." Masterson began pacing the room. "You know I used to be a banker? Down in the financial district. Packaging mortgages."

"Shoulda stuck with it. I hear the foreclosure market is *ripe* for the picking."

"Funny, man. Funny. I like you. But see, that's the thing—you're hitting on a real point. I was one of the guys who helped fuck things up for people. Did some naughty shit. I got rich as everyone got poor. I fiddled while Rome burned. Housing market collapsed like the house of cards that it was but we didn't have long to nest on that, did we? Because that's when the real shit hit the fan. And it showed me—and everybody—just what bullshit the system was. The system was a prison made of illusions, like, like endless walls of circus mirrors. It all crashed. The real crash. The crash of the dead against the living."

"Great story. Can I go now?"

But Masterson ignored him. "But I don't want it to be us versus them anymore. I want us to co-exist. Even if that relationship of coexistance is one based on food and need and hunger. That's okay. Because those things are pure. Hunger is pure. I'm sure you understand that. Being who you are. *What* you are."

Coburn struggled against the hundreds of nails puncturing his flesh and pinning him to the table like a butterfly on a corkboard. His strength still wasn't there—given his guts hanging out of his body and the traces of what was apparently a veterinary anesthetic lingering in his morbid veins, it didn't seem like it would be in reach anytime soon.

"Struggle all you want," Flores said. "We nailed you there pretty good."

"You're going to eat me," the vampire said. That's what this was. What this *had* to be. If the zombies were Grade-E-but-Edible—and hunger was *pure*, as Masterson put it—then a kidnapped vampire was like a fresh slab of filet-fucking-mignon hot off the grill. Though that still didn't explain how they knew who Coburn was, or where he'd be...

Masterson laughed. "Nah. We could. But we won't. The Doc wouldn't like that. The Doc's the one with the plans." He snapped his fingers. "Get Jeepers back in here. Our friend needs another dose."

"Dose? No. Don't put me under again." Those faces. The faces of those he damned—Coburn couldn't abide another second with them. Hundreds of ghosts. Each trapped in a drop of blood. Hallucinations or specters, he didn't know, he didn't *care*, he just didn't want to be locked away in the prison of his own diseased mind with them. He said something he never thought he'd say to these people: "Please."

The wizard Gandalf—or Jeepers, for some reason that remained unclear to Coburn—moved up alongside Coburn with another syringe. Coburn caught a whiff of sage and lavender. *Goddamn hippies.*

"Doped blood," Flores said, looking over Jeepers' slumped shoulder. "We drugged up Fingerman the first time 'cause he loves the ketamine and he's so goofy on it half the time he never falls into the K-Hole anymore. Drugs like that, you're just chasing the dragon. No high is ever as good as the first. Ain't that right, vampire man?"

"Fuck you."

Suddenly Flores' face tightened in a rictus of rage, eyes bugging out of his head in such a way that Coburn thought they might launch out of his head on wobbly springs. "*Fuck you*, man. Fuck! You! Time to go *tits up*, bitch." Flores walked off in a huff, saying, "Dose him, Jeepers."

The wizard shrugged, came at Coburn with the needle.

Soon as it got near Coburn's mouth, he opened his mouth wide and bit down on the needle. It stuck in his tongue and snapped. Jeepers yelped, struggling to wrench open Coburn's jaw—

Which was the wrong move. The vampire reopened his mouth, clamped down a pair of mean canines on the span of flesh between the old wizard's thumb and forefinger—*crunch*—and began to guzzle. Fresh blood—if not entirely clean, as Coburn caught the trace of hash or marijuana hanging out in there somewhere—flooded his mouth as Jeepers screamed like a middle-aged housewife seeing a mouse run across her kitchen floor.

This was the way out. Fresh blood meant a shock to his system. Purge the drugs. He lurched forward with renewed vigor, the nails popping through his flesh and tearing it like ragged leather. Jeepers tried to back away as the monster rose anew, feasting, drinking, making good on his promise to kill Jeepers first (though at present not as painfully as he'd like). Masterson ducked through the curtain, rattling the beads. Flores disappeared down the hall. Fingerman dropped into a fetal crouch and rocked back and forth.

Flee, freaks, flee.

It didn't matter.

All these assholes were going to die today.

Or so he thought.

But then, out of nowhere, came the reedy sylph girl.

She had a Louisville slugger in her hand and a crazy beaming smile on her face. The girl held the bat like she was swinging for the fences.

The bat connected with Coburn's head.

Starbursts erupted in his vision. Streaks of smeary white.

He tried to get back up—

The bat came down on his chest. Then his chin.

Flores launched himself up atop Coburn's body and took a knee. With hands as muscled as the rest of his 'roid-monkey body, Flores jacked open Coburn's now-broken jaw and—

Squirt.

Into the mouth with another jet of bad blood.

Coburn slipped once more into the dark tide. He couldn't tell if Kayla was laughing, or crying, or both. The faces renewed their assault, drowning him in a bucket of his own bilious guilt.

CHAPTER FIVE

Hunters Hunted

THE VAMPIRE WAS right. Soon as Coburn took off leaping from rooftop to rooftop like the shadow from a cloud moving overhead, the zombie throng slowly began shuffling up the street, leaving only a few stragglers behind.

Gil peered over the roof's edge. Creampuff whined by his side.

He felt suddenly overwhelmed and alone. The city was silent. Same way that all the cities were, now: no cars, no helicopters, no constant rumbling murmur of voices and HVAC units and music. Nobody was here to care about him or have him care back. Dead streets, dead city, dead world. Who were they trying to save again, exactly? What was left of humanity? And how many of them were worth a shit?

"I feel alone," he said to Creampuff. "And I miss my daughter."

The dog sat down, stared up.

"Yeah, I hear you. Cut the pity party. Let's hit the bricks, pooch."

WHEN NEXT COBURN opened his eyes, night had fallen and he found himself nailed back to the dining room table. For a half moment he caught a whiff of something sweet and sour hanging in the air—

the scent of jasmine mingling with an eerily-familiar odor of death. Familiar because...

Kayla filled it in for him: *It smells like you.*

At the same time the odor was crawling its way up his nose like a worm, a sound reached his ears that chilled his already cold body:

A howling screech. Containing within it a madness beyond life's margins, a desperate ragged hunger that had no end and gave no quarter.

The scream was far away... but close enough to still be heard.

That sound set off a cascade of images in his mind: rotters drinking his blood, turning into monstrous hell-zombies, the *hunters* who stopped at nothing when it came to getting another taste of Coburn.

How could another hunter exist in the world? All the ones he inadvertently made—and then those that made each other—were gone now. Was there just one? Or had their unstoppable army begun to form anew?

Coburn lay there in the darkness for awhile, trying to parse what he'd heard. A figure drifted beyond the beaded curtain; a shadow upon the sea of shadows. Coburn willed his eyes to see better—normally, he could see in darkness like it was a cloudy day, but right now it seemed that either the ketamine or his day-long exposure to the bleary fireball known as the 'sun' had done his night-sight no good.

Again he smelled jasmine and death.

Stronger, this time.

The figure emerged from behind the curtain.

Now he could see her. She was Asian. Clad in a white doctor's coat. The woman was tall, long limbed, with the elegance of a cellar spider. Flesh pale like a cave cricket and flawless like porcelain—except for the asterisk-shaped crater on her cheek below her left eye. Like someone had taken a chisel to a beautiful doll.

As she approached with confident step, the jasmine smell washed over him.

And so did the smell of death.

She's one of you, Kayla said.

"I've come to take your blood," she said.

"That's awfully matter-of-fact, Doc."

"I see no reason to obfuscate my intentions." She walked the table at his feet, pacing in slow half-moons. He couldn't hear shoes. Was she barefoot?

"You're pretending to me like me."

She frowned. "To be like you how?"

"You know."

"Enlighten me."

He opened his mouth, hissed, let his tongue play across the tip of two plainly-displayed fangs. "See what I'm getting at, China Doll?"

"I'm Korean, and why do you think I'm pretending?"

"Because I'm the only one out there."

"I'm surprised you think so, though I suppose I see why." She seemed done with the conversation. She waved someone on behind the beaded curtain, and here came itchy, twitchy Fingerman, pushing a metal cart with a wooden case atop it.

"Don't you, uhh, need lights?" Fingerman asked.

The woman barely gave him a look. "I can see in the dark even if you cannot. Run along, little rat."

Coburn snorted. "I thought he looked like a rat, too."

But she didn't respond. So much for being friendly.

"What's your name?" he asked her.

"Lydia."

"Nice to meet you, Lydia. I'm—"

"Coburn, yes, I know." She popped the latch on the case—a little brass hook—and opened it. Looked to be something out of medical antiquity. One giant metal syringe. A number of glass containers, each about the size of a stick of dynamite. Old surgical tubing. A shiny metal piece that looked like the head of an octopus with all of its tentacles chopped off at the half-way mark. She began hooking it all together efficiently, silently.

"What's all this nonsense?"

"It's a blood transfusion kit. From the era of the Great War. Would've preferred something more updated, but the hospitals remain host to a continuing plague of the undead." She clipped the octopus head to the tubing, then the tubing to the syringe. Then she did the same the other way: connecting one glass jar to the tubing, and back to the octopus head. "Don't worry. I tested it."

"Tested it."

"Mm. I have test subjects."

"Pigs?"

"Humans. Children, actually."

He laughed, though it was without mirth. "I'm a little confused here, honey. You know that if you were a real bloodsucker you don't need all this fancy crap, right? You just... open your mouth. Let your fangs come out to play. Sink them into somebody's skin like pushing your pinky through a stick of warm butter... mmm. Oooooh-ee. Nothing beats it. Not that you'd know, being a—"

He was about to say pretender, but then Lydia leaned forward, extended her jaw and tilted her head back, and let her fangs show.

As he did, she poked at each with a tongue.

"Satisfied?" she asked. "Good."

Then she went back to setting up the kit.

She told you, boy, Kayla said.

He willed her to shut up.

"So why the kit if you could just drink me dry here and now?"

"The blood is not for me."

She turned her gaze suddenly to the wall. Then to the beaded curtain. Back to Coburn, an unexpected moment of cageyness submerged now beneath that glassy exterior.

Something scratched at his mind like a crow clawing the earth.

"Not for you. Who's it for?"

She didn't answer.

"Who the fuck wants my blood, *Lydia*?"

Still silent. Only the click and squeak of her hands adjusting the apparatus.

What's going on, Coburn?

"I don't even have that much blood in me. If I did I'd be up off this table. I'd be tearing this place to pieces, commanding these freaks to eat one another alive."

Lydia stopped. Finally seemed resolved to say something. "It's not your blood that matters. It's what's inside it."

He went cold. Like someone flushed his system with saline. "I don't know what you're talking about."

"Your blood is different now. You have a guest. I'm here to take her."

Her. Kayla. The cure.

Shitfuck.

Coburn, how does she know that?

No time to think about that now. Panic settled into his supine body like sepsis; that cold feeling of saline turned to a hot rush of acid. "You don't know what you're doing. You don't want to do this."

"Not used to this, are you? The begging. The pleading and wheedling. Usually it'd be your victim, wouldn't it? Begging you for her life. Or begging you to take her life, depending on how badly you tweaked her brain. Trust me. I know." Lydia screwed a massive needle onto the tip of the equally massive syringe. Looked like something used to deliver adrenalin to an elephant's heart. Her gaze flicked again to the windows. Did Coburn sense a nervousness there? "But now you're the one on the slab. You're the one imploring another to save you. Or save the one inside your blood. I wonder what that must be like. To care about another as you do now. The good news for me is, I am not given over to such delicate compunction. It's sad to see you like this, really. It's like watching a wolf limp."

"Are you done talking?" Coburn said. "Because I'm getting tired of hearing your fool mouth flap."

"I am. A rare moment of gregariousness. I suppose I just savor the irony of your situation." An icy smile. "Let us begin."

She gave the needle one last tighten. Moved it toward his neck.

Then: outside, another keening banshee's wail. The hunter, hunting.

Lydia tensed. Syringe held firm in her grip.

Coburn suddenly understood.

"The hunter," he said, clucking his tongue as if to chastise a tardy student. "The hunter's yours, isn't it? You let your guard down. And when you did, some rot-fuck took a bite out of you—not out of your cheek, no, that's from before you turned into the carefree killing machine you are now—and something happened that you didn't figure on. The rot-fuck changed. And now he's out there. Or *she's* out there. Looking like something that kicked its way out of the Devil's own dickhole. Like something that's bringing Hell with it."

"Shut your mouth," she hissed.

"Oooh. Getting testy, now. It's my turn to be the smart one and you don't like that." She turned the syringe downward and he uttered a quick *tut-tut-tut*. "Slow your roll, sister. That thing's on the hunt. And it wants one thing: vampire blood. Yours, if it can manage it. But I suspect mine will do fine. You let one drop of my blood hit the air and that thing will be like a shark scenting prey. It'll come. For you. For me. For all of us. That what you want?"

She hesitated. The needle tip hovering.

Coburn, on the other hand, did not hesitate.

He jerked his body toward—not away from—the needle, letting its tip pop a hole in the side of his neck. He didn't have much blood left, but what he had beaded up at the puncture site like a blood-colored pearl.

It timed out well: only a moment later came another wailing, mournful—and righteously hungry—cry from the distant hunter.

Lydia staggered backward. She dropped the syringe.

Coburn laughed. A dry rasp. Way he saw it: whatever it was she wanted, he did not—and whatever she *didn't* want, well, he'd make certain that came to pass. She was afraid of the hunter? Then he wanted to stoke the fires of that fear.

The other vampire hurried toward the curtain, poking her head through. He heard her barking orders: "Need to move him. Ready another hit of the ketamine. Someone get in there to watch him."

He had little time.

The ketamine was finally gone from his system, leaving only a ghost of its effects behind—he wouldn't be as fast or as capable as usual, but he still had a little of Gandalf's blood left. Enough kindling to start a fire.

He let it burn. Let the blood reach through his system like claw-tipped fingers. He began to rock back and forth—the way they nailed him gave him little room to move, but enough to build momentum, and the table was built for quiet dinners, not rowdy, pissed-off bloodsuckers.

Left. Right. Left. Right. *Left. Riiiight.*

Almost... almost...

Shit!

The table did not tip.

But then—it did something else. The table would not suffer the stress.

Two of the legs on the right side of Coburn's body suddenly snapped like shattered bones, splintering with loud cracks. The force of the table hitting the ground pulled some of the nails from Coburn's flesh.

Not all of them.

But enough.

Coburn snarled, got his right arm free and felt his way underneath his tilted body—he reached out, grabbed the doorframe leading into the hall, and *pulled.* Pain shot through him, every nail popping free with the fresh hell of a cigarette burn, his guts still sloshing around half-outside his body, but then, with the sound of buttons tearing free from a shirt, Coburn freed himself from the table.

Two feet planted in front of him. Dirty feet. Bare. Nails painted neon green, the big toenails sporting anime cat faces.

The reedy sylph brought the bat down again.

But this time, Coburn shot up a hand and caught it in his palm.

Thwack.

"Hit me once," Coburn said, rising to his feet, "shame on *you.* Hit me twice, I tear you open like a human piñata and feast on your blood candy."

He tossed the bat aside. The girl turned to run and he caught her by the hair, snapping her back to him and holding her tight in a cruel embrace. He tilted her head to the side as she struggled, saw the pale freckled stretch of neck—

She's on something, Kayla whispered in the hollows of his mind. *Not ketamine, but something else. She'll slow you down, not speed you up.*

He roared, picked the sylph up, then threw her into the wall; she left a crater in the dry wall and tumbled down on the ground, her body still.

As Gil made his way east through the streets of San Francisco, he heard the hunter's cry echo over the buildings.

It made his blood turn to piss, made his piss turn to ice water. Creampuff darted between Gil's legs, tail tucked low.

His heartbeat galloped like a spurred horse, remembering the lab in Los Angeles: the sound of those things crashing through the ducts, climbing up through the elevator shafts, scrambling up the outside of the building, screaming and wailing as they did so.

It occurred to him, then: they thought the rotters were the end of the world, but they weren't the end. They were just the start of it. The hunters—wretched things of gnashing teeth and razor claw, of extended necks and distended mouths—were the true end of the world. A hurricane of hunger belched up out of Hell.

But then the vampire put an end to them. By putting a bullet in his own brain, Coburn effectively put a bullet in all their brains—giving way to some undead vampire-zombie logic that Gil didn't care to understand.

So now, to hear another hunter…

Thoughts ran wild through his head: Coburn had been bitten. He was too brash, too bold, and got himself in trouble. That was how the hunters were born, wasn't it? One zombie gets a taste for vampire blood and that's it, game over.

And if Coburn was gone, so was Kayla.

He'd already lost her body. Somehow, the vampire was home to her spirit, her soul—even her personality. To lose her again…

It felt like something ripped out of Gil's middle. Like the empty space was filled with bugs and battery acid and a few rusted razors.

Worst of all, it made him feel alone.

This wasn't like him. Gil was the backbone. The leader. The one who kept them all safe. Except now they were all dead and all he had was a red-muzzled rat terrier cowering between his ankles.

Above, the purple evening sky turned darker with the coming of night. The moon rose over the city and Gil pushed on, feeling like a scarecrow absolved of his stuffing. As darkness fell, Gil heard the scuffing of feet on sidewalks and the murmuring groans of the encroaching dead—shapes and silhouettes shuffled ahead and behind, moving faster than usual. They were massing. They'd caught his scent.

The rotters got uppity at night; they grew agitated, gained a very little speed and focus. It was time, then, to go to ground. To hide.

A small voice inside Gil urged him just to stop, to sit down here in the middle of Beach Street, by the white flower delivery van whose side was splattered with blood, by the Mission-style housing with boarded windows, by the pink flowering trees lining the avenue. Sit down—or better yet, *lay* down—and let the zombies come and eat what was left of him.

But he didn't. Gil didn't know why, didn't even want to ponder it. Instead he hurried right, sticking along the houses, trying doors until he found one that opened to him.

COBURN STAGGERED THROUGH the beaded curtain.

Low-lit living room. Couches that didn't match. Bean bags everywhere. Carpet torn asunder. Filth streaking the ceiling and everything smelling like hash and pot and patchouli and semen. Someone (with frankly middling amateur talent) had painted dioramas on all the walls: one of them showed someone that looked like Minister Masterson standing on a hill with his arms wide, a crowd of rotters *and* still-living humans kneeling in the golden showers of his glory. Another offered up a zombie crucified in a combination of Da Vinci's Vitruvian Man and a 'cut of meat' chart at a local butcher's—ribs and fat back and prime cuts. A third image was just a painted ossuary of skeletons and loose bones and Mexican sugar skulls.

Coburn wasn't sure of the narrative, but he could take a few guesses: the people here worshipped the Minister who somehow gave them power over death. That power was nothing fancy, but was a life-giving boon to those who could stomach it. Somehow, these barking moon-spiders had the ability to eat the flesh of the undead without the infection running rampant through them.

Just then: movement behind one of the couches.

A whiff of blood and fear sweat.

And sage. And lavender.

"Gandaaaalf," Coburn said all sing-songy. "Or Jeeeeepers. Or whatever the fuck your naaaaame is. Please come out so I can break all the bones in your body."

The old man arose from behind a couch. The movement introduced a new smell: fear urine that perfectly paired with the fear sweat. The old man's ratty sweat pants showed a wet patch around the crotch and left thigh.

"Please," Jeepers mumbled. "Don't kill me. I'm just doing what I got to so I can stay alive, dude. I—I... you don't know what it's like."

Coburn strode across the room. Confident. Hungry.

"No, no, I know," Coburn said, smiling.

"I'm just an old man. My kids are dead. My grandkids are dead. Please, if you gotta kill me, just don't make it hurt..."

The old man broke down in tears.

He was somebody's Daddy, Kayla said. *You could try to be nice.*

To which Coburn decided: fuck that.

The old man had drugged him. Left him nailed to a table. So that Kayla and the cure could be sucked out of *this* vampire's body by a *different* vampire.

Coburn reached Gandalf, lifted him up by his neck. The old not-wizard's face turned red as tears soaked his cheeks and gathered in that wispy gray beard.

You showed mercy on my people once upon a time, Kayla reminded him.

He reminded her: *We had an arrangement. I was just protecting my food source.*

That excuse doesn't hold up any more, JW.

To which he responded: *Your people didn't stick me with needles after attaching me to a dinner table with a hundred nails.*

My Daddy did shoot you. And leave you for dead at a Wal-Mart.

Coburn growled.

Mercy bloomed within him like an ugly, shriveled flower. He detested it—he did not wear benevolence well. It afforded him only discomfort and self-loathing. But it was there, now, lurking inside him, hateful as it was. This old man wasn't even worth the effort it would take to snap his neck, anyway.

But he still had blood, and Coburn still had needs.

Coburn bent to feed.

Bang.

A gun went off, behind the old man.

Gandalf's chest sprayed red, his blood decorating Coburn's shirt.

Dead blood was not the best blood. Which meant the vampire's meal was... well, if not ruined, then certainly disturbed. Just because you *can* eat your hamburger, after it falls on the floor, doesn't mean you want to.

Besides, now Coburn had a bullet lodged in his breastbone.

He threw the old man's gurgling body forward at whoever had fired the shot—and the 'roided-out thick-necked Hispanic motherfucker stepped to the side as the body crashed against the hardwood floor, bringing up a boxy H&K .45 and peeling off another round at Coburn. The vampire didn't have the speed or interest to move aside. The round clipped Coburn in the meat of the shoulder.

No mercy for this one, he told Kayla. She offered no dissent.

What little blood Coburn had left, he let it burn hot and fast inside the crucible of his body, giving him a preternatural burst of speed. He came up behind Flores, getting an arm around the man's neck and pulling tight.

It was like trying to strangle a bison.

Flores whooped and hollered, began whirling about with Coburn on his back. The thick sonofabitch slammed his body backward, driving the vampire into an old TV stand that now served as home to a collection of bongs and pipes, all of which now crashed to the floor with the sound of tinkling glass.

Flores pistoned an elbow into Coburn's midsection, rupturing the vampire's dead bowels. Blood seeped. The intestines didn't matter, but the blood did.

That's when Flores brought up the .45—clumsy, the way he cocked it over his shoulder thinking to squeeze off a shot at the vampire monkey on his back. Coburn planted a foot back on the ground, got a little leverage, then captured the man's wrist and twisted hard as he could.

He turned the .45 downward.

Got his finger around Flores' trigger finger.

Then: squeeze.

The gun went off, popping a round through Flores' upper thigh. Blood squirted from the hole. The man yowled like a cat whose tail just got run over by a push-mower, and Coburn was not going to waste the opportunity. He slapped the gun away and then planted his mouth on the wound like a thirsty kid at a water fountain, greedily slurping.

Everything was red and warm and beautiful.

With a sudden electric jolt of something else.

Oh, my, Kayla said. *He really was juiced up, wasn't he?*

Flores batted at him, tried to wrench Coburn off.

Coburn felt the burn. The jacked-up tweaked-out steroid rush kicked a hole in his soul. It felt like someone knocked a hornet's nest out of a tree growing in the hollows of his mind. He felt Kayla retreat into shadow.

When Flores stopped batting at him, Coburn kept sucking, felt no more blood reach his mouth. He kept sucking anyway. Felt air and flesh and heard the cracking of bone and—

Frustrated, he pushed Flores backward, then stood quickly, and backhanded the body. The head snapped, spinning on the now-shattered pivot of Flores' spine.

"Neck's not so thick now," Coburn said, chuckling.

Outside somewhere: another howl.

The hunter was coming.

No, Coburn thought. *The hunter is already here.*

CHAPTER SIX

Down Into The Dark

WITH FLORES' BLOOD running rough-shod through his body like a pack of coked-up pit-bulls, Coburn felt his guts twist and clinch and ease back into his body as ribbons of ruined stomach-flesh sought each other out.

He felt like he could punch a hole in the heavens, like he could grab God by the ankle and drag that cruel sonofabitch down here to see what his callous and careless fuckery had wrought upon the world of man.

It was all very clarifying.

And what Coburn knew was that Lydia had to go.

The city was home to a hunter. Hopefully just one. If that thing figured out how to make more of itself—and, Coburn suspected, it would—then once again he'd have a plague of demons to deal with. Only way to ensure the hunter took a big long never-ending dirt-nap was to destroy the source: Lydia the vampire.

Besides, obliterating her into a red pulp would be a pleasure.

Because nobody hurts Kayla.

That thought surprised him.

How protective you've become of me, she said. He heard her giggle— it echoed in the cavern of his skull.

Coburn cracked his knuckles. Felt together again.

He stalked through the house. Hunting.

In the kitchen, he found zombie meat—arms, legs, clumps of unidentified gray flesh—hanging from hooks and hemp rope. Organs piled up in nested wire baskets. Filthy counters sat stocked with soda and liquor bottles filled to the brim with black dead blood and corked or capped. The smell should've been overpowering—strong enough to make a vulture puke. But the walls and cabinets were tiled with little pine-tree air fresheners. Nailed there, just as Coburn had been nailed to the table only ten minutes before.

The rat-man—Fingerman—crouched in the corner. Whimpering. Hiding.

Leave him be, Kayla said.

This time, mercy came easy. If only because Coburn wasn't hungry.

Still. The rat-man could be useful.

The vampire grabbed the ketamine addict by his greasy locks, hoisted him high. "The woman. Tell me where she is, you can keep your face."

"The Doc."

"Yes. *The Doc.*"

"She can hook you up," Fingerman said, eyeballs roving, corneas shaking. He was high right now, wasn't he? Jesus. "Whatever you need, man. Vet drugs. Hospital drugs. Whatever. Oxy, vics, morphine, horse tranqs—"

Coburn shook him so hard the man's teeth clacked together.

"I just want *her*. Where is she?"

Fingerman pointed toward the ground. "Basement, man. Tunnels."

Tunnels?

The vampire tightened his grip around the oily horsetail of hair, demanded to know where the basement was. The rat-man pointed the way: "Around the—*ow*—around the corner." Coburn grunted, which was the closest thing the freak was going to get in terms of gratitude—that and Coburn didn't break a bottle of rancid zombie blood over his head, too. That had to count for something.

Coburn found the basement door. Tried the knob—wouldn't open. Locked, probably. Like that could stop him now. He raised his leg, brought the heel of his boot down on the door-knob, knocking it to the ground.

Then he kicked the door open.

Darkness awaited.

But that was all right. Coburn liked the dark.

Grinning, the vampire descended.

THIS WAS THE *wrong damn house to walk into*, Gil thought. As the undead pawed at the door and boarded-up windows outside, Gil stared at the inside with disgust.

The style was cold, modernist—everything in whites, blacks, grays, with only the occasional splash of bright red (mantle, painting, broken vase, toaster). All hard angles. Nothing soft. Tile and glass and steel.

It echoed how Gil felt about, well, everything right now. Hell, he wanted to commit suicide just being here and having to look at the place.

Strange thing was, it was clean. Dusty, sure. But most houses they'd seen looked like bombs went off. Overturned furniture and dead cats and busted pipes bringing ceilings down to meet the floor. Not this place.

But one thing was troubling: the smell.

It smelled like a rotter's armpit. Wet. Fetid. Above all else: dead.

And yet, no signs of—

Creampuff growled at the steps leading to the second floor.

Gil swallowed. Stepped past the terrier, sliding a bolt into the crossbow and cocking it. The stairs up were steel steps like you'd find on a tractor trailer, suspended from the ceiling by thick dark cables.

No way to go up quietly. Every step a metallic gong.

The stairs shook as he ascended.

The smell? Stronger up here.

He steadied himself on the railing—another cable, this one strung horizontally—and saw Creampuff hop up onto a white leather couch and stare up at Gil with trepidation.

Gil turned, headed down the hallway.

All the while, the roadkill stink growing gnarlier until Gil's eyes were watering and his stomach—which didn't have much more than a few stale Entemann's crumb cakes bobbing around the lake of digestive fluids—churned like a bucket of bad milk in a clumsy man's hand.

At the end of the hall, Gil saw a door cracked open.

He gently tapped it with a foot. It opened with a squeak.

And there he found the source of the stench.

Rotters. Three of them.

Two of them on the bed. Supine. Bound there with an inelegant tangle of nylon rope, extension cords, and twine. One was a man: dark fraying turtleneck, head a mop of Andy Warhol hair, pair of dark frame glasses literally stapled to his mottled face. The other, a woman. Gray blouse with sharp collars. Pair of flowy black pants. No shoes. Toes worn away, leaving only twitching nubs of blackened bone. The two of them hissed and writhed against their bonds.

The third rotter was a child. A young boy of eight or nine with a bowl-cut of black hair and a windbreaker whose fabric went *vip vip vip* every time he moved. One eye dangled out of his head, resting on his swollen chipmunk cheek. The rest of the boy looked relatively well-preserved, for one of the undead.

He, too, was bound up, to a wire-frame office chair. Wheels locked so that it couldn't roll around.

It was someone's family.

The man—the *father*—gurgled. Dead lipless flesh rubbing together. Gil saw a patch of the man's shoulder that had been worn away: the turtleneck gnawed open and the flesh, too. As if on cue, the woman tilted her head toward the father and craned her neck until she could get her chompers around his exposed flesh. She took a few graceless bites and then pulled away again, seemingly dissatisfied by the taste— or, Gil wondered, the lack of nutrition, given that rotters didn't seem to eat one another with any regularity.

The whole scene stirred within him a turbid shit-storm of emotions: it was perplexing (*who did this*), it was grotesque (*couldn't do this to my own family*), it was sweet (*someone cared enough*).

Whatever the case, Gil thought, these people needed to be put to rest. He raised the crossbow. Looked out over the bow sights—a little pink plastic 'V' at the tip of the weapon—and let his finger curl around the trigger.

Something jabbed into the small of his back.

His world lit up. Like it was on fire. A loud fly-wing buzz.

His finger squeezed.

The smell of ozone. And burning. And death.

Gil dropped. The crossbow clattered.

Somewhere, Creampuff barked.

And then a plastic bag pulled tight over his head. As Gil sucked in a hard breath he found plastic in his mouth, around his lips, shutting off his air with a vacuum seal made by his own desperate gasps. His tongue played against it as his body twitched and a sad scream rose up within his throat.

Darkness reached up to claim him.

COBURN WALKED DOWN into darkness.

As he approached the basement, he smelled mold, and a breathy sewage gust. Voices rose up from the shadows, a half-conversation interrupted—

Masterson: "—take me with you, I can help—"

Lydia: "Get away from me. Go deal with the vampire."

Masterson: "Forget him. Forget the others. I'm alive. You're dead. We need each other. I worship you. I—"

Lydia: "It's not me you should be wor—" Pause. "Did you hear that?"

A moment later, she whispered: "*He's here.*"

Oops. Oh, well.

Coburn whistled low and slow to further announce his presence.

"I'm feeling much better now," he called into the dark basement. His eyes adjusted as he reached the bottom of the steps. The basement was just a repository for junk: boxes, debris, a gun rack, a cabinet. And, by the look of it, their bathroom: various fly-clouded buckets sat against the far wall. Reeking.

But what was most interesting was the hole dug out of the wall and floor. Drywall gave way to exposed brick and broken piping. Leading down into whatever tunnels the rat-man had been referring to.

And there, at the mouth of the shattered wall, stood Lydia and Masterson.

"Hey, *guys,*" Coburn said with a low, throaty chuckle. "Geez, I didn't know you came here. The buckets of shit in the corner are *to die for.*

You crazy kids want to get a booth or a table?"

Lydia looked to Masterson. Her gaze locked with his and Coburn could see that the self-proclaimed Minister could not escape. He tried, but couldn't. Something transferred between them—which meant the vampire was dropping her hypno-hoodoo on him. Coburn had no interest in seeing that play out. As Lydia handed something to her cohort, Coburn moved fast.

In his head, Kayla called to him in alarm: *You're not thinking straight. Again.*

He ignored her. Again.

With a sweep of his arms he tossed the Minister aside; the man clattered into a heap of moldy cardboard boxes. Lydia wrenched a brick from its mooring with a sharp crack and brought it against Coburn's head.

He didn't even feel it.

Coburn roared, grabbed her face like it was a bowling ball: thumb in her mouth, two fingers in her eyes, *squeezing* in order to pop the face off her skull. Her eyes started to give way. Pop like swollen grapes.

Then she bit down.

Her teeth cut clean through Coburn's thumb. Through skin, through bone. With the drugs storming through his system, it didn't hurt too much. He even laughed as she spit the thumb out into the tunnel behind her. Her eyes swollen, rimmed with blood, the whites shot through with black.

"Nice job!" he said, giving her a thumbs-up with the hand that had no thumb. Blood wept from the wound.

She kicked him in the stomach. An ungainly, inept kick—nobody had taught her how to fight. Coburn taught himself long ago by getting in fights with any gang thug, robber, rapist, or killer he could find. Humans fought and got hurt just by fighting—too strong a punch meant a broken hand, too high a kick meant your balance was out of whack, and only idiots and assholes went for the headbutt. Headbutt someone, your eyes watered, your head rang like a bell, and dizziness would be your primary reward.

Coburn didn't worry about any of that. His tear ducts were dry as peach pits. His head was as hard as a grave slab.

So he smashed his head into Lydia's face.

Once. Then twice. Then a third time for good measure.

She's a vampire, Kayla reminded him. *Just like you.*

Oh, right. Crap.

Just the same—her nose was shattered and she staggered back into the darkness of the tunnel. Coburn clapped his hands. This was fun. She was green, this one. Young and awkward like a newborn foal. She picked up a brick. Hissed for Masterson. Chucked the brick at Coburn's head—

He leaned left, let the brick sail over.

"Someone really needs to teach you how to fight," he said.

Lydia, nose smashed, eyes bugging out all bloody, shrugged.

"Somebody needs to teach *you* to pay attention," she said.

He heard the scuff of a shoe behind him.

Lydia sprang into the tunnel like a fucking puma, her lithe shadow meeting the deeper shadows within—

Masterson tackled Coburn. Slamming the vampire into the side of the tunnel. As Coburn fell to the ground, Masterson clambered atop his chest. Weeping. Snot-bubbles boiling up out of his nose.

"I used to be somebody," Masterson said. Voice hoarse.

He was holding a grenade. The pin was not at home.

Coburn winced. *Shit.*

Boom, Kayla said, a half-second before the grenade went off.

And the world turned to noise and debris and pain.

The Conversation: #2

WILL I LIVE with him now?

Beats me. Like I know how this works. We're in new territory here, little girl.

Or maybe I'll just die. Maybe I won't exist anymore.

Could be, rabbit. Could be. But I hope not. I really hope not.

Maybe I'll change him like I changed you.

Who said you changed me?

You're so funny sometimes.

Yeah. A real laugh riot.

CHAPTER SEVEN

I Believe That Children Are Our Future

GASP.

Oxygen.

Breath screaming through his throat and filling his lungs—felt cool and hot and good and painful, all in equal measure.

Gil lurched upright. Bag still on his head. But someone had vented a hole where his mouth was, and with every breath the plastic whispered and crinkled.

He reached up, panicked, pawing at the bag. He ripped it off and threw it to the ground like it was a bundle of cottonmouth snakes.

Gil found his own crossbow pointed at his head.

And a dirt-caked child was the one pointing it.

"Get up, dickweed," the boy said. Grungy blond hair covering one eye—a jet of air from pursed lips blew the hair to the side. "I said, *get the fuck up*, bitch."

Gil scrambled backward like a crab.

Something hit him from behind—something heavy, wooden. Cracked him over the head—not hard enough to make him bleed, but hard enough to sting. He turned, saw another kid standing there holding a busted chair leg. It was a girl—hair an unwashed tangle, face streaked with fingers of what looked like ash.

Other children filtered into the room upon hearing the commotion. Another six of them. No teenagers, though a few that looked eleven or twelve, including the boy holding the crossbow aloft. Youngest seemed to be a boy of four or so—a porky mole-cheeked dumpling with hair stuck up and clumped with red as if it had been shellacked with strawberry jam. Gil realized with horror that it probably wasn't strawberry.

His horror deepened when he realized all these kids had weapons. The girl with the chair leg. A pre-teen with bones woven into her pigtails held a folded license plate whose edge was plainly sharpened. A third held a .22 pistol. A fourth had a pair of ice picks, one in each hand. Even the fat little four-year-old dragged an oiled bike chain behind him.

Outside, thunder rumbled. Distant. But closing in.

"You tried to kill my father," Crossbow Kid said.

Gil stammered, cleared his throat. Saw a pair of feet hanging over the edge of the bed—Mother and Father, respectively, both pairs of feet gently twitching and wiggling with the crude facsimile of life. Nearby, the third rotter—the kid with the bowl-cut and cherub-cheeks—spun idly in the office chair.

He stood, saw the crossbow bolt he'd loosed earlier sticking out of the flesh around the father-zombie's collarbone.

"That's your father," Gil said, horrified.

"What of it, dick?"

"Watch your language, kid."

"My name's not *kid*, dick. It's Aiden."

Gil's forehead furrowed. "My name's not *Dick*, Aiden. It's Gil."

"Whatever. You tried to kill my father."

"Yeah," Gil said. "Except I think he's already dead."

That made Aiden angry. He surged forward with the crossbow, which was a mistake—Gil snatched it out of the kid's hand as a bolt flew free and popped into the wall behind him with a *thunk*.

Gil quickly backed against the wall, struggling to find another bolt— but Aiden kicked forward a leather belt covered in loops once meant for bullets but now used to house crossbow arrows.

"You looking for these?" Aiden asked.

The scrawny tween boy pointed the .22 pistol—a long-barrel Browning target weapon—at Gil's chest in an unswerving grip. All he said was: "Dude." Then shook his head disapprovingly, like a parent disappointed in his child.

Gil held up the crossbow, gently set it down on the floor.

"Let's try this again," he said, "my name is Gil. I'm a survivor. Just like you. Now if we can all just put down our weapons and—"

The .22 went off. A sharp snap—the wall coughed up bits of drywall into Gil's cheek and he danced away from it.

Another disapproving shake of the head from Scrawny. "*Dude.*"

Aiden clarified: "He means, I talk. You shut the fuck up. Say one more word, he'll have a bullet rattling around in your head like a marble in a fishbowl. Nod if you understand the words coming out of my mouth."

Every inch of Gil wanted to reach out and snatch up the weapons from these kids and scold the king hell out of 'em. He remembered one time Kayla, thinking someone was breaking in, took a .22 rifle off the gun rack in his bedroom and accidentally shot a hole in the ceiling. Went up through the attic, punched a hole in a junction box, almost started a fire in the insulation. That was when he taught her about gun safety—she never much liked it, but she needed it. The chief lesson he drummed into her head, time and time again: *you never point a gun at another human being unless you mean to kill him.*

Still. This was not the time. So Gil just nodded.

"Like I said: my name's Aiden. The skinny sum-bitch with the Browning Buck Mark Plus aimed at your ball-sack is Pete. Girl who hit you with the chair-leg, that's Ashleigh. Pigtails over there, that's the Princess." The girl waved, smiling big, her bone-woven pigtails bouncing. Aiden gave her a mean look and she stopped waving. Aiden pointed to the boy with the ice-picks. "That's Booboo." Then to a girl with a cleft lip and a sling-shot. "That's Little Mary. Big Mary's not here. That's right. There's more of us. A lot more."

Gil almost spoke, then bit his tongue. He gestured toward the little plump four-year-old.

Aiden narrowed his gaze. "Don't you worry about who he is, old man."

All the children stood around, staring burning holes through Gil. Everyone except the one called the Princess, who stood there smacking her lips and looking blissfully ignorant of the horror in the room before her. Reminded Gil a little of Kayla that way. His heart went sour just thinking about it.

"Your dog's dead," Aiden said.

Gil felt like the oxygen had once more been removed from the room. Like a bag was again over his head and he was struggling to breathe. Once upon a time he hated that vampire's little hellhound, but things had changed. Creampuff was like a board floating in the ocean, to which Gil clinged. And now? Gone?

Aiden continued: "He bit me, so we had to break his neck. Same goes for you if you try anything—"

From downstairs, a bark. A very familiar bark.

Gil felt like he could breathe again.

Aiden's face grew red and he screamed downstairs: "Goddamnit, Charlie! I told you to keep that fucking mutt quiet!" He turned back to Gil. "Fine. I was lying. Whatever. Screw you. Not my fault you—"

Another sound. Not a bark.

Again, the bellow of a distant hunter—a keening, high-pitched screech. The sound made the hairs on Gil's neck reach for the stars. He could see that he wasn't alone. All the kids shifted uncomfortably. They knew what they were hearing.

Princess spoke: "Ellie."

The other kids said the same name in unison: "Ellie..."

They bowed their heads, suddenly somber.

Gil dared speak. "You... you know what made that sound."

"That's Ellie." Aiden nodded. "She was one of us."

COBURN SMELLED PEACHES and cigarettes. Heard Kayla laughing somewhere behind the high-pitched tone humming in his ears. Remembered that the last time he saw someone with a grenade, it was Leelee, Kayla's best friend and almost-doctor and surrogate mother— the pin hit the ground and the grenade took out her and a pack of hunters. And that was the end of that.

I miss her, came Kayla's voice rising out of the fog.

The vampire tried not to think about that.

Instead, he put out his hand, tried to stand, but found that his arm was like that zombie who gutted him—missing below the elbow. He fell, leaning hard on a nub of bone. A barbed spear of white-hot pain shot up from the bone to his shoulder and all the way to his ear.

He rolled over. Into something wet.

Wincing, he sat up, felt along his back for whatever it was—came back with a smear of red. Nearby lay a bowl—no, not a bowl, but a chunk of skull-cap with hair on the bottom. Masterson.

Masterson was everywhere.

The grenade, silly, Kayla said. *Remember that?*

Oh. Right.

At the last moment, before the grenade went off, Coburn turned and dove away from Masterson, pushing that poor dumb human bomb backward. Which explained why Coburn's arm was half-gone.

Now, here he was. Missing an arm. Covered in dust and shattered brick and parts of Masterson. *At least you're not trapped in a Wal-Mart about to be eaten by a crazy super-obese lady*, came Kayla's voice. *Yeah. You never said much about that, but I can see it here with all your other memories. That was pretty gross, JW.*

It was pretty gross.

And this was not as bad as that.

At least he had blood here. It was undignified and made him feel more than a little like a starving dog but...

He bent down, and vacuumed up what was left of Masterson with his lips. Like he was slurping spilled soup from the floor. It was dingy and dirty and losing its nutritive value fast and occasionally he had to spit out spurs of bone or clumps of hair, but blood was blood and this arm wasn't going to regrow itself. (Well, it *would*, but only with the proper urging.)

While siphoning up the liquid parts of the exploded Minister Masterson, Coburn wondered just what the hell that guy's deal was. Thought he was some kind of cult leader. Leading the people toward a—what was it he said? A *symbiosis* with living man and undead asshole. But the truth was, Masterson was just another parasite. This one clinging to Lydia the way a remora fish hangs off the belly of a shark—bottom-feeding scum-sucking trash-picker. Not a leader. Not a 'minister.'

When Coburn was done, he stood.

Grunted. Flexed his toes. Gritted his teeth.

Blood moved to wet the bony end of his arm. Muscle and tendon grew along with it, along with an unfurling flag of too-pink skin.

It was miserable. Felt like his arm was covered in a thousand ants, then dunked in a bucket of boiling water to kill them. Then ants, then boiling water. Over and over again. Until a few minutes went by and he felt fingers—skinless fingers for the moment—wiggling in the open air.

Time, then, to figure out where he was.

He'd gone into the tunnel.

Then used Lydia's head like a bowling ball.

Then Masterson, then *boom*.

And the tunnel mouth closed. A rain of bricks and bone, of dust and dead guy. And now Coburn was looking down the mouth of the tunnel where Lydia had gone. Ahead he saw that this grotto broke into a smaller tunnel—an egg-shaped tunnel of old pale brick that cut across horizontally.

Time to move.

He reached the tunnel. Left or right?

He willed his lungs to pull in air, get a good noseful—he smelled the memory of sewage, not fresh but still married to these walls the way cigarette smoke clings to a sport coat. And beneath it, that hint of jasmine, that touch of death and cold clammy skin. A smell he once thought reserved only for him.

Left, then.

The tunnel did not allow him to stand at full height. He had to crouch, an undignified way to travel if ever there was one. Doubly undignified is how he had to pull himself along, hands falling upon debris that had long lined the brick—much of it stuck there like a lollipop glued to a baby's cheek. Fast food wrappers. Used condoms. He even saw an old red-headed wig plastered to the tunnel wall. None of it breaking down. In a hundred years—a thousand—these will be the remnants of human civilization. The question then became, would anyone even be around to find these things? Or was humanity's ticket punched as its dead fed on its living?

Coburn told himself he hoped humanity *did* stick around, if only so he had something—er, someone—to eat.

Kayla just laughed in the back of his mind, as if she knew better.

Whatever the case, that's why he had to do what he was doing. Had to get to the lab. Had to have them analyze his blood—not just for his own restorative powers but for the healing blood of the very special miracle mystery girl. Her blood was curative. If they could make that into a cure for all mankind, well, that meant his food supply would once more be in good working order.

This was all part of the original deal, he told himself—and told the girl in his head. Protect her. Shepherd her. *Carry her forth*. He did not keep her safe but he could keep what mattered safe: her blood.

She laughed again—the sound of birds chirping, broken glass tinkling.

He ignored her, and pushed on.

Five minutes in, water began trickling past his feet. A silvery rivulet of scum-topped water. It smelled of—

The tunnel vibrated. The growl of distant thunder.

Rain. It smelled of rain.

That was not great news. These sewers no longer worked like they were supposed to. Not that he knew exactly how a sewer system operated, but he was pretty sure that electricity figured into it somewhere down the line. And maintenance. He'd been down beneath New York enough times to know that run-off from the street moved from tunnels like this one into bigger spaces—and from those bigger spaces, the water was pumped away to treatment plants.

No pumps meant the water had nowhere to go.

It would just fill up the tunnels. Some of it might overflow into the bay. But the rest would drown him like a rat. Not that he needed to breathe, but he didn't feel like getting washed into the bay like a dirty soda bottle, either.

He put a little pep in his step. No need to urge his body to do anything crazy yet—he didn't want to waste the blood. But still: faster was better.

Another trembling tumble of thunder from above.

And with it, the sound of a hunter's scream.

It was not as distant as he had hoped.

As the tunnel bent east, Coburn saw ahead of him a murky band of light—a storm-drain looked out onto the streets of San Francisco as rainwater cascaded down in a shimmering sheet. Even as he approached, he heard the susurration of rain grow heavier—from a steady fall to an asphalt-battering downpour.

He neared the storm drain.

An arm shot out of that space. Reaching in from the outside—a lanky, scabby arm, the purple-gray of a faded bruise, the fingers long, *too* long, each tipped with not so much a claw as a curve of sharpened bone poking through the dead flesh. It swiped the air only a few feet in front of Coburn's face, scratching across brick and leaving furrows in the stone.

It was a child's arm.

The hunter shrieked into the storm drain. Coburn saw the beast's face: yes, a child's face, stretched long and thin, the eyes set back in hollow sockets, the mouth a wide-open nest of shark's teeth. Razors laid upon razors. Biting the air. Long tapered tongue licking along the edge of the storm drain the way a dog might lick the rim of his food bowl.

Long dark dirty hair hung in stiff ringlets around her face.

Oh, my god, it's a girl, Kayla said. Coburn could feel the ghost in his head recoil in horror. But not just horror—sadness. And not sympathy, but empathy. As if Kayla saw some part of herself in this girl—dead, now a monster, or part of one.

The hunter spit and licked the walls and gnashed her horrible teeth. A second arm reached in next to the first, both reaching for him.

Coburn felt a stirring of something inside his own mind—a sepulchered carcass of grief and guilt and shame rising from its psychic tomb and shaking off decades of dead and thoughtless dust. Dead girls. Kayla. Rebecca. This one. All his fault. The zombies were him and though this hunter was not his, it still pointed back through time to when he gave the middle finger to the wrong man.

No! No time for that. No time for sympathy or empathy or grief or any of those emotions. They were unproductive. Useless as a short-sleeved straitjacket, worthless as a vestigial organ.

Just as Coburn started to wonder just how he was going to get past the slashing claws and flicking tongue of this child hunter, the creature withdrew her seeking arms and was gone. Whoosh. Leaving only the pouring rain and stomach-grumbles of thunder.

No time like the present. He hurried past the open drain.

Kayla issued an ominous warning: *Remember, JW. Those hunters are smarter than the average rotter.*

It was then that, behind him, he heard an equally ominous noise:

A manhole cover being ripped from its mooring.

Coburn lit a fire in his blood and ran like a sonofabitch.

THEY TOLD GIL about Ellie.

Pete kept the pistol on him as he listened to Aiden tell the story.

"Ellie was one of us. One of the kids who survived. I see the look on your face. You think we'd be the first to go. That we're vulnerable. Well, fuck you, old man. *You're* slow. *You're* the weak one."

Gil wondered why everybody thought he was so old. Then again, he hadn't looked in a mirror in a long time. His fifty-some years probably looked like seventy-some by now. All leather and stubble and raccoon rings around his tired eyes.

Aiden continued: "Kids are quick. Adaptable. Smart in the right ways—doesn't matter if we don't know who the twenty-second president was—"

Grover Cleveland, Gil thought.

"—what matters is what we run faster than you. I'm not saying that all the kids survived. Some kids are real pussies. Their parents start turning to mush-mouthed, brain-eating fucktards and they still want to go and hug Daddy and hold onto Mommy. But those of us who knew the score knew to run. And hide. And we knew *where* to run and *where* to hide. This city has a lot of boltholes."

Gil shot a look at the kid's dead parents on the bed. Shifting. Grunting. And his brother on the chair staring ahead. All preserved. *Saved.* As if a cure might appear one day and return them back to normal—a fairy tale. Or was it? Zombies. Vampires. His own daughter with her miracle blood. Maybe it wasn't so crazy.

It also suggested this kid was a lot more bark than bite.

Wasn't really a great time to say that, though, so Gil let the kid talk.

"Ellie was one of us who made it until—" And here Aiden started to blink fast, like he was maybe trying not to cry. His hands formed into fists at his sides as if the grief were a real thing, as real as the zombies, and he could just knock its block off and send it packing. "Until she wasn't. She got swamped. We pulled her out and up onto a fire escape, but not before they bit her leg. She turned."

"Ellie." A griefstruck whimper from Princess. Who began to sob, crumpling in on herself like a flower dying in fast-forward. Aiden clapped his hands angrily at her and yelled:

"Princess! Shut up! I'm telling a damn story."

The girl only wept harder.

Gil moved over to her—Pete tensed his arm and pointed the pistol with greater and more panicked purpose—but he ignored the gun and went to the girl anyway, pulling her tight against him. She buried her face in his shirt, soaking it through with little-girl tears.

"Go on," Gil said, giving the girl comfort and stifling her tears. "Tell your little story."

"She's crying. I don't like her crying."

"I don't like you being a bully, you little thug. Now keep talking."

Aiden seemed stung.

But damn if it didn't work. Cautiously, he resumed the story: "We... kept Ellie with us for a while. Had her held quick with a catch-pole somebody stole from one of the animal shelters. But over the last couple months, that's when the doctor showed up. Wanting to take more of us away."

"The doctor."

"Uh-huh. She comes around every so often. At first she was nice. Offering us things if we went with her. She said she could take two or three of us on a boat and that she had this lab and there were people there, and it was safe and they had food. I never trusted her."

"You kinda trusted her," Ashleigh said, twirling the chair leg like a slow-motion baton. "I mean, you said—"

"God, Ashleigh, I changed my mind!" He scowled at her. "Fine. I sent some of us off with her at first. But then we never heard anything and I thought the doctor was strange anyway, and so next time she came by I said for everybody to stay here, that we were doing okay on our own and that the adults didn't know safety from a sack of shit. Even still, Javier said he wanted to go with her and it didn't help that she was waving a bag of M&Ms around."

Aiden sat on the edge of the bed, between the wiggling corpse-feet of his two dead parents, as if it was no big thing.

"Wasn't long after that Ellie got bit. And the next time the doc came around, she was pushy. Threatening us. Way she looked at you made you want to go with her even though you didn't want to go with her."

"She had pretty eyes," Pete said, as if lost in a dream.

"But before any of us could follow her, Ellie broke free of the catchpole. Jumped on the doc's back like a monkey. Bit down onto the lady's neck and there was blood everywhere. The lady screamed. Threw Ellie against a dumpster. Ran off like a shot, like a… an Olympic runner. Weird thing was, didn't even look like her neck was bit up. Blood, lots of blood, but no, y'know, wound."

Gil could've guessed the rest of the story, and it went about like he figured. "We got Ellie back with the catch-pole but she changed that night. Got all fuckin' weird. She went from being a dumb zombie to… I dunno. It's like she *saw* us again. But not in a good way. Like in the way a tiger watches you from behind the bars at the zoo. And she got still. Just sat down. Waiting. Zombies don't wait. They smell you and they'll come at you even if that means walking across a street full of broken glass to get at you. She wasn't like that. Not anymore.

"So. We let her go. Threw her behind a door and closed it, pulling the pole out. Then we ran like crazy."

"We still sometimes see her," Booboo said, picking his nose with one hand and using the other to fidget with an ice pick.

Aiden nodded. "We hear her out there. See her, too. She's got a pack of zombos that follow her around like dogs."

Finally, Princess stopped sobbing, progressing to the sniffling-and-hitching-breath phase. She stood next to Gil and rested her dirty cheek on his shoulder. "I miss Ellie. She was a better princess than me."

Gil dared to ask: "This woman. One who Ellie bit. She say where she was taking you kids?"

Aiden said, "Yeah. To Alcatraz. To her lab."

CHAPTER EIGHT

Drowned Rats In A Dead Maze

THE VAMPIRE DARED not look, but the sounds told him everything he needed to know: the hunter dropped into the tunnel behind him, landing with a splash, bone claws and talons clicking on the ancient brick. But the hunter was not alone: other bodies hit the tunnel like sacks of grain dropped out of the back of a pick-up truck. Zombies. Clumsily bumbling into the dark, likely following the focus of their fruitless attention span: the beast in dark ringlets.

As noted, Coburn ran.

You can take her, Kayla said as Coburn hunkered down, clawing his way through the tunnel like a rat driven mad by a parasite. *C'mon, JW. Just one little girl. Remember how well you handled me once upon a time?*

The memory of holding Kayla aloft by her throat struck him. An almost physical blow. With it: another wash of guilt. Acid on the back of his tongue. Acid in the back of his mind. Guilt was for suckers. Shame was for chumps.

Remorse was a line that separated the living and the dead.

The dead had no remorse.

And Coburn reminded himself: he was most certainly dead.

Ahead, the tunnel split—a Y-shaped fork in the path. Coburn quickly sniffed the air, caught at first only the smell of rainwater and broken-down grease and other old chemicals washed from the streets into the sewers, but as he could feel and hear the hunter coming up behind him (a hundred yards, now? seventy-five?), panic twisted through his heart like a rusty screw—

Jasmine. There.

Coburn scrambled down the left-most path.

She's gaining on you, Kayla said.

And she was. The wretched sounds of the pursuing hunter were closer now and closing in fast—the water beneath his feet was starting to form a heavier stream, six, seven inches deep, the walls were growing slick with moisture. His hands slipped, his feet splashed as the water slowed him just enough. It felt like being in a bad dream, except Coburn didn't usually *have* bad dreams. Hell, Coburn usually *was* the bad dream.

Turn. Face her. You're not a runner, JW. You don't flee what scares you. Kayla laughed. *I didn't think anything scared you.*

But this did. This terrified him. Curdled his blood.

Didn't matter now. The hunter was upon him.

She shrieked as she scuttled up behind him, running up the wall on her hands and knees like a spider. Coburn pivoted, spun to meet her as she leaped for him.

The child hunter slammed into his chest, claws digging deep as she shrieked, flecks of rancid spit dotting his face. The pain of her claws was vibrant, alive, an electric misery. As Coburn's head slammed back into the water, rushing into his ears and up the back of his shirt, he saw the little girl up close: a wretched mockery of a child's innocent face, mouth twisted into a shark's grin, eyes the color of infection, neck elongated as if the vertebrae had multiplied.

But that's not the face he saw.

He saw his daughter.

Blinking sweetly as she lay atop him, humming a song.

Light filtering in through gauzy curtains.

A TV going in the background. Something about Ovaltine.

A hard slash of four jagged bone-tip fingers across Coburn's cheek—turning his face into a loose fringe—returned him to reality.

You can't hurt her, Kayla said. *Can you?*

He wanted to. But couldn't. He couldn't hurt this thing that was plainly no longer a child, that had been gutted out by the zombie disease and replaced with the virulent demon borne by the vampire blood—the girl was no longer *in there.*

But you're still in here, Kayla said. *And you're becoming a real boy, Pinocchio.*

Go to hell, Kayla, he thought.

Behind the hunter, the zombies that had fallen in through the manhole were starting to catch up. Crawling on all fours like an old man looking for his fallen glasses. Dragging themselves forward.

They came to feed, too. Vultures hungry for scraps.

Coburn decided to let them have a meal.

GIL STRUGGLED WITH all of it.

The little girl had bitten a—well, what else could it have been? A vampire. Another vampire. Even imagining a world with *two* Coburns damn near made Gil pass out. Doubly troubling was that this vampire seemed somehow connected with the lab they were seeking. What other lab could it be?

All of that didn't add up. Separate puzzle pieces that refused to click together. Only an incomplete picture formed; other parts remained missing.

Just the same, that was bad news. Coburn was out there. So was a hunter. And a second bloodsucker. His daughter's soul caught in the middle.

He remembered what those hunters could do. A vampire biting you was one thing, but zombies biting a vampire—that changed the equation. Things were bad enough with one hunter out there. Gil didn't care to see another rising tide of razor maws and bone claws.

"I'm going out there," Gil said, standing up. "Gimme my arrows back."

Princess clung to his leg.

"Hell I will," Aiden said.

"Kid, I will redden your backside with the back of my hand. You already deserve a good hide-tanning the way you talk to me and your so-called friends here. Now, like I said: arrows. Now."

"Fuck off." The boy lifted his chin toward Pete. "Shoot this turd-farmer."

But Pete didn't move. "I dunno, Aiden."

"Pete!" Aiden whined.

"Just let him go."

Aiden crossed his arms over his chest. Stuck out a pouty chin. "Why you wanna go out there, anyway? Get yourself killed by a swarm of zombos? It's raining like crazy. You won't see ten feet in front of you. And if I guess it right, you're not even from this city. So why go at all?"

"Because I have a..."—he hesitated saying it, but it came out anyway—"*friend* out there. I thought he would've found me by now, but he hasn't. And hearing about your friend Ellie and that... strange woman gives me no comfort. Plus, my... friend is carrying something very important to me."

"*Fine*," Aiden said, kicking over the belt with the crossbow bolts in the loops. "Take 'em and go, you shriveled old douche."

Gil snatched up the belt. Hooked it around his waist.

"I wanna come," Princess said, jumping up and down.

"We could help," Pete said, idly popping the pistol's safety on, off, on, off. Which made Gil increasingly nervous. "We could take you down some of the side-streets where the zombos don't usually hang. They like to gather in the big streets and intersections more than the alleys. For some reason." He shrugged.

"No," Gil said. "*Hell,* no. It's hard enough out there without me having to keep an eye on a pack of little kids."

Princess kicked his shin. "We don't need protecting. You do, mister." Then she smiled sweetly once more and held up the blade fashioned from a sharpened license plate. She stared over its gleaming edge with mad eyes.

"Nobody's going anywhere but him," Aiden said. "You're all staying here."

"Nah. I think we're going," Pete said.

Booboo nodded. The little boy with the bowl-cut hopped up and down, apparently giddy at the notion of wading out into a rain-slick zombie-infested city after nightfall. Which made Gil wonder just how broken these children were.

"I said no," Gil said.

"And *I* said no," Aiden added.

But that didn't seem to matter. The kids stood up and picked up their weapons—chair legs and bike chains and all—and seemed suddenly mobilized for war. All with faces that were either dead to fear or alive with excitement.

Everyone but Aiden. Who sat there. Face reddening.

"You follow me," Gil said, sweeping his finger across the kids, "that's on you. I'm not your father. I'm not your protector. I just want what I want."

The thought struck him, suddenly: *You sound like Coburn.*

Old man.

Hey!

The voice inside his mind: Kayla.

Everything around him seemed slow. Shark teeth crashing together above his head. Descending. Zombies crawling up from both sides. Reaching. Moaning. Gibbering in the tunnel—all sounding like a record played on the wrong speed.

You're not gonna punk out on me, JW.

You got this far.

I'm sorry you killed your daughter.

I'm sorry you killed hundreds of people.

I'm sorry that you're just starting to realize what a terrible person you are.

But you getting dead again isn't going to fix any of that.

All it does is take you out of the picture—and it's a bad picture, JW, a real bad picture. Maybe you haven't looked around, but this sewer may be the nicest place we've been in a while. Everything's gone to hell. Maybe literally, for all I know—the Bible's got some real bad juju in it that matches up pretty well with that happened. All I know is, the world fell down in its own puke. It may not be your fault it's that way, not exactly, but it's still on you. This is your mess. At least a little bit.

And I'm your mess, too. You killed yourself so that I could live, and then I killed myself so that the both of us could carry on.

You leave now, I get dead, too.

And the world just gets hella uglier.

So move your dead butt, JW.

It's not your time. And it's darn sure not mine.

He lurched up. Smashed the hunter to the side, into the brick. The beast cried out in rage and surprise—but no pain. Zombies reached for him as he got up in a low crouch. He put a fist through one. Smashed the other into six inches of rising water and kept pressing until the head caved in like a melon.

The hunter came at him with renewed vigor and he caught the child and smashed her left, and right, and left, and right—flipping her back and forth into the brick sewer tunnel, her arms clawing his, her teeth snapping closed on open air. The sound coming up out of her was like the howl of a tornado—equal parts metallic shriek and freight train bearing down on you.

It cut short, suddenly.

Because Coburn smashed her one more time into the wall.

That wall collapsed.

So did parts of the floor. And the roof.

The vampire and the hunter toppled through open space, along with gallons of hissing rainwater.

Downstairs in the house was another boy named Charlie. Gil didn't know if that was the kid's real name or if they called him that because he had a very distinct Charlie Brown vibe—yellow shirt (no zig zag), round head with fawn-colored hair, a dopey look on his face.

He also had leg braces and a metal cane.

Oh. And a bayonet duct-taped to a broom handle.

Creampuff saw Gil, ran to him. Growled at everyone.

Gil decided to take the terrier with him. But he demanded that they leave the four-year-old behind with Charlie. As they paused at the door, ready to meet whatever waited them on the other side, Princess whispered in Gil's ear that the four-year-old's name was Samuel, and that he was Aiden's little cousin.

And with that, Pete threw open the door.

Before them: a wall of gore-soaked clothing, rotten flesh, and hungry mouths. Zombies pressed forward, seeing a space and trying to fill it, the same way rainwater fills whatever holes and cracks it falls into—they groaned and grunted, their dead mouths filling the air with the stench of rot.

Gil barely had to do a thing. A mailman went down when a .22 bullet punched through its bulging eye and popped out the back of its head like a lead-bellied cricket. A fat lady with her jaw gone found an ice pick shoved up through her ruined sinuses and into her equally-ruined brain. A swift arc from a chair leg and a suit-and-tie rotter's knee went sideways—as the dead man fell to his hands, Ashleigh collapsed his mushy head. Even Princess got in on the action, clambering up Gil like he was a tree and she was a monkey, then screeching with excitement as she slashed left and right with her razor-honed license plate. The top of an old dead man's head came off and he expired with a gush of black blood.

The children were well-practiced at dispatching the dead. As they pushed forward through the pounding rain, clearing a path, Gil saw their system at play—one kid would bring the zombie low by taking out its legs, another would finish the job at the head. "Go for the knees!" one would yell. "Here's the head!" another would cry—a cry born of glee and anger and childish madness.

The pop of bones. The crunch of heads.

The laughter of children.

It was impressive and sickening in equal measure.

And that was how they moved through the dead city. At night. In the rain.

COBURN FOUND HIMSELF plunging deep into a channel of cold water. All was dark, a turbid murk that spoke of rust and shit and swirling brick dust—his hands thrust upward, found rough concrete and water going all the way to the ceiling. He sank down through the space, five feet, ten feet—and again his hands found concrete.

Air forced its way up out of his nose and mouth from the corners of his eyes—bubbles big and small. He didn't need to breathe, and so as the stagnant water forced its way in past his many openings, he felt himself swell slightly—but it gave him no misery, caused him no pain.

He blinked, trying desperately to peer through the dirty channel.

Something moved to his right. Leaving a trail of oily bubbles.

We're not alone.

His ears registered the sounds of movement above and around him. Bricks pirouetted in the murk, hitting bottom. Then came the rotters. Human carcasses given the rough semblance of life, flailing and wordlessly screaming as they sank to the floor, each the truest definition of "dead weight." They could not swim. They could only sink.

But something out there *could* swim.

Another flurry of bubbles. Another fast-moving shadow.

The hunter was comfortable in water. As comfortable as a shark.

Coburn let his body lay flat, stomach-down, against the bottom of the concrete. Then he crept along the curves of the cement, dragging himself with his hands—he found the ankle or head of a sunken rotter, and he pulled himself past the living corpse as the thing floundered about, bubbles pushing out of the rotter's old wounds as putrid flesh accordioned against putrid flesh.

Coburn had no sense of where he was. What was this place? Sewer tunnel above gave way to this below—storage for run-off? If the city still had power (and people), would this water be pumped to treatment stations?

Movement. Stirred water. Dark small shape searching.

She couldn't find him here. Couldn't smell his blood. The hunter was able to move in this space, and could swim with ease like some kind of *hell-dolphin*, but just the same, this was not her domain. That gave him an advantage. Small. But real.

He had to find a way out of here.

Coburn crawled along the bottom, seeking egress.

*   *   *

A MOMENT OF relative calm came to them.

Gil and the children stood under the awning of a laundromat, the rain hammering the ground around them as if the skies held a grudge against the earth. They'd cleared a swath through the rotters and here, on this side street running north to south, the undead herd had thinned—the few that shuffled close ended up with shattered legs and no heads. Gil held the rat terrier under his arm; he didn't want to lose sight of him out here in the weather.

"Where are we going?" Pete yelled to Gil over the rain. Problem was, Gil didn't really know. "My friend was... north of here somewhere. Said he was tracking some people." *To eat.* Gil finished that thought only in his head.

Booboo nervously tapped his ice picks together—*clink-clink-clink.* "Maybe he was looking for those druggies down by Haight and Ashbury."

"Yeah." Pete nodded, taking a moment to pop a fresh magazine into his pistol. He filled Gil in: "There's like, a few pockets of people left in the city—bunch of whackjobs hunkered down in the middle of the city. They're always spaced out on something. Follow some weirdo calling himself the Minister, but he doesn't look like any Minister I've ever seen. Tried to recruit us a while back to serve as runners for I dunno why. But we told them to suck it."

Those must've been the ones Coburn was tracking.

Gil nodded. "Let's go that way."

DARK WATER, BLACK concrete, shapes of struts and beams like bones. Coburn found it all eerily peaceful.

Time and space lost all sense down here. He pulled himself along the bottom for—well, he didn't know. Ten minutes? Ten hours? Ten feet? Ten miles? He'd lost the hunter a while back, or so it seemed, at least. The vampire hadn't spied the creature searching for him—he was free.

You wanted to die back there, Kayla said.

He reminded her that he was already dead.

You know what I mean, JW. You wanted to die in Los Angeles, too. It wasn't just to save us. It was to destroy yourself. Maybe that's why you gave that man the finger way back when in the Big Apple, too. Maybe you wanted to die.

He explained that he was good at what he did—excellent, in fact, and if he wanted to 'die' then he'd jolly well have fucking died a long time ago. He liked who he was just fine, thanks for asking, now would you please shut the fuck up?

My Daddy always said someone who gets defensive like that is that way because they got something they want to hide. Something they ain't telling.

Coburn was about to rebuke her, about to say—er, think—something about how her Daddy was an old grumpy fool, but then he caught movement.

A shape. A little girl's shape.

The hunter.

No, Kayla said. *Look closer.*

Coburn almost felt his heart start beating.

Rebecca.

His daughter.

Floating midway up the concrete wall. Pointing to an open hole—just big enough to wriggle through, head first.

Coburn tried to speak to her, but his voice was lost and all he tasted was the city's polluted rainwater. And then she was gone in a flurry of bubbles; she didn't swim away, but simply dissipated as if she'd never existed.

Starting to see ghosts, JW?

He stayed where he was. Searching the margins of the channel—it went forward and backward, deep into watery shadow, but he couldn't see her anymore. Where had she gone? Was she even real? Or just a hallucination brought on by this sunken sewer pilgrimage?

You better move, dude. Daddy used to say: time waits for no man.

He didn't bother mentioning that time *does* in fact wait for the vampire.

Coburn kicked off the bottom and swam to the hole.

Pop-pop-pop-click.

Pete cried out, dropped the magazine out of the bottom of his pistol and searched for another at his waist—he yelled: "I'm almost out!"

They'd gotten swarmed crossing over Lombard. They couldn't see shit and the rotters came out of nowhere. Didn't help that the road had a lot of cars smashed into one another—made it hard to move, harder to see. Gil clambered up on top of the cars as he and the vampire had done before, but all that did was give him a sign of just how bad it was—they were surrounded, and more were coming, dragging dead legs and reaching out with ruined hands seeking live meat to shove in their hungry mouths.

Worse, that's when Creampuff lost his mind. The dog started twisting and squirming in Gil's grip, sniffing the air and yap-yap-yapping.

Gil couldn't hold on. The animal was wet and hellishly determined to get away—the terrier leapt from Gil's arms, hitting the hood of the red sedan on which they stood before disappearing into the crowd of swarming rotters.

"Creampuff!" Gil called once, twice, and again until his voice was rough and raw. "Goddamn dog!"

A pot-bellied trucker zombie started to come up over the car trunk and Gil put an arrow in the lumpy bastard's forehead—he rolled off the car and was gone, the arrow gone with him. Atop a silver SUV he saw Princess and Pete standing together—Pete fired off judicious shots, and any time a rotter got close, Princess knelt down and chopped him in the brain.

Gil heard Creampuff barking somewhere. His first thought was, *Hell with him.* Stupid dog. Doesn't want to stay alive? Wants to take the worst possible moment to go hunt a… rat or a squirrel? Fine, so be it. The dog liked the vampire more than him, anyway.

That thought hit Gil again: *the dog liked the vampire more.*

Oh. Holy hell.

"We need to follow the dog!" Gil hollered, over the din of moaning zombies and .22 pistol-fire and roaring rain.

Gil clipped a zombie missing half its face with the side of his crossbow and used the gap to hop down off the car.

But as he did, the half-faced rotter thrust up a searching hand and caught his ankle—Gil's world yanked sideways as he fell to the asphalt. He let go of the crossbow, thrust out his hands and caught asphalt against his palms—the sting went through his fingers and up his arms as the rest of his body followed, hitting the street. He cried out. Dirty sore-laden feet surrounded him. Rotters reached. He turned over, swatted—one started gnawing, the blackened teeth having no luck getting through his pant-leg.

Gil pushed one away. Kicked another. Felt his world grow smaller, hedged in by rotters swarming over him like ants upon an overturned beetle.

It all happened so fast and yet so very, very slowly.

He pushed one away.

Another moved in—not fast, not cunning, just clumsily lurching forward in the sudden vacancy. A woman. Nose hanging off her face like gristle from a steak. A brittle mop of hair framing her puffy cheeks.

Her teeth sank into the meat of his palm.

And then her head collapsed with the hard *whaaang* of a shovel.

Gil pulled all his limbs in, fresh blood running from the bite-mark. It didn't hurt, not much—his hands were too numb from falling, from the shock of it all. As he turtled in, he saw a shovel-blade sweep in again, taking out legs and smashing heads. As one zombie's head snapped to the side, exposing a soggy trachea and severing its spine, Gil caught a glimpse of Aiden.

Aiden, with the shovel.

The other kids filled the space—wooden chair-legs and stabbing picks and Pete bashing in heads with the butt of his Buck Mark.

Gil quickly rolled over, got to his feet, tucked his hand away into his sleeve. Felt the blood soak through.

Don't think about it. Forget the bite. Forget the ticking clock. Shut up. Eyes forward, old man. Your daughter needs you.

He snatched up his crossbow.

Aiden came up alongside him, shovel black with the ichor that passed for undead blood. "Figured you'd need my help."

Gil nodded. "We did." He cleared his throat. "I did. Thanks."

Aiden saw Gil hiding his hand. "Your hand."

The boy tensed. Gripped the shovel tight.

"I'm good," Gil said, mustering a brave face to carry the lie. "I hurt it in the fall. Fell on a piece of glass." Not a hard lie to swallow—the streets were littered with debris, including the remnants from shattered car and home windows.

"Good," Aiden said. "I'd hate to have to fuck you up."

"Yeah."

"Sorry about before."

"It's fine."

"We better move. Find your friend. The zombos won't be long in the coming." Somewhere down the street, Creampuff barked: an insistent *me! me! me!* yapping that Gil would know anywhere. He nodded to Aiden, to all the kids, and then took point and hurried forth ahead of his own dread thoughts.

CHAPTER NINE

The Hills Of San Francisco

THE MANHOLE COVER launched from its mooring, flipping up in the air like an errant pancake. It hit the street, cracking the asphalt and rolling into a mini-van, where it promptly dented the bumper with a *bang*.

The vampire Coburn emerged from the hole.

Stinking. Dripping. Bleeding.

He dropped to his hands and knees and barfed up sewer water. Gave each nostril one good blow, too—a snot rocket of muck spattered the earth.

Rain fell on him.

It felt good. Made him feel like a new man. Blah blah blah, baptism and washing away sins and rebirth and whatever.

Then he looked up.

"Oh, goddamnit," he growled. "Really?"

The chorus of gathered dead gurgled and drooled in response. Coburn found himself in the middle of an intersection atop one of San Francisco's trademark hills—tree-lined streets and parked cars and a trolley track running up one hill and down the next. And all around him, crowds of the doomed and demised.

The dead noticed him, now.

Began moving toward him through the rain. A shrinking circumference of rotting flesh ready to crush him and tear him asunder.

Worse, as if to rub not merely salt in the wound but battery acid and fire ants and a whole fucking *salt lick*, Coburn heard the shriek of the child hunter rise from the manhole cover. He'd crawled his way out of the transport channel and back into the brick tunnels and up through the hole in the street, and now his foe was about to do the same.

But that shriek bought him a moment. As it rose up out of the hole, the encroaching tide of starving dead stopped, cocking their heads like confused beasts.

Speaking of a confused beast—

Coburn saw a darting streak of white shoot out from between rotters.

Creampuff bowled into him, then regained his footing, claiming a spot between Coburn's boots and settling into a low growl.

"Well, looky here," Coburn said. "What's up, you little rat turd?"

The dog gave him a wide-eyed look, then resumed growl.

"Uh-huh. Nice to see you too, pooch. Not a real great time to show up, though, since I think we're both about to become dinner."

The dog seemed unfazed. Curiously, Coburn took strength from this.

Then: Another howl rose from the open manhole.

Child's hands—corrupted, tipped with sharp bone—emerged from the hole like a fly wriggling free of a wound. The little girl's face surfaced, crooked needle teeth exposed in a lip-curling snarl.

The hunter had arrived.

That's when everything went batshit.

THE VAMPIRE BARELY had time to parse what was happening.

The hunter leapt from the hole like a hungry flea, bowling into Coburn's back and knocking him flat.

Ahead, the zombies surged forward, toward him—

But then rotters started falling.

They tilted hard, legs taken out from under them. As they fell forward, backward, to the side, they were kindly absolved of their heads and brains.

The givers of said absolution?

Children.

One with a shovel. One with—knives? Little girls. Little boys. Pre-teens. Human. Definitely human. He could smell their blood.

Don't get any ideas, Kayla said. *They're not your own personal protein bars.*

Coburn didn't get too long of a look. The hunter dug its claws into his back and pushed him to the ground. His nose ground against the city street. His teeth biting blacktop. He pawed behind him, tried to stand, but again his head smashed into the asphalt—claws gripped the back of his head, dug in beneath the scalp…

Another flash of white. Creampuff got in on the action, making guerilla strikes from the margins. The dog darted in and out with that trademark terrier speed, nipping at the hunter—taking chunks of ear and flesh from jaw—before leaping just out of reach from the monster's swiping talon.

It gave Coburn the opening he needed. The vampire twisted his body, dumping the hunter to the ground.

He was able to again behold the scene—

This time, with a new—well, old—player.

Gil shouldered his way through a pair of rotters. Crossbow bolt through one's eye. Swing of the bow to collapse the second's head.

Their eyes met, vampire and man. They shared a friendly nod amidst chaos.

Coburn felt Kayla in his mind. Excited. Jubilant, even.

The moment did not last.

The girl with the chair leg—her face marred with streaks of ash, ash that looked purposeful, like a kind of war-paint—spun into the questing hands of a jawless rotter. The creature's hands found her throat. Pulled her close.

Gil saw. Screamed.

The fiend drew her upward to its seeking mouth—

For Coburn, that looked all too familiar.

He did not know this girl. Did not care anything for her outside a small ember of gratitude for coming in here and saving his pale ass.

But he knew his daughter. He knew Kayla. Knew he had failed them both.

Coburn moved. Point A to Point B in a half a blink of a reptile's eye— and when he came upon the monster holding the little girl, its mouth so close to her throat its fattened raw beef of a tongue was pressed against her skin, Coburn let the momentum of his preternatural speed carry through to the back of his hand.

The rotter's head cracked, spun off the shoulders the way one might spin the cap off a cheap whiskey bottle. Black blood aerosolized.

The girl fell.

Coburn caught her.

Her throat was torn out.

No! came Kayla's voice. *Just the rotter's blood.*

The girl blinked.

The gore slid from her neck, plopping to the ground in the middle of the fracas. Washed away by the rain. The girl stared up at Coburn with eyes moist with wonder and terror.

"What are you?" she asked. A small voice, but Coburn could hear.

He answered the only way he could: "I don't know."

Then he set her down. Picked up her gore-clumped chair leg, handed it to her. Next thing he knew, Gil's back was to his own.

The zombies had again stopped. Formed a circle around them. Staring not at their prey but at the one they believed to be their master:

The child hunter was up. Claws dripping.

At the beast's feet lay Creampuff. White coat gone red. There on the ground like a broken toy before the child who played too rough.

A surge of anger bubbled up inside Coburn.

His dog. That was *his* dog. Nobody—man, woman, child, or reanimated dead thing with vampire's blood churning through its nightmare veins—messed with his dog. Shit. Shit!

We're doomed, came Kayla's voice. Echoing through his head. *Doomed... doomed... doomed.*

It was as if Gil could hear her.

Because the old man said, "I have an idea."

And then he brought up the crossbow, splitting some fool rotter's head, and hurried over to a minivan parked cock-eyed at the corner.

The child hunter started toward Coburn.

But then another child stepped in the way. Blond shaggy hair, hanging over his face. He parted the hair with his fingers, then held out his hands.

"Ellie," the kid said. "It's me. Aiden."

The hunter hissed. Offered no recognition. Took a step forward.

"Kid," Coburn growled.

But Aiden took another step forward. "I want to help you. You should come home. With the rest of us. Look. We're all here."

"*Kid,*" Coburn said again, this time more insistent. The other kids called to him, too—told him not to do that, to stop, to get away.

"That's not Ellie," the tall boy with the bloodied pistol said. Desperate. Voice cracking. Sadness there.

The hunter moved fast.

So did Coburn.

They met Aiden in the middle. Coburn swept the kid up, turned his body. The hunter's claws again dug into the meat of his back, but with his free hand he grabbed behind the mutant and flipped her forward into a crowd of rotters—undead bowling in the hell-born apocalypse.

Aiden cried out. In that cry a great abyss where grief suddenly rose up like a terrible wind. As the boy collapsed onto his hands and knees, sobbing, Coburn saw Gil had shattered the driver-side window of the mini-van and was sitting in the front seat—he whooped, yelled for everyone to get in.

Coburn understood the plan.

He herded the children toward the minivan as the hunter scrambled to its feet, claws clicking on blacktop and teeth clacking together.

It stood as the kids entered the minivan through the backdoor.

Coburn hurried back for the dog.

"Coburn!" Gil yelled. "No time!"

But there had to be time. He scooped the pooch up. Smelled the blood. Felt the crass and callous demon of hunger send up a tickling finger to tighten his jaw, make him think about eating the dog here and now, fulfilling the animal's long-ago purpose of being a road-trip snack in case the vampire needed it. Sick. Shameful. But that was the demon.

What mattered though was:

The dog was still breathing.

Barely. Shallow. A low whine from the back of its throat. The dog's side perforated with puncture marks from the monster's claws.

Coburn heard Gil calling to him again. The vampire turned back toward the van, saw that once more the beast stood between him and his goal.

Fuck that.

He couldn't kill this kid, or rather, this thing-that-was-no-longer-a-kid.

He had enough presence of mind to realize that now. It was a cowardice born of guilt, a roadblock in his way because of those he'd hurt and lost. Even though this thing was no longer human. Even though this *girl*—Ellie—was gone and the body now filled by a devil of desire and thirst and cruelty, Coburn still couldn't kill her. Or it. Or whatever it was.

But he was getting to that mini-van, goddamnit.

Creampuff looked up at Coburn. Blood trickling from his muzzle.

The hunter's patience was at an end. The beast bolted toward him. Claws out. Jaw unhinging like a snake's—mouth wide, too wide, its lashing tongue licking the rain and tasting the air.

Coburn held his ground.

And when the beast was close enough—he took one big step back.

Over the open manhole.

The hunter did not fall through the manhole, not entirely—but one of its legs did disappear into that space and the beast fell forward, cracking its head on the macadam and yowling in rage and anguish. Needle teeth broke off and scattered like the knucklebones cast by a diviner.

Coburn used the body as a stepping stone and bolted toward the van.

The zombies surged again. The mesmerism of the hunter, interrupted. They pushed forth toward the van. Slapping wetly against its side. Rocking it.

The vampire gave himself one last boost—

And shouldered hard right into the back of the vehicle.

The van started to lurch forward.

There they were, at the top of a hill. On Hyde Street. Down the hill—north, though you couldn't see it in the dark and through the rain—was the bay. Where they had been hoping to get to all along.

Coburn clambered atop the van as it started to roll down the hill with Gil at the wheel, steering out of the way of parked and abandoned cars, clipping zombies and letting the wheels pop their limbs and heads like blood-gorged ticks.

The van picked up speed, bounding away in escape.

Coburn heard the wretched cry of the hunter.

Wounded. Stung. Starving.

Always starving.

He looked behind him, and in a small blessing could not see the beast.

CHAPTER TEN

Dead End

THE VAN BOUNDED down the hill, steering to narrowly dodge debris and skirt other cars. Some of the rotters saw them pass, tried to follow, slapped at the vehicle as it passed—but they were too slow, too stupid, to matter.

They bounded pasted a gutted Starbucks. An overgrown park. Boutique hotels and shuttered restaurants. And all around them, dead people: some still moving, others just corpses burned or gutted or gone from suicide. In cars. On street corners. Hanging half out of windows.

All the while, Coburn clung to the roof-rack of the mini-van with one hand, shushing Creampuff and stroking the little dog's head with the other. The animal panted. Heavy. Too heavy. Blood wetting Coburn's arms.

Soon the great Hyde Street hill evened out—*please keep your arms and legs inside the ride*, Coburn thought, calling to mind a fleeting memory of Coney Island that he did not expect and could not follow—and since Gil had the van in neutral, there wasn't much he could do but steer it straight into a parked car to stop it. Not before mowing over a DEAD END sign. Which Coburn hoped was not somehow prescient.

* * *

THE RAIN LIGHTENED, but just the same they all poured out of the van and huddled under the tattered awning of some bullshit maritime souvenir shop with wooden pirates standing vigil out front.

The kid—Aiden—looked wrecked. Gutted. Hell, they all did. A little girl with pigtails came up to Coburn and gently patted Creampuff's head.

"This is your stop," Aiden said. Staring at a faraway point. "You better go. Zombos won't be long in coming."

Pete pointed past the storefront and toward the maritime tourist complex of Fisherman's Wharf. "Follow this out, it'll take you to the end of the Hyde Street pier. You'll find some old dinghies tied up. We use them to fish sometimes."

"Ew," the little pig-tailed girl said. "Fish, yuck."

"What about you?" Gil asked. "You could come with us."

"To Alcatraz?" Aiden asked. "No, thanks. We've got our place here."

Coburn held Creampuff close, furrowed his brow. "Wait. Who said jack and shit about Alcatraz?"

"Better play catch up, old man," Aiden said. "You're looking for a lab, right? Alcatraz is it."

"Rude little prick," Coburn said.

"Takes one to know one," the kid answered.

That was probably true.

It was then they said their goodbyes. The kids all shook Gil's hand—though the pig-tailed one who the others called 'Princess' leapt up and hugged him like he was her long-lost grandfather. Coburn stood off to the side, gently scratching Creampuff's ear.

Fact you can do anything gentle is a surprise, came Kayla's voice, which had been silent since the fracas on the hill.

Coburn grunted.

Then felt someone standing near him. One of the midgets.

"Thanks for saving my life," the girl with the dirty face said; chair leg tucked under her arm. "Hope your puppy's okay."

"Yeah. Me, too."

"Later."

"Later, kid."

The children left. Darting off around the corner, in the rain. Disappearing. A pack of apocalypse orphans—although, the vampire had to admit, they had better control of things than most of the adults they encountered.

"You ready?" Gil asked.

"Sure," Coburn said.

But he was pretty sure it was a lie.

He had no idea how unready he really was.

The Conversation: #3

CAN YOU STILL hear me?

A little.

But I'm fading, aren't I?

I don't want to talk about that.

You don't want to talk about a lot of things.

Ain't I a bitch?

But these could be our last moments together. Tell me, John Wesley. Tell me about what you regret. Tell me about what you love.

I regret nothing. And I love only myself.

Now you're just being stupid.

It's how I roll.

Won't you miss me?

I'll miss you. But it won't matter because I'll be dead. Dead for good. Dead and done and fucked four ways from Friday.

I'll miss you, too.

Yeah.

CHAPTER ELEVEN

The Devil's Island

THE DINGHY BOBBED in the bay. The thunder was distant, now. The bulk of the storm had moved out to sea again, leaving behind only a grimy mist of rain falling oily against their skin.

The vampire had Gil row for a minute.

He set the dog in his lap. The animal no longer looked up at him. His breathing was fast, shallow—like watching a rabbit die from fright. The holes in his side were pretty bad. Went deep.

The dog was dying.

Coburn said as much.

Gil looked back. Mouth in a sad, straight line.

"Not that I'm a doctor or anything," Coburn said.

"Be nice to have Leelee here," Gil said.

"Yeah. Yeah it would."

The dinghy continued. Alcatraz in the distance, a shadowy rock growing larger and larger as they approached.

The dog's breath came in hitches now—inconsistent, unsteady, uneven. Gil spoke up again: "Remember. Leelee got bit. Kayla saved her. Right then and there."

"That she did."

Gil turned around. Set the oars down. "No, you're not listening. Her blood. Kayla's blood. It's *your* blood now. Give the damn dog some of your stuff." Gil looked down at the dog. "But you better hurry."

Coburn sank his teeth into the tip of his thump, ripping the flesh of the thumb-pad clean off. Then he thrust it into the dog's mouth and used his free hand to massage the hand, way you'd urge milk from a cow's udder.

The dog's tongue lapped at the wound. Weakly, but there it was.

Then the dog stopped breathing.

Coburn shook the dog. "No, no, get up. Wait. Shit. Fuck!" He shot a hate-fueled gaze at Gil. "You did this. You told me it would work. You said—"

The dog shuddered suddenly, took in a great gasp of air.

The tail started going. Just a light *thwip thwip thwip* against the inside of Coburn's arm. The eyes focused again. The breathing returned. Still shallow. Still weak as wind blowing around a piece of tissue paper.

But it was there.

Then Creampuff pissed on Coburn's lap. Probably not an act of spite. Probably.

"Dog pissed on me," Coburn said.

"Maybe you deserved it," Gil said. "Maybe he's trying to make you smell better. Because let me tell you, you smell like shit. Literally. Like shit."

"You don't smell so good yourself." Coburn held the dog close. "You planning on telling me you got bit?" The infection had a smell. Cheesy. Curdled. *Parfum de rotter.*

Inside Coburn's mind, Kayla woke up at that—he heard her shout for her father as if the old man could actually hear her psychic projection.

Then he heard her crying.

"I got bit," Gil said. "So what."

"Here." Coburn thrust out his still-bleeding thumb. "Drink up. Worked on the dog. I guess. Go on. Drinky, drinky. Suck my thumb, little baby."

"Better than 'old man,' I guess." But Gil didn't move. Instead he stared ahead, still rowing, and said: "Something you need to know about Kayla. Something Kayla needs to know, too."

Daddy?

"She's listening. But first—" Coburn gestured with the bloody thumb.

Still Gil didn't move.

"It's about when she was born. She wasn't born right. When she came out, she was—"

A gunshot split the air in the distance, echoed over the bay, and the bullet punched the water about three feet off the right side of the boat. Coburn said, "Jesus Christ. Fuckin' assholes think we're an invading army or some shit." He stood up in the boat. Waved his arms. "Hey! Fuckos! We're here to help! We've got something—"

"Coburn, don't stand up in the—"

Another gunshot.

The bullet clipped Coburn's hip—shattering bone and coming out through his buttock. His leg gave out and his body pivoted, and he tumbled over into the water with a heaving splash.

More bullets followed him into the water. Watery lines as the slugs punched the space above his head—lead minnows leaving little bubbles. The underside of the boat drifted away, churned by the oars. Gil was leaving him—not a shock, and not unwarranted since he was being shot at, too.

The vampire could take care of himself. The old man knew that.

Probably.

Coburn, feeling mighty pissed off, swam.

KAYLA'S VOICE: AN endless chatter of crows inside his mind. *Daddy! Please let him be all right. What was he going to tell you? What's wrong with me?*

Coburn couldn't help but answer: *You're dead. That's what's wrong with you.*

In return he once more heard her weeping.

Damnit.

He swam through the dark water, losing track of the boat and eventually pulling himself up on the rocky shore of Alcatraz Island. All around him—trees, rocks, the remnant of an old brick wall here and, further up, a warped chain-link fence. Beyond all that, the silhouette of the prison itself, all hard angles and severe lines. Uncle Sam's Devil's Island.

The wind kicked up over the water, buffeting him, and as he shook himself dry like a common cur, someone called to him from further up.

Standing on a cement platform about fifty yards away:

Lydia, oh, Lydia, oh, have you met Lydia.

Gil knelt next to her. She held a rifle to his head. Remington 700 by the look of it. Bolt-action. High-caliber.

Double damnit.

"Up here," she called. "Unless you want your friend's brains to paint the concrete." She pushed the gun forward, the barrel jabbing Gil hard in the temple.

Please, save my Daddy. Don't you fail me, JW. Don't you dare.

Coburn knew he could get away from her. Be like a cockroach slipping away under a fridge. All these trees. Under the cover of night. Could sneak up on Lydia from behind, kick her heart straight out of her damn chest. But then Gil would be dead and Kayla would be inconsolable and—

"I'm coming," he called. "Just settle the fuck down up there."

Grudgingly—and grumpily—Coburn found the walkway and plodded up the steps, boots squishing as he did. When he got closer, he could see Creampuff laying next to Gil. Still with the shallow breathing. But the bleeding had stopped.

Lydia stood tall. But she was only feigning triumph. All about her, the miasma of fear hung like a cloud of gnats.

"You're afraid of me," he said, grinning.

"You're not the one I'm afraid of."

"Well. Let's get this over with. My friend and I hear that this is your lab. That why you wanted my blood? Synthesize a cure? Should've just said something. That's what I want, too. Instead you have your Jonestown drug cult fuckos nail me to a table until you show up? Not cool, lady. Not cool."

Lydia laughed. Not a happy sound. A high-pitched trill, anxious and angry and simulating delight. "Lab. Well. Guess you caught me, then."

"So drop the gun."

"I don't think so."

Coburn tried a little voodoo. Tried to stare deep, past the darks of her eyes and into her brain where he could pluck those strings and make her a puppet for his monster theater. "I said *drop the gun*, honey."

She *tsk-tsk-tsk*ed him. "You really think that works on me?"

"Boy's gotta try."

She kneed Gil in the back. Told him to stand, then march. "You too." Coburn reached for the dog, but she pressed the gun against the back of Gil's head. "Leave the mongrel behind."

"Fine. But you're not making me feel real friendly."

Another laugh.

THE LIGHTS COME on: fluorescents overhead snapping to life with a pop and a hum. The prison awakens out of the dark, but to Coburn it looks less like a prison and more like a cathedral of rust-colored bones. The femur of corroded railings, the radius and ulna and jail bars, the fingerbones meshed together caging the lights above their heads.

Inside each cell: beds, IV poles, metal and wooden carts with all manner of medical equipment both modern and antiquated. Toward the back, Coburn saw equipment like he saw in the Los Angeles lab: centrifuges and cabinets of beakers and a big metal box with a window in the side and a place to stick your hands into some rubber gloves—a place where you could manipulate dangerous chemicals or, who knows, a pissed off wolverine, without getting your hands destroyed.

But nobody was here.

And the smell...

The odor of corpses. The perfume of spattered blood. Hidden beneath an invisible façade of harsh nose-burning antiseptics.

This lab was dead. Dead like Lydia. Dead like that Ellie girl who bit her and turned into a monster. Dead like the rest of the world.

Kayla wasn't sobbing in his head. She was whimpering. Receding to the furthest-flung corners of his mind.

"Coburn..." Gil said.

"I know, Gil."

"This is a dead place."

"I said I know, Gil."

Lydia pushed them forward with the barrel of the gun. "Did you really think that I was operating some lab? Saving the world? Please. Those days are done."

Coburn's blood felt hot. Set to a low simmer, galloping on toward a boil.

"I *thought*," he began, "that you were like me. Doing what you had to do to survive. Saving the human race is, for us, like the humans making sure their cow-herd doesn't have mad cow disease. Not sure if you noticed, but the blood supply out there's gone a little *sour*, Doc. Figured you wanted to save people to save yourself."

"That what you're doing, John Wesley? I know different."

Those words. Sounded like Kayla's words coming from Lydia's mouth. Didn't make sense. The mercury in Coburn's thermometer cracked the glass, shot a hot arc of angry blood straight to his brain.

Lydia didn't know what hit her.

Coburn grabbed the barrel of the gun. Anchored his boots to the hard prison floor, put everything he had into it and swung her skinny ass into the metal bars with a *clang*. Her hand let go of the gun, and he spun it like a cheerleader flipping a baton and turned the barrel on her. Bead between her eyes.

She slid to the floor and sat there. Long dark hair framing her face. Framing that smile.

"How'd you know my name?" he asked.

But she didn't have to answer.

Footsteps echoed down between the cells.

A voice, so familiar and so uncomfortable—like a tongue pushing through flesh and bone and slithering into the white of one's marrow.

"Hi, John."

Coburn wheeled with the rifle and started firing.

CHAPTER TWELVE

Heart Of Glass

PULL TRIGGER. JACK bolt. Eject shell. New shell. Pull trigger.

Four times.

Boom. Boom. Boom. Boom.

Ears ringing. Air stinking with the acrid smoke of a discharged weapon.

Blondie kept coming. Arms out in faux-beneficence. Cleft lip like an axe wound pulling his lips into a twisted sneer beneath his smashed nose. Above that, a pair of blue, blue eyes glittering like sapphires.

In his chest: four holes. A little blood dribbling out of each.

Coburn jacked the bolt again. Fired dry. *Click.*

"Would it be in poor taste to clap?" the vampire asked. "I'm going to do it anyway because, wow, look at that grouping." He brought his hands together in a slow-motion applause. The clap echoed.

It's him, Kayla said. Waves of fear radiated from her, like ripples of pondwater after a stone interrupted the surface.

Coburn's fear matched her own.

"You can't kill me," Blondie said. "Besides the fact I'm already dead, that is. You put an end to me, well. You know how *that* story goes."

(*"It's one of those old immutable laws,"* Blondie said, *making a face that might've been a grin, might've been a sneer. "Kill the maker and you kill the monsters he made.")*

Lydia stood. Worked her way behind them, pacing like a starving puma. Gil threw a sideways glance at Coburn: "You mind telling me what's happening?"

But Blondie was the one who answered, as he approached: "Good question, Gil. It is Gil, isn't it?"

"How the hell you know my name?"

"I know all. My blood is his blood. I gave unto him so that he may live. But he's got another guest in there, now. Another ghost in the red." Blondie showed his curved fangs. Ran a too-pale tongue along one. "I've been waiting for you, John. Been sitting there in the back of your dreams. Silent and stoic. A gargoyle looking down from above and watching the movement of the tiny people below."

Coburn felt his hands tighten around the stock of the rifle. The wood split with a bony *snap*. "You fuck. What happened here? Where's the lab?"

Blondie stopped about ten feet away. Whistled. "I had to kill all those people, John. All that hope-for-the-future nonsense? Curdles the blood. Optimism has no place in this world, not any more. The lights are out. The playground is for us monsters, now. Too bad you can't have the fun I have."

"I figured you for smart," Coburn said, seething. "But you're dumb as a bucket of guts. As I was telling your mistake here—" He tossed a thumb at Lydia, behind him.

"Your sister, if you will—"

"Fuck you. Like I was telling her, we need people. Food supply. Blood. In case you missed that part?"

"See, that's the thing. You were always a fine predator, John. Don't think I haven't been watching you these many decades. You hunted. Killed. *Fed.* Good for you. But me, I don't hunt because I need to. I hunt because I want to. You kill and ditch the bodies. I keep them alive long as I can. I hurt them. I roll around in their misery like a dog in mud, covering myself in their glorious scent. You're a predator, okay, fine. But I'm a monster. I'm the Devil, John. And this is my world, now."

Coburn tilted his head left, then right, let the neck-joints crackle and pop. He said, "I'm tired of you talking."

Then he moved.

Put everything he had behind the thrown fist—enough blood and gusto to turn his arm into a piston that would punch a hole clean through the smug motherfucker's chest, driving splinters of breastbone through the monster's heart as Coburn shoved the organ right out through the space between the bastard's shoulder blades.

That didn't happen.

Blondie caught the fist with both hands like he was fielding a football. Then gave a hard twist. Coburn's arm shattered like a corkscrewed twig.

He fell to the ground, and for good measure Blondie completed the football visual and gave Coburn's head a hard punt.

Coburn's jaw broke in a half-dozen places. Unmoored and loose in his skin. Tried to speak. Came out as anguished babble.

Gil did not sit idly by.

Or, at least, he tried not to. He moved forward, an ungainly and foolish assault, and found himself lifted off his feet by the vampire Lydia. Who held Gil's neck in the crook of her arm 'til the man's legs went slack.

JW, they're hurting my Daddy.

He told her that he knew, and had other things to worry about right now.

You fix this.

Right now he couldn't fix shit. He urged the blood to repair his cracked jaw and splintered arm. Blondie knelt down by his side. Patted him on the head, way he'd patted Creampuff so many times.

"I'll say this, John. You do have a point about the food supply. I'll give you that. It's hard out there. I'm torn. On the one hand, watching the world die and come back to life—the weak herd of humanity replaced with my children, children made from your blood which is my blood—it thrills me. One of the few things that can thrill me. So much so I'm not ready to give up my front row seat. But that means I need to eat, and fresh blood isn't so readily available. I have Lydia bring me children sometimes—and as you know, I am nothing if not a fan of the misery of youth—but it's not enough. My hunger is long. My patience? *Short.* And lo and behold, what happens is—"

Blondie, it seemed, liked to hear himself talk. Lost in the sound of his own voice like a—what was it? Dog rolling around in mud.

Coburn saw the opportunity.

Seized it by the balls.

His jaw was still fucked, but his arm was better. He surged up, snapping an elbow into Blondie's jaw—

Or, that's what should have happened. But it didn't. Blondie caught it. Twisted the arm again so that it snapped. Then slammed Coburn's face hard into the concrete. Once. Twice. Blush of bright blood behind Coburn's eyes as his own teeth and fangs jettisoned down the back of his throat.

"Feisty," Blondie said. "I'm very proud. But that matters little. As I was saying, little rabbit, what happens is you end up gulping down the blood of some miracle baby, some little twit with the healing power of the heavens, and next thing I know, you're changed. Weaker of spirit, maybe, but stronger of blood. You don't need to feed as much. The hunger doesn't cloud your vision. And you can move around during the day. You know the last time I saw the sun? I don't. I literally don't. That memory is lost to me. But now that I know I can have it again, I want it. I really, really want it."

He picked up Coburn the way an old maid picks up one of her many fat cats—under the arms, shoulders shrugging. It was hard to see Blondie, since half of Coburn's skull was broken like a candy dish, his eyes pinched by rolls of skin and shards of bone. But he could see Blondie's puckered sneer.

"I want her," Blondie said. "I want what she gave you."

"Fbuh myoo," Coburn said, and gamely spit a loose tooth against Blondie's forehead—*ptoo.*

Blondie grabbed Coburn's head. Racked it back.

Then sank his fangs deep.

CHAPTER THIRTEEN

Conversation, Continued

RED LIGHT BLOOMED in darkness. Stop light. Exit sign. Supernova. Television screen smeared with someone's blood.

Faces tottered atop shadow bodies. Faces of victims. Coburn's victims. Cheeks of porcelain. Eggshell chins. Bone China. Cracking, splitting, pieces falling to the ground and turning to fat flies with red eyes who fly away.

Kayla sat on a recliner. Drinking a glass of Scotch. Smoking one of her Virginia Slim cigarettes she wasn't supposed to have.

Peaches and nicotine.

"You still didn't say it," Kayla said.

Coburn—not just Coburn, but John Wesley Coburn, a man in slacks and a cardigan wearing penny loafers to warm his feet—grunted. "Say what?"

"You know what."

"I'll miss you too, Kayla."

Behind Kayla's chair, another little girl appeared—Rebecca, running around, giggling, pigtails bouncing. In and out of shadow. Like she can't see all the faces and bodies disappearing around her.

"My baby girl," John said.

"She'll be gone soon, too."

"I don't want that."

Kayla shrugged. Blew a gauzy plume of smoke. "I'm cold. And tired."

"I'm sorry."

"Are you?"

"What's that supposed to mean?"

"I mean, are you really sorry?"

Coburn narrowed his eyes. "What are we talking about, here? Sorry about you being cold and tired here in the house inside my head? Or sorry about something bigger? Something deeper?"

"About anything."

"I don't really know."

Kayla sipped the Scotch, wrinkled her nose and brow like she just took a hit of vinegar. "You used to drink this stuff? Somebody should put a Mister Yuck sticker on it."

Again Rebecca appeared. Circled Kayla's chair the way a moth circles a porch light—same glow, too. But then: back to shadow.

Coburn was about to speak, but Kayla interrupted.

"Listen, JW, this is poop-or-get-out-of-the-outhouse time. I gotta know how committed you are to all this. Because I'm not feeling real good about our chances. I'm thinking your friend with the split lip and the white-blonde hair has it right. This is just a place for monsters, now. We found one lab and it went to hell. We found the second lab and it had already been swallowed up by the Devil you know. Creampuff's halfway dead. So's my Daddy. We've got not one but two other vampires, and we're trapped on a prison island outside a dead city."

"What's that have to do with—"

"You feeling sorry? Dude, look around. You killed a lot of people. Still would and still want to. My resolve is starting to shake in its boots. I'm thinking, maybe I was wrong about you. Maybe I was always wrong. Maybe you're never gonna be a better man than you are right now—maybe you're always the monster and I should just let you and me and your baby girl go home. Maybe there's no John Wesley left in here like I thought. Maybe there's just Coburn."

"Fuck you."

"See? That's what I'm talking about."

"I don't need to feel bad about who I am or what I've done."

"Don't you? Because feels to me like you want to save people—real people, living people—then you gotta want it. Gotta want it in a way that means they're more than just little blood-bags tottering around. Can't just be a man-sized mosquito anymore, JW."

He snorted. "Ends justify the means."

"Do they? Do they really?"

Again Rebecca did a circuit around the chair. This time, her throat was ripped open. The front of her shirt like an apron of blood.

"I want to talk to my daughter." Coburn stepped in front of the girl's next loop but—poof, she was gone.

"You can't. Because you killed her. Girl doesn't want to talk to you. Little girl's supposed to trust her father, like I trust mine. But she doesn't and so that door's closed to you."

"I never meant to kill her. He did this to me."

"Blondie? Life sucks. He did that to you. But you did it to her."

He caught a glimpse—Rebecca, hiding behind the chair, staring over with wide bright eyes. Suddenly those eyes cracked like marbles hit with hammers. She fell to pieces. Turned to fat-bellied flies.

Coburn dropped to his knees. "She's gone now."

"She's with him."

"Then I should go, too." He ground his teeth so hard they started to break. Fingernails into his palms. Knees hard into the ground. Wet tears. Red tears. "Let's all just go. If she's in Hell, then that's where I want to be."

"Me first," Kayla said. And then she broke apart like the ash from her cigarette and was gone.

CHAPTER FOURTEEN

Eject Or Die

COBURN HIT THE ground. Bloodless and broken.

Blondie pulled away, clawing at his throat, his mouth, his head. Fingers fishing around the edges of his eyes, a wail rising up out of his throat that sounded like someone torturing a coyote.

Coburn watched it. From inside his own head.

I'm still here, he said to Kayla. *Still me.*

But no answer came back to him.

He couldn't feel her there.

Blondie backed against one jail cell. Began bashing his skull against the bars—*whang-whang-whang-whang.* Howling.

"I want her back," Coburn said. To everybody. To nobody.

He started to drag himself forward. Palms slapping flat on cement, pressing down, pulling himself forward inch by miserable inch.

His searching hands found his maker. Coburn pulled himself up.

"*I want her back,*" he gurgled.

Blondie just screamed.

A hand fell on his shoulder. Cold. A whiff of jasmine.

"What did you do to him?" Lydia cried, and spun Coburn around. Her face was a rictus of rage. Fangs out.

A spire of wood shot through her chest. Then disappeared again. She blinked.

Coburn rasped: "The brain. *The brain.*"

With trembling hands, Gil jammed the shattered rifle spear through her temple. Coburn caught sight of the man's face: Gil looked like hell.

But then, Lydia's eyes went glassy and rolled back and she collapsed like a scarecrow without a cross to hang on. She died like one of the hunters: skin going red, then black, blistering like a hot dog left too long on the grill. From her head-hole a jet of ropy red blood splashed out, turned glossy and dark like motor oil.

Soon she was just a stain with a pile of clothing and skin sitting atop it.

Coburn had never seen another vampire die before.

Huh.

He liked it enough, he wanted to see it again.

He grabbed Blondie. Jacked him against the cell bars. A rain of rust flaked off into that platinum hair.

Blondie's incoherent wails resolved into a few decipherable words: "Hate her hate her hate her hate her *her presence burns.*"

"That's my girl." Coburn forced a smile. It was like moving mountains. He did it anyway. "Now give her back."

With one good arm, Coburn did as was done to him: forced the head back. His own mouth was smashed to bits—fangs just jagged stumps in his mouth. They'd regrow, but not here, not now.

Instead, he raised his ruined arm. A jagged sliver of bone poked from the forearm. He jabbed it hard into Blondie's neck.

Then placed his mouth over the wound and drank.

He felt them come back to him.

In the rush of blood, in that horse-kick of jetting red, there they were.

His ghosts. His dead.

They gave him wings and they were his anchor. They ruined him. They elevated him. They were his and his alone. He owned them.

He heard his daughter's giggles.

He smelled peaches and cigarettes.

My girls.

*   *   *

COBURN COULD SMELL it. The sun was coming up.

Fueled by some twisted combination of rage and bliss, revenge and madness, he dragged his maker by his too-blonde hair past the cells, kicking and screaming. The other vampire seemed weak, empty now of Kayla but still broken somehow, like a fractured wind-up toy limping in circles.

Bam. With a heavy boot, Coburn kicked open the front door. He dragged Blondie out, tossed him down over the railing and onto the rocks below. He heard his foe's back snap. That sound gave him great pleasure.

Coburn, fueled by the blood of his maker, leapt over the railing.

He landed with both feet on Blondie's chest.

Ribs and breastbone cratered with a crunch.

Blondie sobbed. His face slick with crimson.

Coburn held him there. Across the bay, east toward Oakland, the horizon became a pink smear like someone spilled a convenience store slushie across it—it glowed brighter and brighter until the top of the sun's head poked out.

Smoke smoldered from Blondie's hair.

"Kill me," Blondie said.

"Happily," Coburn growled.

"She's like a poison." Bubbles of blood welled on Blondie's empurpled lips.

"She's my poison."

And it was then that she spoke to Coburn.

You can't kill him, JW.

Bullshit, he thought, as wisps of smoke licked the top of the other vampire's head. Coburn smelled the reek of burning hair. Pale flesh started to char.

Kill the maker. Kill the monsters.

He told her, good.

That means you.

Good.

That means me.

Fuck.

That means Rebecca.

Fuck, fuck, fuck!

Coburn hauled the man to his feet. Heat came off him in waves. The backs of his ears started to turn lobster red, then black, then gray.

"You get to live," Coburn growled. "Or whatever it is we do. This is your reprieve. But remember her beauty. Her innocence. Remember her sweet, irritating voice inside your head—and realize it's worse now that she's gone."

"Please. Let me burn."

"Not today. But one day."

And Coburn marched out to the water and threw the vampire in.

The monster hit the water with the sound of a red hot skillet run under the faucet—steam rose with a brief boil of bubbles.

Then the body was gone.

But Coburn was still here.

And, it turned out, so was Creampuff. As Coburn turned to walk back up to the prison, he found Creampuff sitting there. Still looking rough as a gym sock that went through a house-fire, but there and alive and giving him a cocky look.

The vampire scooped him up.

INSIDE, GIL LAY on the floor, dead.

But then he stirred. Groaning. Sitting up. Looking like death on a hot plate. Creampuff trotter over, licked his hand. Gil gave the pooch a nod.

"He's alive?" Gil said. "And you too?"

"Mm," Coburn grunted. "Looks like."

"Am I alive?"

"I guess. Figured that bite would've taken you by now."

"Not yet. But I sure feel like the underwear around a rotter's rotten ass."

Coburn shrugged. "You look like that, too. Except maybe with the elastic all blown out."

"Thanks." Gil offered a weak thumbs-up.

"Hey. Think nothing of it."

Coburn offered his hand. "Here. Let's get you up. Get you some blood."

"You think there's another lab out there somewhere?" Gil took the hand. "CDC? Big Pharma? Scientists, doctors, someone?"

"If there is, we'll find it."

Gil suddenly said: "Kayla was stillborn." He must've seen the blank and bewildered look on the vampire's face, so he kept talking. "That's what I was going to tell you—and tell her—before. She was born dead. And she was dead for forty-seven minutes. They tried resuscitating her. Nothing. Guess they were about ready to..." Gil drew a deep breath, almost fell over before Coburn steadied him. "Ready to bag her and tag her. But then she took a big gulp of air and shot up on the table. They tried to tell us it was natural, that some stillborns do that—though rarely forty-seven minutes after the fact—but then she took another gulp, and another, and next thing you know her purple face turned red as a beet as she let out the biggest damn squall in four counties. She was dead. But then she lived."

Inside, Coburn felt Kayla stirring, restless, like a bird in a cage.

She didn't say anything.

Maybe she didn't have to.

ABOUT THE AUTHOR

CHUCK WENDIG IS a novelist, screenwriter and self-described 'pen monkey.' He sold his first story when he was 18. After working in the computer and role-playing game industries he began scripting TV and film projects, including a horror film script which won him a place at the prestigious *Sundance Screenwriter Lab* 2010.

He's written too much. He should probably stop. Give him a wide berth, as he might be drunk and untrustworthy. He currently lives in the wilds of Pennsyltucky with wife, dog, and newborn progeny.

Double Dead was Chuck's first novel and he has since gone on to write a slew of best-sellers including the Miriam Black series of books and *Star Wars: Aftermath*.

www.terribleminds.com

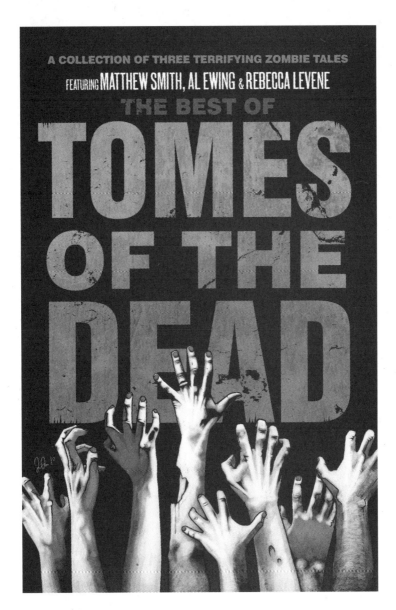

THE ZOMBIE APOCALYPSE STARTS HERE...

The masters of flesh-munchingly, gut-wrenchingly, eyeball-poppingly great zombie fiction bring you three of the best books from the first years of the critically-acclaimed Tomes of the Dead line. In The Words of Their Roaring a gang lord struggles to take power in a London overrun by the zombie hordes, in I, Zombie an undead Private Eye works on his toughest case yet and uncovers the terrible truth behind his true identity, and in Anno Mortis a female gladiator uncovers a plot to breach the barrier between life and death in Ancient Rome.

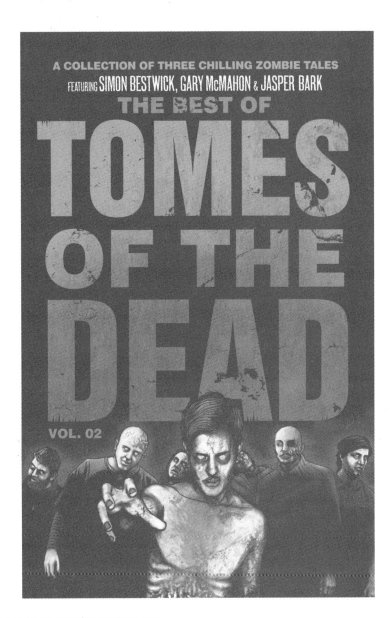

A COLLECTION OF THREE CHILLING ZOMBIE TALES

FEATURING SIMON BESTWICK, GARY McMAHON & JASPER BARK

THE BEST OF

TOMES OF THE DEAD

VOL. 02

BEWARE THE MARCH OF THE UNDEAD!

The masters of flesh-munchingly, gut-wrenchingly, eyeball-poppingly great zombie fiction bring you three more of the best stand-alone books from their critically-acclaimed Tomes of the Dead line. In Tide of Souls a drowned world is beset by the undead and a supernatural threat nobody could ever have imagined, in Hungry Hearts a rookie policeman must choose between the woman he loves and the world he is sworn to protect, and in Way of the Barefoot Zombie a lifestyle guru can give you everything you want as long as you're willing to embrace your inner zombie.

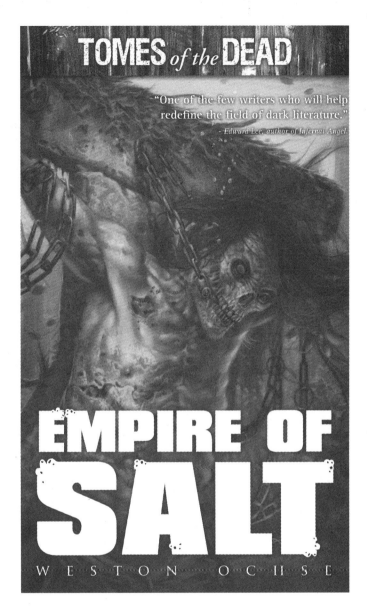

A DREAD TIDE!

The Olivers have a chance to make a new home by the Salton Sea. Looking forward to Californiab fun, sun and adventure they are unprepared for the ecological devastation they find. The sea is rotting, the town of Bombay Beach is dying and the citizens are like bait, waiting to be plucked from their homes by what comes from the sea. For just off the coast something lies in wait, a government secret gone wrong, a deadly experiment that has created a breed of zombie like no other.

Beware the coming of the green, the townsfolk say. Beware the coming of the night!

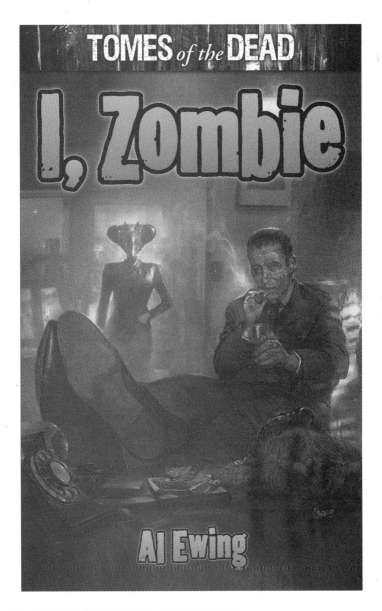

MY NAME IS JOHN DOE. I'VE BEEN DEAD FOR TEN YEARS."

I have no heartbeat, no breath, no smell, just cold, clammy flesh animated by something I don't understand. So I sell my dead flesh to the highest bidder. If the price is right, I'll kill for you, steal for you, or save your life for you. There's no mystery you can't hire me to solveƐ apart from this one. The bent copper torn apart in his flat by something not quite human. The hidden rooms underneath the Tower of London. The hollow-eyed boxer, Morse, and strange, strange Mr Smith with his head full of the future. And the secret they found. The secret of who I am. A secret so big and black and terrible that it changed everything we thought we knew about existence. And now I'm the only person who can stop the end of all life on this planet...

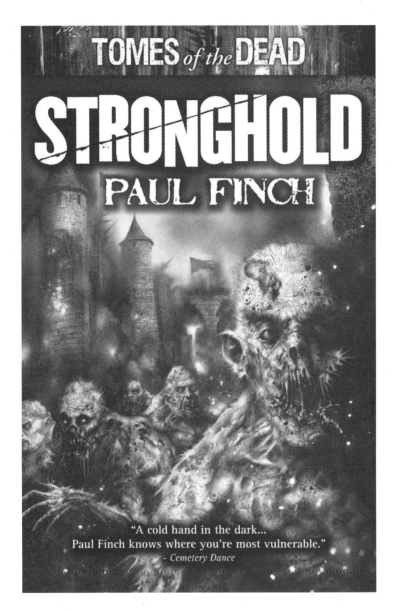

TOMES *of the* DEAD

STRONGHOLD

PAUL FINCH

"A cold hand in the dark...
Paul Finch knows where you're most vulnerable."
- *Cemetery Dance*

SIEGE OF THE DEAD!

Ranulf, a young English knight sent to recapture Grogen Castle from Welsh rebels, comes into conflict with his leaders over their brutal methods. Unbeknownst to any of them, the native druids are planning a devastating counterattack, using an ancient artifact to summon an army that even the castle's superstitious medieval defenders could never have imagined. Grogen Castle, seemingly impregnable to assault – armed with fiendish devices to slaughter would-be attackers in their multitudes – is besieged by countless, tireless soldiers forged from bone and raddled flesh. As lives are held in the balance, Ranulf must defy his masters and rescue the daughter of his enemy, but hope lasts only so long as the stronghold holds out against the legions of the angry dead...

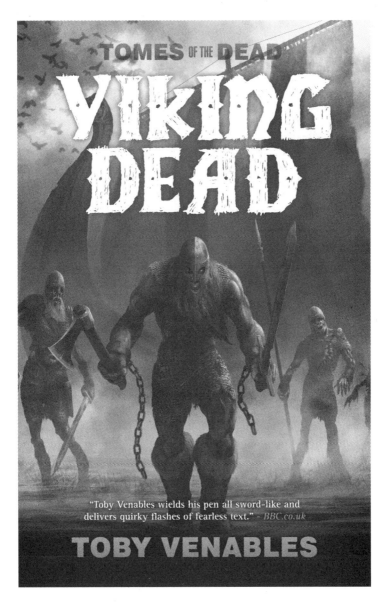

TOMES OF THE DEAD

VIKING DEAD

"Toby Venables wields his pen all sword-like and delivers quirky flashes of fearless text." - *BBC.co.uk*

TOBY VENABLES

THE SHIP OF THE DEAD

Northern Europe, 976 AD. Bjólf and the viking crew of the ship Hrafn flee up an unknown river after a bitter battle, only to find themselves in a bleak land of pestilence. The dead don't lie down, but become draugr – the undead – returning to feed on the flesh of their kin. Terrible stories are told of a dark castle in a hidden fjord, and of black ships that come raiding with invincible draugr berserkers. And no sooner has Bjólf resolved to leave, than the black ships appear...

Now stranded, his men cursed by the contagion of walking death, Bjólf has one choice: fight his way through a forest teeming with zombies, invade the castle and find the secret of the horrific condition – or submit to an eternity of shambling, soulless undeath!